ALL THE PAIN OF PROMISES

HILLARY RAYMER

❀ Formatted with Vellum

For the ones whose souls are summoned by the sea

CONTENT WARNINGS

- Adult Language
- Explicit Sexual Content/Sexual Themes
- Brief off page mention of SA
- Violence
- Death of a Family Member
- Poisoning
- Mental Abuse

se Celestine

CHAPTER ONE

Solarius Starstorm's wedding was perfect.

It was small and quiet, exactly how he would've preferred it, and the sun was already making its descent across the western sky, leaving ribbons of sapphire between stretches of gray clouds. He bristled against the stiff gust of wind that came in off the coast, carrying the scent of the sea, where the waves capped in frothy white peaks. Bouquets of white roses, frosted red berries, and green ferns topped with stardust shivered in the frigid breeze, while bundles of carved driftwood were aglow with faerie fire, spitting flames into the coming night to make certain everyone attending stayed warm. He hadn't expected it to be quite so cold, but *someone* had demanded they marry on a beach even though it was nearly the damn Winter Solstice.

Unfortunately, that was exactly where Solarius found himself now.

On a beach, his new boots sunk into blush-pink sand, while tiny snowflakes tumbled down from the early evening sky like pieces of forgotten lace.

Again, it was a pretty fucking perfect wedding, save for one minor detail.

His bride.

Lady Narissa Seaborne was *not* the female Solarius wanted to marry.

In fact, if he'd gotten his way, he would have remained a bachelor for the rest of his days, because it never failed that any time he found himself romantically involved with a female, he always ended up with a broken heart. Sure, he'd shattered plenty of hearts along the way, but at least he was up-front in the matter. Before he warmed any beds or found himself between the thighs of a willing female, he made sure each of them knew he would be gone before dawn. He never stayed long, waiting until they were gently dozing in his arms before making his stealthy escape. But the two times he'd wanted more, the two times he'd been almost desperate to claim one female for the rest of his life, he'd had his heart ripped from his chest. Gutted. Smashed. Stomped upon as though it were muck during a summer rainstorm.

And Narissa Seaborne just so happened to be one of the two who had ruined him.

But it was fine.

Nothing a bottle of spiced whiskey and mindless sex with a needy female wouldn't fix.

He supposed if it had been anyone else standing across from him, he might have been a little keener on the idea of marriage. Especially since he had no say in the matter. If only his eldest brother had seen fit to match him up with a darling wife whose charm and demeanor were practically confectionary. She would have a sugarplum smile and bake sweetly decadent desserts, and perhaps most importantly, she would enjoy his company both in and out of the bedroom. But alas, Ariesian had chosen to curse him with the one female in all of Aeramere who absolutely hated him.

And Narissa, stars bless her, was neither sweet nor enjoyable.

She was an ocean made of fire.

Tumultuous and dangerous.

Instead of worrying about whether he'd gain too much weight by eating whatever tasty little treats she made, he was more concerned with whether or not she planned on poisoning him tonight. As he'd most recently learned, she was rather adept and quite skilled in the art of potions and herbs.

And now, as he stared down into her eyes that reminded him of frostbitten seas, he wondered what the fuck he did wrong. *She* was the one who destroyed the beautiful thing between them, she was the one who wrecked him, who drove a dagger of cold iron right into his heart. Yet somehow, she had the nerve, the absolute audacity, to act as though it was all his fault.

Solarius scoffed.

He wasn't the one who had been caught tangled in satin sheets with someone else.

Even as the unbidden thought stole into his mind, the even more unwanted memory came with it, and he gritted his teeth.

He blinked, shoving it away, back into the dark depths of his tortured soul where it belonged. Steadying himself, he took a breath, hating the way his lungs seized the moment his gaze landed on her again.

Stars, she was fucking beautiful.

Her wedding gown reminded him of crushed aquamarine, it glittered and sparkled in the rise of hazy moonlight. The sleeves were long and sheer, ballooning down her arms before tapering at her delicate wrists. It cut low, swooping across her bosom, embellished with swirls and incandescent gems. Tiny snowflakes clung to her lashes and her long, golden waves. She'd pinned half of her hair back, and woven pale pink flowers into the tresses and twisted plaits. Despite the frosty temperature, she still looked kissed by the sun, her cheeks rosy and sea swept. Gold rings, some of them studded with turquoise stones, adorned her thumbs and fingers, though one finger in particular remained bare.

He supposed he'd have to remedy that at some point, but if she didn't force the issue or seem too bothered to go without one, then he was in no hurry to make such a bold claim. Everyone who was anyone in Aeramere knew he was getting married, anyway. A ring on Narissa's finger wouldn't change anything.

But then she smiled up at him, and it was so radiant, so positively arresting that for a moment, he forgot himself. Her tempting scent of exotic florals, sandalwood, and the sea lured him, beckoned him. Solarius almost reached for her. It would've been so easy to wrap one arm around her waist and drag her flush against him, but instead he shoved his hands into his pockets and rocked back on his heels, away from her.

Something cold plunged straight into his chest.

Regret. Anguish.

He couldn't be sure.

He was too distracted by her glossy lips. They were painted a pearly pink color and when they curved, all he could focus on was imagining how they would taste. Like strawberry cream candy. Or maybe fizzy fruit wine. But then she spoke, and her words knocked him right back into the reality he didn't want to endure.

"I would rather drown in a tidal wave of my own making, my lungs filling with the salt of the sea, than ever have to take you as my husband."

Ah...there she is.

Such a naughty midnight siren.

"Poetic." Solarius grinned and flashed her a wink. Her pale green eyes, lined with kohl and dusted with gold, expanded in a silent challenge, and he rose to greet it. "I would rather watch the moon burn into oblivion and fall from the sky than ever be forced to marry you."

Narissa's smile turned venomous, and the rosy hue of her cheeks deepened. "Charming."

A male coughed loudly, clearing his throat, and Solarius glanced over his shoulder, barely sparing his brother a glance. What else was to be expected? He'd been forced into a marriage with a lady who was all silk and flower petals around everyone else, but who was daggers and poison to him.

Ariesian simply arched a severe brow, his expression one of blatant displeasure. Solarius's brother was *not* amused. He folded his arms over his chest, his scowl deepening.

"You're supposed to be saying your vows."

Right. Vows. Those pesky affirmations of eternal devotion and adoration.

It was a good thing the fae could fucking lie.

Narissa huffed out a breath, the winter chill in the air causing it to mist before her. Slivers of moonlight slanted through the wispy clouds and dainty flakes, highlighting half of her in its ethereal glow. She tucked one golden wave of hair behind her ear, drawing Solarius's gaze to where silvery blue tattoos of waves graced the pointed tip, illuminated by the light of the moon. He'd never noticed it before, how those tiny tattoos seemed to glow when showered in the affection of moonlight, and it was something he found oddly curious considering lunar magic just so happened to be his specialty.

Solarius wondered what other parts of her glimmered in the midnight hours.

"I, Narissa Seaborne…" Her tone was lulling and dreamy, and something about it made his blood hum in approval. He quite enjoyed it when she sounded like a siren of the sea. "Take you, Solarius Starstorm, as my…husband."

Her vows were simple.

Plain.

But he didn't miss the catch in the back of her throat, the jumping of her pulse, or the tremble in her voice.

He stole another haphazard glance around the small outdoor space, and the cluster of people watching them blurred together in a shift of messy colors. He hooked a finger into the collar of his shirt and tugged, loosening his tie, until he caught the knowing eyes of his sister, Novalise. She sat in the front row, one hand curled around the arm of her husband, Lord Asher Firebane, the other folded neatly in her lap. Her smile was soft and when she dipped her chin just slightly, a tumble of lavender hair fell over her shoulders. Novalise nodded once, a gentle nudge of encouragement.

Right.

He could do this.

More than that, he *had* to, as Ariesian had given him no other option.

Solarius's gaze slid back to Narissa and suddenly it was just her. Only her. Those frosty ocean eyes focused intently on him, but they weren't hardened with resentment, they were clear and soulful, and if he lingered too long in their depths, he would drown.

An icy breeze skated in over the cresting waves, loosing a golden curl so it whipped across Narissa's face. Before Solarius could stop himself, he reached out and captured the silky strand, tucking it gently behind the tip of her ear. The back of his knuckles barely grazed her cheek and Narissa shivered, her teeth grazing her glossy bottom lip.

Solarius tracked the movement.

Forcing himself to look away from her lush lips and back into her mesmerizing eyes, he spoke.

"I, Solarius Starstorm Celestine, take you, Narissa Seaborne…" He swallowed around the lump of some unrecognizable emotion. "As my wife."

There would be no explosion of magic over their heads when they sealed their destiny with a kiss. There would be no magnificent display of fate, of shimmering moonlight and sparkling tides. Their union was simply a means to an end, a burden forced upon them both to strengthen their respective houses before the apparent war looming on the horizon. If Solarius had his way, he'd stop it before it ever reached Aeramere's shores.

But with the attack during Novalise and Asher's wedding last autumn, he feared it was already here.

Well, it was best to make it official. At least now Ariesian could focus on marrying off the rest of their siblings and leave him alone.

Solarius leaned down to kiss Narissa and validate their marriage, expecting a featherlight brush of the lips and nothing more, when the minx turned at the last moment and gave him her cheek instead.

Shocked gasps and murmurs of disquiet swelled, reverberating through him like a slap across the face.

The slight was unfathomable.

Narissa had publicly humiliated him, and the sting of shame crawled up the back of his neck.

The stars could die and give way to an eternal night before he ever let her get away with such an insult.

Solarius grabbed her then, anchoring one hand to the small of her back while the other fastened to her hip. He hauled her close, crushing all breath of space between them, and her back bowed as she arched away from him in silent protest. For a second, he thought she'd be rigid in his arms or try to shove him back. But she felt the same as she did all those years before, supple and pliant, like her body had been crafted to mold perfectly against his own.

An angry line furrowed across her brow, causing the corner of his mouth to curve.

He leaned in close until it was almost scandalous in nature, then trailed his lips over her ear all the way to the delicately pointed tip where those tiny incandescent wave tattoos glowed only for him.

"Tell me, Rissa love," he whispered, his mouth feathering kisses where pretty pearls pierced her ears. She shivered in his arms, and the breathy little sound she made was enough to send him to his knees. Her eyes fluttered closed and he held her tighter, enjoying the way she melted into him. Her scent overwhelmed him. Tempted him. Damned him. "Where else do you shine beneath the moonlight? Is it only your ears?"

Her eyes flew open.

His gaze dipped intentionally to the curve of her breasts, then returned to her face. "Or do you have glowing tattoos elsewhere as well?"

Her scowl deepened and her sun-kissed cheeks blushed the most beautiful shade of ruby he'd ever seen.

"*That*," Narissa hissed through a clenched jaw, adjusting her hair so it covered her ears, "is none of your business, my lord."

"It is now." Solarius flashed her a wolfish grin. "Everything about you is my business, *wife*."

He had every intention of dropping her, of letting her go so she fell onto her cute little ass in the sand with all of their family watching. Because more than anything, he wanted her to feel a similar burn of mortification.

But Ariesian must have sensed his intentions, because he was by Narissa's side with lightning speed, snaring her by the elbow as soon as Solarius let go. She wobbled and tipped to one side, her heels sinking into the sand, arms flailing in an effort to keep her balance. Narissa yelped but Ariesian kept her upright, his seething death glare fixated on Solarius.

He told himself he didn't care if his eldest brother was furious with him, if he'd acted like a sulking child, if his conduct was hardly becoming of a lord of Aeramere. His own wife had refused to kiss him after they recited their vows, which would only serve to spark rumors and half-truths. It was bad enough all of society knew he and Narissa were on less than amicable terms, but now her blatant denial of him would only incite speculation about their obviously unhappy marriage and dredge up the failings of their past courtship. Both of which he preferred to avoid completely.

Solarius returned his hands to his pockets and rolled his neck, sparing Narissa one more long look. She was flushed with the stain of embarrassment, her brow was pinched, and the pale green of her eyes simmered like a blazing ocean.

Behind her, the sea frothed with rage and the waves lashed the shore.

She was furious.

Good, it was easier to have Narissa pissed off and loathing him with every fiber of her being than it was to see her despondent and melancholy.

Ariesian's scowl of disappointment bored into Solarius, and he caved beneath the pressure of his upbringing. Grinding his teeth until they were sure to turn to dust, Solarius offered his arm to escort Narissa into the ballroom of House Azurvend, where they would have to dance and pretend to actually like one another for the remainder of the evening. Surprisingly enough, she accepted his proffered arm, hooking her hand into the crook of his elbow. Her smile was pure radiance, though a bit tight at the corners. It never faltered, not even as they passed a cluster of females whose obnoxiously loud whispers were barely disguised behind their gloved hands.

"Just so we're clear, my lord." Narissa's velvety siren-like voice floated up to him, and again he found his gaze drawn to her mouth. "I will never forgive you."

His lips quirked. "For what? Nearly dropping you on your bottom in the sand on our wedding day?"

"No." She drew up short, her eyes a volatile storm of emotions he couldn't even begin to place. Her bottom lip quivered, but she held her ground and dropped his arm. "For stealing from me the one thing I never should have given you in the first place."

Solarius stared at her, then opened his mouth to demand an explanation, because he knew for a fact he'd not taken anything from her. But Narissa was already stalking up the sea-worn path to where House Azurvend stood luminous against a backdrop of turquoise waters, darkening sapphire skies, and frosted snowflakes, leaving him alone in his own damning misery.

Stars above, he needed a drink.

Preferably one not laced with poison by his darling new wife.

CHAPTER TWO

$\mathcal{N}$arissa gripped the edge of the porcelain sink, her stomach churning violently, her nails tapping a restless rhythm that echoed softly through the empty bathing suite. She blew out a low, shallow breath, struggling to maintain her composure, while dreamy music floated from the ballroom beyond. She dared a hesitant look at herself in the gilded mirror encrusted with bits of aqua sea glass and met the watery gaze of her own reflection. For a brief moment, she worried she might be horribly ill.

She'd done it.

She'd married Lord Solarius Starstorm, the one male she had pined after for years, yet instead of feeling overcome with joy and elation, her nerves were coiled tightly with dread. The constant swell of anxiety left her unwell.

Narissa lowered her chin and sucked in another greedy gulp of air.

Her wedding gown was suffocating. The soft and decadent chiffon stuck to her skin, smothering her. She'd needed a moment to collect herself after their vows, to keep herself from crying in front of him. Humiliation spread through her once more, a ruthless blush staining her cheeks. Solarius had every intention of dropping her, of letting her topple into the sand without a care. She'd seen it in his eyes a second before he let her go. Lucky for her, his eldest brother Ariesian had seen his intent as well and caught her by the elbow.

Despite wanting to slap him across the face for such churlish behavior, Narissa couldn't be furious with him. Not really. She was the one who had offered him her cheek instead of her lips when he attempted to seal their vows with a kiss. It wasn't that she didn't *want* to kiss him. In fact, her desires were quite the opposite. But she was absolutely terrified. Solarius had been the epitome of an honorable lord during their courtship a few years prior—he'd been attentive, chivalrous, and exceptionally refined. So much so, that he never kissed her then, either. But Narissa told herself that the moment their lips met, their magic would claim one another, and Solarius would be her mate. Her perfect match in every sense of the word. For how could he possibly be anything else?

The enchanting moon and the alluring tides called to one another, such a fate was designed before even the rise of stars. And Solarius, he had moonlight running through his veins. She'd witnessed his power firsthand, the forceful yet wondrous sphere he called the lunarstorm. When he was engulfed in the magic of the moon and all of her phases, when he'd been doused in that glow of silvery light, Narissa's blood stirred. Her tidal magic awoke, beckoned to the surface by Solarius's unintentional summons. She'd known then, if she were to ever kiss him, they would be bound together for an eternity.

But kissing Solarius was something she could never bring herself to do.

Not after…not after all she'd endured from him. Not after he stole her heart, then crushed it with a vengeful fist. He'd done the unthinkable, the callous and cruel. And the wound he'd left behind on her soul had never fully healed. She was wed to a male who used her to get what he wanted, then abandoned her without a second thought.

So, she'd been left with no choice and had refused to kiss him at their wedding. She'd insulted him plainly in front of their families and friends, and perhaps worse, before most of Aeramere's nobles. There was no doubt rumors would circulate through all five houses and reach every corner of the realm, as most of the lords and ladies loved nothing more than to gossip. It was bad enough Queen Elowyn had failed to make an appearance at their wedding, especially considering she and Lady Trysta Starstorm, Solarius's mother, had been friends for a number of years. Now, the whispers would only strengthen.

They would call her a tease for denying him a kiss.

He would be offered pity and sympathy for marrying such a snobbish wife, and Narissa had no doubt it was only a matter of time before Solarius received propositions from plenty of other females who were ready and willing to warm his bed.

Her stomach soured at the thought.

She sniffled then, the tingling sensation in her nose building until a single tear slipped from her eye. She watched in the mirror as it rolled down her cheek, forming a perfect, opalescent pearl.

Narissa let it fall.

Only when her tears were tied to an emotion did they turn to pearls, otherwise they remained simple beads of saltwater. And that particular teardrop was bound to sorrow.

The pearl hit the ground at her feet, bouncing and tinkling like faerie bells, before it rolled across the smooth teal floor into a forgotten corner.

She sucked in another shuddering breath, her insides seizing against the crush of despair that refused to relinquish its hold.

"Narissa?" a delicate, feminine voice called out quietly.

Turning around quickly, Narissa swiped at her eyes to prevent any more tears or pearls from escaping, and came face to face with Lady Sarelle Starstorm.

Her beautiful midnight hair was twisted into a thick plait over one shoulder with moonstone charms woven through the inky strands. Her gown was simple yet svelte, the cobalt satin swept off her shoulders and hugged her waist before pooling at her feet in a sea of evening blue. Diamonds studded the long sleeves and a small constellation tattoo outlining three mountain peaks was formed over her heart. When she tilted her head, the stardust smearing her cheeks sparkled like the night sky.

"Are you well?" Sarelle asked, her deep sapphire eyes darkening with concern.

Sarelle was one of Solarius's four sisters. There were eight Starstorm siblings in total, and Narissa always found herself oddly jealous of the large, lovely, and welcoming family. She had no brothers or sisters and had been orphaned at a young age. When her parents died, it was her eldest cousin Reif Marintide who took her in and cared for her, who ensured she had a home and a place in society.

Unfortunately, it was also Reif who agreed with Lord Ariesian Starstorm to marry her off to Solarius.

Narissa clasped her hands before her, fiddling with the dozens of gold rings wrapped around her thumbs and fingers. "I'm not entirely sure. I worry I won't be well ever again."

Sarelle's features softened, and a ghost of a smile graced her lips. "It's going to be okay, you'll see. I know Solarius can be difficult and frustrating, but I promise, his heart is good."

Narissa once thought so, too. But that was before…

"How can I possibly face him?" She ducked her head, her golden waves tumbling around her like a gilded waterfall. "Solarius cannot stand me. My very presence infuriates him. You saw the look on his face when I gave him my cheek."

"It was a bit harsh to deny him." Sarelle winced and pressed her painted red lips together. "Why didn't you kiss him?"

"Because…" Narissa opened her mouth but words, the *right* words, failed her. "Because I didn't want to imagine something that might not be there."

Because she didn't want to fall in love with him. She didn't want to be fated to him, not after what he did to her.

"I understand." Sarelle reached out and looped their arms together. Slowly and with practiced confidence, she guided Narissa back out into the ballroom of House Azurvend, where it looked as though a seaside wonderland had been kissed by winter.

Mosaic tiles the color of ocean mist and shimmering sand swirled across the floor, shaping crashing waves and winding shorelines. Sprigs of holly wrapped around golden pillars, the tips of their prickly evergreen leaves dusted with frost. Icy blue waterfalls cascaded down the circular balconies, flowing into serpentine streams that surrounded the main floor where couples danced and twirled to a jovial tune. Sea glass snowflakes floated overhead, each one in varying shades of turquoise, soft rose, pale green, and light blue. Faerie fire glinted from carved sconces of driftwood lining the walls, musicians were seated on a small dais, their beautiful melody echoing through the vast ballroom, and the air was scented with stunning bouquets of winterblooms and lush berries.

"Sometimes," Sarelle whispered, pulling Narissa close to her side as they passed a group of haughty nobles with Prince Aspen Willowblade standing among them. "We have no choice but to pretend."

The prince's cold green gaze tracked Sarelle's every movement.

Narissa was well aware of what her friend was implying, of course. Sarelle was trying to catch Prince Aspen's eye in an effort to learn of his rather secretive plans. There were rumors he intended to overthrow his mother and take the throne for himself, but Narissa knew very little about the matter. She did, however, know that Sarelle agreed to be part of a grand scheme to woo the prince and feign interest in him to earn his favor and, thus, his confidence. It was a dangerous game she was playing, one that could possibly end in a lashing or worse, if she got found out. Especially since the prince was considered cruel beyond measure and in possession of a rather wretched personality. But given the way Prince Aspen's eyes followed Sarelle through the room, Narissa suspected her plan was working.

Sarelle would gain the prince's affection, and Ariesian would put a stop to their relationship before an engagement could come to fruition.

But Narissa didn't want to pretend to be in love with Solarius.

She wanted a love match. Or better yet, she wanted the one to whom she was fated to love her in return.

"It wasn't supposed to be like this," she muttered, more to herself than Sarelle as her gaze flicked around the ballroom, refusing to linger in one place too long for fear of meeting any knowing stares.

Sarelle clamped Narissa's hand where it rested in the crook of her arm as they continued their methodical walk about the ballroom. She squeezed gently, offering quiet encouragement.

"I was supposed to fall in love." Narissa wouldn't mention that she *had* fallen in love and had never quite fallen out, which was why it made Solarius's betrayal of her heart all the more painful. "I was supposed to marry someone whose soul spoke to mine, whose magic chose mine."

A sigh escaped from her pinched lungs, like a harbored, fading daydream. "I was supposed to be happy."

Narissa's voice broke on the last word, and Sarelle stumbled to a stop as Solarius stepped directly into their path.

Again, Narissa's breath caught. For an entirely different reason.

It simply was not fair that someone who despised her should be so devastatingly handsome.

Solarius stood before them with his hands shoved into the pockets of his sleek black pants. He wore a slim black coat that accentuated his lean, muscular frame. Beneath the coat was a crisp white shirt and the top three buttons were undone, revealing a glimpse of the constellation tattoo shaped like a trident marking his heart. His hair was mussed, the silver strands with inky black tips were haphazard and windblown, like he'd just stepped in from the beach. He angled his head, his sharp jawline drawing her gaze as he watched her beneath a pair of drawn brows, his eyes molten like liquid silver.

Breaking tides, it would be far easier to continue to loathe him if he wasn't so ridiculously perfect to look upon. But of course, he would choose that moment to appear, to overhear her distress. She wouldn't be at all surprised if he attempted to exploit her feelings later. Besides, he'd done far worse already.

"Narissa." Solarius's smooth, rich voice caused her stomach to flip and the way he spoke her full name softened her knees. He slipped one hand from his pocket and held it out to her, palm up. "Would you dance with me?"

Before Narissa could object, before she could muster a plausible excuse, Sarelle was already removing Narissa's hand from her elbow and placing it in Solarius's offered one. Her smile was kind and reassuring, but it did little to ease the gnawing anxiety that was devouring Narissa from the inside out.

Solarius's thumb grazed the back of her hand as he led her out onto the ballroom's main floor, and Narissa bit her bottom lip to keep it from trembling. He lifted her arm with ease, twirling her once as the beginning strings of a new song hummed through the room. Spinning her into him, his left hand claimed her waist while his right hand clasped her own, extending their arms in preparation for a waltz. He pressed her in close, until her breasts were crushed against the solid wall of his chest, until their bodies were molded to one another, until their breaths mingled. His commanding touch sent a wave of warmth coursing through her veins, a wonderfully splendid sensation, and one she wouldn't allow herself to enjoy. For it was just as Sarelle had said, sometimes they had no choice but to pretend.

And Solarius Starstorm was putting on one hell of a show.

He guided her into the dance, each step fluid and graceful like they were meant to be in one another's arms. She ignored the way he wove their fingers together, the way every spin left her lightheaded and longing for an emotion she could never claim. Her gown flowed around them like a sea of aquamarine, and for one fleeting moment, she felt weightless, like Solarius could carry her and she would never have to let go. But then his hand slid to the small of her back, diminishing every shred of space between them, and she sucked in a sharp breath.

Narissa immediately regretted it.

His scent overwhelmed her.

He smelled of delicious citrus, warm spices, and a splash of bay rum. Every so often, she caught a hint of it on the air, whether it be a sifting breeze along Azurvend's seaside village or lingering in a room long after Solarius had departed. His scent haunted her. Tormented her. Having to spend the remainder of her days with him would be agony. Raw, torturous agony.

His lips grazed her temple as he maneuvered her around the ballroom, and the way his whisper caressed her skin sent her pulse skittering wildly. "Are you unhappy?"

So, she'd been correct in her assumption. Solarius *had* overheard her conversation with Sarelle. No matter. Her words were nothing to be ashamed of, and she was allowed to wallow in her feelings of misery and misfortune. She would not, however, express such sentiments to her new husband.

"My happiness was not written into our marriage contract, my lord." Narissa spoke with an air of indifference, refusing to meet his penetrating gaze. "Therefore, it matters not what I feel, as my emotions are no longer relevant."

Solarius's grip on her tightened so severely that she was left gasping. Her eyes flew to his, only to find him glowering with that same kind of disdain she'd seen from him every time they were forced into the company of one another.

"You are mistaken, my lady." His voice dropped so low she almost couldn't hear him over the whimsical music. "Your happiness matters greatly, and your emotions will always be relevant."

"Just not to you," she snapped, shoving another unbidden memory from her mind. She glared up at him, shielding her heart from his pretty little promises. She'd made that mistake once, she would not do so again. "Do not act as though my feelings matter to you, not when we both know it is the furthest thing from the truth."

Solarius stilled then, drawing up short in the middle of the ballroom and keeping her firmly in his hold. They were so close to one another, the rise and fall of their chests matched a steady rhythm, and she was certain his heartbeat was a perfect echo of her own. His dark brows narrowed, and she didn't miss the way his eyes flitted over her face as though he was searching for something that was missing. He pressed two fingers beneath her chin, tilting her face up to him.

"If you have a mind to say something, then speak now and freely, my lady." His thumb dragged across her bottom lip, tugging lightly. "Otherwise, I would suggest you hold your tongue until we are in the privacy of our chambers."

"Why?" Narissa asked, vaguely aware of the other lords and ladies who were now feigning a dance while circling around them like vultures. "Afraid they'll see you for the insufferable scoundrel you are?"

"My reputation is already well-known." He flashed a wicked smile. "It is you who will finally be seen for what you are."

"And what's that?" she taunted, ready to absorb whatever barb he threw at her.

Solarius hesitated. His irritated gaze dipped to her mouth as though he was tracing the lines and committing the curves to his memory. Her tongue darted out, the gloss she wore tasted faintly of vanilla, and he tracked the movement. He leaned in, lips slightly parted, and a spike of fear left her frozen in his arms. If he kissed her, she would never survive.

But then he blinked and drew back, as though coming to his senses.

"Nothing, Narissa." He released her as the final chords of an enchanting melody faded away in the background. "Absolutely nothing."

Narissa stared at him, unable to form words, her mind emptying of every sharpened retort. She could have handled an insult, could have brushed off any number of offenses. Yet to be so singularly diminished, to be relegated to *nothing*, carved open some long-buried wound inside of her.

Solarius didn't deserve her tears. Or the pearls that would inevitably form from them.

"If you'd excuse me, my lord." She dipped into a formal curtsy, holding his tense gaze the entire time. "I suddenly find myself no longer in want of your company."

He opened his mouth to object, but she spun on one heel, her gown billowing around her as she moved toward the refreshments table positioned along the opposite wall of the ballroom. She kept her footfalls soft and delicate, offering a practiced smile to any guests who sent questioning looks her way. Not once did she stumble. Not once did she falter. She kept her composure until she reached the table and grabbed a glass of winter berry wine.

Narissa sniffed the burgundy contents and tried not to wince.

While the scent of berries and spice was quite distinct, it was overpowered by the alarmingly strong smell of red wine.

She rarely indulged in libations, but tonight called for an exception.

Lifting the glass to her lips and surveying the decadent ballroom over the crystal rim, she took a hesitant sip.

Bursting flavors of cranberries, orange, cinnamon, and clove danced across her tongue in a surprisingly delicious blend. The beverage was much more pleasant than she expected, and she drank it far faster than she intended. Warmth bloomed in her belly and chest, her fingers tingled, and her thoughts went fuzzy. A lovely numbness spread through her, and she reached for another glass of the warm wine.

Yes, Narissa thought as she smiled to herself, she rather liked the idea of being numb.

CHAPTER THREE

Solarius stood with his brothers, Tovian and Nyxian, on the opposite side of the ballroom with an untouched drink in his hand.

His brothers were distracting him with stories of their sea-faring adventures. Having recently returned to Aeramere after months of worldly travel with Aran Ruhdneah, a High Prince of Faeven, and having been to far more places than Solarius thought possible, they were finally home.

"Tell me again about the female who broke our dear Tovian's heart," Solarius murmured, his gaze trained on Narissa, whose exquisite and ladylike form was now hiccupping and teetering off balance. She'd already consumed two glasses of winter berry wine, which was two too many. Because Narissa never drank.

"It was absolutely devastating. You should have seen poor Tov. He was ready to carry her back to Aeramere and make her his wife." Nyxian clutched one hand to his chest, the scar cutting down the left side of his face only serving to highlight his wickedly sarcastic smile. "Her name was Everinne, and she was damningly beautiful. Nothing at all the like the ladies of Aeramere. Pretty eyes, curves where it mattered, legs for miles—"

"Watch it," Tovian warned, dipping his head so a swath of midnight blue hair fell across the front of his face. "She may not be a lady of Aeramere, but you will mind how you speak about females."

"Of course. Apologies, dear brother." Nyxian feigned a look of remorse, then turned to Solarius and winked. Conspiratorial little shit. "She had eyes the color of the eastern Arcasian Sea, like pools of turquoise flecked with the gold of the sun. Her breasts were two perfectly round orbs of creamy flesh, tanned like—"

Nyxian grunted in pain.

Tovian jabbed his elbow into Nyxian's ribcage with enough force that he doubled over as a grating laugh wheezed out of him. Solarius had the decency to maintain an even expression, but his lips twitched in spite of himself.

"Fuck off, Nyx." Tovian glowered and his face—which had tanned considerably on their voyage—heated to a reddish shade of untempered rage. "I was in love with her."

Solarius clicked his tongue in amusement. "I'm somewhat surprised she was charmed by you, Tov. Usually it's Nyx who wins over the ladies in record time."

"I have no doubt I would've stolen her heart and broken it," Nyxian declared. His rakish charisma knew no bounds. But he folded his arms over his chest and arched one dark brow. "However, Tovian lured her in with his signature move."

"Oh, really?" Solarius mused, running his thumb along his jaw to hide his smirk. "And what move is that?"

If Tovian was known for anything, it was being an esteemed lord with a mild manner and refined taste. He was respectful. Attentive. Courteous in every sense of the word.

"The inside the wrist kiss." Nyxian clapped Tovian soundly on the back. "Works every time."

Interesting.

Solarius would file that bit of information away for later. Perhaps he would attempt such a move on Narissa.

At once, heightened awareness fired through him, and his gaze latched onto her again. This time he caught her sitting on one of the shell-encrusted ledges lining the small streams coursing through the ballroom, and she appeared dangerously close to falling in.

A piece of him had broken when he overheard her tell Sarelle she was unhappy. It wasn't as though he expected anything less, neither of them *wanted* this marriage, but if they had any hope of survival, they would have to find a means to tolerate one another. And that included being cordial and somewhat content.

He had tried to extend her some grace.

Her feelings, thoughts, and emotions absolutely mattered. Just because they'd been forced into an arranged marriage didn't mean they had to be miserable.

But showing Narissa a shred of kindness had been the equivalent of attempting to pet a feral cat. She hissed, showed her claws, and would have tried to scratch him across the face.

So, he'd chosen to let her walk away, which only led to her wallowing in copious amounts of winter berry wine.

"Sol." A soft, sparkling voice called from behind him.

Solarius turned to find Sarelle, her hands clasped together. She was spinning a silver ring around her finger—the focal point was coated in stardust and diamonds and looked eerily similar to a tiny wolf skull.

"Hello, sister." He leaned forward slightly to inspect it. "Is that an animal skull on your finger?"

Sarelle immediately tucked her hands behind her back. "I don't want to discuss it."

He levied her with a wary look. "Very well..."

"Sol." She entreated him again, her sapphire eyes pleading. "You must do something."

"Must I?" he asked, already knowing why Sarelle had approached him. "Lady Narissa has made her sentiments quite clear. She wants nothing to do with me."

Rubbing her lips together, Sarelle's gaze flicked to Narissa, then back to him. The female in question was now stumbling toward the balcony, tripping over the hem of her wedding gown with every step.

"Solarius, please." A small wrinkle of concern furrowed across her brow. "I don't know what transpired between the two of you during your courtship, and I will not ask as it is not my place, but Narissa is obviously hurting. I beg of you, save her from further shame this evening."

"Further shame?"

Solarius glanced around the ballroom as Narissa lurched past a group of ladies whose blatant snickers of disdain could be heard over the strumming of music. His insides simmered at their mocking sneers and vicious glares. He handed Sarelle his untouched drink and popped his jaw.

"Fine." He rolled his neck, mentally preparing for whatever battle he was bound to face with his new bride. "I'll go fetch her."

Sarelle offered him her gratitude, but Solarius was already stalking toward Narissa, who had vanished through one of the stained glass doors leading to the outdoors, hunting her like predator to prey. He had no idea if she would actually listen to him, he'd never witnessed a drunk Narissa before. For all he knew, she may very well try to toss him over the balcony's edge.

He made brief eye contact with Ariesian, who was in a deep conversation with their youngest sister, Creslyn, and her new husband, Drake Kalstrand. Solarius had no doubt he would be privy to the information they discussed at a later time, but knowing Ariesian, he wouldn't want to sully Solarius's wedding night with talks of treason. Ariesian tilted his head, just slightly, to where their mother stood upon a small dais in Prince Aspen's company. Trysta was rambling on about something, gesturing over the grandeur as though she was somehow responsible for any of it, while Prince Aspen maintained an expression of tedious boredom, his gaze fixated on something or someone at the back of the ballroom.

The hairs along the back of Solarius's neck prickled and his skin crawled.

He didn't care if he shared the same blood as his mother, he didn't trust her in the least.

Stalking past the dais, he shoved open the majestic stained glass door depicting a mighty ocean wave crashing against the shore, and was assaulted by the frigid winter air.

There was Narissa, showered in the silvery wash of the winter moon, with a flurry of snowflakes dancing around her. The pale blue wave tattoos on her ears glowed, and he caught glimpses of another decorating her spine before it disappeared beneath the seam of her dress. Her wild golden curls whipped around her as she gripped the smooth, gilded railing with both hands. She was trembling, though whether from the cold or some other source, he couldn't be sure, and every so often her shoulders gave a violent shake. Over the whisper of the wind and the call of the sea, Solarius could just hear the faint tinkling of bells.

Not bells.

Pearls.

Ivory pearls bounced off the stone balcony, the sound of it was almost enough to rip his heart from his chest.

Narissa was crying.

Fuck.

He approached her slowly, as to not frighten her, and tucked his hands behind his back. "Rissa."

She spun around and his lungs seized.

She was tragically beautiful. Dark damp lashes framed her frozen green eyes. Her cheeks and the tip of her nose were rosy from the cold, and when her glossy bottom lip quivered, he wanted to bite it between his teeth to keep it from trembling. He longed to reach out and tuck one of those loose strands of hair back behind her delicately pointed ear. He wanted to capture her face and kiss her until such sadness no longer haunted her, until she was warm, and soft, and wanton in his arms.

But stubborn pride kept his hands firmly behind his back, fists clenched.

"Forgive me, my lord." Narissa sniffled, then hiccuped, swiping hastily at her cheeks. "I just...I needed..."

She waved one hand furiously between them. "Air."

Solarius rocked back onto his heels, the corner of his mouth tugging upward. "I'm rather fond of air myself."

She ignored his quip, continuing to wipe the tears from her cheeks before they could turn into pearls. She huffed out a breath, the air misting before her, and hugged her arms around her body, swaying toward him.

Solarius gently cupped her by the elbow, steadying her. "Perhaps we should retire for the evening?"

That was *definitely* the wrong thing to say.

Narissa blinked and her icy green gaze narrowed. She damn near froze his heart from the inside out with those eyes.

"Oh yes," she drawled, her siren-like voice slurring on the words. "Of course."

She attempted to yank her elbow free from his hold, but Solarius only tightened his grip and dragged her closer.

"Best to get the deed over with then, hm?" She smacked at his chest with her other hand in a pathetic attempt for release. "Make it well and truly official?"

"Narissa..." he warned, but this time when she yanked away from him, he let her go. For every few stumbling steps she took, he closed the distance between them in one stride.

"It's fine." She drew the word out and waved another flippant hand through the air. "I'll go to your bed willingly since it is now my duty as your wife but expect nothing else from me."

Did she actually think he would bed her *unwillingly*?

Solarius frowned as he stalked across the balcony after her. "Wait just a damn minute, if you think—"

Narissa whirled on him, hair flying like golden ribbons, snow clinging to her lashes, and the pale green of her eyes burned hot with defiance.

"Rest assured, my lord. I am quite used to males spreading my thighs to take what they want, then leaving me before the sun breaks the horizon."

The fuck?

Solarius drew up short. His chest expanded on a breath of rage, and fury pumped through his veins. If someone had taken advantage of Narissa, if someone had dared to lay a hand upon her, they would know his wrath. All he needed was a name and he would end them without hesitation.

"Who?" he demanded, reaching for her arm.

But Narissa dodged his grasp, and the look she sent him was one of pure loathing. *"You."*

Before he could require an explanation as to what in the blazing stars she was talking about, Narissa was already spinning away and stomping, albeit stumbling, back toward the ballroom.

"Oh no, you don't." Solarius lunged and snared her by the waist, hauling her back. "You've already made quite the spectacle of yourself this evening."

He twisted her in his arms so she faced him, then scooped her up and tossed her over his shoulder.

"Put me down!" She swatted at his back, but honestly, he would have been in more pain if he'd been attacked by a swarm of butterflies.

"Not a chance," he mumbled, wrapping an arm snugly around her wiggling thighs.

He couldn't very wall waltz back into the ballroom with Narissa tossed over his shoulder like a satchel of sand, mostly because he didn't particularly care to give the lords and ladies of society anymore of a reason to snare them in their vines of vicious rumors.

There had to be another way.

His gaze skimmed the outdoor balcony until he caught sight of Reif Marintide lounging against an exterior alcove. A sconce of faerie fire illuminated his silhouette, the flames flickering in the biting wind. He stifled a yawn, then jerked his head to the right, where a winding stone staircase wrapped around a pearlescent tower that shone like moonlight.

"Straight up." Reif swirled his glass of whiskey, the ice clinking together softly. "Her room is the first door on the left."

"Right." Solarius nodded in gratitude. "Thanks for that."

He flashed a winning smile. "Anytime."

Narissa huffed as Solarius carried her past him.

"Traitor," she hissed.

Reif scoffed and took a sip of his drink. "You don't know the meaning of the word, sweet cousin."

Solarius started up the stairs with Narissa tossed over his shoulder, taking them two at a time. He thoroughly expected her to keep pounding on his back, but it seemed as though she had settled and finally resigned herself to her fate.

"You know," she said, heaving a dramatic sigh, "I am quite capable of walking."

He had seen the way she wobbled and tripped over her skirts on the balcony. She might have been in possession of two feet, but her balance had disappeared along with the last of the winter berry wine.

"Unlikely," he countered, adjusting her in his hold as he reached the door at the top of the stairwell. He grabbed the bronze handle, pushed open the ornate wooden door, and was immediately assaulted by oceanic wonder.

Narissa's bedchamber was a dreamy, calming escape. An ode to Azuralis, the sea goddess herself. The walls were the softest hue of blue, embedded with shimmering pearls and crushed sea glass. Gilded scales stamped the deep turquoise flooring and in the far corner, the hearth was flanked by two small waterfalls set in marble reminiscent of a dazzling sunset. A curving bench was positioned beneath a magnificent stained glass window, the brilliant colors depicting two sirens separated by their own desires—one remained below the surface of the sea, surrounded by a forest of coral, while the other was perched upon a stone by the shore, her gaze trained on the moon. Overheard, the tower reached a point, and there a chandelier carved from driftwood floated as though being carried by invisible waves.

But it was her bed that held his attention.

It was large and sumptuous, draped with a thick blush comforter, a canopy of pale teal, and a pile of downy pillows.

Carefully, Solarius set Narissa on the ground. "This is quite the place you have here."

"Yes, well. It is somewhat of a safe haven for me, and I would prefer it if you did not ruin it." She crossed her arms out of spite, then tipped to one side.

He made to catch her, but she swatted at him and gripped the gilded spire of her bedpost. "I am perfectly fine, my lord."

"Whatever you say, my lady." Solarius lifted both hands in surrender, then shoved them into the pockets of his pants. If she wanted to teeter around her bedroom and risk toppling into the hearth, that was her prerogative. He stepped back, giving her some space, then canted his head to one side. "I thought I was supposed to be the one who was drunk tonight."

She cut him down with a fiery glare, her nails digging into the bedpost supporting her weight. Her expression shifted and the change happened so quickly, he almost didn't register it. One moment, she looked like she wanted to stab him in the eye with a seashell, and in the next, she appeared pensive and troubled.

Narissa dropped onto the bed, gently swinging her legs so her shoes embellished with milky blue gemstones slipped from her feet and tumbled to the floor. "This is all your fault."

Tension coiled through Solarius, tightening his shoulders and stiffening his spine. He locked his jaw. "By all means, Rissa love, tell me again how I've ruined your life. How positively miserable you are. How much you loathe my very existence."

Apparently, for some crime he did not commit.

She sighed again, but it was more despondent this time. Shoving off the bed, she tiptoed toward her mirror, her brow puckering at her reflection.

"Sometimes I hate you." Her voice was quiet and there was a quivery break, the slightest catch in her breath, like she wanted to expand on her statement, then thought better of it.

Instead, she reached her hands behind her back and started fumbling with the laces of her gown.

Solarius inhaled sharply. "What are you doing?"

"I thought…" Narissa twisted, struggling to untie the ribbons. She reached one hand over her head while the other grasped blindly behind her back. "That is to say, I assumed we…"

She met his gaze in the reflection of the mirror, and his scowl only deepened.

If she honestly thought so little of him as to assume he would bed her while she could barely remain upright, she was sorely mistaken.

Solarius Starstorm Celestine was many things, but he was *not* a bastard. He would never take advantage of a female, wife or not.

He balled his hands into fists, keeping them tucked into his pockets so she couldn't see the furious effect her assumption held over him. "I have no intention of being intimate with you tonight, Narissa. You'll be incoherent by the time your pretty little head hits that stack of pillows upon your bed."

She snatched what looked to be a silk robe off the back of a velvet chair, but all Solarius could see was a brief glimpse of teal fabric and a hint of lace.

"And I have no intention of remaining in this gown all night. I would prefer to sleep in something more comfortable." This time, Narissa turned, glancing at him from over her shoulder.

Golden blonde waves tumbled around her bare shoulders and when those eyes, frosty green and framed with dark, wispy lashes, found him, his heart almost stopped.

"Will you help me?" she asked softly, gathering her sea-swept hair to one side, exposing the column of her sun-kissed neck, where her flesh looked entirely too kissable. "Please?"

Solarius's jaw locked tight.

Fuck, he was in trouble.

CHAPTER FOUR

*N*arissa immediately regretted her request for Solarius's assistance.

He looked as though she'd slapped him across the face. Eyes wide, mouth slightly agape. He was stunned into silence, and she couldn't determine if he was more appalled or disgusted by the fact that she'd asked him for help.

Her cheeks flamed, and she dipped her head so her waves tumbled forward to disguise her mortification. Perhaps the winter berry wine had emboldened her a little too much.

"Forgive me, my lord." She grasped blindly for the ribbons lacing up the back of her wedding gown. "I'm quite certain I can manage on my own."

She dared a quick glance at him in the mirror, just enough to catch him blink. He shook his head once, as though clearing his thoughts, like he wasn't exactly listening to her.

"My apologies." His voice was hoarse. He closed the distance between them in two strides, coming to stand behind her, the nearness of his presence sending a swarm of butterflies fluttering through her stomach. Hooking a finger in the collar of his shirt, he gave it a hard tug, then cleared his throat. "I would be more than obliged to help you…undress."

Narissa held her breath, tension flooding her veins as he reached for her. She listed to the left, catching the side of the mirror for support in a desperate attempt to cling to the last shreds of her dignity. She expected him to untie the ribbons as quickly as possible to rid himself of her company, but he surprised her instead by carefully plucking the flowers from her hair.

Solarius set the small collection of pink blossoms on her vanity, then loosened her tresses with his hands, gently running his fingers through the woven plaits. Tingles of delight shivered across her skin, and Narissa gripped the gilded mirror's edge to keep her balance. Her nails dug into the finely carved wood while the pads of his fingers lightly massaged her scalp, easing the tangled knots of tension so the strain of her muscles melted away. Her eyes drifted closed and she softly sighed, relishing the tenderness of his touch.

It would be so simple, so easy to lean into him. To sway backward so she was pressed against him, completely losing herself in the moment. And for one brief glimpse of time, she could imagine their courtship hadn't ended in tumultuous disaster, and that their new marriage could rival even the greatest of love stories.

Of course, those were only dreams and silent wishes.

When Solarius gathered her unruly waves and draped them over one shoulder, his fingers grazing the length of her neck, Narissa's eyes flew open.

And she found him watching her with burning intensity, the silver of his gaze molten with an emotion she didn't understand. It heated her thoroughly, scorching her from the inside until she thought she would melt into a puddle at his feet. His calloused hand slid around her throat, following the smooth line to her jaw, before tilting her head just slightly. He bent down, his mouth hovering near the pointed tip of her ear, his warm breath fanning along her cheek. Goosebumps pebbled her flesh when he leaned closer, his lips brushing over the shell of her ear. A breathy gasp escaped her, and her lungs pulled tight, making it almost impossible to breathe.

With his other hand, he pinched the pearl earring she wore

between his thumb and forefinger, and she imagined he was quite capable of squeezing other things as well.

"Would you like for me to remove your earrings?" he asked, his voice a rough scrape that caused her nipples to harden in anticipation.

Narissa trembled and shook her head, the movement nearly imperceptible, because she couldn't tear her gaze away from his in the reflection.

His hands fell away, flexing at his sides.

She watched him watch her, his eyes skimming the length of her body, lingering on dip of her hips, the swell of her breasts, and the hollow of her throat for so long a furious blush scalded her. She almost squirmed beneath his lazy, albeit seductive, assessment until finally his attention landed on the web of ribbons binding her into the lace corset.

With the skill of a practiced lover, Solarius slowly worked the laces of her dress. He was methodical, pulling the ribbons one at a time, his gaze flicking to hers each time another piece of silk was unbound. His featherlight touches teased and tormented her in a provocative conversation of stolen glances and silent challenge. Each of them quietly goaded the other to see who would flinch first, who would pull away, who would take it a step further. Narissa's stomach clenched as his knuckles grazed her newly exposed flesh, and when he traced the tattoos marking her spine with one finger, trailing all the way to the curve of her backside, she bit the inside of her cheek to keep from sighing with longing.

She didn't care if he hated her.

She didn't care if she was supposed to hate him.

In that moment, with the tension between them so thick she could've sliced through it with a blade, Narissa would have given anything to have Solarius's hands on her.

He slid his thumbs beneath the fabric bunching at her shoulders and gradually nudged the gown down the length of her arms, so it slipped from her body and pooled at her feet in a puddle of sea foam silk.

Narissa shivered as he drank in every inch of her. She was fully nude, save for the scrap of triangular blue satin covering her most intimate area, and when she turned to face him, the silver of his eyes darkened to a fathomless stormy gray.

The fire in the hearth sparked and spat, the flickering glow highlighting only half of his face, illuminating the raw hunger in his gaze.

She tucked her bottom lip beneath her teeth, and he tracked the movement, fixating on her mouth for a moment before stepping in closer so the fine fabric of his coat lightly scraped her nipples. Her pulse skittered, beating wildly, so loud she swore he could hear it between her rapid, uneven breathing. Every agonizing second was wrought with confusion as her mind spiraled. Never before had she seen him look at her like that—like she was some forbidden piece of fruit, like he wanted to devour her whole. Heat pooled low in her belly, and she clenched her hands into small fists and locked her spine, the air between them thinning, causing her head to spin.

Or perhaps it was the winter berry wine.

Narissa swayed on her feet.

"Easy, Rissa." Solarius hooked one arm around her waist and the other under her knees, lifting her off her feet. "Time for bed."

Bed.

Her head lolled against his shoulder, and suddenly it was rather difficult to keep her eyes open. In fact, she found it quite comfortable to be carried in his arms, even if it was only a few short strides before he laid her on the bed.

Narissa sank into the cushiony mattress, surrounded by a mountain of fluffy pillows. Solarius draped the thick velvet comforter over her naked form, tucking it in around her legs to ensure she stayed warm. She snuggled into the plush softness, tugging the comforter up to her chin, and though her lids were heavy with exhaustion and possibly the effects of too much alcohol, she peered up at him.

"You don't want me." The words were out of her mouth before she could stop them. They weren't exactly a question, nor were they a statement of fact. If anything, it was a mild observation.

Solarius leaned against her bedpost, and the sheer layers of teal chiffon hanging from the canopy rippled around him like gentle ocean waves. He clicked his tongue and crossed his arms over his chest.

"You know nothing about what I want." There was no malice in his tone, but more of a somber acknowledgement.

"But I thought…" She yawned then, curling deeper into the comfort of her bed. "It was your intent to get the deed over with, as you so aptly put it."

"I will not bed you tonight, Narissa. Not when you're in such an inebriated state." He roughed the back of his knuckles along his jaw, his gaze drifting away from her to the stained glass windows. "Another night, perhaps."

Yes.

They would have plenty of those together, an endless stream of sleepless nights that bled into hostile days filled with the strain of their new marriage.

It sounded positively lovely.

Solarius shoved off the bedpost and headed for the door. Narissa clutched the comforter to her chest to keep from reaching for him, counting his steps as he walked away from her.

"Are you leaving?" she asked, trying to keep the desperation from her voice.

He stilled, barely sparing her a glance from over his shoulder. She couldn't read his expression in the dim glow of firelight, but his silhouette was taut with tension. He didn't appear to move or breathe. He simply stood there, contemplating, and when he finally spoke, the words floated across the room to her on a rough whisper.

"Do you want me to leave?" Again, he flexed his hands.

"Not particularly." Her response was hushed and lacking its usual confidence.

Narissa knew Solarius didn't care for her, just as she knew he would rather be anywhere else than in her bedroom. But for one night, she could pretend…because she was so tired of being alone.

He turned to face her fully then, his eyes expanding into radiant pools of silver. Arching one brow, he pinned her with a cautious, scrutinizing look. "You wish for me to stay?"

She shrugged beneath the covers, the velvet comforter sliding down her shoulder. To Solarius's credit, his gaze never left her face. "It *is* our wedding night."

Solarius straightened, running a hand through the silvery black strands of his hair. "Very well."

He removed his boots first and set them by the hearth, then shrugged out of his coat, laying it neatly over the back of the winged chair. From her cocooned position on the bed, she shamelessly admired everything about him. She liked the way the top buttons of his collared shirt were undone, giving her glimpses of his muscled chest. She enjoyed watching him roll his sleeves, fastening them above his toned forearms. He was recklessly handsome in an imperfect, careless sort of way. Maybe it was the way his hair always looked slightly mussed, like he thoughtlessly shoved a hand through it. Or perhaps it was the way his shirt was always a little wrinkled, as though he'd grabbed it from the floor after a night of drinking and merriment. Either way, his haphazard, yet delectably roguish appearance, always gave Narissa's heart cause to skitter.

Solarius stretched out on the bed alongside her, kicking one ankle over the other, and tucked his hands behind his head as he sank into the mountain of pillows. He lay on top of the comforter and Narissa rolled over to face him, gnawing on her bottom lip.

His gaze was trained on the delicate canopy above them, and she wondered if perhaps he was accustomed to stargazing at night. She imagined his bedroom at House Celestine had a ceiling made of glass so he could admire the moon and the stars as they shifted across the skies. Unfortunately for him, right now his only view was a swath of shimmering turquoise fabric.

A sigh of discontent escaped her and her eyes fluttered closed with the pull of exhaustion. With no promises, no expectations, and no hope for the future, she murmured, "Goodnight, my lord."

Narissa was already halfway to the realm of dreams when Solarius's rough whisper caressed her cheek.

"Goodnight...my lady.

CHAPTER FIVE

*N*arissa was in horrific agony.

Her temples were throbbing, a relentless ache that she could feel deep in her bones. Though her eyes were squeezed shut, she could sense the blinding light of mid-morning pouring in through the stained glass window, warming her face. But she didn't want to open her eyes, she didn't want to remember that she was trapped in a loveless marriage with a male who could barely tolerate being in the same room as her.

The memory of the way Solarius looked at her in the mirror while he undressed her sent a rush of nausea coursing through Narissa. Then again, it likely had less to do with him and more to do with the fact that she was recovering from her overindulgence. Her blood pumped through her veins like sludge, her mouth felt as though she'd rinsed it with a handful of sand from the beach, and each time she moved, her stomach sloshed with the remnants of last night's winter berry wine. She winced, cautiously stretching one arm out to the other side of the bed, only to find it cold and empty.

Of course, Solarius had left her. She honestly shouldn't be surprised, nor should she have expected anything less. On second thought, it might be best for her to hold no expectations of him or their relationship whatsoever. Then she would never be disappointed.

On a groan, Narissa eased herself up into a sitting position and blinked open her eyes against the harsh stream of sunlight. Rude, that it should be such a beautiful day when she was feeling so feeble and out of sorts. She swiped under her eyes, wincing when kohl mixed with a sheen of gold from the previous day's liner smudged her fingertips. A cursory glance in the floor-length gilded mirror left her cringing and scowling at her own reflection in distaste.

She was an absolute mess.

Her waves were frizzy and chaotic, much like how they looked after the downpour of a summer storm. The skin beneath her eyes was smeared with leftover kohl and golden powder, so she looked like she'd taken a vicious punch to the face and had been graced with glistening bruises. Her lips were dry and papery, cracked like crisp parchment, and she was in desperate need of a hot shower to rejuvenate her aching body. Even a soak in her tub would be lovely, though it would not be as easy to wash her hair.

Narissa clambered out of bed and nearly tripped over a pair of boots.

She scowled down at the offending shoes, reaching blindly for her satin robe.

Boots, she realized, that did *not* belong to her.

Her heart stuttered as she grabbed the robe from the chair nearest her vanity. She wrapped it snugly around herself, tying it at the waist, and raked a hand through her messy waves. It was then she heard the rushing of water over the ambient trickle of waterfalls flanking the hearth. She scanned the rest of her room, noting the sleek coat slung over the wingback chair, along with the pair of pants and rumpled shirt deposited on its seat cushion.

Solarius had not abandoned her after all.

He was currently in her bathing suite, likely naked, wet, and positively glorious, standing beneath a stream of scalding water.

She padded lightly across the hardwood floor, careful not to make too much noise. Curls of steam slipped from beneath the closed door, warming her toes. Pressing both hands to its carved surface, she placed her ear against the door and listened. At first, there was only the hiss of water as it bounced off the marble, but then it was accompanied by a low, shockingly delightful baritone.

Solarius was *singing*.

Narissa pulled back, confusion marring her brow.

She didn't know he could sing.

It was surprising, all things considered. His voice was deep and lulling, a melodic cadence with enough seduction to soften her knees. She sighed, entranced by the spell of his song as the words wove a story of dancing stars and painted skies. Maybe, if they ever managed to tolerate one another for more than five minutes, they could play a duet some time. After all, Narissa was quite proficient at the harp.

Without warning, the water shut off and she startled, lurching away from the door.

Her gaze shot around the room and she hesitated, torn between bravery and cowardice. She could jump back into bed and pretend to still be asleep—hopefully he would fall for it—or she could waltz into the adjoining bathing suite without hesitation and freshen up as planned. If she chose the bed option, she could keep her eyes closed until he finally left and avoid any sort of confrontation. Whereas if she opted to walk right into the bathing suite, she might be forced into conversation, and considering he was most definitely naked at this very moment...

She took one step toward the bed and paused.

No.

This was *her* room. She had just as much right to be in there as him, and she didn't care if her unannounced arrival made him uncomfortable.

Narissa smoothed her unruly hair and shoved open the door.

It smacked soundly into something solid on the other side, jarring her. She put her shoulder into it, forcing it open, only to see Solarius stumble backward.

"Fuck." He winced and grabbed his shoulder, the towel he held falling to the ground in a heap of white, like snow.

Narissa couldn't help but stare at the ridiculously gorgeous male standing before her, fully nude. He was more perfect than she remembered. Perfect chest. Perfect abdomen. Perfect...

Her gaze dipped to his waist, then a bit further, and she yelped.

"Sweet shores, I am *so* sorry. I didn't mean to—" She covered her eyes with her hands, whipping around to grant him some privacy, and slammed right into the door.

"Ow!" she cried, clutching the side of her head where pain ricocheted through her temple. The ache spread to the back of her neck, and she whimpered.

"Shit." Solarius muttered, his hand coming to the small of her back. "Are you okay?"

"I...I think so." Narissa lightly rubbed her head, hoping a bruise wouldn't form. She looked bad enough already. "Tides below, that hurt."

She twisted to face him, suddenly remembering he'd been injured by the door as well. "Wait, are *you* okay?"

He'd wrapped the white towel around his waist, knotting it just below his navel, where tiny beads of water sluiced down his deliciously carved hips. She couldn't decide if she was relieved or disappointed. Either way, she was once again rewarded with a rather splendid view of his tempting body. Her gaze trailed over every inch of his flesh, noting the constellation tattoo resembling a trident across his heart, and the moon phases marking his right arm, stopping just above his elbow.

Solarius shoved his damp hair from his face, and the corner of his mouth lifted. "I'll survive."

Well, that made one of them.

Narissa swallowed, blaming the rise of heat in her cheeks on the blanket of steam engulfing her, because the flush of her body had absolutely nothing to do with the male standing in front of her.

She turned a bit, careful to avoid the door. "I'll just—"

"No, it's fine." Solarius attempted to step past her, and they both moved to the same side. "I'm done, you should..."

Narissa pivoted and he matched her, each of them carefully trying to avoid the other while mimicking one another's movements.

Solarius grinned, then captured her by the waist with both hands.

She grabbed his wrists, and a gasp slipped between her lips when he lifted her off the ground. In one fluid motion, he spun her around, switching their places—so she stood within the bathing suite and he was by the door.

"Thank you for the dance." He smirked, the silver of his eyes flashing with mirth, then closed the door soundly behind him.

Narissa waited exactly five seconds before collapsing against it.

She could still feel the warmth from his hands burning through the silk of her robe. Now, she somehow had to shower without imagining those same exceedingly capable hands roving all over her body.

A huff of annoyance escaped her.

Her intent was laughable.

Narissa would never be able to ignore the feel of his touch, just as she knew the image of him fully nude would be at the forefront of her mind for the remainder of the day.

Perhaps even longer.

CHAPTER SIX

Solarius dressed, grateful he'd had the foresight to request fresh clothing well after Narissa had finally fallen asleep. He tucked in his navy silk shirt and smoothed the pleats of his smoky gray pants. Even though he went through the same motions he did every day—lacing his boots, rolling his cuffs, adjusting the collar—his mind was racing.

He could not stop thinking about the fact that Narissa was in the bathing suite, merely one door away, and that she was completely naked.

The faint hint of floral soap wafted from under the door, which meant she was probably lathered in sudsy bubbles, all silky and slippery. And thanks to the fact that he'd helped her undress last night, he knew *exactly* what she looked like beneath all those layers of silk and chiffon. Skin that looked as though it had been kissed by the sun, a slender waist and full hips, breasts that would undoubtedly fit perfectly into each of his hands, and the jewels piercing her navel had been the icing on the cake. It had taken every last shred of his willpower not to trail a finger from the hollow of her neck to those flimsy little panties and rip them right off her.

But he was a lord of Starstorm blood, born of righteousness and chivalry, and so he'd politely kept his hands to himself.

His thoughts, however, were another matter entirely, and were proving much more difficult to control.

Do not think about her naked.

Do not think about her naked.

Do not think about her naked.

His cock twitched.

Solarius swore.

Stars above, he had to get out of this room and put more than a door of distance between them.

He stalked over to the bathing suite, rapping twice against the hardwood. "Narissa?"

Her soft voice floated from the other side. "Yes?"

"I'm going to the dining hall to grab breakfast for us, and I'll bring it up to your room." He shoved his hands into the pockets of his pants and rocked back onto his heels. "And I'm also going to see if I can find something for your headache."

A pause, then, "What makes you think I have a headache?"

Aside from the obscene amount of alcohol she ingested the night before?

He shifted on his feet, keeping that thought to himself. "You just smacked your head on the door. I'd say it's a lucky guess."

Rolling his eyes to the driftwood chandelier hanging from the ceiling, Solarius didn't wait for her to respond and strode out of the bedroom in search of food.

He was pleased to discover there was another winding staircase that led from Narissa's room to the interior of the house instead of the balcony, especially considering the wind gusting off the coast was brutally cold. Tiny waves frothed, their white caps crashing into the shore, and he wondered how often the tides were in sync with Narissa's mood. That notion alone sent his thoughts spiraling back to those ethereal wave tattoos marking the tips of her ears as well as her spine. It was fascinating that they would glow a silvery blue in the wash of moonlight, it was even more curious how he'd never noticed them before.

Or perhaps he'd just failed to pay attention.

Apparently, his memory was lacking.

Narissa had made an outrageous claim against his honor last night, alleging they'd been intimate together, only for him to discard her like days old rubbish.

But she was severely mistaken.

Solarius had never had sex with Narissa. If he had, he would fucking *remember*, and he sure as stars wouldn't abandon her in a cold bed the next day. No, he would show her the most sensual kind of affection, worshiping every beautiful, desirable inch of her until she was trembling with longing. Until he was the only one capable of sating her needs. Then he would make her come so hard, the moon would fall out of the damn sky.

Something he should be doing right at this very moment, he thought with a rush of bitterness. Considering they were newly married.

Instead, he was fetching her breakfast and finding something to alleviate the agony from the night before, all because he'd broken their previous courtship and she'd broken his heart. He'd never publicly spoken ill of Narissa after their courtship ended, nor had he commented on the cause of such discord. No one needed to know Solarius had caught her in bed with Lord Calfair Skyhelm, one of his oldest and now former friends, but his lack of explanation hadn't kept the rumors away. They spread like wildfire, growing more absurd and outrageous with every whisper, until the truth of the matter was lost to an ocean of lies and misjudgment.

Stars be damned, even Narissa seemed to have forgotten that she was the one at fault for their resentful estrangement.

With his mood dampened by unwelcome memories, Solarius wandered aimlessly through the corridors of ivory pillars embedded with turquoise shells, following the deep blue floor that rippled with every step, like walking upon waves. The curving ceilings depicted painted murals of sirens and swirling seas, of jagged cliffs and rough shorelines.

Solarius wasn't incredibly familiar with the layout of House Azurvend. He wasn't exactly friends with Lord Reif Marintide, nor did he often visit Aeramere's esteemed coastal city. While the swirling staircases and soothing waterfalls were pleasing to the eye, they made it difficult to discern which way he was going. It didn't matter if Solarius passed more than one servant who certainly could have given him directions, he refused to look like a foolish husband who'd yet to be given a proper tour of his new wife's residence. Once he made it to the main level, he simply followed the scent of fresh biscuits, candied fruits, and spiced beef.

Eventually, he discovered the dining hall where Reif was already enjoying a late breakfast.

The lord of House Azurvend was lounging in a chair near the dining table with his legs stretched out before him, one ankle kicked over the other. His pants were the color of sand, and his crisp shirt reminded Solarius of warmer days. It was a bright, sparkling kind of blue and Reif had paired it with a trim cream-colored vest embellished with waves of shimmering thread. He held a cup of steaming tea in his hands and his dark blond hair fell across one side of his face when he lifted it to his mouth.

"Morning," he drawled, watching Solarius from over the rim of porcelain as he took a sip.

"Morning." Solarius gestured to the spread of food on the table. "Do you mind if I take a plate up to Narissa? She's feeling a little...unwell."

"Unwell?" Reif straightened and sat up, his brows pinching together. "Does she need a healer?"

"No, not exactly. More like she needs a remedy from all the alcohol she ingested last night." Solarius rubbed one hand along the back of his neck as a rush of heat scored his chest. "And this morning she, ah, ran into a door."

He wouldn't dare tell Reif that the main cause for Narissa's possible head injury was because she'd walked in on him fully nude in the bathing suite. And fully erect. Granted, it wasn't his fault he'd woken up like that, but he hoped a shower would give him time to get his blood pumping to somewhere other than his cock. Unfortunately for Solarius, the longer he stood in the shower, the more he couldn't stop thinking about the way Narissa had curled against him during the night, or the way her hair had tickled his chin. Or how those breathy little sighs she made while sleeping sent his entire body vibrating with longing.

And the way her pretty eyes drank him in when she stormed into the bathing suite had only served to bolster his ego.

A tiny spark of hope ignited inside of him.

"Ran into a door, eh?" Reif mused, the corner of his mouth ticking upward into a knowing grin. "Is that what we're calling it these days?"

Solarius choked on a laugh and grabbed a plate from the stack at the far end of the table. He would neither confirm nor deny Reif's assumptions. His relationship with Narissa was already precarious, like they were balancing on opposite ends of a tightrope across a gaping chasm. One wrong move, and they would both fall to their doom.

"Must have been quite the evening." Reif stood then and pushed in his chair. "I'll send a maid up with a brew for Narissa, it works wonders for post-alcohol ailments."

Solarius nodded once. "I'm grateful."

His gaze swept across the wide variety of food spread over the table. There were bowls of fruit drizzled with honey, platters of seasoned potatoes and fried meats. A tiered tray was overflowing with miniature teacakes, and baskets of warm biscuits were loosely covered with a cloth, the steam rising from them. There were at least four different types of sweetened jams, and it was then Solarius realized he had no idea what Narissa preferred.

Did she like raspberry and lemon jam? Or was the spiced orange her favorite? Did she even like biscuits?

He supposed he would have to fill the plate with some of everything.

"I almost forgot." Reif set down his cup of tea and pulled a silver envelope from his vest. "Ariesian left this for you last night."

He set it carefully on the edge of the plate.

"Right." Solarius's finger itched to rip off the wax seal depicting the Faerie Star flanked by two outward facing crescent moons—his family's crest. He was beyond curious to see if his eldest brother had acquired any more information regarding the strained relationship between Queen Elowyn of Aeramere and her son, Prince Aspen, and whether or not their beautiful realm would descend into war and chaos. But alas, it would have to wait, as he had a very hungry and likely rather angry bride awaiting his return upstairs.

Solarius gave Reif a slight nod. "Thank you."

"Anytime." Reif waved away his gratitude with ease. "Oh, and one more thing."

Solarius grabbed a spoon, preparing to load a helping of the seasoned potatoes onto the plate, then paused.

"Narissa has a penchant for sweets." Reif inclined his head toward the tiered tray of tiny colorful cakes. "In case you were wondering."

"Duly noted."

A brief flash of amusement flickered over Reif's face before he strolled out of the dining hall, whistling an old tune about the goddess of the sea and her love for the moon.

After Reif left the room, Solarius started loading up the plate with food—meat and potatoes for himself, and sweet treats for Narissa.

If she wanted to eat cake for breakfast, who was he to stop her?

CHAPTER SEVEN

After what felt like an eternity, Solarius finally found his way back to Narissa's rooms.

Balancing the plate of food with one hand, he hesitated on the other side of the bedroom door. He debated knocking to announce his arrival, then thought better of it and nudged the door open. If there was one thing for certain, he never knew what to expect with her.

But he realized fairly quickly that he better get used to her taking his breath away.

Because that's exactly what she did.

Solarius walked right in, then drew up short, nearly tripping over his own two feet.

Narissa was seated upon the bed with her knees pulled up and feet bare, a day dress spilling around her like sun glinting off the crystalline sea. Her ruffled skirts were a shade of pale turquoise that glinted gold in the light, and the white bodice billowed like cresting waves off her shoulders. The sleeves were long and loose, and though her garments were completely unadorned, Solarius swore he'd never seen anything more beautiful in his life. She wore her sunlit hair down in wild waves, and with the exception of the gold rings on almost every finger, she wore no other jewels. A book was splayed open in her lap, and she scraped her teeth along her bottom lip while she read, a habit he found oddly endearing. When she licked her finger to turn the page, he almost dropped the entire plate of food on the floor.

His muttered curse drew her attention and she glanced up, slamming the book closed.

"My lord." She shoved the book into the pearlescent drawer of her nightstand and sat up, crossing her legs beneath her. "You're back."

"Yes." He cleared his throat and slowly moved toward the bed, carefully setting the plate between them. "I brought food."

Solarius inwardly cringed.

I brought food.

What a stupidly obvious thing to say.

"I can see that." Narissa tilted her head, her waves tumbling over one shoulder and he had half a mind to sweep them back, just for an excuse to touch her.

His throat worked, but words would not form. There was something different about her, something so inexplicably eye-catching that he couldn't quite name what held him utterly captivated.

She blinked, those frosty green eyes watching him stare at her, and he realized they were not lined with kohl. She wore no shimmering powder or paint, yet her lips were a natural rosy pink. There were no ornaments or charms in her hair, no excessive glamour or fabrics with dazzling designs meant to draw a male's eye.

This was the real Narissa, in her purest form. The one she kept hidden from the rest of society. The one she may have inadvertently revealed only to him.

And he fucking loved it.

"You look beautiful." He shook his head once and sat down on the opposite side of the bed. "Are. You *are* beautiful. My lady."

Stars above, he could not even *speak* properly around her today. She had affected him somehow, her very presence made him feel as though he was lost in an ocean of wonder, and for her he would gladly drown.

"Thank you." Her voice was soft yet clipped, as though she wasn't entirely sure if she should accept his compliment or not. Like perhaps she didn't truly believe him.

Not that he could blame her, their relationship was built off stony insults and harsh insinuations. It had been forged in the fires of disparagement, honeyed words and flattery were lost between them.

They ate together in mostly companionable silence, with a few casual remarks about the weather and Narissa's fondness for sweets.

"Are you going to open that?" she asked, nodding to the letter in his hand. She popped her thumb into her mouth, sucking off a bit of icing.

Solarius swallowed a groan of desire and spared her a glance.

"I was..." His voice trailed off when he realized she had a smear of creamy blue icing clinging to her bottom lip. He grinned. "You've got something just there."

He tapped his own lip, then reached out, his gaze flicking to hers. "May I?"

She nodded once, her pale green eyes darting to his mouth.

Solarius gently cupped the right side of her face with his fingertips, then dragged his thumb across her lip, swiping away the remnants of the sugary residue. When he licked the icing from his thumb, wishing he was tasting something else, her eyes rounded and a distinctive blush flooded her cheeks.

She edged back, away from him, and blew out a harsh breath.

She hates me, he reminded himself.

And damn it, he should hate her as well. Narissa had been the one to play him for a fool, to lead him into thinking there was something good and wonderful between them before seeking solace in the arms of Calfair Skyhelm. Solarius was the one who'd been humiliated, the one deemed an "unlovable rake" by society, because he couldn't manage to hold the interest of one of Aeramere's sweetest souls.

Sweet, indeed.

Solarius had been on the receiving end of Narissa's venomous mouth more times than he could count. So why then could he not quit thinking of her? He shouldn't be imagining her writhing beneath him while he teased and taunted her into oblivion. He shouldn't want to die from the poison of her velvety lips or melt into the satin of her skin. It would be unusually cruel to coerce her into thinking there was attraction between them just to what, pretend they were happily married?

Eventually, he would have to bed Narissa, but it would not be done out of obligation. No, the first time he filled her, he wanted her wet and willing. And he would claim her in such a way, no other male would ever compare.

He plucked the envelope from Ariesian off the plate and tore it open.

Solarius unfolded the piece of parchment and skimmed his brother's bold, clean script.

"What's it say?" Narissa asked as she drew her knees to her chest and wrapped her arms around them.

Narissa was privy to a good bit of knowledge where the possible coup of Queen Elowyn by Prince Aspen was concerned. After all, she'd been there when those wretched creatures attacked House Celestine during Novalise and Asher's wedding. She'd witnessed first-hand the destruction they'd caused, just as she'd seen how Queen Elowyn's magic failed to assist them in their time of need. Shockingly enough, it had been Prince Aspen who sent the fiends back to whatever earthly hell in which they belonged—though some believed he created them as a diversion to distract from his intent to overthrow his mother. If the prince painted himself in a good light by saving Celestine from those foul beings born of tainted magic, then he would no longer look suspect.

But Solarius wasn't about to be deceived by such tactics.

Prince Aspen had come to their aid, yes, but he'd also done so in the form of the Eyrewolfe, a massive wolf-like beast with a skull for a head and large curving horns. If the prince could keep *that* a secret from his subjects, there was no telling what other matters remained undisclosed.

"Ariesian is reminding me that we're invited to House Celestine for the annual Yuletide Ball." Which Solarius knew meant they would go not only to make an appearance, but that it would also be one of the first times he and Narissa were seen out by society. Their behavior would be telling. "And he has asked me to join him in a game of starshoot."

Her brow quirked, a flicker of amusement passing over her face. "Starshoot?"

Solarius grinned, the fondness of the memory flooding him. "It was a game we played with my father when we were younger. He could create anything from the stars, so he would make constellations in different animal forms and we would shoot them with bows and arrows made of stardust. But that was before—"

Before he died.

Before Lord Zenos Starstorm Celestine, who was strong, powerful, and exceptionally brilliant, had fallen asleep one night and never awoken.

Queen Elowyn had carried out a brief investigation into his cause of death, but the royal healers declared there was no foul play within a few days, and so he was buried beneath the stars, leaving behind a wife and eight children. Already his legacy was forgotten by everyone, save for those born of his blood.

But Solarius did not believe his father had left this life due to natural causes. Fae did not simply go to sleep and never wake up. That was an affliction in the mortal realms, something suffered by humans. For a fae to fall into an eternal slumber, it would have to be forced or sought out with precise intention. A charm, perhaps. A poison or tonic. Lord Asher Firebane's mother came to mind, as she willingly ended her own life after her bastard of a husband died.

Yet Solarius knew without a doubt that Zenos Starstorm would never in the span of centuries take his own life. If anything, his father was far too stubborn for such a demise.

Something warm and soft covered Solarius's hand and his mind quieted.

"Sol?" Narissa's lulling voice summoned him from the chaos of his thoughts.

He glanced down to see her hand covering his own, where he

clenched the bed linens so tightly his fingers curled into fists. She stroked the pad of her fingers across his knuckles. It was a gentle sweep, back and forth, and he found it oddly soothing.

"Apologies, my lady." He forced his hand to relax beneath her touch.

"Would you like to talk about it?" Her tone was achingly tender, and his heart strained in response.

Solarius shook his head, not wanting to discuss his demons. Even if she was showing him a kindness, he had no desire to share his inner turmoil with Narissa. At least not until they explored whatever personal tension was brewing between them. It would seem their past courtship was not quite how either of them remembered, and he had every intention of having that conversation with her soon, even if that meant she would show her claws and teeth.

"Another time." He eased away from her and shoved off the bed. "Anyway, Tovian is the one who possesses such magic now. Since he and Nyxian have returned and settled after their seafaring travels, I imagine Ariesian is keen to have us all together for some sort of brotherly bonding."

"You're leaving then." It wasn't quite a question as it was a statement, and Narissa refused to meet his gaze, busying herself with the glistening ruffles of her skirt instead.

"Yes, only for a short while." When she failed to look at him again, he shifted his weight and shoved his hands into his pockets. "Do you not have any dalliances or social gatherings of your own to attend? I would assume you have any number of ladylike matters requiring your attention."

"I...of course." Narissa snapped off each word, and when she finally lifted her face, her eyes were shadowed and her full lips were pressed into a hard line. "Of course."

Something about the look on her face set him on edge, almost worried him. But he shrugged off his concern. Knowing Narissa, she was probably contemplating his death. "I shall return in time for dinner. I promise."

Her smile was pinched.

Part of him wanted to haul her into his arms and kiss that cross look right off her face. The other part of him knew better. Best to wait for her fury to calm, lest he try to kiss her and end up drowning in the wave of her wrath.

"I'll be back before nightfall." Solarius took one more long look at her before leaving. Her legs were pulled to her chest, her chin resting upon her knees. She was staring at the stained glass window, the depiction of the sirens and their separate desires holding her captive.

Narissa sighed and refused to look his direction.

Solarius accepted his dismissal with the grace of a scorned lord. He turned on one heel and walked out of her bedchamber without another word.

CHAPTER EIGHT

nnoyance fired through Narissa.

She supposed she ought to be grateful that Solarius had decided to leave her alone, yet instead she found herself oddly vexed by his abrupt departure. They had not yet been married for a full cycle of the sun, and already he couldn't wait to get away from her.

Which was fine, she didn't require his companionship.

Narissa had grown rather used to spending time by herself.

She would attend to her *ladylike matters* while he gallivanted off with his brothers to shoot constellations out of the sky—a sport which sounded far more exciting than anything she could imagine. Solarius probably thought she intended to busy herself with knitting, or drawing, or spending obscene amounts of money at the shops in Azurvend while sharing bits of gossip with other noble ladies. But in truth, she had no one to share her innermost thoughts and secrets with, she was without a close confidante or dearest friend. Despite being taken in by Reif after the death of her parents, her relationship with her cousin was one of agreeable cordiality. As Lord of House Azurvend, Reif was far too preoccupied with his own schedule and responsibilities to pay her much attention, so Narissa found her own ways to amuse herself in the long stretches of time she spent alone.

She collected the near-empty plate and set it on the nightstand, then padded across the floor to where a small, bronze siren statue was fixed to the far wall. Wrapping one hand around the siren's tail, she pulled gently and the hidden door gave way, groaning open to reveal a dimly lit secret room.

The space was smaller than her bedroom, but it was cozy, and it was the one place in all of Aeramere where she truly felt at peace. Where she could lock herself away and pretend the rest of the world had ceased to exist.

Dried herbs hanging from long pieces of twine decorated the rough stone walls, and wooden shelves were crowded with vases of sugar vine, bloodroot, and ash wood. Jars filled with cloud mist, illuminance algae, and moonflower nectar were right beside baskets of citrus peppers, syrenshade, and a random assortment of mushrooms from House Terensel. Her smooth worktable was crowded with bowls of crushed coral, sea glass, along with a mortar, pestle, and a scratched-up cauldron. Wooden shelves displayed Narissa's prized collections of potions, salves, and sensual elixirs—the latter of which she sold to the ladies of Aeramere by means of clandestine meetings—because Reif would be horrified if he discovered she was brewing tonics designed to enhance a female's sexual prowess.

Narissa cleared some room on her worktable and lit a small fire beneath the cauldron. She poured in a small amount of lotus oil, just enough for it to simmer, then set to work grinding some winter rose petals with her mortar and pestle. She added a few drops of smoky vanilla to the crushed flowers, blending them together until her wrist and shoulder ached, then combined them with the lotus oil in the cauldron. Grabbing a wooden spoon from the shelf behind her, she stirred the contents while tiny bubbles gurgled and popped, and a warm, sultry scent hung heavy in the air.

Despite the cold outside temperatures and the wind rattling the panes of the framed window overlooking the sea, beads of sweat dampened Narissa's brow. The cotton sleeves of her day dress clung to her skin, and she shoved them up to her elbows as she continued to mix the elixir. For one fleeting moment, she considered concocting a love potion. Perhaps then Solarius would come to his senses, even if he was only charmed into believing it.

Narissa laughed softly at the absurdity of the idea. She shook her head once, the golden waves of her hair frizzing slightly in the thick air. Tucking an errant strand behind her ear, she reached for a bottle of pearl dust, then paused when two feminine voices sounded from inside of her bedchamber.

She stilled, listening as the maids who set to work tidying her room also felt the need to share their opinions on Narissa's relationship with Solarius.

"I don't know what he sees in Lady Narissa," one with a nasal, high-pitched voice proclaimed. "She's hardly beautiful. In fact, I would call her rather plain."

"I heard their union was contracted by Lord Starstorm and Lord Marintide." The second maid had more of a husky voice, as though she'd swallowed a handful of rocks. "Lord Solarius probably doesn't even love her."

"I pity him," the first responded, snorting with derision. "How tragic for someone as handsome and charming as Lord Solarius to be bound to such a delicately tedious female who prefers potions to parties."

"She always was a bit of a wallflower."

"Well, if Lord Solarius is looking for a more bountiful garden, my gates are certainly open."

The maids giggled, their mocking laughter echoing through the small crevices of the stone wall, gradually filling Narissa with a sense of immeasurable dread. She pressed the heel of her palm to her chest to alleviate the building pressure there, rubbing in slow circles while she took one steadying breath after another.

Cruelty knew no bounds.

Narissa wasn't ignorant—she was well aware that her perceived love for the solitary and her quirky hobbies made her a less than desirable mate to most. Yet the truth of it was she didn't *enjoy* being alone. It was simply a matter of fact. She never experienced a proper introduction to society after the death of her parents, and it was a difficult task to find companions of worth as most ladies of Aeramere were rather fond of gossip and lacking in trustworthiness. In truth, the only female Narissa would consider an honorable friend was Lady Sarelle Starstorm, and not even she knew the truth behind Narissa and Solarius's abrupt and failed courtship.

Admittedly, their reasons for ending things were murky at best. Narissa had no desire to slander his reputation or character, so she stewed in silent contempt instead, only voicing her dislike for him when the need arose. However, Solarius seemed trapped in a world of delusion, choosing to direct his anger for his own misgivings at her instead of himself. Naturally, outlandish rumors surrounded their falling out, with neither Narissa nor Solarius confirming or denying anything. She was never certain why Solarius remained silent on the matter, but for Narissa, her pride had been bruised and her heart had been broken.

Shame cut her deeply, like a blade forged of cold iron.

After all, it was her secret to keep. If she didn't want all of Aeramere to know that Solarius had charmed his way into her bed, taken her virtue, then refused to speak to her again...then that was her business.

She owed no one an explanation.

And for Solarius to act as though he'd done nothing wrong, like she was somehow at fault...well it filled her with a kind of blinding rage, which was why she gave him her absolute worst any time they were stuck with one another for company.

Anger, insults, attitude, and saucy comments were all she could do to protect her fragile heart from him.

Narissa sighed, letting the contents in the cauldron simmer over the open flame. Eventually the maids finished their cleaning and finally went about the rest of their daily tasks, but Narissa didn't return to her bedchamber. Instead, she enclosed herself in her room of potions and practicality, a place where she could control every aspect around her. Where nothing was left to chance or fate. She toiled over the cauldron for hours, perfecting the special oil blend until her eyes began to water, and she lost all track of time.

"I thought I might find you in here."

Narissa's head snapped up at the masculine voice and her gaze zeroed in on the entry where Reif lounged against the arching wall. The cuffs of his blue shirt were rolled, and his loose tan pants were tucked into his shiny onyx boots. One finger was hooked in the collar of the well-worn coat slung over his shoulder and his sandy blond hair was mussed and swept over half his face, as though he'd just stepped inside from off the beach.

Reif lifted a single brow in question. "Care to explain why you're hiding away from the world the day after your wedding?"

"Not particularly." Narissa pressed her lips together and doused the flame beneath the cauldron with a spritz of water, just enough to smother the small fire into nothing but damp embers and curling ribbons of smoke.

"I would have thought you were spending time with Lord Solarius all day," he drawled, pushing away from the uneven stone wall. "So, you can imagine my surprise when I learned he has been out from House Azurvend since mid-morning and you were not with him."

Narissa let her shoulders rise and fall in nonchalance. She had perfected the art of showcasing indifference. "Lord Solarius returned to House Celestine at his brother's request. The invitation was not extended to me."

Reif's brows pulled together into a frown. "Is that a fact?"

"So it would seem." She wiped her hands on a towel and eyed the concoction she'd crafted. It would need to cool before she could ladle it into the proper vials. Her gaze flicked back to her cousin and the unfortunate topic at hand. "I imagine his siblings will always take precedence."

Reif made a derisive sort of noise, his boots clicking soundly across the floor as he approached her workspace. "I'm inclined to disagree with you, Narissa. Last night, for the entirety of the evening, Lord Solarius couldn't manage to keep his eyes off you."

Only because she was incredibly drunk and he didn't want her embarrassing behavior to stain their marriage.

Narissa blew out a breath, sending a ruffle of her wavy hair fluttering into her face. She flattened her palms against the wooden table and leaned forward, glaring up at Reif. "While I appreciate your reassurance, dear cousin, your pitiful attempts at matchmaking are nothing more than a waste of breath. Lord Solarius does not desire me in that way."

Maybe he did once. But that was before he got what he wanted then renounced her completely.

"If I am destined to be in a loveless marriage, then I will make the most of it." She gathered up some wilted winter rose petals and deposited them into a small glass jar for safekeeping. "But I will not go so far as to humiliate myself by thinking he values me."

Solarius may have claimed her feelings mattered, but his actions that morning spoke otherwise.

Reif rapped one knuckle along the edge of her worktable and when she looked over at him, his mossy green eyes were shrewd and gleaming. "There is one thing that will serve you well, so long as you don't forget it."

"Oh?" Narissa tilted her head to one side, planting both hands on her hips. "And what's that?"

Because of course she needed advice from her cousin on how best to win the heart of her husband, a male who clearly could not stand the ground she walked upon.

"Solarius Starstorm is quite possessive in nature. He does not like to share, nor does he want anyone touching what belongs to him." Reif smiled broadly, as though he'd made some sort of revolutionary discovery.

Narissa was not impressed. She suffered him a very loud, drawn-out sigh. "What are you suggesting, Reif?"

He bent forward conspiratorially, his whisper grating and full of absurd bravado. "Only that if you entertain the attention of another male, it won't be long until Lord Solarius arrives to defend what's his...which is you, of course."

Unfazed, Narissa stared at her cousin.

"That's it? That's your masterful bit of guidance?" She rolled her eyes to the ceiling, then raked her fingers through her hair. How horribly unoriginal. "You think I should try and make him jealous?"

It was quite possibly the most male scrap of guidance ever—impractical and utterly useless.

But Reif's response gave her pause.

"Not quite." He held up one finger with a solemn shake of his head. "You should make him realize what he has before it's lost to him."

Narissa wasn't entirely sure if that was a compliment, but it certainly sounded like one, so she decided to accept it. "I'll consider your suggestion, Reif. Thank you."

He inclined his head. "Freshen up and come to dinner, I've invited some guests from House Terensel. They should be arriving any moment."

"House Terensel?"

But before Narissa could ask who was joining them for dinner, Reif was already strolling back down the small corridor and she was left alone with her thoughts.

Outside, the sky was alight with hues of crimson, gold, and blush. The sun would dip across the western horizon quickly as it so often did in the throes of winter, and twilight would descend before giving way to the midnight hours.

Solarius's words prodded at the back of her mind.

"I shall return before nightfall. I promise."

Narissa scoffed, stalking from the potions room to her bedchamber, already knowing this would not be the only time Solarius failed to keep his word. She would simply have to prepare herself for the inevitable pain that followed his string of broken promises.

CHAPTER NINE

The sun was bleeding across the sky, smearing hues of gold with indigo as nightfall approached, and Solarius was keenly aware that he was breaking his promise to Narissa.

Shit.

He was going to be late and there was no way he would be back in time for dinner. Guilt swarmed him. It wasn't as though he was proud of being unable to keep his word. On the contrary, he usually held himself to exemplary standards, most specifically in terms of loyalty, honor, and respect. But he was currently with his brothers—Ariesian, Tovian, and Nyxian—and the three of them hadn't had this much fun together in what felt like years. Add in a few bottles of spiced whiskey and they were having a damn good time.

Solarius's breath misted before him as he loosed a heavy sigh, the biting winter wind slapping at his face while he stood on a ledge of the Moonfall Peaks overlooking Celestine. The fading sun sparked off the high mountains, casting them in a sheen of golden violet, their sharp peaks coated in a heavy layer of snow. His thick woolen coat blocked most of the chill, but he'd long ago lost most of the feeling in his fingers from gripping his bow.

He twirled the bow once, admiring its exceptional quality. The limbs were curved and crafted from midnight stars, solid in form yet shimmering like the night sky. Its string was a thread of glittering starlight and each arrow, though navy in color, looked like they'd been forged from a sea of stars.

Tovian had absolutely outdone himself. He possessed the rare ability to create anything from the stars, a gift he'd inherited from their father, and his aptitude for his magic had only increased with every passing year. His designs were masterful works of art, fabricated from celestial ribbons of wonder, and woven together to form anything born of the imagination.

Solarius wondered if Tovian harbored a more powerful magic as well, much like his other siblings. Perhaps he could control another aspect of the starstorm, similar to Novalise.

He debated asking him about it when Nyxian's jovial voice dragged him back from his thoughts.

"Come on, Tov!" Nyxian shouted, a wide grin stretching across his face as he raised a glass of whiskey in one hand and his bow with the other. "Give us another one!"

Tovian laughed, smoothing back his sweep of deep blue hair. "Alright, alright. Let me think."

He rolled his neck once, his breath puffing before him in the frigid night air. Clamping his palms together, Tovian slowly stretched his arms apart, an arc of chaotic stars and streaks of fire expanding between his hands. Angling one elbow back with his fingers splayed wide, he catapulted the explosion of stars into the open night sky. The tiny sparks of fire and magic swirled and raced throughout the darkening heavens, taking the shape of a magnificent raven. The bird-like constellation fluttered between wispy gray clouds, swooping and soaring around the mountain peaks.

Ariesian stepped up beside Solarius, a look of determination cut across his brow. He notched his arrow of stardust and took aim, his gaze unwavering as the glittering raven glided over a canvas of ink.

"Mine." He loosed the arrow with perfect form and it shot across the pitch, striking the raven's heart. A cascading waterfall of dark teal and golden stars tumbled toward the earth, the sparkling remnants of a fallen constellation.

"Better make a wish." Tovian jerked his head to where the stars were fizzling and burning out before they reached the jagged mountaintops.

Ariesian scoffed, slinging his bow over one shoulder. His gaze scanned the night sky once more, watching as the last star burned out completely. "I never make wishes on fallen stars."

No one mentioned that was Caelian's area of expertise, especially not after the situation involving Kjeld Holtstrom. Their second youngest sister had made a grave misjudgment by putting her wants and desires above the hands of fate. It was a terrible error and one she would pay for… dearly. Kjeld Holtstrom was Drake Kalstrand's former general and closest friend, and he'd willingly sacrificed his life to save Solarius's youngest sister, Creslyn. Yet instead of allowing Kjeld to claim a warrior's death, Caelian stepped in and saved his life by making a wish upon a falling star.

Or rather…multiple wishes.

Caelian's magic was the ability to grant wishes upon stars, and she had used her power for selfish reasons, caring not for the soul subjected to her bidding. It would have been manageable if Caelian had only wished for Kjeld to live, but she sought more than just his survival. She wished for many things and not once did she ask for Kjeld's consent in the matter. Her brazen assumptions altered the course of his destiny—Caelian had single-handedly changed the man's entire life, and he was in no rush to forgive her for it.

It was a sore spot of discussion and disappointment for Ariesian, so Solarius cleared his throat in an effort to redirect the somber nature of the conversation.

"You never were the hopelessly romantic one." He jabbed Ariesian in the ribs lightly with his elbow. "That title has always belonged to our Tov."

Tovian's face fell, his easy smile fading into a faint scowl. "A lot of good it did me."

Nyxian slung his arm around Tovian's shoulders, his carefree grin widening. "Go easy on yourself, Tov. It's not as though you were jilted for a fae of common birth. She chose a prince, for star's sake."

Tovian summoned his magic, gathering more stars between his palms. They burned brighter this time, flaring with the rise of his emotions. He launched them overhead, the twinkling orbs shifting into the constellation of a prancing fox. "What use is romance if it ends in heartbreak?"

Solarius shifted his weight, shuffling his feet over the rocky terrain of the mountain's ledge. "We've all had our hearts broken, Tovian."

"Not me." Nyxian positioned his arrow on the notch of his bow and steadied his aim. In the next moment he set it loose, turning away from his mark to face them. "I break hearts before they can break mine."

The arrow pierced the leaping fox and gleaming stars of emerald and copper spilled toward the rigid line of mountains.

Solarius rolled his eyes. *Show-off.*

"What about you?" Tovian asked Ariesian, collecting another cluster of brilliant stars in his hands.

Ariesian stiffened and adjusted the sleeves of his coat, flicking away an invisible fleck of dirt. He cocked his head to one side. "What about me?"

Tovian shrugged then, his teeth scraping along his bottom lip as he considered his words. He launched the bundle of stars into the swath of darkness overhead. "Ever had your heart broken?"

"No," Ariesian answered, his tone devoid of any emotion.

Solarius cracked a smile and smacked Ariesian soundly on the back. "That's because he doesn't have one."

His eldest brother shot him a hard look. "Har har."

The dazzling constellation above them took the shape of a siren diving through waves of starlight.

Solarius hesitated, stepping away from Ariesian, and Tovian clicked his tongue.

"Might want to catch her before she swims away." He nodded toward the stunning display.

As if on his command, the siren constellation arched backward into another crashing wave moving across the sky.

Shit.

Solarius plucked an arrow from the quiver at his back, blowing out a low breath as he carefully notched it on the bow. Magic danced along his near-frozen fingertips as flickers of Tovian's power skated over his skin. He could feel the intensity of his younger brother's gaze upon him, watching him as he took aim. Solarius gripped the arrow, pulling his arm back, tracking the siren as she leapt and dove through the sky. The moon gleamed like an orb of silver, shrouded behind wispy veils of clouds, highlighting her every move.

It would be easy to summon his own power, to use the strength of the moon to outshine the constellation, to blast it into oblivion until it was all but forgotten.

But he could do nothing of the sort, not with all three of his brothers watching.

Solarius released the arrow, holding his breath as its sharpened starlit point pierced the siren's heart and an explosion of gold and turquoise tumbled toward the earth.

He let the quiver slide from his shoulder and dropped the bow gently onto the ground. "I have to go."

"Already?" Tovian's brow pulled together, and he glanced to where the remnants of stars burned out completely. "But we're just getting started."

Solarius grabbed his gloves from a nearby pile of rocks and pulled them on. Almost at once, the fur lining them warmed his frozen fingers. His breath misted before him as he shoved his hands into his pockets. "Yes, but seeing as I'm the only one of us who is married now, I've been saddled with other duties."

Nyxian strolled toward him, his loud, full laugh echoing through the mountains. "Because fucking Lady Narissa Seaborne is *such* a chore."

Something dark twisted inside Solarius and he closed the distance between them in one stride. He matched Nyxian easily in height and met his youngest brother with a murderous glare. When he spoke, his voice was rough, like he'd swallowed a handful of gravel. Low and dangerous. "Mind your tongue when you speak of my wife."

Nyxian threw both hands up in innocence. "I didn't mean any harm, I simply—"

Ariesian swatted him on the back of the head, a scowl marring his face.

"Just because Mother claims you're star-touched, does *not* mean you can act like a complete ass." He gripped the front of Nyxian's collar and jerked him forward, his expression one of practiced malice. "You are a lord of House Celestine and you will conduct yourself as one. You treat Lady Narissa the same way you would one of your sisters, with respect. As you would defend them, you defend her. Do I make myself clear?"

"Yes, Aries. Of course." Nyxian ducked his head, his unruly dark blue hair tumbling across his forehead, hiding his scarred eye from view. Ariesian released him, and he sheepishly adjusted his coat, then tucked his hands behind his back like a scorned child. "Apologies, Sol. It won't happen again."

"See that it doesn't." Solarius softened, unable to be too furious with any of his brothers for long. "Otherwise I'll tell every female in Aeramere that you're in the market for a wife."

Nyxian's jaw dropped and the slash of sapphire cutting through the silver of his left eye darkened. "You wouldn't dare."

Solarius grinned, rolling his neck from one side to the other. It had been quite some time since he'd found himself in a brawl with one of his brothers, and his fists were ready. "Try me."

Ariesian chose that moment to step between them, folding his arms across his chest. "Solarius, go home to your wife. I'm sure she's patiently awaiting your arrival."

Tovian and Nyxian snickered, but Ariesian's head whipped in their direction and he cut them down, silencing them both with a single look.

"Do I need to arrange marriages for the two of you as well?" His voice rumbled like menacing thunder and the stars trembled.

"I hear Lilith is on the hunt for a husband," Solarius added to the impending threat.

Tovian blanched, all color fading from his face. "Absolutely not."

Nyxian, on the other hand, looked slightly more perturbed about the matter, a prominent scowl sketching across his brow. "Over my dead body."

Lilith Vylera was a well-known succubus whose notorious bedroom activities had gifted her with a reputation, one that touted her incredible skills behind closed doors. She'd been eyeing the brothers of House Celestine for quite some time, but she'd yet to snare one of them in her sultry clutches. In truth, they were all slightly intimidated and terrified by her as she lacked social decorum and was constantly flooding conversation with sexual innuendo.

"That's what I thought." Ariesian clapped Solarius on the back, turning him away from Tovian and Nyxian in a casual manner that suggested they had more important matters to discuss.

Solarius dipped his head slightly and lowered his voice. "Are they aware to take care regarding their conversations around Mother?"

Ariesian nodded once. "They are indeed. I informed them both of our suspicions. Nyxian was more than concerned when he learned Mother botched Novalise's star reading and lied about her power. They both agreed to keep quiet and play the part of proper lords of Aeramere in her presence."

The matriarch of House Celestine, Lady Trysta Starstorm, had roused Solarius's guard last Midsummer when she'd failed to conduct a proper star reading for their sister, Novalise. It merely confirmed that Trysta had been manipulating star readings over the years. On the surface, such an act would appear harmless, but when coupled with the fact that Trysta blatantly tried to hide Novalise's true magic and was actively working to pair their other sister Sarelle with the duplicitous Prince Aspen, it cast their mother in a less than complimentary glow. There was hardly anyone Solarius trusted less at the moment than his own mother.

There were other reasons from the past as to why he was skeptical of his mother, but those came with painful memories.

"Good." Solarius cast a backward glance over his shoulder to find Tovian and Nyxian already preparing for another round of starshoot. "Is there anything else I should know?"

"Not yet." There was an edge to Ariesian's tone, a sharp kind of coldness like the bitter wind sweeping through the valley of Celestine. "It's been unusually quiet."

Never a good sign.

They'd grown accustomed to the rumors, to the rising swells of unrest throughout Aeramere calling for Queen Elowyn's removal, much of which was believed to be circulated by her own son, Prince Aspen. Solarius supposed the celebration of Winter Solstice could be cause for the sudden stretch of peace across the realm, but he wouldn't allow such a feigned sense of respite to cloud his judgement or slip through his defenses. If war was coming to Aeramere, they would need to be prepared, and given the current state of affairs in their realm, they stood no chance of victory. Every house had blindly stood by Queen Elowyn, believing her promises of safety and ever-lasting peace, thinking they were protected by a shield of immeasurable power, only to uncover that the Veil enveloping Aeramere was nothing more than a common glamour.

They were, in a word, fucked.

Perhaps this unexpected length of quiet was a blessing.

"If you require my assistance, you know how to reach me." Solarius offered Ariesian a mock salute.

"That I do, though you should be enjoying these next few weeks with your new bride." Ariesian's dark brow arched in silent question. He would never speak the words, would never verbally humiliate Solarius, but the unspoken inquiry left him shifting his weight from side to side and his gaze slid to the uneven ground beneath his feet. At some point, he and Narissa would have to consummate their marriage, otherwise the contract between their houses would not stand.

"I see." Ariesian tucked his hands behind his back, his chest expanding. "Perhaps you and Narissa need some time alone. Together. Away from everyone else."

A honeymoon, a fortnight of forced marital bliss, where they would have to spend every waking moment with one another. Where they would have to do absurd things other couples conquered long ago, like getting to know each other, figuring out one another's likes and dislikes, learning their habits and hobbies. But talking to Lady Narissa Seaborne was like trying to trek across the jagged mountaintops of the Moonfall Peaks—dangerous and oftentimes a promise of death.

Solarius rocked back onto his heels and tiny rocks slid beneath his feet. "Seems like a rather daunting challenge when expectations are so high."

Ariesian's brows quirked again.

"The Yuletide Ball. This." Solarius gestured to their brothers and the vast sky. "Why call me away from House Azurvend only to bid me to spend time with Narissa?"

The corner of Ariesian's mouth lifted in what could almost be considered a smirk. "To see if you would actually show up."

"Of course I would." Solarius shoved his hands into his pockets, stiffening against another frosty gust of wind. "You're family."

Ariesian's fraud of a smirk faded as soon as Solarius spoke, and the faint shadows of disappointment haunted his eyes. "Narissa is your family now, and she should be your priority. Your duty is to her, not to me."

Solarius stared at his brother. "But—"

Ariesian lifted one hand.

"You will always be a lord of House Celestine." He angled his head so his sleek silver hair fell across his face. "You still are, but now you also have Lady Narissa Seaborne Celestine by your side. She is as much a part of this family as you are, but she deserves more from you, Solarius. More than you've given her."

Solarius's temper spiked and he clenched his fists. His jaw popped.

"You don't even know the half of it," he muttered.

"Pardon?" Ariesian asked, leaning closer.

"Nothing." Solarius shook his head. It was incredibly difficult to be kind and caring to someone who couldn't stand to even share the same air as him. "She hates me, you know? And I don't even know what I've done wrong."

Ariesian shrugged with the nonchalance of a lord who cared for nothing and no one, a far cry from his usual demeanor. "So, make her fall in love with you again."

Solarius almost choked. "It's not so easy."

Ariesian brushed off his concern with a wave of his hand. "Falling in love is the easiest thing in the world, Sol. Staying in love, however, is far more difficult. It requires work and effort from both parties, every hour of every day. And marriage is about finding new ways to show you love someone, especially if you want it to last an eternity."

"Damn you for being so wretchedly brilliant," Solarius mumbled, his previously ill temper fading into something that felt more like remorse.

"Damn you for expecting anything less from me." Ariesian cocked half a smile, then turned on his heel and headed back toward Tovian and Nyxian, who were shooting dozens of starlit arrows into the sky with reckless abandon.

Solarius watched them for a moment longer, then expeditiously made his way back to House Azurvend armed with a new outlook regarding his recent marriage.

He was going to make his wife fall in love with him.

CHAPTER TEN

inner with Reif, along with a few nobles from House Terensel, had come and gone. Narissa had been obliging, as was expected of her. She's suffered through idle small talk about the bitter winter season, and she'd remained dutifully quiet when their guests tiptoed around the volatile topic of Queen Elowyn and her son, Prince Aspen. Now, Narissa was perched on the edge of a stiff wingback chair near the hearth, pretending to be interested in a conversation about a hedge maze between Reif and Lord Florian Arborvin. Apparently the maze was filled with topiaries that were brought to life with magic, their ultimate purpose to chase and terrify the participants. Even more shocking was the fact that it was exceedingly popular. To his credit, Lord Florian appeared as disinterested in the discussion as Narissa felt.

Her gaze wandered to the ornate window etched in frost overlooking the Arcasian Sea. Darkness blanketed the sky like spilled ink and still Solarius had not yet returned.

Narissa wondered if perhaps this would be the first of many broken promises from him.

It never failed that even when she was in a room filled with her peers, she always managed to feel completely alone. Not quite an outcast, just simply unseen. Invisible. Both she and Reif had been the only children of their parents, and when her mother and father passed in a freak carriage accident, Reif was already saddled with lordly duties, and left her to her own devices. She was perfectly capable of occupying her time. More often than not she busied herself in the secret wing of her room concocting potions and sorting herbs, or she lost herself to the wondrous melody of her harp. Despite her unchaperoned upbringing, Narissa made every effort to be the epitome of a proper lady. She rarely took up space, she blended in perfectly with the gilded papered walls of nearly every ballroom, and it was a rare occasion she was ever on the receiving end of any untoward behavior.

Save for in the case of Lord Solarius Starstorm.

For whatever reason, be it the cruelty of fate or the animosity of the stars, that male ignited her temper and set fire to her soul.

Both of which were precisely two more reasons why she absolutely could not stand him.

Her mind drifted to when they first met, when Solarius plucked her from obscurity at House Galefell's Featherlight Ball and danced with her upon candy pink clouds set against the backdrop of a lavender sky. Her knees had softened each time he flashed her one of his charming smiles and she'd been unable to tear her gaze away from the liquid silver of his eyes. Solarius had captivated her with his chivalrous nature, with his amusing manner, with the intensity with which he spoke to her, as though he hung upon her every word and breath, desperate for more.

Narissa shook the memory away and swallowed a sigh.

Rising from her seat, she excused herself from the dull tedium of hedge maze talk, intent on finding another more stimulating pursuit, but not before Reif pinned her with a look of concern.

She attempted to placate him with a smile, and though he nodded once, approving her leave, she knew she would have to face his questions later.

Narissa went in search of an escape and found it in the music room down the hall, in the form of her beloved harp.

The walls were a rich navy with metallic gold swirls imprinted along the baseboards. Rich flooring showcased a pianoforte, a violin, a lute, a few other woodwind instruments, and her harp. Silver faerie fire glowed within a crystal chandelier, giving the space an ethereal feel like being underwater. The harp was situated in the far corner near the bay window overlooking the sea, and a familiar kind of serenity drifted over her when she seated herself behind it to play.

Her dark aqua evening dress spilled open at the slit when she braced the harp between her knees, anchoring the instrument against her right shoulder. Made of sleek cherrywood, it had been a gift from Reif for her birthday seven years prior, and she'd instantly taken a liking to it. She loved the way her fingers floated over the strings, plucking them with delicate accuracy, creating the most delightful melodies. Every song reminded her of the sea, the harmonious rise and fall of waves, the gentle lull and the mystical call that spoke to the magic flowing through her veins.

Narissa's eyes fluttered closed and the tips of her fingers glided over the harp's strings.

The song poured from within her, every chord an ode to the long-buried ache she kept hidden away from the world. She played nimbly, allowing her fingers to catch and feather the strings with poignant perfection. The haunting tune echoed through the stillness of the room, carrying upward to the vaulted ceiling where it lingered like a forgotten memory. She played only the good notes, a devastating medley of major and minor chords, and each strum pierced her chest like an arrow launched from a bow. It would have made a splendid aria, a wondrous refrain of foolishly broken hearts, and tragic lost love.

A single tear slipped from her cheek, and she felt the cool surface of a pearl before it bounced off the wooden floor and rolled away.

"You look absolutely captivating when you play the harp, Lady Narissa."

Her eyes flew open, and she found Lord Florian standing in the doorway of the music room. He bent down and picked up the runaway pearl, pinching it between his fingers in careful examination. He was handsome, devastatingly charming, and moved with a sort of casual grace. His hair was shaved on the sides with short, tight midnight coils on top. He kept a neatly trimmed beard and the collar of his sage shirt was opened slightly, revealing a swath of flawless, rich brown skin. A thin gold chain hung from his neck and tiny emerald studs glittered from his pointed ears.

Lord Florian set the pearl on a table full of scattered sheet music, tucked his hands into the pockets of his pants, and strolled toward her.

"Thank you, my lord." Narissa offered him a kind smile, she was rarely paid such high compliments. "I wasn't aware anyone was listening."

"I couldn't quite help myself." He angled his head, studying her with a warmth that wasn't at all intimidating. Instead, he watched her as though he was simply amazed by her. "Your talent is rather immeasurable."

A blush crept into Narissa's cheeks. "You flatter me, my lord."

A faint line furrowed across Lord Florian's brow. "No, my lady. I merely speak the truth. I am most impressed by your musical accomplishment."

Narissa knew she could play well, but she hardly considered herself a great proficient. When she failed to respond, Lord Florian presented her with another question.

"Tell me, my lady." He pressed his lips together, considering. "Do you know *Aeramere's Amore?*"

"I do, yes." She was quite fond of the song and had played it a handful of times, though it was incredibly difficult.

"Would you play it for me?" he asked and lowered himself onto the leather settee near her. Candles flickered throughout the room, highlighting the intensity of his golden eyes. "It's my favorite."

"Oh, well..." Narissa hesitated. It wasn't that she lacked confidence, but *Aeramere's Amore* was a rather...sensual song. It was intimate. Passionate. Something reserved for lovers. "I'm not sure I could—"

"I know it's complex and requires the utmost care and precision."

Lord Florian gestured to her harp and flashed her a winning smile. "But I would be honored if you gave it a try."

Narissa loosed a breath, her teeth snagging on her bottom lip. "Very well, my lord."

Pleased, Lord Florian settled back, crossing one ankle over his knee, and Narissa played.

This time, she did not close her eyes. She remained focused, her fingers moving over the strings as though she were plucking wisps of silk from the sky. Keeping time, she lightly tapped one foot against the wood floor while Lord Florian strummed his fingers against the arm of the settee. A faint smile lifted the corner of his mouth and though he continued to watch her, his gaze was distant, as if the song had taken hold of his mind and transported him to another time. The amorous melody flowed through the space, soft and elegant, cocooning them in a bubble of musical splendor.

Until Solarius stalked into the room and froze, shattering the beauty she'd created.

Narissa ignored him, wetting her lips, determined to continue the song without interruption. Her fingers nimbly plucked the strings for the crescendo, her heart thundering in her chest, overpowering the music of the harp as Solarius strode closer, coming to stand just behind her. She played by memory now, becoming acutely aware of his every move even though she could hardly see him from the corner of her eye. She sensed his breathing, felt the faintest graze of his fingertips as he toyed with the ends of her hair. His scent clouded her mind, tore through her in a thousand different directions, and she held her breath, striking the final notes of *Aeramere's Amore*.

Lord Florian's applause shook the fog from her mind and she jolted, ready to lurch upright and put as much space between herself and Solarius as possible. But just as she made to stand, his hand clamped down upon her shoulder, keeping her in place.

"Well done, Lady Narissa." Lord Florian stood, practically beaming with awe. "I have not been serenaded like that in an age. You are exceptionally talented."

"Thank you, my lord." She gave him her best smile. "You are too kind."

Lord Florian's melted gold gaze landed on Solarius. "Your wife is truly exceptional, her gift in the musical arts is phenomenal. You must be incredibly proud, Lord Solarius."

Solarius's hand tightened on her shoulder. "Indeed."

Narissa bit back the tart remark lingering on her tongue and schooled her expression into one of smooth neutrality. It took every ounce of self-control not to roll her eyes toward the vaulted ceiling.

Solarius didn't even know she could *play*.

"Lady Narissa, would you be willing to play the harp at the Festival of Roses?" Lord Florian produced a rosebud that bloomed fully in the palm of his hand, each petal scripted with rose gold ink—a formal invitation to House Terensel's springtime ball. "I would love to have your music be the star of the evening."

Narissa ducked her head, blushing furiously. "I, that is, I'm not certain—"

"At least tell me you'll consider it." Lord Florian offered her another one of his winsome grins.

She sighed then, not particularly wanting to be the center of attention at the Festival of Roses but not wanting to offend Lord Florian, either. Perhaps she could decline his offer gently in a few days. "Very well, my lord. I shall give it some thought."

"Please do." Lord Florian bowed then. "I bid you both goodnight."

He left the music room, whistling the tune of *Aereamere's Amore*, and once he was completely out of earshot, Narissa smacked Solarius's hand from her shoulder.

"Are you quite finished being a self-righteous prick?" She shrugged out of his hold. "I would very much like to stand and stretch my legs."

Solarius released her then, tucking both of his hands behind his back. "Do you make a habit of playing the harp for males seeking your company?"

Narissa almost choked. What a crude insinuation. She whirled on him then, smoothing the wrinkles from the skirt of her gown, and gave him a vicious smile. "Only when they ask sweetly."

Solarius damn near erupted with rage. Color flooded his cheeks and his silver eyes turned molten. There was a distinctive pop of his jaw, and though he stood painfully still, she didn't miss the way his upper arms flexed with tempered fury.

Reif was right.

Solarius was incredibly overprotective and possessive. As much as Narissa was loath to admit it, she supposed such a reaction could work in her favor if she wanted his attention. Not that she was keen on making him jealous, but if there were no other options, then at least she had a last resort.

"Don't be so dramatic." She waved off his anger with an air of flippancy. "It's not as though it matters. Everyone knows Lord Florian prefers males over females. He just so happens to possess a love for music as well."

"I hear he prefers the company of both," Solarius grumbled, folding his arms over his chest.

Narissa shrugged, ignoring his complaint, and turned to leave.

"Where are you going?" There was something in Solarius's voice that gave her pause, like an underlying twinge of worry.

Impossible.

He stopped worrying about her the moment he walked away from her and never looked back.

Narissa tossed a glance at him from over her shoulder, lifting it in feigned disinterest. "Well, you've made it quite clear that you would prefer to be anywhere else than with me, so I figured I would leave you to it."

She turned from him then, heading for the door of the music room, when Solarius's hand snared her wrist. He hauled her backward so quickly, she almost stumbled into him. Her back smacked into the solid wall of his chest and though his grip remained loose, she knew he had no intention of letting her walk away so easily.

Solarius hooked a finger around one of her golden locks, sweeping it back from her neck so the warmth of his breath tickled her ear.

"You didn't answer my question," he murmured, his fingers idly stroking the inside of her wrist.

She turned her head to face him, crushing the flutter of butterflies swarming in her belly, when she realized their lips were a stolen kiss apart. They were so close, their noses almost touched. If she wanted, she could rise onto her toes and trace the line of his lips with her tongue, committing the fullness of them to her memory. She imagined he tasted of warm spiced whiskey, of sleepless nights and silky tangled sheets, of frozen moonlight and desire.

His free hand moved to her waist, and he wrapped an arm around her, keeping her pressed close against him.

Their breaths mingled—hers slightly gasping and uneven, his calm and steady.

Her gaze flicked to the melted silver of his eyes and his pupils expanded, heated by an emotion she recognized all too well. She blinked, focusing on his mouth instead, his next words lingering in the space between their lips.

"Where are you going?" he repeated quietly.

Narissa's knees trembled, and she locked her spine, refusing to sway. She would not give into his charms. She *could* not.

She lifted her chin, and his eyes dipped to her mouth. "Somewhere far away from you."

Solarius grinned.

His hands slid from her waist to her hips, gripping her. Tilting his head to the side, his silver hair with blackened tips fell over half of his face. In the low, otherworldly light of the music room, she could almost give into the temptation of being a truly married couple, of pretending there was no past between them, of imagining a future of happily ever afters. The light bounced off his handsome face, dousing him in a glow that almost weakened her, one that almost knocked down all her carefully crafted defenses.

"What if I wanted to go with you?" he asked, so earnestly she nearly fell for his scheme.

Nearly believed him.

"Then I would say too bad." Narissa twisted out of his arms, breaking the spell he held over her. "You do not get to pick and choose when you want my time or affection. I spent most of the day alone already and you cared not how I passed my hours. Therefore, it would stand to reason that where I go now and what I do next is none of your concern."

She dropped into a curtsy, refusing to acknowledge the questions harbored in his hardened gaze. "If you would excuse me, my lord. There is somewhere else I would rather be."

Narissa left him then, knowing Solarius watched her as she walked away, and though it twisted a blade through that soul-deep ache in her heart, she refused to look back.

CHAPTER ELEVEN

*D*amn it.

Solarius watched Narissa walk away from him again, her hips swaying in measured time to the beating of his heart.

Anger simmered through his veins. He was supposed to be charming and irresistible. He should have swept her into his arms, whispered sweet nothings into her ear, then kissed her until she could no longer recall her own name. But he'd screwed it up already. His plan to woo his wife, to somehow make her fall in love with him, had backfired in record time. All he'd accomplished was pissing her off once again.

In retrospect, he probably should have started their conversation with an apology for his tardiness instead of questioning her loyalty. But alas, he'd been burned by her before, so he couldn't help it if his guard was up.

It wasn't much of an excuse. In fact, it was rather pathetic.

Fine.

He'd give her a head start.

Solarius counted to thirty, then followed her faint, lingering scent. The delicate floral smell mingling with sandalwood and sea air and was practically an aphrodisiac to his senses. It was tantalizing. Tempting. Enough to make his mouth water.

So, he kept his pace slow and quietly tracked her through the expansive corridors of House Azurvend. He passed through open-air walkways, beneath arches embedded with sea glass, where the bitter wind smacked at his cheeks, then descended a staircase of sandstone into the lower levels of the house. Here the air was somehow thick and warm, as though the humidity of the summer continued to thrive despite the cloak of winter blanketing the outdoors. He rounded a corner and drew up short, mesmerized by the scene unfolding before him.

It appeared to be a cove of some kind, or maybe even a lagoon. Tide pools of crystalline turquoise water were surrounded by large, smooth rocks, protecting them from the crashing waves of the Arcasian Sea just beyond. Ribbons of steam unfurled from the sparkling surface of the pools, the heat emanating from them enough to slightly dampen Solarius's shirt. Gaping openings of crumbling rock in the ceiling allowed for the brilliant wash of moonlight to spill into the cove, shrouding the space in a silver glow. He inched closer, peering from around a pillar of ivory quartz, and swore he'd never seen anything more lovely in his life.

There was Narissa, kneeling near the edge of one of the pools, gathering some sort of green plant from the surface of an uneven stone. Her wavy hair was a mess and piled high on top of her head into a lopsided bun with a few loose tendrils curling around her neck. She absently tucked one behind her ear and Solarius swallowed hard, captivated by her every movement. Narissa stood, balancing precariously on the uneven ledge of rock as she collected the pieces of vine-like sea kelp in a small wicker basket. Glimmering pink flowers bloomed wherever moonlight touched them, the petals closing in the flash of shade, then opening again at her touch. It was fascinating, watching the grace with which she worked, but her absolute ease did nothing to soothe his nerves.

The tide was high, spilling over some of the rocks and crashing into the steaming pools. Foam and seawater soaked the hem of Narissa's dress and when her footing slipped, Solarius's heart stopped completely.

He lurched forward, ready to rescue her from certain death, but Narissa righted herself as though she hadn't almost been swept out to sea and hopped over each rock's slippery surface until she was safely standing upon the sandy ground.

Solarius could only stare.

She was incredibly nimble for a lady, and his mind wandered to what other sorts of activities she might be exceptionally good at—preferably those that took place in the bedroom.

Narissa set down her basket, her gaze drawn to the open sea beyond the swell of waves and the boundary of rocks.

Solarius silently debated leaving without saying a word. She was clearly in her element, and he had no doubt making his presence known would only sour her mood. To be honest, he was growing rather tired of constantly being the reason for her scowl. And her tears. He imagined what it might be like to be on the receiving end of one of her rare smiles, the ones she reserved for those she truly loved. She would glow, illuminated from within like those radiant pearls that fell down her cheeks, iridescent and rare.

He ducked his head and turned to go, freezing the second her hands reached for the laces of her gown.

Solarius didn't move. He didn't breathe.

Narissa fumbled for a moment, then gradually tugged the sheer sleeves of her dress until the soft fabric fell from her shoulders, then further still, exposing the golden hue of her flesh. Aqua satin covered in tiny diamonds tumbled to the ground, pooling around her ankles like an ethereal ocean.

Solarius had seen her naked before, stars above, he'd undressed her on their wedding night. But this was different. *She* was different. In this moment, she was uninhibited. Unafraid. She was composed and confident. She pulled a pin embellished with black pearls from her hair, and the unruly tresses tumbled to the middle of her back. Narissa was flawless—every curve, every dip, every inch of her golden skin was perfect. His wife was fucking magic.

She stepped out of the discarded gown and his jaw clenched when she lowered herself into the tide pool. Goosebumps pebbled over her skin, her nipples hardened, and Solarius forgot how to breathe. Crystal blue water lapped at her calves and thighs, then her hips and waist. She arched slightly, easing back to float on the warm pool's surface, and closed her eyes. The rings on her fingers sparkled as she languidly moved her hands through the water. Her wild blonde hair fanned out like gilded ribbons, tiny waves rippled, and she looked exactly like Azuralis.

The goddess of the sea.

His constellation in the night sky, the one that marked his heart.

He summoned his magic then, cradling moonlight with his hand, then pouring it over her nude form in tiny rivers of silver. His blood thrummed, the power of the moon encapsulating his very being, its light and darkness desperate for something more. For something he couldn't quite find.

The wave tattoos on the pointed tips of Narissa's ears glowed, a gleaming bluish-purple hue, and Solarius knew the ones swirling down her spine were illuminated as well.

Leaning against the pillar so it supported the brunt of his weight, he watched her float, thoroughly enchanted.

"Are you going to spy on me all evening?" she asked, her eyes still closed. "Or have you come to insult me again?"

Her scornful remark should have set his teeth on edge, should have baited him to fire back with some snide comment, for that seemed to be the way of their conversations. But here, with her defining the very meaning of the word breathtaking, Solarius couldn't find the words.

"Apologies, Narissa." He shoved off the pillar, following the sandy path to the tide pool, ensuring his footfalls were loud enough for her to hear. "I can't seem to stop staring at you."

Slowly, she stood upright once more, her frosty ocean eyes watching him as he made his way down the trail toward her. Turquoise waters coasted just above the swell of her breasts, and he didn't miss the way her chest heaved in an unsteady breath. She tracked him, sliding her tongue along her bottom lip, then scraping it with her teeth.

"I just…" Solarius paused at the edge of the tidal pool, tucking one hand into his pocket. He reached out, dragging two fingers through the air as he angled the rush of moonlight so it cascaded around her like a waterfall. He tilted his head to one side, admiring his work, admiring her, and shrugged. "I'm finding it rather difficult to collect my thoughts at the moment."

Narissa's cautious gaze flitted over him. "Is that a compliment, my lord?"

Her soft, lusty voice was enough to bring him to his knees, to beg forgiveness for an offense he had never committed.

He cleared his throat, never breaking her gaze. "The highest, my lady."

Beats of heavy silence passed between them, measured only by the intake of their breaths and the crashing of gentle waves.

Narissa shoved her hair back from her face, the gold strands already drying into reckless, messy waves. "You could join me…if you like."

Solarius hesitated.

There was no doubt in his mind that if he entered that damn tide pool, he would do something stupid. Like touch her. Or kiss her. Or be completely unable to keep his hands to himself. Worse though, he wouldn't want Narissa to feel obligated to return such gestures or resent him for it later. However, if he refused to join her now, if he walked away like he *knew* he should, then he would destroy the olive branch she'd carefully extended to him.

Torn, he said nothing, and slowly removed his boots.

He untucked his shirt next, taking care to unfasten each button one at a time, then tossed it behind him over a slab of rock. Reaching for the waistband of his pants, he let them fall, and though he thoroughly expected Narissa to blush furiously, he was surprised to find her studying him. Her pale green eyes swept over his body, her head tilted in concentration, her brow just barely pinched as she watched him sink into the tide pool.

The water was shockingly warm, it soothed his muscles and relaxed his bones. Salty sea air mixed with the calming scent of mint, and for the first time in a long time, Solarius felt at peace. Curls of steam separated him from Narissa like a thin curtain of mist, and he waded toward her, gradually closing the distance between them. Gravelly pebbles at the bottom of the tidal pool sifted beneath his feet as he neared her, but she didn't back away from him, even though each breath she drew was painfully shallow. Solarius kept his hands fisted at his sides in an effort to keep himself from touching her, standing close enough for the tips of her hardened nipples to gently graze his chest.

The faintest touch sent all the blood rushing to his cock, and he locked his jaw, his nails biting into the rough skin of his palms.

"My lord," she whispered.

Agony coursed through him. "My lady."

Narissa wet her lips, tugging on the corner of her bottom lip with her teeth.

"Have you always had this tattoo?" she asked, reaching for him with one hand. Her fingers drifted around his upper arm, her thumb gliding over the silky black ink marking him. The phases of the moon were tattooed upon his right arm, from his shoulder to his elbow, and the way she caressed his bicep weakened him completely. His cock thickened and he swallowed a groan.

Damn her and her siren song voice.

"Yes." It was far more difficult to get the word out than he thought, like he was trying to speak with a wad of cotton in his mouth.

"Mm." Her fingertips moved to his chest, to his heart, lightly tracing the smaller tattoo there. "This one looks like a trident."

"It is." His pulse was thundering now, echoing through his ears, rushing with the pumping of his blood. "I was born under the star sign of Azuralis, the goddess of the sea. In the night sky, you can find her by the trident of stars stretching toward the moon from the sea. It is her constellation that marks my heart."

"I see." Narissa's eyes flashed to him, her face unreadable in the swath of dim light. "Almost like serendipity."

"Almost," he ground out, desperation clawing at him.

She was so close he could taste her scent on the air. It teased him, taunted him with images of midnight pleasures and stolen kisses. Each time she shifted in the water, another rush of desire, of longing, pulsed through him. His restraint wavered. Every unintentional yet sublimely delicate touch scraped away another layer of his cool composure.

Narissa had to know, stars above, she *had* to know the effect she had on him. If anything, she had to be able to feel the hardness of his shaft between them.

"What about your tattoos?" Solarius asked, silently hoping the conversation would dull his need to claim her.

She gathered her hair, twisting it over one shoulder.

"My tattoos aren't anything special. They're merely waves along my ears and down my spine." The swirls of ink illuminated, radiant and lovely, in the light of the moon. "For the most part, no one even knows they're there. They're practically invisible. Only in the wash of moonlight do they glow, only then are they seen."

There was something about the way Narissa said the words, the way she spoke them with a ringing hollowness. A broken sort of emptiness.

It snapped something inside Solarius, left him aching, so his heart twinged, and he longed to take away whatever caused her such pain. Such agony.

Solarius grabbed her then. He palmed the back of her thighs and hoisted her up, pressing her damp body against his own. She molded against him easily, weaving her arms around his neck, her fingers playing with the ends of his hair. Her skin was like satin, soft and perfect, everything he'd imagined when she tormented his dreams night after night. Silvery moonlight bounced off the rippling water, reflecting prisms of turquoise and sapphire. Solarius hefted her higher, ensuring he held a good grip on her bottom, and she locked her arms tight around him.

Finally, his midnight siren was in his arms.

He'd lost track of the number of times he'd dreamed of her, longed for her, begged the stars to let him have her.

Narissa threaded her fingers through his hair, twining and tugging. Solarius's gaze flicked up to her pretty face, where her rosy gold cheeks flushed, emotion banked deep in the endless sea of her eyes.

All he wanted was a kiss. Just one. A taste. A promise of all he lost when she chose Calfair over him.

Solarius tilted his head back, angling his face to hers, and whispered into the space between them. "Let me kiss you, Rissa love."

Her answering inhale was all the permission he needed.

Solarius didn't hesitate. He claimed those luscious lips of hers, prying them open with the tip of his tongue, and then he drowned.

The rush of power between them was unlike anything he'd ever felt before, a damning swell, wave after crashing wave of emboldened magic. Moonfire exploded, a phantasmic burst of energy that pulled the mesmerizing strength of the tides right into him. He could hear the call of the ocean, the way it sang for the moonlight, the way it blended with the blood running through his veins. Solarius tightened his grip, unable to break their kiss, fusing their mouths together in maddening desperation.

Something wrenched around his heart and pulled, nearly ripping it from his chest.

The wild magic of the tides collided with the controlled chaos of the moon, claiming one another in a damning bond of their souls.

Solarius knew the exact moment the thread binding him to Narissa snapped into place. It was as though he'd been awakened from a years' long slumber. Awareness flooded him, overwhelmed him. Her thoughts whipped through him like a whirlwind, her racing heart pumped blood through his veins, her scent, her essence, her very being, were ingrained into his soul.

Narissa belonged to him.

And he belonged to her.

Without warning, Narissa lurched backward, freeing herself from his hold. She stumbled through the pool, clambering away from him.

Her eyes were round with something that could either be considered shock or horror, and he wasn't entirely sure he wanted to know the answer.

"I knew it." Narissa clutched her heart and climbed out of the tide pool, grabbing her gown but abandoning her shoes. Her voice broke. "I *knew* it."

"Narissa!" Solarius called after her, but she didn't stop. Instead, she took off at a full sprint, running toward the entrance of another smaller cove.

And she didn't turn around.

"Narissa!" Solarius leapt out of the pool, striking his toe against a jagged rock. Pain splintered up his leg, but he ignored it. "Fuck. Rissa, wait!"

Naked, freezing, and alone with a damn erection, Solarius watched as Narissa disappeared into the mouth of the cove. He yanked on his pants and dropped onto one of the rocks, his frustration mounting. Her words replayed in his mind, and he couldn't escape the heartbreak in her voice.

I knew it.

That's what she'd said.

Solarius blew out a rough breath and dragged one hand through his hair.

Narissa had known they were mates. Somehow, she'd known…and she'd been so repulsed and put off by the notion that she'd fled. No wonder she'd avoided kissing him for so long, she knew their magic would claim one another. And the very thought of it revolted her. The lingering pain of the bond stretched between them and a dull ache formed in his chest. Mating bonds weren't exactly meant to be ignored. Yet Narissa had run off and now he was left feeling the heated sting of her rejection.

Perhaps this was the sort of agony Novalise had suffered when Asher originally denied their bond as well.

Solarius groaned and scrubbed a hand over his face—making Narissa fall in love with him had become exponentially more difficult.

CHAPTER TWELVE

arissa did not sleep.

Instead, she braced one hand on her hip and rubbed the other over her heart, where the bond warmed, spreading through her chest. A few tears slipped free once she was finally out of his sight, but she'd almost tripped over a pearl that rolled beneath her bare feet. She hated how she was in tune to his thoughts, to his emotions, to the steady beating of his heart. She could follow the bond between them and know it would lead her back to him, but that would defeat the purpose of intentionally trying to evade him. Solarius was aimlessly wandering the halls of House Azurvend, same as her, though his thoughts weren't quite as tormented as her own.

She attempted to barricade her mind, carefully building a wall so he wouldn't be privy to her innermost thoughts. It should hold so long as she didn't let down her defenses.

Narissa shook her head, scolding herself.

Of course, she had to do something so foolish as kiss him. But breaking tides, he'd been so tempting. And when he'd picked her up in the pool, and every inch of him had been pressed against every inch of her, how could she possibly do anything else?

One careless moment of weakness and she'd bonded herself to

Lord Solarius Starstorm. It didn't matter if he was all she ever wanted, all she ever dreamed of, because he'd made himself perfectly clear quite some time ago.

He did *not* want her.

And Narissa highly doubted an arranged marriage and an accidental bond would be enough to change his mind.

The moment the sun broke the horizon, Narissa burrowed herself into a thick fur coat and headed down to the beach. The wind bit through her heavy skirts and she wished she'd been smart enough to grab an extra layer for added warmth. She looped a wicker basket over one arm and her leather boots sank deep into the damp sand with each step. Eventually the call of the ocean drowned out the howl of the wind, but it did little to erase the frigid air from smacking her cheeks and whipping her hair.

Narissa sniffed, pressing her lips together as she bent down to gather some fresh herbs and plants for her potions. She rummaged through the overgrowth near the shoreline, collecting stems of sun thistle and jaded aura flowers. Every so often she paused to grab some seashells that caught her eye. Some were shaped like swirling cones, others reminded her of tiny fans. They ranged in color too—washed white, pearlescent blue, and the shimmer of a melted sunset. She rinsed away the grit and sand, dipping them in the waves that came to kiss the shore.

Even as she rolled over the word "kiss" then quickly tried to shove it into the recesses of her despairing thoughts, an image of Solarius popped into her mind.

The devastated look in his eyes as he held her, the way the silver of them burned hot the moment he lifted her into his arms.

And the kiss...oh sweet shores, *that kiss.*

Solarius had not been gentle or kind, he hadn't taken his time exploring her. No, he'd wanted to claim and conquer. His mouth slashed over hers, demanding she accept all he was willing to give. His tongue tangled with hers, tasting and devouring, drawing out her inhibitions. When his grip on her bottom tightened, when he squeezed her flesh, possessing her with his hands, Narissa had unraveled. She'd melted into him, knowing she was made for him. And the way his cock nestled so pleasantly between her legs while she was in his arms...if she'd adjusted herself just a bit, angled herself a little differently, he would have filled her completely.

His body was more cut than she remembered. Muscular and toned, she'd wanted nothing more than to lick every solid inch of him. Especially his rather impressive cock. She definitely didn't recall him being quite so large when she first lay with him, but then again, most of that evening was an uncomfortable blur.

Warmth pooled low in her belly and goosebumps that had absolutely nothing to do with the cold riddled her flesh. Her nipples hardened, straining against the confines of her gown.

Narissa stood and blew out a breath, lifting her face to the sky so the bitter wind could cool her cheeks.

If she wasn't careful, she'd let her guard down, and Solarius would know *exactly* what she was thinking about...he would know exactly what she wanted.

"Again, I find you without your husband," a familiar male voice called over the rushing waves.

Narissa spun around to face her cousin, schooling her expression into one of bored neutrality. "Reif, we've been over this. My time is of no value to him."

She lifted her basket, displaying the contents of plants and shells as though it was some kind of proof. "He doesn't care about me."

Reif strolled toward her, kicking up sand in his wake. His hands were tucked into the pockets of his heavy overcoat, and he dipped his chin as he approached, unfazed by her explanation. "He told you that, did he?"

Narissa bit her lip. "Well, not in those words."

The lie tasted foul in her mouth. In fact, Solarius told her quite the opposite. He claimed her time, her emotions, her feelings...that all of her mattered. But his promises were easily made and easily broken, just like the crust of a pie.

Reif shoved his wavy blond hair back from his face, his eyes softening. "Then he said he didn't want to spend time with you?"

"Ah…" Another moment when she'd shut Solarius down completely. He'd asked to go with her when she left the music room, and again she'd denied him. She'd left him, until he'd followed her to the tide pools. But now Reif was staring at her like she was an ever-growing thorn in his side. "We're simply not compatible."

Reif rocked back onto his heels, digging them deeper into the sand. He roughed his knuckles along the line of his jaw, his gaze drifting to the horizon to the east. "I suppose it's kind of difficult to come to such a decision when you never spend time with one another."

"He doesn't want me, Reif." Exasperation splintered through her, but even though she believed the words she spoke once before, now she wasn't entirely sure. Last night, those fleeting moments they shared in the tide pool spoke silent volumes. If anything, it cemented the fact that Solarius absolutely wanted her, at least physically, but she was terrified of losing her heart to him again. Narissa clutched the basket to her waist, stiffening against the gusting breeze. She grasped for the final excuse and tossed it to him. "Solarius is the one who ended our courtship, not me."

Reif leveled her with a singular, questioning look. "Why?"

"Why what?"

"Why did he end your courtship?"

An excellent question, one that had haunted her midnights nearly as much as his face.

"I…I don't know." The memory would bleed Narissa's heart until it failed to beat. Her chest ached, and she took a steady breath, fearful that Solarius would sense her dread. "I always assumed it was because he got what he wanted and saw no use for me anymore."

Reif arched one brow, the corner of his mouth quirking. "So, you never asked?"

Shame filled her. It wasn't as though she never thought about asking Solarius why he left her, because she had, many times. But the truth of the matter was that she was terrified of the answer. She didn't want to know if he'd grown tired of her, if he didn't want her, or worse, if he'd found someone else. To protect her heart, she'd channeled that fear into anger, which had morphed into a twisted loathing.

"Do you think you're undeserving of an answer?" Reif pressed.

Narissa lifted her chin. "Of course not."

Reif shrugged and started to walk away.

"Then maybe you should find out," he called from over his shoulder as he sauntered up the beach back toward the house.

Narissa scowled.

Damn her cousin for using sound logic.

Dinner was painfully awkward.

Narissa had managed to dodge Solarius and escape his alluring gaze for the majority of the day, but now he was seated directly across from her, and the knowing look in his eyes held her captive. Every so often he would glance down at his plate of seared fish and roasted vegetables, then he would blink and lift his gaze to her. The way he stared at her from beneath those somber brows caused her skin to prickle with delightful awareness. His silver hair with its inky tips fell across his face, covering one eye and giving him an air of seductive mystery. The midnight blue shirt he wore was flecked with silver thread, and he'd rolled the sleeves to reveal inches of corded muscle and veined forearms. He'd become an unavoidable distraction, the kind she could no longer simply ignore.

To make matters worse, the mating bond seemed to expand and warm, coiling around her heart like the strangling vines of writhing bane. It pulled and stretched, toying with her volatile emotions. The need for attention, the urgency to be touched by Solarius, thrummed through every inch of her, wound her nerves so tightly she thought she might combust. Mating bonds were incredible things, fueling the lust for desire and the ache to do the unthinkable. Warmth spread through Narissa, and a distinctive heat left her tingling and aching. Crossing one leg over the other, she twisted her napkin in her lap. She swiped her tongue along her bottom lip, finding herself incredibly parched. It was possible she was dying of thirst. Solarius licked a drop of sauce from his fork, and she almost whimpered. It was a raw kind of torture, being bonded to the male who'd broken her heart.

Narissa wanted nothing more than to crawl across the table, seat herself in front of him with her legs spread, and plead with him to feast upon her instead.

Solarius choked on his water.

His gaze snared on her, and the silver of his eyes turned molten, heated with raw hunger.

Narissa blanched, slumping into her seat. The flush of embarrassment scalded her cheeks as the realization slowly sank in.

He'd heard her

Breaking tides, Solarius had *heard* her thoughts, and it was too late to take them back. He'd been given a full view of her mind. Narissa ducked her head, wishing she could turn into a puddle and melt through the wooden floorboards, never to be seen again.

"This is absurd." Reif grabbed his glass of whiskey and took a hefty swig, draining the contents. Planting one elbow firmly on the table, he gestured toward them with the empty glass. "The two of you need to sort this nonsense out immediately."

Now it was Narissa's turn to hastily swallow down her mortification.

Only death would have been less humiliating than having one's cousin assume the reason for the strained silence at the dinner table was because of a martial spat and not at all due to the ridiculously heavy sexual tension.

Narissa shrank even further into her chair. Disappearing in a crowded ballroom and making herself scarcely noticeable against a backdrop of flowery papered walls was far easier than trying to blend in with the fabric of her cushioned seat.

Solarius, on the other hand, remained unmoving. His gaze had not strayed from her. In fact, Narissa wasn't even certain he had blinked. He was unwavering, the entirety of his focus resting solely upon her.

Reif rapped his knuckles on the table. "Lord Starstorm had the right idea."

At the mention of Ariesian's title, Solarius snapped out of his entranced state, his head swinging in Reif's direction. "Pardon?"

"I tried to tell him we shouldn't force it, but I'm beginning to see he was correct in his early suggestion." Reif leaned back in his chair, his fingers steepled in a way that made him look as though he was plotting their future demise. He made a sort of *tsk*ing noise and shook his head, shoving a hand through his unkempt dark blond hair. "A mandatory honeymoon is exactly what the two of you need."

"What?" Narissa yelped, at the same time Solarius attempted to negotiate with him.

"Reif, please. I assure you that is the *last* thing we need."

For the first time in quite a while, Narissa found herself in agreement with Solarius. It would be a complete disaster if the two of them were required to spend time alone together. Being sent off to some horribly romantic location, then left with no other option but to pretend to enjoy one another's company would end in disaster. They would be sequestered in the same room and Narissa wouldn't know a moment of peace because the bond would ensure Solarius—and every glorious inch of his body—consumed all of her thoughts.

Narissa simply would not survive it.

She would absolutely perish.

But Reif remained undeterred.

"No. This back-and-forth silent treatment has gone on long enough. House Azurvend and House Celestine have reputations to uphold, and I shall not have these petty quarrels sullying our good names." He gently rapped one fist upon the table, enunciating the finality of his decision. "I will have your bags packed at once. You leave tonight."

A wave of nausea slammed into Narissa, and she blew out a low, shaky breath. "And where, may I ask, is our destination?"

"Windsong. In Galefell," Reif responded, cutting at the flaky grilled fish on his plate.

"Galefell," Narissa repeated numbly, sparing a wary glance in Solarius's direction.

His mood instantly soured. A line of vexation marred his brow and his jaw popped. He lifted the whiskey glass in his hand and swirled the golden contents, his knuckles whitening with each churn. The silver of his eyes had cooled to the shade of cold iron. Of course he was agitated, House Galefell was the home of Calfair Skyhelm, his former best friend. The two had a falling out some time ago, and though Narissa wasn't entirely certain of the details, she did know Solarius kept his grudge against the sky lord closely guarded.

"There are plenty of ways to spend your time together." Reif ticked off each idea on one of his fingers. "They have those fancy boat rides through the sky, their entertainment district is quite magical, not to mention Eponians are bred there, so perhaps you might take riding lessons."

Solarius scoffed. "I am more than capable of riding an Eponian."

Narissa, on the other hand, was certainly not. The winged horses were beautiful, but she found them slightly intimidating. Not only that, but she much preferred to be on the ground or near the water's edge. Flying through the sky—whether on horseback or in the safety of a carriage—was her least favorite activity.

"But most importantly," Reif continued, ignoring Solarius's protest, "maybe the two of you will learn how to tolerate one another. I would hardly expect you to fall in love, but for the sake of both our families, perhaps you could make a little more effort. We are supposed to be uniting our houses, not dividing them. Lay your past quarrels to rest, before your abhorrence of each other ruins all we've worked to achieve."

Narissa stood abruptly. Her mouth fell open, but she snapped it shut when her cousin shoved back from the table and stalked from the dining room, leaving them to suffer in the resounding silence of his fading footfalls.

Reif had never once raised his voice to her, nor had she ever seen him angry, but his mounting frustration was palpable. It hung heavily in the air, suffocating her. The last thing she wanted was to disappoint Reif, especially since he willingly took her in after the death of her parents.

But a honeymoon?

With Solarius?

Narissa's knees weakened, and she gripped the edge of the table with both hands to keep herself from swaying. Honeymoons came with certain promises…certain expectations. She blanched, sucking in a shallow breath, her chest heaving.

Solarius rose, cocking his head to one side as he eyed her. "How are you faring, Rissa love? You look slightly ill."

Bile scalded the back of her throat, and she dug her nails into the wooden surface of the table. "I am."

He clicked his tongue, then knocked back the remnants of his whiskey. His gaze raked over her, peeling away the layers of protection she'd constructed around herself. "Does the thought of spending time with me really make you physically sick?"

The accusation was harsh, scraping away her resolve.

She shook her head, pressing her lips together. "It's not that."

Her grating whisper clawed at the ache forming between her temples.

Solarius rose, planted his hands on the table's edge, and leaned forward. He matched her motions. The lines of his face reminded her of granite, hard and unwavering. "Then by all means, enlighten me."

Narissa shook her head. She didn't want to have this conversation. Not here. Not now. She didn't want to relive the painful memories of their past. Her lungs caved and she grasped at her wavering confidence. Usually, she had no problem giving him a lashing of the tongue, but for some reason—be it the pressure of the bond or some other undiscovered reason—she couldn't find the strength to face him.

"It's nothing," she muttered, denying him the opportunity for an argument.

"You're lying," he countered, and she kept her gaze focused on her half-eaten plate of food, unable to meet his eye.

"Perhaps."

"Damn it, Narissa!" Solarius slammed one fist upon the table, splintering the wood and rattling the dishes. She jumped, her eyes flying to him, only to find the unstable emotions of anger and desperation colliding on his face. "Tell me, Rissa. Right now. Why do you hate me? What have I done to deserve such loathing from you?"

Narissa met his menacing glare with one of her own, her resolve snapping. "You broke my heart, Sol!"

"And you broke mine!" He shoved both hands through his hair so the messy pieces fell across his face, then he threw his arms out wide. "Yet here I am, trying to make this work."

Her bottom lip began to tremble, and she bit it until the pain made her gasp. "Impossible."

"What's impossible?" he demanded.

"I couldn't have possibly broken your heart, Solarius." Narissa clenched her jaw and lifted her chin, the threat of tears causing her vision to swim. "It was never mine."

CHAPTER THIRTEEN

The silence between Solarius and Narissa was unfathomable. The quiet in the carriage interrupted only by the whistling winter wind.

The stillness stretched like a gaping chasm, cold and empty. One day it was as though they were traversing a rickety bridge, determined to meet in the middle. Then the next they were ripped apart, standing on opposite ledges, overlooking the widening expanse between them. Not even the echo of his voice could reach her. At this rate, Narissa would never fall in love with him.

Now, they were on their way to Windsong, where they would undoubtedly be forced to exchange pleasantries with Calfair Skyhelm. If that bastard of a lord knew Solarius was arriving in Galefell, he would drive a well-placed wedge between Solarius and Narissa. Besides, he was the reason their courtship ended in shambles.

Anger rumbled through his chest.

Not so long ago, or perhaps not long enough, Calfair had been his best friend. They'd spent the majority of their youth together, from racing Eponians in the middle of the night during a rainstorm, to pouring soap into Celestine's fountains and watching bubbles pop and coat the city in sudsy stardust, to drunken escapades that involved daring one another to see who could drink the most whiskey.

Solarius always won that game.

But with each passing year, their audacious friendship evolved into a tiresome rivalry. It seemed that no matter what Solarius did, Calfair had to best him. Whenever they skipped rocks at Silvermist Lake in the warmer seasons, it was a ruthless game to see whose stones bounced the furthest across the lake's sapphire surface. And in the winter, when Silvermist Lake froze solid, it became a battle to see who could break the ice with the largest rock first. If Solarius placed first in fencing, Calfair would tout he'd been triumphant in swordplay. Eventually their competitiveness spilled into their personal lives as well—who danced with more ladies at a ball and who stole the most kisses in the gardens.

All of that changed when Solarius set his sights on Narissa.

He wanted her, and only her, his conflicts with Calfair be damned. It had been a mistake, a terrible lapse in judgement.

Solarius had made the unfortunate assumption that if he was serious about courting a female, then perhaps Calfair would stand down and see that their feud was coming to an end. After all, they couldn't be esteemed bachelors forever. While a lofty dream, it was not the way of things in Aeramere. A lord was destined to take a wife, just as ladies were bound to find a husband. He'd almost bought a ring for her, had a thoroughly planned proposal that filled him with nauseating anxiety. Just in case. Everything Solarius ever wanted, he'd found in Narissa.

That was until he'd discovered her with Calfair in a secluded bedroom of House Galefell during a Midsummer ball. The door had been left unlocked, as though Calfair wanted Solarius to find them, like he'd planned to bed Narissa the whole time. It had been the final match he never saw coming. He'd said nothing afterward, choosing instead to save face and shield their reputations from any outlandish rumors. But Solarius had lost his best friend and the female he wanted to marry in the same night.

So, no. He wasn't too keen on being sent to Windsong.

Calfair was the last fucking fae he wanted to see while he was trying to woo his wife.

Solarius glanced over at Narissa seated beside him in the carriage.

She was gripping the edge of the leather seat so tightly he thought for certain her nails would tear through the thick fabric. Her back was painfully straight, her arms were locked by her side, and every muscle of her body seemed stiff with agonizing tension. The pale green of her eyes expanded, and her gaze darting from one sleek window to the other. The frantic beating of her heart pulsed through his own veins and his brow furrowed. He didn't think their most recent dispute was cause for her to act as though the world was going to come crashing down around her, but then the carriage caught a gust of wind and bounced lightly upon the stiff evening breeze.

Narissa yelped, clutched at his upper arm with both hands, and squeezed her eyes shut.

Stars above, she wasn't still mad at him.

She was *afraid.*

All the air left her in a rush and her eyes flew open. She let go of him at once, but Solarius grabbed her hand, keeping it wrapped tightly around his arm. He squeezed her fingers in reassurance, noting how small and delicate they were in the strength of his grip, admiring the pretty gold bands she wore. Perhaps he would give her one to add to her collection one day. Narissa tried to tug away one more time but he held on, refusing to let her go. If she was scared of flying, then the least he could do was offer her comfort, whether she wanted it from him or not.

"Are you alright?" he asked, keeping his voice low and soft.

She shook her head and curled her fingers into the fabric of his coat. "No. I hate flying."

"Fear not, I won't let anything happen to you." Solarius gave her hand another reassuring squeeze. "Besides, what could be safer than riding in a carriage pulled by winged Eponians?"

When those frosty green eyes looked up at him, glazed with a familiar sheen, he saw the deeply planted root of her fear.

"My parents…"

Her harsh whisper struck him with remorse, and he silently cursed himself for being so thoughtless with his words. He should have known better. For her sake, he should've taken more care.

Of course Narissa hated flying, she'd lost both of her parents in a carriage accident. It was a rare occurrence to be sure, but devastating, nevertheless. Lord and Lady Seaborne were returning to Azurvend from House Emberspire after the Firelight Festival when their carriage was caught in a sudden summer storm. A bolt of lightning startled the Eponians and the driver lost control, sending them careening toward the ground. At some point, the carriage detached from the shaft and the driver was able to save himself and the Eponians, but Narissa's parents were lost in the crash.

She was only a child when it happened.

Solarius gently stroked the bond the way he might caress her during the midnight hours.

Narissa gasped when he attuned to her labored breathing, she shuddered when he filled her with his heartbeat, when the might of the moon danced with the tides. Their magic drifted toward one another lazily, a lulling sway, like the languid way the waves returned time and again to kiss the shore. This was not the same violent clash as before, it was a welcome kind of serenity. She turned into him as the carriage jostled to one side, pressing her forehead to his shoulder, inhaling sharply while her body remained rigid and stiff with fright.

Carefully, Solarius reached for her mind. *"Rissa."*

She stiffened against him.

At first, there was only deafening quiet, but then he heard the lullaby of her voice.

"Yes, my lord?"

Solarius casually ran one hand up and down her spine in an effort to calm her. *"I was merely curious if the bonded mind sharing actually worked."*

Narissa leaned back, her grip on his arm loosening slightly. She arched one golden blonde brow. "Apparently it does."

"Right," he agreed, nodding once. She hadn't smacked at his hand yet, nor had she inched away from him, so he continued with his plan. "Can you see my thoughts?"

Solarius opened his mind to her, and Narissa suffered him a sigh.

She folded her hands in her lap, but he liked her closeness, enjoying the way her thigh brushed his own. "You're wondering how much longer until we arrive at Windsong."

"What about now?" he asked, pressing a different thought upon her, showing her exactly what was on his mind.

A pretty blush stained the rosy gold of her cheeks, and she ducked her head.

He wanted her to see their shared kiss in the tide pool from his perspective, wanted her to realize the power she held over him, wanted her to understand his mild obsession with her. That kiss had been his undoing. Her lips were a drug, intoxicating and potent. Had she denied him, he would've gladly dropped to his knees and begged her for a kiss. The mating bond snapping into place was the icing on the cake, serving only to amplify his fixation on her. Half the time, the words coming out of his mouth defied those feelings, but Solarius had been unable to quit his mind of Narissa since Ariesian first announced their engagement. It didn't matter if Calfair had her first, he *still* wanted her.

He would always want her.

Solarius cupped her chin, lifting her face, his gaze instantly dipping to where her pink lips parted in surprise. He lowered his voice, then murmured, "And now?"

A breathy little noise escaped her.

This time, he invaded her thoughts with everything he had *wanted* to do to her in that tide pool. If she'd let him, if she hadn't run from him, he would have worshipped her like the moon. Gazed upon her like the stars. Unraveled her like the endless night. He'd wanted the freedom to feel her everywhere, to let his hands explore every soft inch of her velvety skin. With her legs locked around his waist and her arms woven around his neck, it would have been so easy to lift her hips, to slide into her, to claim her beneath the silky shower of moonlight.

Solarius's blood hummed in anticipation and his magic flared, calling to her.

Her scent overwhelmed him. He wanted to lick the air. To taste her on his tongue.

"Can I touch you?" he asked, forcing each word out with feigned composure. He would lose his damn mind if she refused him.

Narissa's teeth snagged on her bottom lip, and his cock swelled in response. "I don't think—"

Stars above, she would slay him with her rejection.

"Please, Rissa love." He wasn't above begging, not when it came to her. "You consume my thoughts. You reign over my dreams. I know I've said awful, hurtful things, and despite the resentment between us, I am driven to the brink of madness just by looking at you."

"Solarius…" The tone in her voice set him on edge, as though she intended to rebuff him. But then she did the unthinkable. Narissa angled herself toward him and that small gesture ignited a spark of hope inside the frozen walls of his chest.

"I beg of you, Narissa." He searched her face, praying his needs, his desires were not one-sided. In the shrouded darkness of the carriage, with slants of moonlight splintering in through the foggy windows, he caught a glimpse of longing in her eyes. "Let me taste the poison of your lips, let me feel the satin of your skin beneath my palms. One more shared moment is all I ask."

She pressed her lips together in consideration and his hands stole around her hips as he swallowed a groan.

"Let me kiss you, Rissa love."

She loosed another pinched sigh. "I hate it when you call me that."

Solarius grinned. "I know."

The corner of her mouth twitched. Almost a smile. Stars above, how long had it been since he'd actually seen her smile? Or heard her laugh? He couldn't recall the last time, and that thought alone caused his chest to heave, the stabbing ache expanding with each breath. His lungs seized, and the erratic beating of his heart echoed in his ears to the rushing of his blood. He needed her like he needed air. Without her, he simply would not survive. "Let us have this moment, then I promise you can hate me again tomorrow."

Her lashes fluttered like the wispy wings of a tiny butterfly, and she looked up at him. "You promise?"

Solarius nodded in earnest. "Yes. I promise."

Narissa reached out, tucking a few fallen strands of his hair back behind his ear. Her fingertips feathered along his cheek, lingering at his jaw.

"Okay," she agreed quietly. "One more moment."

"Blessed stars," he groaned, and plucked her off the seat beside him, dragging her across his lap so she straddled him.

Solarius snared one arm around her waist to support her while his other hand captured the back of her neck. Her squeal of surprise sent a bolt of desire coursing through him, and when his mouth slashed across her plump, pink lips and she readily opened for him, he knew one more kiss would never be enough.

He wanted all of her.

Forever.

CHAPTER FOURTEEN

$\mathcal{N}$arissa knew she was making a detrimental mistake.

Sprawled across Solarius's lap with her velvet skirts tangled around her was just asking for trouble, especially when his capable hands snaked beneath her warming layers to glide up and over her bare thighs. Goosebumps pebbled her flesh and she shivered, causing him to tighten his hold on her. She threaded her fingers through his silky hair, admiring the way the soft strands blended from bright silver to inky black. Even though her mind was screaming at her, begging her to stop, her heart was not in the mood to listen.

He did prove to be a most welcome distraction from her fear of flying.

She anchored herself to him, deciding right then that his mouth was magic, and if he was indeed attempting to divert her attention so that she was no longer terrified of falling out of the sky, then she would allow it.

His tongue swept through her mouth, and she liked how he tasted faintly of mint and whiskey. She committed the flavor of him to her memory. Kissing Solarius was like fighting against the currents—each time she tried to swim to the shoreline, to save herself, he dragged her back out to the sea. And she was ready to let him drown her. Her magic sang the song of a thousand sirens, summoning the beauty of the moon. She let the silvery glow of moonlight wash over her, relishing the way her skin seemed to tingle beneath its affection. The union of their magic was a hypnotic symphony, and she knew every note by heart.

Solarius's hands skated farther up her legs and his thumbs traced the scrap of lace she wore, sliding beneath the thin barrier of fabric. He hooked one finger around the strap, pulled, then let it snap against her hips.

Narissa gasped, breaking their kiss, and he seized the opportunity to plant a trail of kisses from her neck to the top of her breasts.

The teal gown she wore cut low, the satin corset doing very little to disguise her ample bosom. It cinched her waist and shoved her breasts together, granting him easy access. He scraped his teeth along her round flesh and Narissa's head fell back, a desperate moan slipping from her. She twisted her fingers through his hair, her heart skittering inside her chest as he molded his hands to her bottom and squeezed.

"We shouldn't do this," she murmured, melting into him despite her better judgement.

Solarius made a noncommittal sound, one hand sliding to the small of her back while the other settled between her thighs.

"I don't even like you, Sol."

She gripped his shoulders for balance and ground her hips against him, feeling the hardness of his shaft straining against his pants. An excited thrill whipped through her, knowing she was capable of arousing him. Not that she doubted her abilities, but it gave her a wonderful sort of satisfaction to know she could still have such an effect on him. Just imagining the full length of him filling her caused delicious heat to blossom inside of her. She rocked herself against him again, craving the friction their bodies created.

"Fuck." His silver eyes flashed to her face, glazed with lust. "Oh, trust me. I'm aware."

Narissa pressed her lips together, lowering her mouth to the tip of his pointed ear. She let her breath float past him as she whispered, "I don't think you are."

"Then tell me." He nudged the lace aside, slowly stroking his knuckles up and down her center. She was already slick, but he pretended not to notice. "Tell me all the things you hate about me."

Narissa almost whimpered, her nails digging into his coat as she attempted to angle herself, to quietly plead with him to touch her.

"Tell me," he repeated, except this time it was more of a demand.

She met the intensity of his gaze, understanding that he wouldn't go further, he wouldn't touch her where she wanted until she did exactly as she was told.

Very well, two could play this game.

"I hate your cocky smirk, and I hate how you always know what to say to get under my skin." She rolled her hips, and he pressed his thumb to her clit, rubbing small, tantalizing circles.

"Is that the best you've got?" he drawled.

"No." Narissa shook her head, biting her bottom lip. Solarius tracked the movement, his eyes expanding with tempered heat, and the bond started to throb, sending torturous vibrations through her. "I hate the way you look at me. Like I'm coveted. And I hate that you can see right into my soul."

"Hmm." The hand fastened to the small of her back tensed, and Solarius extended two fingers along her slit, still refusing to enter. His jaw clenched as he watched her. "Is that all? You're sure there is nothing else you'd like to add?"

She was panting now, every inch of her was on fire, prickling with awareness. And it was all his fault. He knew exactly what he was doing, stringing her along, teasing her with sensual promises yet denying her at the same time. Narissa was no fool. She knew Solarius was well versed in the art of seduction, and now he was proving the extent of his damning talents. Worse, the proof of his own desire continued to nudge against her, and there was nothing she could do about it. Tremors of anticipation wrecked her, and she was flushed with longing, with the agonizing need for release, yet he continued to edge her on. Perhaps he was better at this game than she thought.

"I hate the way our magic chose each other. I hate how you know exactly where to touch me." Narissa sucked in a ragged breath when his mouth melded to the side of her throat. Her voice was scarcely audible as she said, "I hate how you weaken me."

He pushed two fingers inside of her and she almost came undone right then. It had been far too long since the last time she'd experienced any sort of pleasure. Weeks, maybe. Months? She could no longer recall.

"And?" he taunted.

And…Solarius was asking her a question.

Narissa blinked, struggling to remember what she was supposed to be doing.

He nudged his fingers a little further.

Ah, yes. Listing things she hated. About him.

"And I hate that you're my husband." The lie was bitter on her tongue, but his touch was an aphrodisiac, better even than the most well-blended mixture of purple moon lotus. No herbal remedy or potion would ever leave her so aroused, so positively stimulated, so perfectly sated as him. So, in a pitiful effort to earn more of his attention, she spewed another lie. "I hate that we're bound to one another for eternity."

A low chuckle rumbled through his chest, and she never realized how much she enjoyed the sound of it.

"Is that so?" He pressed another kiss to her neck, bit softly, then swiped his tongue to ease the sting. "Because I think you're lying to me."

The carriage dipped on another gust of wind, and a spike of fear pierced Narissa's heart. She shrieked, clutching at him, but Solarius was quicker. He shoved those two fingers deep inside of her, curling them slightly, then withdrew, repeating the motion over and over. His other hand continued to firmly hold her in place on his lap and each time the howling wind jostled the carriage, he pumped her faster. Harder. So she was caught somewhere between the crippling edge of panic and the soaring heights of sexual gratification.

His tongue flicked the lobe of her ear, toying with the hoop dangling there, and his raspy voice caused her nipples to harden until they ached. "You're so wet, Rissa love. But I thought you hated me?"

"I do," she cried, bouncing on his hand, needing more. She was so, so close.

"Then say it." He dragged teeth along her jaw, moving to nip at her lip, and his movements slowed inside of her. "Because if you tell me you love me, I'll never believe you."

A grievous emotion seized her then, twisted around the bond and yanked, so she thought her soul would be ripped from her chest. Tears spilled down her cheeks, blurring her vision. His torment knew no bounds.

"I hate you." Narissa choked the words out, leaving her throat raw. Solarius caught one of her tears with his tongue.

His fingers stilled completely and his gaze darkened, a line harboring between his brows. "Saltwater."

"Sol, please," she begged. "Please don't stop."

Seconds ticked by before he spoke. His face was a mask of indifference and his mind was silent. He angled his head to one side and his throat worked. "Are you lying to me?"

"No." She shook her head violently, frantic for him to continue. Throwing her arms around his neck, silent tears continuing to fall, she looked him in the eyes and lied again. "I h-hate you."

Solarius clicked his tongue. "That's what I thought."

Narissa couldn't see his face. The moon had vanished behind a blanket of clouds, and though the night sky was a hazy shade of sapphire ink, the carriage was swathed in darkness. There was only the two of them, their shared breaths, and the feverish beating of their hearts.

He didn't make her wait anymore, he drove her straight to oblivion. His fingers slipped in and out of her with practiced ease, his thumb applying the perfect amount of pressure, so in the next moment she fractured, splintering into a hundred pieces. The orgasm rocked her and she collapsed on top of him, sucking in greedy gulps of air. Her body thrummed as she recovered, and she tried not to notice the way Solarius adjusted her skirts, or the way he smoothed her frizzy waves. The way he seemed to genuinely care.

The carriage rumbled to a stop as it landed on solid ground, but the air between them was still ripe with tension, with everything she had said and everything he had not. Narissa eased back as the lights from Windsong poured into the carriage, drenching them both in a golden glow. Yet she couldn't make herself climb off his lap.

And to her surprise, he did not remove her.

Instead, he leaned his head back against the leather seat and reached for her face, wiping away the dried saltwater upon her cheeks.

Solarius said nothing, but the look in his eyes was filled with a thousand emotions she couldn't quite place. The bond was eerily silent, save for an overwhelming knowledge, a profound understanding. He knew she was lying. Those tears she'd let fall were not tied to a true emotion.

Because Narissa didn't hate him.

Not even a little bit.

Not at all.

In fact, it was unfortunately quite the opposite, and the very existence of such a thought would be her ultimate ruin.

CHAPTER FIFTEEN

 indsong was a collection of stone and wood cottages clustered together on the mountains overlooking Galefell. Solarius had only ever visited Windsong twice before, both times during the Midsummer season for some wedding he'd been forced to attend, and back then the landscape had been lush with evergreens, wildflowers, and the rugged peaks of lightly snow-capped mountains. The weather had been warm with a cool breeze, a stark contrast to the bitter winter temperatures he and Narissa currently faced. Now the mountains were banked in snow and the icy pines stood frozen against the biting wind. Gilded lampposts burning bright with faerie fire illuminated the cobblestone path up to their assigned cottage, and to be honest, it was grander than he expected.

He took stock of the cozy two-story cottage—a balcony wrapped around the upper level, there was a stone patio off the side with furniture seated around a roaring fire pit, and through the many windows he could make out the glow of dozens of lanterns and candles. A bough of holly stretched across the front entrance, and though it looked large and expansive from the outside, he knew there was only one bedroom.

Not that sharing a bed with his wife would be a problem, but after their little carriage interlude, it had been a struggle for Solarius to stay focused on anything else.

He'd lost track of the number of times he'd imagined Narissa writhing beneath him, but witnessing her do it on top of him was another kind of fantasy altogether. She'd left him stricken and hard as a fucking rock, but stars above, it had been worth it to see her fall apart in his arms. It was like watching decadence unfold—her flushed rosy cheeks, the breathy little sounds she made, the way she clung to him while she rode him, chasing her release. His only regret was that it had been his fingers that brought her pleasure and not his cock.

Now, he was standing outside the cottage they would be sharing for the next fortnight, trying to wrap his head around the fact that his wife had blatantly lied to him.

There had been nothing more arousing than when Narissa was seated upon his lap, declaring all the things she hated about him while simultaneously being edged toward climax. But then she'd started to cry, leaving streaks of saltwater drying down her face, and he'd known she wasn't telling him the truth. He had a small collection of pearls in a jar on top of his dresser, each of them a former tear belonging to Narissa, each of them also completely his fault. He'd expected a pearl or two to fall in the carriage, but none had formed, which meant those tears weren't connected to a genuine emotion.

Narissa was lying.

She didn't hate him. At least, not honestly.

He shoved his hands into his pockets, his gaze sliding over her.

Narissa was bundled into a furry coat that dusted the cold ground like frothy ocean foam. Her nose was pink from the chill outside, but her swollen lips were from him. Haphazard golden waves tumbled down her back, lightly sprinkled with falling snow, and her smile was brighter than the moon as she gazed up at their welcoming little cottage.

But that beautiful, beaming smile faltered when she looked over at him.

"Ready?" she asked, an air of indifference in her voice, and Solarius couldn't read the emotion banking deep in her eyes. She gripped the bronze key tightly in her gloved hand and while he debated sneaking into her mind through the bond, he thought better of it when she huffed out a breath of frozen air and went to unlock the door.

He followed her inside and was once again struck by Narissa's beauty.

She twirled around in a small circle, admiring the splendor of the room. A massive stone fireplace roared to life, surrounded by comfortable seating and fur-lined blankets. Her heeled boots clicked against the hardwood floor and her eyes danced when they landed on tiny shimmery clear vases overflowing with soft flora positioned on nearly every surface. But it was the way her coat slipped from her shoulders that gave him pause, the way wonder caused her deep pink lips to part on a gasp, how her delight in the natural made it impossible to tear his gaze away from her.

Narissa carefully removed her gloves, trailing her fingers along the back of a leather sofa. She looked up, sighing in contentment when she caught sight of the chandelier that looked as though it was made from the lining of clouds—fused iridescent glass.

"It's..." Her voice was strangely quiet. "So much more than I expected."

Solarius swallowed around the sudden lump in his throat and nodded. "Yes. Quite."

She glanced in his direction then, only to catch him staring at her, and scarlet stained her cheeks. Her lips pressed together in a firm line, and then she forced a long, exaggerated yawn.

"Well," she declared loudly, "I'm having difficulty keeping my eyes open."

Not him.

Solarius was wired. Currents of energy were running through him, filling him with a kind of torturous awareness. He couldn't silence his thoughts. He couldn't clear his mind. He just kept replaying the image of Narissa on his lap, the one moment she'd been willing to give him, only to have it shattered by her lies. He could have handled her hatred of him if it had at least been honest, but she was hiding the truth of her feelings from him. And he was determined to find out why, because if there was one thing he simply could *not* tolerate, it was intentional deception.

He had enough exaggerations and falsehoods surrounding his family, he didn't want it to leach into his personal affairs with his wife as well.

Solarius waited until the maid assigned to their cottage hauled in their luggage, then made her way to the servants' quarters in the adjacent building. Once the door closed soundly behind her, he faced his wife and asked, "Tired, Rissa love?"

The nickname did the trick. Her eyes ignited, those pools of green burning away the frost and simmering like an ocean of fire.

"Yes." She spoke through a clenched jaw, and he didn't miss the way she held her gloves in fisted hands. "I am."

"Then perhaps we should retire for the evening?" he mused, shoving his hands into the pockets of his heavy overcoat. He didn't intend to imply any sort of innuendo or hidden meaning behind his words, but he much preferred her when she was feisty. She spoke her mind then, she never held back. So, if he poked her a bit to get a rise out of her, then so be it.

"Unless you're afraid to sleep with me?" Solarius arched a singular brow and sauntered toward her.

"I'm not afraid." Narissa stiffened, and he tucked his hands behind his back.

He approached her slowly, standing close enough so that if she wanted space between them, she would have to be the one to step back. To step away. Besides, he didn't exactly tower over her by any means, but his height did offer him an excellent vantage point. One glance downward and he was greeted by the swell of her perfectly splendid breasts. Her delicious scent of sandalwood, salty sea air, and heady florals wafted over him, and he reached between them, tracing the delicate deep cut line of her gown with one finger.

She sucked in a sharp breath, her skin flushing beneath his intimate assessment.

Solarius wasn't sure why she was acting so reserved. Usually she met him head-on with a vicious smile and a sharp tongue. Yet now she was almost apprehensive. There was hesitance in the way she couldn't quite meet his eyes, and it drove him mad. He rather liked her when she was demanding and forceful, when she glared at him as though he was the last person in the world she wanted to see, when her verbal assaults left him desperate for more of her.

Unless, of course, it was all an act. An exceptional performance for reasons still unknown to him.

He bent lower, brushing his lips along the lobe of her ear, taking great pleasure when she shivered against him. Her hands moved between them, her fingers curling into the lapel of his coat.

"Let me kiss you, Rissa love," he whispered, skating his lips up to the tip of her ear. "Let me take you to bed."

Another one of those tempting sounds slipped from between her lips and his cock throbbed to life. She swayed into him and his hand slid around to the small of her back, dipping lower. He pressed her firmly against him, so she would know the exact effect she had on him, and like a naughty midnight siren, she ground her hips into his bulging shaft.

"Let me taste you," Solarius groaned. He would absolutely beg again if necessary. Anything to finally be able to feel her fully, with nothing between them but sweat and skin. "Let me fill you."

"Sol." His name on her lips was hardly more than a strained whimper. The bond flared to life, but Narissa's fingers unfurled and she pressed her hands against the solid wall of his chest. "I…I can't."

Solarius locked his jaw, inhaling deeply, then slowly recovered from his mate's refusal. Again, she was determined to deny him. Not that he was owed intercourse or any other kind of intimacy with her, but stars be damned, certainly she had to at least *feel* something for him. Even if her attraction toward him was strictly because of the bond, he told himself that would be enough, that he would find a way to manage a purely physical relationship. If she didn't want to give him her heart, he would accept that, but not without trying.

Not without begging.

"Tell me why." He spoke every word with soothing tenderness. He wanted to understand her reasoning, but more than that, he needed to know why she was continuously putting up a wall around herself, why she wasn't allowing herself to get too close to him. "If you're nervous, I promise I'll worship every inch of you to keep you calm. If you're worried it might hurt, I promise we'll go as slow as you need."

Narissa shook her head, a familiar sheen glazing her eyes.

Fuck.

"It's not that." She sniffed once and a tear slid down her cheek. "I'm just…"

Solarius caught the small pearl and shoved it into his pocket before it could hit the floor. "What is it then, Rissa? Tell me. Please. Help me understand."

Her chest shuddered and she wrapped her arms around herself, taking a step back. Coldness expanded between them. She gnawed on her bottom lip, her eyes darting all over the room, looking anywhere but at him.

"Rissa," he urged.

She squeezed her eyes shut, and when she opened them, they were filled with a vast and deep hurt that hollowed out his heart. He'd never seen so much sorrow, so much agony, all of it kept safely hidden away by a façade of aversion.

"If I do this, if I share this part of me with you now…I'll never forgive myself."

Solarius stared at her.

That was not at all what he was expecting her to say.

"I don't understand." Again he stepped forward, and this time she quickly stepped back, not allowing him to get too close.

She threw her hands up between them, warding him off. Her eyes continued to shine but no tears fell as she said, "I'm not enough for you, Sol. I wasn't the first time, and I know—"

"Wait a damn minute." His blood ran cold, like someone shoved a dagger made of ice right into his chest. "What do you mean, *the first time?*"

Narissa's lips parted, and a tiny frown crinkled her usually smooth brow. She was twisting her gloves in her hands now, wrinkling the fine fabric. Her gaze darted to the floor, but then she rolled her shoulders back and raised her chin.

"The first time we were intimate."

Solarius's mouth fell open, and then he snapped it shut. His mind was reeling, unable to process the words she said, because they were an outright lie. He pinched the bridge of his nose with his thumb and forefinger, trying to make sense of the scene unfolding before him, but a gnawing sense of unease, of growing disquiet, coursed through him.

"The most intimate we've ever been was when you were sprawled across my lap in the back of that carriage." He jerked his thumb toward the door for emphasis, and with painstaking slowness, he closed the distance between them. A sick, twisted sensation wrenched through his gut. "So, I will ask again. What first time?"

Devastation etched into her pretty face and the flames flickering in the hearth cast her in a mask of shadow and light, haunting her with a chilling sort of beauty.

"The first time we had sex, Solarius." Her voice was hoarse and scraping, raw with temper. "Do you truly not remember?"

Shock slammed into him and that roiling knot of dread scalded the back of his throat.

"Narissa, I never..." He raised both of his hands and staggered backward. Surely he had to be losing his mind, she was gravely mistaken. He let his arms fall to his sides, dumbfounded by her declaration. "We never had sex."

"Yes, we did!" She threw her gloves at him, then stormed toward him like a little ball of sea-swept fury. Fisting both of her hands on her hips, she glared at him, rage funneling down the bond. "I gave myself to you, Sol!"

He grabbed her wrists and hauled her to him, if anything to keep her from attacking him. "No. No, you didn't. It wasn't me."

Solarius ignored the fact that her accusation stung his pride—it hurt beyond measure that she would confuse him with Calfair. But he pulled her in, breathed her in, and the truth spilled from him like he'd consumed too much honeyed wine.

"Trust me, Narissa. I would have remembered if we slept together, because only an act of fate would be enough to pry me from between your legs."

Narissa blushed furiously, and he shuffled her wrists to one hand, keeping her in place, then captured her chin with his free hand. He lifted her face to his, lost himself in those eyes of hers.

"And it would have been my fucking honor to be your first."

"*Your only*," he whispered into her mind.

"But, but it was you." Her tears were falling freely now, tiny white and pink pearls bounced off the hardwood floor, tinkling like faerie bells. "I saw you with my own eyes."

"It wasn't me, Narissa." Solarius pressed a kiss to each one of her knuckles. "I swear to the stars it wasn't me."

She was trembling now, violently shaking in his arms. Her chest heaved, and she gasped for air like she couldn't quite breathe. Broken sobs and incoherent words escaped her, and he gathered her into his arms, tucked her head beneath his chin, keeping her in his fierce grip. The scenario of that night replayed in her mind, a chaotic whirlwind of color and voices, of discordant music, and darkened corners. Every image, every word bled before him, the wretched result of what happened when he left Narissa alone at House Galefell for less than a quarter of an hour. Through her eyes, he witnessed the blurry, muddled memory of what she was forced to endure when he wasn't there to protect her.

A venomous rage unlike anything he'd ever known surged through his veins, and with his wife breaking down in his arms, Solarius was only certain of one thing.

He was going to kill Calfair Skyhelm.

CHAPTER SIXTEEN

*N*arissa had never seen Solarius so furious, so full of such cold, ruthless rage. The ice radiating from him forced her to take a step back, to put space between them. Magic exploded around him, a violent vortex of moonlit shards and pulsing lunar power. Streaks of blazing silver ripped through the air as the might of the moon threatened to break free from his control. His chest was heaving with harsh, scraping breaths and his fists were clenched by his sides, his knuckles a ghastly shade of white. He rolled his neck, the resounding crack enough to make Narissa's skin crawl. The silver of his eyes was molten, heated by uncontrollable anger. When he finally spoke, his voice was low and grating, rough like he'd swallowed a mouthful of gravel.

"I'm going to kill him." Solarius popped his jaw and his chest expanded, his magic amplifying. "I'm going to fucking kill him."

"Who?" Narissa squeaked, her own magic churning, bubbling to the surface. She crossed her arms over her chest to keep the pull of the tides at bay.

It was bad enough her own husband didn't remember sleeping with her, but now he seemed positively murderous, and she had no idea what had spurred such a volatile response. If anything, she should be upset with *him*, not the other way around. He was the one at fault, the one who spoiled their previous relationship.

Solarius turned his deadly eyes on her. "Lord Calfair Skyhelm."

Narissa blanched, concern flickering through her. "He is a friend of yours, is he not?"

"He was…" The lunarstorm surrounding Solarius ebbed, the chaos of the moon settled, and Narissa's soul calmed.

"Was?" Her brow furrowed slightly. "What happened?"

Solarius didn't even blink. "He slept with my wife."

Narissa balked at the accusation, her own frustration igniting. "No! How could you say such a thing? How could you make such a wretched claim against me? I never betrayed you. Ever."

Because she loved him, and now she realized even that was a mistake.

"I know that…now." Solarius shoved his hands into the pockets of pants, his mouth pressed into a firm line, and the wrinkle across his brow deepened. "But it was not me who took you to bed during that Midsummer ball in House Galefell all those nights ago. It was Calfair."

"What?" Narissa's voice sounded hollow to her ears, a painful echo. The dawning of an abysmal realization.

"Think about that night, Narissa. Try and recall every detail you can." While Solarius was the epitome of level-headed composure, his eyes told another story. They were begging her, pleading with her to remember.

It was a decadent ball thrown in the honor of the Midsummer season, when quite literally everyone in Aeramere was on the hunt for a mate. House Galefell was known for their lavish parties, and that particular one was no exception. While most events were hosted later in the evening and carried on well into early morning the next day, this festivity began at the golden hour, when the sky was set on fire by the gilded rays of the setting sun so all of Galefell looked dipped in gold. It was a spectacular sight to behold, but when Narissa tried to focus on the more specific details, she found her memory blurry and somewhat out of focus.

"We were at House Galefell for a late Midsummer celebration.

There was cloud dancing." She knew, because though Solarius was courting her then, she was again plastered to the wall like a flower and left without a dance partner. "I waited for you, but you were called away by someone of more importance, I suppose."

"Stop that immediately," Solarius demanded, snatching her chin and tilting her head so she was forced to look up at him. "Do not diminish yourself. Do not think yourself unworthy of my time or attention."

"Easier said than done, my lord." Narissa jerked, yanking herself free from his hold. "Whether you intended to abandon me in search of other pursuits is neither here nor there. What matters is I was alone, at least until Lord Calfair…"

Acid roiled in her stomach and her gut clenched as a swell of nausea swept through her.

"Until he *what?*" Solarius uttered the last word with such finality, Narissa was certain she could feel all the blood drain from her face.

"He gave me a glass of wine while I waited for you. He said it would keep the edge off." She shook her head once, pressing the tips of her fingers to her temples in an effort to ease the pounding ache growing there.

Images from that night were hazy, the wine was the color of crushed black cherries. She rarely drank, but in that moment, she'd been so overwhelmed by disappointment and her own loneliness that she'd allowed herself a moment of weakness to indulge. Narissa knocked back the contents without a second thought, not realizing that the scent profile of the wine didn't quite match the flavor.

"The wine," she repeated numbly, her gaze slowly trekking over Solarius until it reached his face. "It tasted like muddled cherries and spice, but it smelled of dragon root."

Dragon root. The warm, earthy scent should have been her first clue. The queasy feeling settling in her stomach expanded and her lungs seized.

"Dragon root?" Solarius crowded her, cupping both sides of her face with his hands. His touch was cool, her skin was hot. "What's dragon root?"

"It's a plant with leaves that mimic dragon scales. But the roots, if ground into a fine powder, have been known to cause hallucinations of the one thing you desire most." Narissa grabbed Solarius's wrists and pushed away from him.

She'd been drugged.

Calfair had *drugged* her.

Narissa sucked in a garbled, gasping breath. She was suffocating, even the air was seemingly laced with poison. Her vision swam, a watery version of the world around her, and when she spun away from Solarius, everything tilted. She stumbled into a slim, curving bronze tower filled with books, sending them cascading to the floor. The beating of her heart was so loud, she could scarcely hear Solarius calling to her. Fingers fisted into the heavy silk of her gown, she pulled, the ripping of fabric not nearly enough to disguise the broken sobs erupting from her chest. She wanted to tear the flesh from her bones, to mutilate herself so severely, that the bastard of a lord never dared to look upon her again.

Calfair had *touched* her.

He'd coerced her. He'd stolen her virtue while pretending to be Solarius.

Bile scalded the back of her throat and Narissa heaved, her nails digging into the back of the plush sofa for support. She could sense Solarius hovering near her, the layers of his scent wrapped around her like a comforting blanket, but the chill in her blood would remain forever. She did not think she would ever be warm again. Not even the security of the bond was enough to save her, to soothe the agony restricting the beating of her heart. Her body had been violated, her mind deceived. Each ragged breath caused her chest to burn as though it had been set aflame, like she'd been scorched from the inside out.

She reached back behind her, her numb fingers fumbling with the ribbons of her gown.

"I can't…" she choked out. "I can't get it off."

"What do you need?" Solarius asked, desperation pinching his tone. "What can I do?"

"Get it…get it off me." She tore at the sleeves, her nails grazing skin. "Get it off, please."

"Okay. Just breathe, Rissa." He reached for the velvet laces, but he wasn't moving fast enough.

"Get it off me! Get it off, now!" Narissa clawed at the elaborate dress, hating that there were so many beads and buttons and utterly useless bows. "Please, Sol. Get it off."

This time, he didn't hesitate.

He hooked his fingers into the front of her bodice and tore, ripping the seams in half, sending beads scattering all over the cottage floor. He yanked the rest of the gown off her, freeing her from its smothering confines. Gathering the crumpled heap of fabric in his arms, he stalked into the kitchen and shoved the ruined dress into a waste bin. When he returned, his eyes rounded with worry.

"Narissa…your body…"

She clamped her hands over her face, mortified beyond measure. "I don't wish to talk about my body at the moment."

"No. Rissa. Something is wrong." Solarius's rough palms gently cupped her elbows, the faintest of touches. "You're covered in red splotches."

"What?"

Her hands fell away, and she glanced down between them. Sure enough, her tanned skin was mottled with angry, red welts. The agonizing panic coursing through her, the insufferable turmoil racing through her mind, had revealed itself in the form of uncomfortable blotches spreading across her arms, abdomen, and legs.

Solarius released her. "What can I do for you? What do you need?"

Narissa needed to wake up. She needed this to all be some horrific nightmare, for being tricked into bed by that wretched Lord Calfair was far worse than thinking Solarius had broken her heart.

"A shower," she croaked, her voice hoarse and cracking.

It did not matter if what she'd experienced with Calfair happened ages ago, the halting realization left her feeling unclean, like she wanted to scrub every part of her he touched until she was raw and bleeding. She would stand beneath a spray of scalding water, hot enough to melt away her flesh. She craved numbness, wished she could wallow in a sea of empty feelings where she was merely a husk of a soul. Perhaps if she broke down, if she sobbed and wailed, then maybe she could slowly start to recover. To rebuild her confidence. Instead, she only felt a growing sense of anger seeping with vengeance.

"Okay." Solarius nodded, guiding her toward the main bedroom, his hand lightly hovering near the small of her back. "Let's get you in the shower."

Once inside the bedroom, Narissa slipped out of her shoes and lowered herself to the edge of the bed while Solarius started the shower in the connecting bathing suite. Thick curls of steam instantly poured into the bedroom, as though he knew she wanted the water to burn the memories away. She stared at a spot on the floor, the one where the whorls and grains on the wood faintly resembled drifting clouds, vaguely aware of Solarius, who stood ready to jump into action if she so much as blinked the wrong way. Tension rolled off him in heavy waves and while the warm bond blossomed inside her chest, it did nothing to soothe her soul.

He shoved one hand through his hair, shifting his weight back and forth.

Narissa knew what he was thinking—his thoughts were not nearly as chaotic as hers, but they were incredibly divisive. He was torn between staying and caring for her and murdering Lord Calfair Skyhelm in cold blood.

"You desired me." Solarius's words were weak and carved with uncertainty, like he didn't quite believe it to be true. "That's why you have hated me all this time, that's why you could not stand to be in the same room as me. Because you thought it was I who bedded, then abandoned you."

The truth of his words hung between them, carved out by foolish assumption, blatant acceptance, and erroneous resentment.

"Yes." Narissa did not look at him, her eyes did not stray from the swirling clouds engraved upon the hardwood floor. "You never told me why you wanted to end our courtship. You just left."

Again, he shifted his weight, unease filling the space between them.

"I saw you with Calfair."

Her gaze shot to him then, cold and ruthless. She dug her nails into the soft bedding to keep from doing something she might regret…like slapping him across his wretchedly handsome face.

"That is not an excuse," she snapped, no longer caring if venom laced her tone. "Years, Sol. I blamed myself for what happened between us for *years*. When in fact I was exploited by your so-called best friend and all the while you made me think I was somehow unworthy of you."

His shoulders bunched and his hands curled into fists. She could see his anger simmering beneath the surface, feel it pushing down the bond. A swath of hair fell across his forehead, just covering one eye, but she could plainly see the silver of his gaze harden.

"How do you think I felt, Narissa? I saw you fucking my best friend!" He threw his arms out and paced in a small circle, gesturing to nothing and everything all at once. "What was I supposed to do? Barge in and haul him off of you?"

"Yes!" Narissa no longer cared if she was shouting, if her wrath and pain poured from the whole of her heart. She lurched off the bed, rammed one pointed nail directly into the solid wall of his chest. "That is *exactly* what you should have done! Then we would have realized I'd been drugged, and you wouldn't have been stupid enough to think I could ever love anyone but you!"

Solarius's mouth fell open. He stared at her, the expression on his face one she didn't quite recognize. But right now, he was the last person in all of Aeramere she wanted to see.

"Rissa…"

"Out." She pointed to the door of the bedroom and spoke with deadly calm. With poised authority. "Get out."

"Narissa, please. Can we just—"

"No." She couldn't look at him again, otherwise she would cave, she would give in to him, and she couldn't afford to have her resolve weaken. Not yet. "I need to think. I need to breathe. And I can't do that with you here."

"Narissa."

"If you don't leave, I will." Narissa squeezed her eyes shut and took a steady breath, inhaling the citrus steam filling the space between them. "Please, Solarius. I need a moment to myself."

His mouth was pressed into a firm line, but he said nothing. He gave her one sharp nod, turned on his heel, and left her alone in the bedroom, closing the door quietly behind him.

One, two, three, four...

Inhale.

Five, six, seven...

Exhale.

Eight...nine...

On ten, Narissa screamed. She screamed until her throat ached, until the last shriek of rage was choked out of her on a heaving sob. And when she stepped into the searing shower, she made a silent vow to herself that she would never allow another to take advantage of her. She would rise with the powerful ocean tides, she would be the cresting waves, the dangerous currents.

And Calfair would pay for his transgressions against her.

CHAPTER SEVENTEEN

wice.

Twice now, Solarius had seen his wife naked. Twice, he hadn't been able to touch her. At least, not in the way he so desperately wanted.

Solarius stared at the closed door, the only obstacle preventing him from running back into that damned bedroom and hauling Narissa into his arms.

Her screams nearly broke him. The sound was unlike anything he'd ever heard before. Raw. Gritty. They would haunt his dreams.

But he stayed away, exactly as she asked of him.

He couldn't be sure, but it sounded like she was in the shower now. Her soft murmurings drifted through the closed door, and while it seemed like she was calm, her emotions told a different story. Every so often the bond flared to life and he felt her rage, her grief and sorrow keenly. As though those very same feelings belonged to him. Yet there was nothing he could do to ease her pain, to offer her any semblance of comfort.

Worst of all, she'd been right.

He should have stormed into that room and pulled Calfair off her.

He should never have doubted her. He should have been there for her, should have *saved* her.

Because she had loved him.

Solarius replayed that bit of information over in his head again.

"You wouldn't have been stupid enough to think I could ever love anyone but you."

Narissa loved him. Maybe not now, but she had once, and he'd let her down. He'd broken her heart and left her to fend for herself against a monster in disguise.

His mind drifted to when the autumn season encompassed all of Aeramere, when he'd been deep in his cups during Embernyte, and hating every aspect of his life. He thought about how Reif approached him and warned him of Calfair, of how Solarius how found his prick of a former friend cornering Narissa, attempting to coerce her to the gardens beyond the ballroom.

A new kind of fury burned to life inside of Solarius.

Calfair had shamelessly tried to seduce Narissa again and all that time Solarius stupidly thought she wanted the bastard's attentions.

He sucked in a sharp breath, cracking each of his knuckles one at a time.

Solarius needed a drink, otherwise he was going to do something he would regret, and it involved ensuring Calfair Skyhelm could no longer draw a single fucking breath.

☽✶☾

AFTER A BRIEF, albeit bumpy carriage ride from Windsong, Solarius stepped out into Galefell, the city nestled high in the sky among the clouds.

Galefell was a stunning floating island hovering along Aeramere's northwestern coast. It was the home of the Eponians, the majestic winged horses that pulled the carriages through skies, making travel between all five houses expedient and uncomplicated. Shops and homes decorated the soft landscape, swelling in various heights with frosted rooftops, swirling ivory pillars, all connected by ornate bridges made from stained glass. Though it was nightfall, the curving streets were illuminated with gilded lanterns drifting through the air, each one filled with sparkling faerie fire. Fluffy clouds banked around the whole of the city, reflecting hues of lavender and icy blue set against the backdrop of an inky starlit sky.

Solarius burrowed himself into his coat, ducking his head against the bitter chill gusting up from the Chantara Sea. The frigid breeze carried the scent of night jasmine, frozen mountains, and the faintest tang of the ocean. Conversations buzzed around him as air fae bundled in fur-lined coats strolled through the bustling city, slipping in and out of stores and eateries, seemingly not at all bothered by the snow-laden ground or cold temperatures. Solarius didn't mind the winter season, but it was certainly not his most favorite.

He ducked into the nearest tavern to escape the constant chill and was instantly surrounded by the overcrowded warmth of too many bodies crammed into a small space, coupled with the smell of stale alcohol and expensive perfume. A scowl etched its way across his brow as he maneuvered through the lively tavern bursting with raucous laughter and low-hanging lights. Behind the bar was a shim-mery glass sign with mist moving through it that read, The Thunder-cloud. Every so often thunder would rumble throughout the tavern, the crowd would erupt in a chorus of cheers, and sparkling cider would pour from a fountain shaped like a cloud near the back.

A couple weeks ago, the Thundercloud would have been his preferred type of locale—loud and obnoxious, brimming with bad decisions, and the perfect place to drink oneself into oblivion.

Alas, that was no longer the case.

Now, he found himself in search of a single stiff drink to alleviate the overwhelming urge to murder his former best friend.

Solarius sidled up to the bar, inserting himself between a dour female whose frown rippled across her brow in heavy lines, and a robust male with beads of sweat clinging to his forehead and neck.

Grimacing, Solarius ordered a spiced whiskey, intent on keeping to himself. He was grateful none of the Thundercloud's patrons looked familiar as he was hardly in the mood for company. Instead, all he wanted to do was punch Calfair hard enough to knock his smug smile off his face. He also considered taking great delight in breaking every bone in his body.

By some horrible yet hostile twist of fate, a gust of wind blew open the door to the Thundercloud and in strode Calfair with two of his crude cronies.

Calfair's dark, coiffed hair was swept back from his face, slick like it had been coated in luster oil. His cheekbones were too sharp, his smile too wide. Solarius knew many ladies considered him quite the catch, most of them gushing about his flawless skin or striking black eyes. But Calfair's handsome looks were strictly a veneer, a perfected glamour to disguise the venomous serpent hiding in plain sight. He wore a pristine white shirt tucked into perfectly tapered light pants and his cruel grin was made predominantly worse by the pitiful excuse for facial hair sprouting from his chin.

If Solarius didn't know any better, he would have sworn Calfair plucked his own pubic hair and then attached the black sprouts to his face.

"Then I made her dance for me until her pretty feet bled." Calfair's boisterous voice drew the attention of almost every soul in the tavern. No doubt he was talking about the horrors he inflicted upon his pets —the mortals he kept in cages hidden within the pristine walls of House Galefell. "I debated bringing her to our next ball, but I fear she'll be dead by then."

Calfair chuckled darkly.

Seething rage pumped through Solarius's veins. He knocked back his shot of whiskey, then crushed the empty glass in his hand. Shards of broken glass cut into his palm, and scarlet oozed between his knuckles. He ignored the pain pulsing from his palm and pushed back from his seat. Shoving his way through the crowd of bodies, he discarded his overcoat onto the back of an empty chair and quietly rolled the sleeves of his shirt, buttoning them into place.

Calfair's glossy black eyes found him.

"Solarius." His name fell somewhere between a greeting and disgust, and Calfair flashed him a caustic smirk. "Can't say I expected to see you here, old friend. I would have thought you'd be busy enjoying your new wife. A bit too free spirited for my liking...great tits, though."

Uncomfortable laughter rang out, but Solarius heard nothing save for the rushing of his own blood. Closing the distance between them in two long strides, he met Calfair with a callous glare, standing so close, he could smell the ale tainting his breath.

"Do not *ever* speak of Narissa again," Solarius warned.

"Or what?"

"Or I'll fucking kill you."

The mocking amusement in Calfair's eyes dimmed to cold understanding. "Ah...figured it out then, did you?"

Solarius popped his jaw. "That you drugged Narissa, then stole her virtue by pretending to be me?" His fists coiled tightly, ready to strike. "Yeah. I figured it out."

"Too bad for you I got there first," Calfair chided, then he tapped one finger against his chin, considering. "Tell me, have you bedded her yet?"

Calfair ran his tongue along his teeth, and at Solarius's silence, a sadistic smile stretched across his face. "No? So, you haven't heard that sweet little sound she makes when she finds release? Pity. Though it no longer matters. She may spread her legs for you, but we both know it will only be my face she sees from now on...good luck with that."

Blind rage pummeled Solarius and he slammed his fist into Calfair's face with so much force, the bastard's head snapped back and blood spurted from his busted mouth. Calfair stumbled back, staring at the crimson stains littering his crisp white shirt, and launched himself toward Solarius. Screams and shouts filled the Thundercloud, but he was ready. His other fist hooked through the air and the satisfying sound of bone crunching against Calfair's too-straight nose fueled him with even more fury.

They grappled, taking vicious swings at one another while attempting to throw the other to the ground. At one point, Calfair's head bounced off the granite bar and Solarius thought for certain the prick would finally stay down, take his beating like a proper lord, and leave before he humiliated himself further. But he hauled himself upright and sent a gust of wind barreling into Solarius. He flew through the air, slamming into anything in his path, until his back met a wooden table, splintering it in half. Pain ricocheted through his body, a silent scream of agony that tore from his shoulder to his spine.

His own lunar magic roared to life, ready to bring down the wrath of the midnight heavens, but Solarius suppressed the surge of power.

He shook off the discomfort and launched himself at Calfair, prepared to mutilate him with nothing more than his bare fists. If that lousy excuse for a fae needed to cheat and use his magic because he was losing, then Solarius would make sure his defeat marred his honor for the rest of his days.

He got in one more vengeful hit, the might of his elbow colliding with the underside of Calfair's jaw, before someone's hand clamped around his fist.

"What the—" Solarius whipped around to face the offender. He had every intention to tell them off for interfering, but instead found his brother-in-law staring back at him.

Drake Kalstrand stood just behind Solarius, the play of light in the tavern bouncing off every surface but him, leaving Drake cloaked in a touch of darkness. His mouth was set in a firm line, and the leathers he wore were a far cry from the polished appearance of other males, lending him an air of intimidation. For a brief moment, Solarius thought Drake meant to rebuke him for fighting in public—if Ariesian had been the one to discover him, he would never hear the end of it—but the focus of Drake's deadly glare was aimed at Calfair.

"Take a breath." Drake released him then, adjusting the roughened strap of leather bound across his chest, the one decorated with a varying assortment of daggers.

"He's still standing." Solarius wiped his mouth with the back of his hand, blood smearing his skin.

"That may be…" Drake glanced in his direction and rolled his shoulders back, the depths of his eyes reflecting a kind of commiseration, as though he understood just how much Solarius wanted to end Calfair's life. "But I'm afraid I cannot allow you to kill him."

"Why not?" Solarius barely recognized his own voice. He flexed his hands, chest heaving, heart pounding.

"It would be in poor taste."

Solarius cut Drake with a look of severity. "What are you talking about, Drake?"

Again, the god of shadow and prophecy's lethal glare slid back to Calfair. "You would sully the Starstorm family name if you kill your future in-law."

"I beg your pardon?" Solarius's gaze swung back to Calfair, and the jerk had the audacity to flash another cutting smirk—bloodied mouth, bruised face, and all.

Solarius shook his head, wincing as it throbbed along his temples.

Impossible. There was no way Ariesian would promise Sarelle to Calfair, not when she was supposed to be pretending to persuade Prince Aspen to court her. Stars above, Calfair was almost as bad as the prince himself, and Solarius was ashamed he'd ever been friends with the miscreant in the first place. Calfair was an absolute scoundrel. A selfish, cocky asshole who enjoyed tormenting those he deemed beneath him.

"That's right, Lord Solarius." Smugness dripped from the sarcastic use of his title and Calfair spat a disgusting mixture of saliva and blood onto the tavern floor. "Your brother and my father are working on uniting one of your brothers with my sister."

Solarius's jaw dropped and he snapped it shut.

If Nyxian didn't already know, he would likely find out soon enough, and once he did would lose his stars-damned mind. Tovian would be the one to take the news in stride and accept his fate, but Nyxian…he would fight. There were two things in this world Nyxian simply could not stand. The first, being told what to do. The second, the uncanny idea of sleeping with one female for the rest of his life.

Solarius stole a glance at Drake, who nodded once in confirmation, and a riotous stream of curses filtered through his mind. The last thing he wanted was to have any kind of connection, marital by name or otherwise, to this bastard.

Calfair sauntered forward, but there was no mistaking the way he winced and favored his left leg as he walked. "So, run home to your little wife before she finds her way into my bed again."

Solarius lurched toward him, but Drake's arm shot out with blinding quickness, preventing any further movement.

Drake grabbed a fistful of Calfair's shirt and hoisted him into the air for everyone in the tavern to see. "I suggest you shut your mouth, Skyhelm. Before I cut off your cock and shove it down your throat."

Solarius bit the inside of his cheek to keep from grinning. Most might assume that was nothing more than a vicious threat, but if anything, it was a promise. After all, Drake had conducted that exact exploit on a man who dared to lay a hand on Solarius's youngest sister, Creslyn.

"You wouldn't—" Calfair choked out.

"Try me," Drake countered.

Shadows swarmed, engulfing the space around them, leaching it of warmth and replacing it with a permeating cold that sank deep into Solarius's bones. Gasps and a few startled cries echoed throughout the Thundercloud, and the fear of those who stood nearby was so palpable, he could almost taste it on his tongue.

"Leave." Drake commanded Calfair like he would one of his notorious dragons. "Now."

He dropped him without a second thought and Calfair staggered backward, smoothing his wrinkled shirt, and lifting his chin with a sense of feigned authority.

Calfair scoffed once, sent a vitriolic look in Solarius's direction, then turned around and stomped out of the Thundercloud, all while trying to disguise his limp.

Solarius straightened, though it wasn't like he was much better off. In fact, he was fairly certain the impact with that damn table had broken a rib or two. Maybe three. But it had been well worth it. He loved a good brawl, specifically those without magic, the ones where it was only a matter of brute strength and bare knuckles. It gave him a kind of delicious satisfaction, making the hideous bruises and broken bones all the more rewarding. Despite the shock of pain reverberating throughout his busted body, Solarius locked his spine and accepted the glass of whiskey that Drake shoved into his hand.

He would never admit it out loud, and while he didn't particularly care for Drake, his loyalty to Creslyn and their family was unrivaled. Which was why he didn't argue when Drake clinked his own glass of whiskey against Solarius's and they knocked back their drinks in unison. The warm, cinnamon flavor burned the back of his throat, and he tapped the empty glass on the bar's smooth surface, debating having another.

Rolling his neck once, he continued to twirl and tap the glass. "How did you know I was here?"

"I didn't." Drake shrugged, lifting one hand in the bartender's direction to signal another round. "That was pure luck."

"Mm." Solarius licked his bottom lip and hissed as the metallic tang of blood coated the tip of his tongue. "Getting myself into a bar fight doesn't really strike me as something important enough to be revealed in one of your prophecies."

The corner of Drake's mouth twitched, but it vanished just as quickly. "Not quite."

"Then what are you doing here?" Curiosity piqued, Solarius feigned indifference. Drake rarely left Creslyn's side, not unless it was absolutely necessary and of the utmost importance. "If not stopping me from ending the life of that miserable piece of shit?"

Another nonchalant shrug.

"Nothing."

"Bullshit."

Drake collected the two new shots of whiskey and slid one in Solarius's direction. "I am tracking someone of interest. Someone who has no business being in Galefell."

Tracking, indeed.

Drake could move between shadows. He was like a wraith, undetectable until it was too late.

They raised their glasses again, knocking them together once more before downing the fiery contents.

"Who?" Solarius asked, not at all expecting a response from the impassive god.

Drake's eyes darkened.

"Your mother."

CHAPTER EIGHTEEN

Despite the pale glow of morning sunlight streaming in through the cottage's window, Narissa knew the other side of the bed would be cold.

Solarius had not returned.

She thought for certain he would come back before dawn. She'd woken up multiple times during the night, stretching one arm out just to see, only to grasp nothing. His half of the bed remained empty. A tiny part of her hoped he would be asleep on the sofa in the cozy living area, but she knew she wouldn't find him there. The bond quickly diminished that small glimmer of optimism—he was gone.

Truth be told, she was not entirely sure she wanted to know where he spent the night. She didn't want to think about whose arms he may have stumbled into, or dwell upon what sort of circumstances might have found him.

Sighing but choosing not to despair, Narissa climbed out of bed and carefully considered her options. She could explore the cottage, which admittedly would not take long and seemed like the more uninspiring choice, or she could muster up a pluck of bravery and venture into Galefell alone.

The decision made itself, and Narissa chose a gown of heavy teal silk with sapphire lace overlay along the hem. Iridescent crystals in the shape of flowing waves embellished the waist and the modest bodice was complete with sheer long sleeves that draped off her shoulders. Nude stockings reached the top of her thighs, and she paired them with shiny black boots. Not ideal for trekking through snow-covered streets, but at least they looked pretty. She adorned her fingers with multiple gold rings—some thin and delicate, others decorated with turquoise gems—and grabbed some gold hoops as well as a necklace made from rainbow-hued seashells.

Narissa moved through the deafening stillness of the cottage, careful not to make too much noise, as though one sound from her would disturb the already painful quiet.

Her gaze betrayed her, darting to the plush sofa positioned across from the roaring hearth. It was empty, no strewn blankets, not a pillow out of place.

Narissa tugged on her wool overcoat, fastening the buttons slowly, glancing at the main entrance after each one.

She knew there was a servant or two assigned to their cottage at Windsong, but Narissa was beginning to think they were invisible. Either that, or they'd made themselves scarce after her and Solarius's argument last night. Not that it mattered, she doubted they were much for conversation. Most of the servants at House Azurvend acted as though she didn't exist or were always startled to discover she was in the room with them. Over the years, they had become quite adept at ignoring her.

Which was fine, she reminded herself.

This was nothing she was not already accustomed to overcoming. Loneliness suited her just fine.

Narissa would hire a coach to bring her to Galefell's city center, and while she was there, she would shop around for some flowers and herbs not often found in Azurvend. She would not replay that harrowing night where Calfair used her for one of his revolting schemes. If she thought on it too much, her subconscious would scream at her for being a fool, because surely she would have noticed how Calfair hadn't kissed her, how the way he carried himself was nothing at all like Solarius, how his touch was all wrong. So no, she would not worry that her eyes were still puffy from too many tears and lack of sleep. And she certainly would not dread the fact that her husband had not yet returned to her.

She would hold her head high.

She would face whatever storm she was forced to weather.

And if she purchased a few leaves of nightfern, then so be it.

BY THE TIME the mid-morning sun kissed the glistening rooftops of the alluring floating isle of Galefell, Narissa found herself tucked inside a welcoming cafe nestled against a wall of luminous ivory roses with a steaming cup of orange clove tea. She treated herself to a delicious cherry tart—a pastry of crisp, flaky dough filled with sweetened cherry cream and topped with a drizzle of melted chocolate. The cafe was the exact sort of place where she felt most comfortable. It exuded warmth with its pastel papered walls and blooming silver vines.

She absently stirred her tea, admiring the way the golden liquid glimmered like stardust, when two shadows fell across her table.

Narissa glanced up to find two females gazing down at her, one with a smile bright enough to put the sun to shame, and the other who looked as though she'd bitten into a particularly sour lemon. She recognized the one with the smile as Lady Aria Skyhelm, Calfair's younger sister, and though she did not know the name of her surly companion, there was something oddly familiar about her.

Lady Aria was absolutely stunning, and the polar opposite of her elder brother. Her flawless bronze skin glowed with ethereal beauty, kohl and golden powder lined her rich amber eyes, and her shiny black hair was swept up into an intricate style of curls and braids so that it was piled high then tumbled over one shoulder. The gown she wore looked as though it had been crafted from the sunrise. Gold bound the strapless bodice and waist as long layers of blush, peach, cream, and the palest blue rippled around her. A cloak of white fur was pinned at her neck and when she tilted her head to one side, the diamonds cascading down her pointed ears twinkled in the morning sunlight.

"May we join you?" Lady Aria asked, her smile never faltering.

"Of course." Narissa gestured to the empty seats across from her as pinpricks of uncertainty needled along her spine. She was not accustomed to anyone ever asking to be in her company willingly. Then again, it was a rare occasion when she was actually noticed.

Lady Aria slid into the high-back chair with practiced ease, her movements sleek and graceful. While the female accompanying her remained austere and excessively prim, as though her spine was made of steel.

"You're Lady Narissa Seaborne, are you not?" Lady Aria's sultry voice dropped to a conspiratorial whisper.

It was interesting how so many nobles had already seemingly forgotten that Narissa was now married to a lord of House Celestine. Or perhaps they heard the rumors of their small wedding ceremony and chose to dismiss it as nothing worthy of note. Or maybe they simply forgot.

"I am." Narissa nodded once. "And you're Lady Aria Skyhelm."

"Indeed."

Lady Aria's perfectly manicured nails, sharpened to a point and painted a pretty nude shade, tapped the table between them. Her eyes flicked to the female accompanying her and when she made no effort to introduce them, Narissa assumed the stuffy female was either a lady's maid or a chaperone. Though the latter seemed unlikely, as it had been some time since any lady of Aeramere had been required to have a chaperone. Still, Narissa could have sworn she'd seen the lady's maid somewhere before, she just couldn't remember where.

"I had no idea you were visiting Galefell. Are you here with Lord Marintide?" There was nothing malicious or spiteful in Lady Aria's tone, in fact, she seemed genuinely curious.

But Narissa chose then to politely correct her assumption, as she did not care to be incorrectly relegated to a lifetime of spinsterhood. By the tides, she was *married*, and everyone should know it.

"Actually, I'm on honeymoon." She offered Lady Aria a dazzling smile of her own, hoping it was enough to disguise all the hurt and pain staining her heart.

Lady Aria blinked, her thick lashes fluttering. "Honeymoon?"

"Yes. With my husband." Narissa dipped her chin at Lady Aria's look of confusion. "Lord Solarius Starstorm."

"Lord Solarius?" Her dark brows rose in surprise, and without warning, she reached out and squeezed Narissa's hand. "Oh, how delightful! Calfair failed to mention your engagement, so I had no idea you were even betrothed!"

Narissa bit back on the urge to snort with derision, and she was thankful for her own self-control because Lady Aria's sincere kindness was overwhelming, easing some of her inner turmoil.

"Well done, Lady Narissa." She winked then and gave her hand another squeeze before leaning back. "Lord Solarius is quite the catch."

There was no quip. No insult. No backhanded compliment.

Just pure, unaltered kindness.

Lady Aria tossed her head once, so her curls and braids of silky black hair glinted like obsidian in the morning light. "So, tell me, Lady Narissa, are you enjoying your stay?"

"We've only just arrived last night."

While Lady Aria's smile did not falter, her lady's maid stole a doubtful look in Narissa direction before turning her attention once again to where she kept her hands folded in her lap. Only then did Narissa realize how it must look for her to be out and about without Solarius by her side.

"I just figured I would come into the city from Windsong to see if I can find any flowers or herbs not readily available to me in Azurvend. I didn't want to bore Sol with my genteel hobbies." Narissa held up the cherry tart. "But then I was distracted by this delectable treat."

Lady Aria's laughter filled the air, reminding Narissa vaguely of satin and smoke. "I don't blame you in the least. You simply must try the sunrise meringues before you leave Galefell. They are positively divine."

"I will be sure to do that." Narissa pinched off a piece of the cherry tart and popped it into her mouth, chewing slowly, still unsure why Lady Aria was taking the time to converse with her.

Lady Aria leaned forward, propping her elbows upon the table, and gently twirled one finger through the air.

At once, the scent of wisteria, sun-drenched lilacs, and orange blossom wrapped around Narissa, clinging to her skin like the warm heat of summer. An incandescent bubble of magic, an imperceptible glamour, encompassed her and Lady Aria. The soft music floating throughout the cafe was muffled, the already quiet conversations of other patrons were dulled to near nothingness, while everything within the bubble was amplified. Her breath. Her heartbeat.

She stretched one hand out slowly, but her palm did not penetrate the iridescent barrier. It was like pressing against a solid globe of glass. She was trapped.

Narissa sucked in a breath, her gaze meeting Lady Aria's benevolent eyes.

"Don't worry, Lady Narissa. No one can hear us anymore." Her nose crinkled in distaste when she looked over at her lady's maid. She huffed once, then bit the corner of her bottom lip. "I find myself in need of a potion. Or an elixir of some sort."

Narissa instantly relaxed.

Ah.

So, Lady Aria was in need of her services...she wasn't trying to humiliate or demoralize her. She just didn't want anyone to eavesdrop on their conversation. A rather clever tactic.

With her interest piqued, Narissa took a sip of her tea, then asked, "What sort of potion?"

"I have it on good authority that Calfair is attempting to match me with one of the Starstorm brothers." She inspected her nails as though she couldn't be bothered with such nonsense.

"Would that be such a bad thing?" Narissa asked cautiously.

Lady Aria's amber eyes twinkled with mischief. "Yes. If it is not the one I want."

Narissa's back snapped straight at her blatant admission. "Oh. I see. And, um, you would need a potion to...?"

"To discern whether or not Calfair is lying."

"A truth serum, then."

"Yes!" Lady Aria's painted nails clicked against the table in rapid tandem, her excitement building. "That is exactly what I need. This is my future, and he's playing with it like it's one of his stupid little games. I want to be able to ask him questions and receive honesty in response. I refuse to let my life be dictated by a spoiled male heir who has never once had to be held accountable for his own actions."

Narissa flinched.

Though they weren't meant for her directly, Lady Aria's words stung, cutting open that wound she'd been trying to repair overnight. But all of that would change, eventually. Calfair would be held accountable soon enough. Narissa had no intention of allowing him to get away with the crime he committed against her.

"A truth serum..." Narissa mulled the idea over. Certainly she could put together the necessary ingredients, perhaps even have it ready in a day or so. It would not need long to steep as truth serums were a powerful substance. That being said, she might even have one in her personal collection which would eliminate the need to craft one altogether. "I will see what I can do. It shouldn't take me long to blend."

"Wonderful. The price is of no consequence, bill me as you need." Lady Aria waved one hand through the air like she was pretending to fix her hair, and the bubble of magic fell away. "I'm hosting a ball tomorrow evening and would be honored if you and Lord Solarius would attend."

Then she winked.

The sign that she wanted the truth serum by tomorrow night.

Very well.

Narissa nodded once even as her gut sank and her heart tumbled into its acidic pit of despair. The tea soured. The cherry tart left her suddenly most unwell.

"I would be delighted." The lie burned the tip of her tongue.

Attending a ball at House Galefell where she was sure to be in the presence of Lord Calfair sounded like the least delightful thing ever. And there was absolutely no way Solarius would attend. If anything, Narissa would have to find a way to sneak off to the ball without his notice, deliver the serum to Lady Aria, then return to Windsong before she was missed. No part of her makeshift plan sounded at all like it would work, but she knew firsthand what it was like to have her future planned without her consent, and it was a kind of silent suffering she would not wish upon her worst enemy.

"Lovely." Lady Aria rose, then dipped into a slight curtsy. "Come along, Hespira. Let us not waste any more of Lady Narissa's time."

The lady's maid stood dutifully without sparing Narissa a single glance, but still, she rolled the name over in her mind.

Hespira.

Narissa swore she knew the face, but the name was completely wrong. Well, if she couldn't remember, then she supposed it wasn't terribly important. Maybe it would come to her later, but right now she was quite giddy with the prospect of concocting a truth serum. Gathering up her belongings, she took a final sip of tea, then walked out into the bright, snowy streets of Galefell.

CHAPTER NINETEEN

Solarius hadn't intended to stay out all night, in fact, his aching body started screaming hours ago for him to find his way back to Windsong and into Narissa's bed, but crushing Calfair's face with his fist had only temporarily relieved some of his seething rage.

He'd been shocked when Drake chose to remain at the Thunder-cloud with him and indulge in a few drinks, considering their amity was forced by way of marriage. If it wasn't for his sister, Creslyn, Solarius would have attempted to take Drake's life on more than one occasion. Granted, he would have failed miserably with Drake being a god of shadow and prophecy, but he would have put up one hell of a fight.

Despite Drake's ability to be a smug asshole the majority of the time, he did have his uses. Walking through shadows, for example, was incredibly convenient. Not to mention his ability to venture into the shadow realm and scroll through prophecies the same way one might casually flip through a book. It was how Solarius's family learned war was coming to Aeramere, through one of Drake's prophe-cies. But prophecies were not written in the stars. They could change and be altered, they could transform, if by nothing more than an act of fate.

If Solarius could find a way to prevent his world from descending into chaos and ruin, he would do it.

Even if it meant betraying his own mother.

Drake had learned that Trysta Starstorm was a current guest at House Galefell, a bit of knowledge that was most peculiar, seeing as how his mother and Lord Aeolus Skyhelm were far from friendly. Whenever Queen Elowyn held her High Council, they were at each other's throats, bickering over which House deserved more protection from the uprisings led in Prince Aspen's favor. All of which had been oddly silenced since the prince decimated a ghastly number of corrupt magical creatures who attacked during Novalise and Asher's wedding a few months prior. He'd simply slammed his fist into the ground and vanquished them without a second thought.

All rumors of an uprising were dispelled after that impressive display of power.

Solarius buried his chin into his overcoat as he trudged through the snow-covered streets of Galefell in search of a carriage to return him to Windsong. He kept his head down, focusing solely on his footsteps in the hopes of not drawing any unwanted attention. Drake was already headed north toward the majestic house sitting in the clouds to see about gaining an audience with Lord Skyhelm. An unlikely feat as House Galefell owed House Celestine no favors. Then again, Drake usually got what he wanted, so perhaps it would be a successful trip for him after all.

A soft whinny sounded from the other side of the street and Solarius darted toward the waiting Eponians when something soft plowed right into him.

"Oh, I beg your pardon." The alluring voice from his dreams floated up to him and he grabbed the female's shoulders. The bond surged to life, heating him thoroughly.

"Narissa?"

Her gaze flew to him, lashes fluttering, lips parting.

Concern pulled his brows into a scowl. "What are you doing here?"

She shifted, trying to loose herself from his hold, but he kept his grip firm.

She huffed once, her breath misting before her. "I figured I would enjoy my own company and explore Galefell, since my husband chose to stay out all night."

A couple passed by arm in arm, their curious gazes lingering a little too long for Solarius's liking. His hands instantly slid from Narissa's shoulders to her wrists, drawing her closer. Her fingers were cold so he covered hers with his own, holding them against his chest.

"You kicked me out," he murmured quietly, his thumb tracing idle circles across her knuckles.

"Of the *room*. Not the cottage." She pressed her lips into a smooth line, plastering a carefully crafted smile to her face before looking up at him. "I did not think you would leave and just—"

Her little gasp did something to his heart.

"You're hurt." Narissa's icy green eyes softened, and she tenderly touched the cut on his bottom lip and the bruising beneath his eye. Her soft fingertips caused his heart to pound and his blood to pump straight to his cock. "What happened?"

He shrugged, keeping his emotions in check, determined to stay nonchalant. There was no reason to worry her, no reason to tell her he almost beat Calfair into a bloody pulp, that he would have ended him right there if Drake hadn't stepped in and hauled him back.

Solarius rubbed his lips together, wincing when the cut split open again. "I got into a fight."

"Mm." Her pretty pink lips pursed in consideration, and it took every last bit of his willpower not to lower his head and kiss her. Then she hooked her arm through his, tucking herself into his side like she belonged there and said, "Come along. We should get you cleaned up before anyone starts to talk."

Too late for that, Solarius thought with a sardonic grin.

News of his brawl with Calfair would be widespread and would probably reach Ariesian's ears before they even got back to Windsong. Not that he would be punished for such an offense. Solarius had no doubt that once he explained his side of the story, Ariesian would agree that Calfair's ass beating was well worth it and very much deserved. Ariesian might be the responsible, stoic firstborn son, but if there was one thing he would never tolerate, it was a slight against his family.

And Calfair drugging Narissa then fucking her was definitely an insult.

The carriage ride back to Windsong was blissfully silent.

It wasn't as though he didn't want Narissa to talk, he actually loved the sound of her voice, but a pounding ache had formed at the base of his neck and then proceeded to dig its claws into his temples. He didn't know if it was from the few injuries he'd suffered, too much alcohol, or not enough sleep. Likely a combination of all three.

Narissa led him to the main living area and ordered him to sit on the sofa before the roaring hearth. As the heat from the fire seeped into his bones, he watched in amazed silence as she disappeared to the bedroom, returning a few moments later with the necessary supplies to take care of him. A soft green towel was tossed over her shoulder, and she carried a small bowl of warm water in one hand, with a few jars tucked into her crook of her free arm. Setting everything on the glossy wooden end table, she shoved back the sleeves of her gown, then gathered her wild tresses, twisting them on top of her head into a messy, lopsided bun. A handful of loose strands curled around the nape of her neck, while a few more framed her face.

Solarius swore he'd never seen anything so fucking beautiful in his entire life.

She dipped the towel into the warm water, soaking it, then squeezing out the excess liquid. And when she dropped to her knees, situating herself between his legs to dab at the cut on his lip, his shaft hardened to the point of pain.

"This might hurt." She leaned forward slightly and braced one hand on his thigh to balance herself. Her touch may as well have seared away his clothing. She dabbed the warm towel to his mouth, her full breasts brushing against the bulge in his pants, and he bit back a groan so it sounded like more of a feral growl.

He clenched his fists to keep from touching her, his nails biting into the skin of his palms.

Her brows pinched together and her tongue darted out, wetting her bottom lip, and damn the stars, he couldn't tear his gaze away from her mouth.

"I told you it would sting," she chided, pressing the towel to the top of his cheekbone.

Solarius almost laughed, but he didn't want to piss her off, and he definitely didn't want her to leave. Narissa thought he was in pain from his injuries, which was adorable, all things considered. But she had no idea her soft little touches, her absolute nearness, were driving him mad with desire. He wanted to stretch out on the sofa, pluck her off the ground, and have her sit right on his face.

Narissa's cheeks flamed, and she made a squeaking type of noise.

It was then he remembered the bond, the way they could see one another's thoughts, project their emotions upon each other.

"What's wrong, Rissa love?" His magic stroked the bond as he slipped into her mind, and he was rewarded with another breathy little gasp. *"Are you afraid to have me feast between your thighs?"*

A look of determination washed over her face, but she refused to meet his gaze. She tossed the towel over the arm of the sofa and opened a jar of healing salve. Using her middle finger, she scooped out a small amount and applied it to the bruising beneath his eye. It smelled medicinal, like ginger and lemon, but it was nothing compared to the tempting scent of *her*.

"No, my lord. I am not afraid." She trailed her fingertips along his jaw, like she was committing the shape of his face to her memory. *"Though I do think you might suffocate from such an endeavor."*

Solarius laughed. "Trust me, my lady, I will not suffocate. But if by chance such an unlikely event occurred, then I could think of no nobler way to die."

The corner of her lips tipped up and she shook her head. Those wild, fallen waves that slipped loose from her bun teased him. Tormented him. A furious dark pink blush bled into her cheeks, and he wondered if the rest of her body flushed just as beautifully.

She leaned back, placing her hands on her knees, and studied him. "Are you hurt elsewhere?"

His broken ribs were fucking killing him, but his pride kept him from admitting as much to her. "No."

"Liar." Her retort held a bite, and she flicked her fingers forward, urging him to remove his shirt. "Nice try. Let me see."

"It's fine, I promise. It'll heal up soon enough with—"

"Solarius." Narissa crossed her arms in an attempt to scorn him, but all it did was cause the tops of her sun-kissed breasts to spill over the beaded bodice of her gown. "Take. It. Off."

He grinned wildly, yanking the hem of his shirt out of his pants. "If you wanted me to take off my shirt, Rissa love, all you had to do was ask."

Her eyes rolled to the cavernous ceiling of the cottage and then she was leaning forward again, her fingers nimbly working away at the button of his shirt, a tiny line of annoyance etched across her brow.

He longed to kiss it away.

When the fabric of his shirt fell open, Narissa's eyes widened in horror, her golden skin blanched, and she clamped one hand over her mouth.

"Sol…" His name was a whispered prayer coming from her, yet her tone was tainted with sympathy. "You must have broken at least three ribs."

Solarius didn't mention she was probably right. Calfair's cheap magic shot definitely messed him up more than he cared to admit. He glanced down at the damage and gritted his teeth. His skin was mottled with splotches of dark purple, angry red, and sickening blue green. The bruising was horrendous, spreading all over most of his right side to his hip. The pain emanating from that area of his body was a stabbing ache, like a freshly forged dagger was embedded in his bone. He sucked in a sharp breath, hissing when she lightly splayed her palm over his discolored flesh.

Narissa opened another jar of salve. This one was a pale green color and smelled distinctly of fresh earth and grass. "You're lucky you're still standing, my lord."

"You should see the other guy."

Her fiery ocean gaze flicked to his face, and he flashed her his most charming smile.

"It's not funny," she muttered, scooping out some of the ointment with two fingers and delicately applying it to his injury.

He watched her work, staring at her capable hands, at all the pretty rings she wore glinting in the warm firelight. He imagined those same elegant fingers gripping his cock, stroking and pumping him, guiding him inside her wet heat. She was so close, surely it was obvious to her now. Surely she could see the way his cock stiffened, damn near *reached* for her, but she just kept gliding those velvety hands of hers over his abdomen, oblivious to his torture. Solarius squeezed his eyes shut and let his head roll back against the sofa. His shaft strained against the confines of his pants. Stars above, if she kept touching him like that, he was going to explode right here. And he wouldn't even fucking care, because then Narissa would know *exactly* the kind of effect she had on him.

"I should…" Hesitation clung to every word. "I, um…if you would excuse me, my lord."

"My lady." His voice was hoarse, and he inhaled a ragged breath.

Solarius felt her pull away. But he did not open his eyes, and he did not stop her. Because if he begged her to stay, he'd be unable to control himself, and he'd fuck her until she could no longer walk. But she deserved more than that from him. Narissa deserved better. She deserved to be cherished. To be honored. And he wanted to worship her, he wanted to take his time admiring every inch of her body. When she finally gave herself to him, he would treasure each breathless moment.

So he would wait, until there was everything and nothing left to say, until he earned the love and trust of his wife.

CHAPTER TWENTY

Narissa could not get away from Solarius fast enough.

She bolted to the opposite side of the cottage, toward the bedroom. Once safely inside, she closed the door and let her body sag against it, let the strength of the hardwood support her flustered state. Shoving back her messy, fallen waves, she took a slow, steadying breath and rested her palms against her abdomen.

She was *not* blind and she was most certainly not oblivious to the fact that he was so plainly aroused by her presence. It was flattering beyond measure to know she had such an effect on him, and truth be told, she'd been forced to squeeze her thighs together more than once while she kneeled before him. But sweet shores, it was his eyes that did it to her.

The way he looked at her, like she hung the moon and danced among the stars. Had he always looked at her like that? Her mind said *no* while her heart whispered *yes*, and there was no denying that shred of truth. She saw the heat simmering in his gaze each time they argued, each time they hurtled snide, uncaring insults at one another. And every time, she ignored it. Every time, she pretended it was rage lurking there instead of lust. But when she tended to Solarius's face and broken ribs, his silver gaze was molten, swirling with the charge of desire and longing, and she would gladly have lost herself in those endless pools of liquid moonlight.

Admittedly, it had been slightly rude of her to leave him so abruptly.

Narissa shoved away from the door. Planting both hands on her hips, she paced the small length of the room.

She wanted to be angry with him for unknowingly letting Calfair take advantage of her. She wanted to be frustrated thinking of all the heartache they could have been spared if he hadn't been foolish enough to think she chose Calfair over him.

The mere thought of it made her skin crawl.

Narissa heaved a breath of irritation and lifted the bronze handle on her trunk. She rummaged through her belongings, gently shoving aside neatly folded piles of satin slips and lacy undergarments until she found what she was looking for. Tucked beneath the exquisite nightgowns and bundles of fancy unmentionables was a long, rectangular wooden box. Narissa carefully flipped both brass latches and opened the lid to find her collection of tonics, serums, potions, and elixirs all carefully cushioned against a bed of sapphire velvet. A dozen corked glass bottles and vials were individually labeled with tiny parchment tags in her tidy handwriting. Running her fingers over the bottom row, her pointer finger paused on a vial filled with a shimmery bright green liquid and a tag that read "veritas serum."

Her mouth pulled to one side as she considered Lady Aria's request.

She was grateful her personal supply of concoctions had made the trip from Azurvend to Galefell, and though she hated to part with the truth serum—for one never knew when such a potion would be useful—it would be far simpler to give this one to Lady Aria as opposed to brewing another one here.

Narissa sensed him before he spoke.

She snapped the lid shut and glanced up to find Solarius standing in the doorway of the bedroom. He looked rumpled and positively delicious with his shirt wrinkled and unbuttoned, hanging open to reveal the full expanse of his chest and solid abdomen. Her gaze trailed over him appreciatively, taking in the dip of his hips where his pants were slung low, admiring all the pieces of him she struggled to ignore when she slathered that healing ointment over his beautifully crafted body. Solarius grabbed the door frame with one hand, leaning slightly to the right while his other was carefully splayed over his injured ribs.

Narissa rubbed her lips together and replaced her box of potions, then stood, dropping into an awkward curtsy. "My lord."

"My lady." His voice was thick with restraint. He stared at her, seconds ticking by with painful slowness as the yearning in his gaze kept her rooted in place.

Toying with the long sleeves of her gown, Narissa waded through the tension between them. "Did you require something?"

He blinked. "I was wondering if you would like to sit outside with me?"

"In the cold?"

"It's snowing." Solarius released the frame of the door and rolled his shoulders back. "I could start the fire."

Narissa's brow quirked in amusement. "You? Start a fire? That is Asher's realm of expertise, is it not?"

Novalise's husband wielded frostfire, and while Narissa knew her brother-in-law was quite capable of producing fire, she was not so sure her husband harbored that same skill set.

He shrugged, rolling her humor off his shoulder. "I'm certain I can figure it out."

Narissa stole a glance out the window. The sky was gray and ominous, and large chunks of fluffy snow fell from the sky like pieces of finely woven cotton. It could be nice to sit around a fire and watch the snow fall.

Her gaze flicked back to him. "On one condition."

Hope washed over his expression, and for a moment he looked more youthful than she'd ever seen him. "Anything."

"Can we get something to eat?" she asked. "I'm starving."

Solarius grinned, heart-stopping and devastating all at once, and

Narissa was reminded of why she fell in love with him in the first place.

NARISSA SAT CUDDLED NEXT to Solarius beneath a pile of fur blankets on a cushioned settee as heavy flakes continued to fall from the gray winter sky. The balcony of the second floor stretched overhead, shielding them from the swirling snowfall, but making for a spectacular view of the mountains. Their dark gray outlines slanted across the horizon, the peaks a brilliant white against a backdrop of slate. Narissa shared an overstuffed footstool with Solarius, their legs outstretched near the stone pit where flames of faerie fire crackled and snapped, dancing with the tumbling snowflakes.

She secretly enjoyed the way his long legs brushed against hers with every slight movement, every casual adjustment.

Shockingly enough, Solarius had managed to light the fire without any assistance, and Narissa would not deny she was quite impressed. Especially when the haunting play of shadow and light illuminated him in a way that made him look both tempting and treacherous. But now she was curled into a plush pillow, her body just breaths from the heat of his own, and a platter of delicious treats was spread before them. There was a variety of dried meats and aged cheeses, cloudberry spread and crackers, pistachio wafers, and a bowl of olives. There was also a tiered tray filled with tiny cakes, frosted cookies, and sugared berries.

She popped one of the little cakes into her mouth, shimmying her shoulders and humming to herself as the flavors of rich raspberry and vanilla cream filled her with a sense of contentment.

Solarius's brow lifted in amusement, the corner of his mouth tugging up one side. He tossed an olive into the air, then caught it in his mouth, and Narissa rolled her lips to keep from giggling like a lovesick youth.

He reached for another olive. "I appreciate the fact that you love food as much as I do."

Narissa smirked and grabbed a one of the thick chocolatey cookies decorated with frosting and took a hefty bite. She sighed as she chewed, her gaze sliding to meet Solarius who was sitting back, watching her, his grin widening with mirth.

She licked a smudge of frosting off one finger. "Good food nurtures the soul. Why should I concern myself with regulated portions or the size of my waist when there are delicious cookies to enjoy?"

Solarius lifted his glass of warm apple cider. "I'll drink to that."

As the snow continued to tumble down from the darkening sky, Narissa snuggled further into blankets, aware of the way she sought the nearness of Solarius's body for warmth. He stretched one arm out, letting it fall around her shoulders as he pulled her in closer. His scent enveloped her, the layers of fresh citrus, warm spices, and the tempting hint of bay rum soothed her, and she inhaled again, breathing him into her lungs. The bond hummed between them, a gentle nudge, a comforting reminder. Yet the pleasant solitude and ease of being with him was overrun with his racing mind.

Despite his relaxed, effortless outward appearance, his thoughts would not settle.

"The chaos of your mind will not calm, Solarius." Narissa turned her head so it rested on top of his chest, and he was forced to look down at her tucked beneath his arm. "If there is something you must know, then ask."

"What's your favorite season?"

She blinked up at him. That was not at all what she expected.

Narissa twisted the fur fibers of the blanket between her fingers. "Well, I love the longest days of Midsummer. When the air is heady and clings to my skin, when I can no longer tame my ridiculously wavy hair. I love how the sun takes forever to bleed across the sky, then paints it in hues of pink and gold. It's hot and a little sticky, and only the fall of twilight offers reprieve."

She peered over at him and found his gaze focused solely on her mouth.

"Do you have a favorite season?" she asked, more breathless than she ought to be considering she was curled into his side and not exerting any kind of energy.

His eyes continued to linger on her mouth, and her skin heated beneath the intensity of his gaze.

"I like summer, too." The pads of his fingers strummed her skin in lazy strokes along her collarbone. "What's your favorite color?"

Narissa was grateful for the distraction of another question because his teasing touches sent a rush of blistering heat straight to her core. She swallowed hard. "That one is tricky."

He chuckled. "Is it?"

"Yes." She angled her face so their lips were a breath apart, so if she looked closely enough, she could see the silver of his eyes darken, could witness his pupils expand every time he looked at her. "I have so many."

"Tell me about them," he murmured.

"I love the color pink, but my favorite is a delicate blush shade, like the beach of Azurvend. And I like blue, but only when it's mixed with green, like the waves of the Arcasian Sea or the aquamarine beads on my favorite pair of earrings." The last words shuddered out of her. "What's your favorite color?"

"Your eyes." He said it with such assurance, without hesitation or thought, that a blush colored her cheeks. Solarius reached out with one hand, gliding two fingers beneath her chin, tilting her face up to meet him. "They remind me of a frostbitten ocean set on fire."

"Oh." Her cheeks burned and his compliment left her flushed.

But he didn't back down and she didn't pull away.

Time seemed to disappear when she was with him, there was no dawn and no dusk. It was like being caught in a void, where hours were measured in stolen glances and longing stares, and seconds were nothing more than faint breaths and quickened heartbeats. Each moment was an eternity, carved into the memory of her mind.

Solarius's hand trailed up the side of her face, cupping her cheek like she was treasured, and she melted into him like clay, ready to be molded and sculpted. He hummed an evocative tune, one that tickled her subconscious and made her fingers itch to play her harp.

"I love that song," Narissa whispered into the space between their mouths.

"I know." His thumb traced her bottom lip, and her body ignited, set aflame by his touch. "Music is everything the heart cannot say."

In the next breath, the lyrics drifted down the bond as he sang them into her mind.

"And so two souls were set adrift,
One to the heavens, the other to the sea,
And I stood alone on that treacherous cliff
Whispering to the night, come back to me."

Her magic soared, the summoning of the tides racing toward the lure of moonlight. He lowered his head and Narissa curled her fingers into his shirt, drawing him near. He kept his grip firm as he dragged her closer, so she was almost sprawled across his reclined body in a tangle of blankets and skirts. His free hand slid beneath the fur blanket and grabbed her thigh, hiking it up over his lap. A shiver of delight raced down her spine.

"Are you cold?" he asked, his lips moving over hers as he spoke.

"Not exactly."

"Me too."

It was a nonsensical response and Narissa didn't care. All she wanted, all she craved, was the feel of Solarius's mouth on hers.

"Lord Solarius." A female voice squeaked, piercing the moment, deflating the sexual tension, and the servant assigned to their cottage, who'd all but made herself scarce for the majority of their stay, suddenly appeared at the most inopportune moment. "A letter, my lord. From House Celestine."

"Fuck," Solarius murmured against Narissa's mouth, and she bit back a grin.

He hefted her into his arms and stood, cradling her against his chest with a pile of blankets trailing around them. "Come on, Rissa love. I know you said you weren't cold, but your lips are turning blue, and I much prefer them pink."

CHAPTER TWENTY-ONE

Narissa tried not to be disappointed by Solarius's decision to not touch her and failed miserably.

When they came inside from the snowy outdoors, he had a warm bath drawn for her, then retreated to the main living area…where he stayed for the duration of the night. Not once did he ask if she might enjoy his company or if he could share the bed with her. He was solemn and reserved, and the swift change in his behavior was jarring. He behaved perfectly, like a proper lord of Aeramere, yet not at all like a husband. So she'd slept in the immense bed by herself. Alone. Again.

She supposed it had something to do with the letter he received from House Celestine, and though he had not divulged any of its contents to her, she did not miss the way his knuckles whitened while reading it or how his jaw ticked when he crumpled it with one hand and tossed it into the nearest waste bin.

The next morning was no better.

In fact, she thought it was worse.

They spent most of the day exploring Galefell and all the while Solarius remained terribly agreeable. It was strange, not being at odds with one another, not bickering or tossing out well-intended jabs. He rarely spoke to her as they wandered the streets, browsing shops, and when they stopped in a bakery so Narissa could grab more of those delicious tiny cakes, he didn't even notice when she intentionally left a dollop of pink frosting on her lips. Solarius wasn't exactly cold to her, but more overly formidable. At the same time, he was completely oblivious to the effect he had on her throughout the day.

His little touches left her wired, so her skin tingled with constant anticipation. When his hand moved to the small of her back, she felt the distinctive tug of longing in her core. If he gently took her elbow to guide her to another area of the streets, her knees softened and her heart skittered out of control. She was acutely aware of him, her body entirely in tune to him. To his chivalrous movements, his incoherent murmurs, his complete and utter distraction. Yes, he was with her, but he was going through the motions. His mind was somewhere else altogether, and he'd built a shield around his thoughts, one not even the bond could break.

By the time they returned to Windsong, Narissa was done with his foolishness.

She no longer felt guilty about sneaking off to House Galefell to deliver the truth serum to Lady Aria. Though balls and parties were one of her least favorite things to do, she was almost looking forward to the music and drone of incessant chatter, as anything was better than the suffocating silence of a withdrawn and distracted Solarius.

Narissa fisted her hands on her hips as she watched him.

He was sitting on the sofa, staring into the flames of faerie fire sparking in the hearth, with a small cup of hot cider balanced upon his knee. Gold flecks of the snapping fire reflected in the distant silver of his eyes, and Narissa pressed her lips together, refusing to waste any more time.

"If you don't mind, I'm going to swim fully nude in the hot springs behind the cottage." Narissa didn't even know if hot springs existed in Windsong, but her words had the desired effect, because Solarius blinked, and continued to stare absently into the hearth.

"Of course," he muttered, barely hearing her.

She scowled then, her eyes flicking to the charming blown-glass chandelier floating above them. Mist billowed and swirled through the ribbons of fused glass like shimmering clouds, and for a moment she wished Solarius was coming to the ball at House Galefell, for surely there would be dancing, and it had been so long since she'd been swept around a ballroom on enchanted clouds.

But Solarius didn't move from his frozen position on the sofa. He was so lost in his own thoughts, he wouldn't even know she was gone. On a sigh of disappointment, Narissa fled to the main bedchamber to dress for the evening.

She chose a gown of dark pink, the shade reminiscent of Azurvend sunrises right before sunlight crested the sea's horizon. The satin bodice plunged in the front, revealing the piercing in her navel, and dipped dangerously low in the back. Thin straps embellished with diamonds held the sparkling fabric in place, and the decadent skirts fell around her like a waterfall. She opted for a collar of tiny pink sapphires, matching earrings, and a gold ring for almost every finger. Her gown wasn't incredibly thick, so nude thigh-high stockings were an absolute necessity to keep her somewhat warm, and she decided on heels the color of warm sand. She snatched the vial of truth serum from her collection and tucked it into the low waist of her gown, concealing it from view.

Though empowered with her choice to attend Lady Aria's ball on her own, she didn't quite possess the bravery required to leave out the front door.

Narissa grabbed a pair of gloves, wrapped her velvet-lined cloak around her shoulders, then left through the back entrance of the cottage.

She wouldn't dally at House Galefell, she had every intention of finding Lady Aria directly upon her arrival to deliver the truth serum, then make a quick escape. Besides, she was quite good at being stealthy. This was not the first time she would mill about a ball unnoticed. Hopefully Calfair would be too busy chasing other ladies to even notice her. Considering the only reason he paid her any attention at all was because of Solarius, it shouldn't be too difficult to avoid him.

Slipping out into the frigid night, Narissa swallowed down the knot of fear clogging the back of her throat that had nothing to do with facing Calfair and everything to do with flying alone in a carriage pulled by Eponians. But the only way to reach House Galefell was through the sky, and though it was bound to be an expedient trip, Narissa couldn't quite overcome the terror that seized her muscles as soon as she stepped inside the waiting coach.

Once the door shut soundly behind her and she was seated, Narissa squeezed her eyes shut, held her breath, and whispered a plea to the stars to keep her safe.

House Galefell was exactly as Narissa remembered.

Lavish. Whimsical. And dripping with excess.

The ethereal ballroom was brimming with lords and ladies in their finest—swishing skirts of lace and silk, trim coats and bold vests, all in a varying assortment of jewel toned hues. In retrospect, perhaps she should have asked Lady Aria if there was a theme for the evening, because her bold gown of deep rose stood out like pearl in a bed of crushed shells. It might be more burdensome to move about inconspicuously than she originally imagined. Shades of emerald, sapphire, and amethyst swirled throughout the magnificent ballroom where couples danced upon charmed clouds that hovered in the air and moved to the melody of the music.

It was quite possibly the most beautiful sight she had ever witnessed.

"Lady Narissa, darling!"

The smoky feminine voice of Lady Aria cut through Narissa's spellbound haze, drawing her attention to one of the more crowded corners of the room. Following the sound of her voice, Narissa spied Lady Aria surrounded by a surplus of male suitors, each of them stumbling and fawning over her exquisite beauty. Be it a bored, flat smile or a disinterested roll of her eyes, they fought and elbowed one another to see who could gain her attention next.

Lady Aria flicked her wrist, and they parted for her as easily as Narissa split the tides. When Lady Aria shimmied past their bold advances, it was plain to see why they were so captivated by her. She was dressed in a strapless gown of liquid gold that molded to her every curve, the cut of the bodice so low that Narissa worried one wrong move and her assets would spill from the gorgeous fabric, scandalizing everyone in attendance. Her midnight hair was unadorned, kohl lined her rich amber eyes, gold dusted her bronze bare shoulders, and her lips were painted ruby.

She was striking in every sense of the word.

Lady Aria abandoned her flock of admirers and headed for Narissa, the faintest waves of powerful magic rippling around her.

She grabbed Narissa's hands, lightly kissing the air near each of her cheeks. "I'm so glad you could make it, you look positively radiant."

"Oh." Narissa flushed and ducked her head. "Thank you, Lady Aria. You are quite breathtaking yourself. Though I am afraid I can't stay long."

"Nonsense! We're only just getting started." She waved one flippant hand through the air, gesturing to where the swell of music lifted the clouds higher. "Where is your husband?"

Narissa tugged at the collar of pink sapphires wrapped snugly around her neck, they were somehow too tight. She'd never had a problem with them before, yet now it felt as though they were strangling her. "Ah, you see, Lord Solarius is the reason I cannot stay."

Lady Aria's gaze narrowed and her lips pulled to one side in distaste.

"Not that he forbade me," Narissa supplied quickly, the need to defend her husband suddenly fierce, and she stole a hasty glance over one shoulder. "Solarius would never. That being said, he and Calfair had a bit of a falling out. I don't believe they are on speaking terms."

Lady Aria's raspy laugh filled the air between them, and she planted her palm over the swell of her bosom. "Oh, yes. I am well aware. Lord Solarius demolished Calfair in a fight at the Thunder-cloud the other evening. It was a well-deserved beating, if you ask me."

Narissa's mouth fell open and she quickly snapped it shut as the missing pieces of the puzzle slowly fell into place. Solarius had gotten into a fight, but he didn't say with who. Narissa had been so distraught by his injuries and caring for him, she never even thought to ask. She didn't know if Solarius went in search of Lord Calfair, or if was by some stroke of dumb luck, or if the fates just chose chaos that night.

A nearly invisible line of concern etched its way across Lady Aria's forehead. "Did you not know?"

"Oh, of course! I patched up Solarius afterward." It was only a half-truth and Narissa shoved one hand through her messy waves, pretending she was privy to every aspect of Solarius's life. "But he wouldn't tell me what they fought about."

Because she already knew, as much as she hated to admit it.

Lady Aria's shoulders rose, then fell in disinterest, and she inspected her perfectly manicured nails.

"Your guess is as good as mine, darling. Usually Calfair loves to boast about such squabbles, but I suppose he chose to slink into the shadows on this matter because he was so humiliated and humbled." Her ruby lips curved into a caustic smirk. "A public beating can bruise a male's ego."

Narissa smiled in return, grateful there had not been much discussion about her being the reason for their brawl. While she was enjoying Lady Aria's company, she also knew that since Lord Calfair had been horribly embarrassed, he was sure to be in a dreadful mood, and she wanted to be as far away from House Galefell as possible. Determined to finish her task and retreat to Windsong, Narissa rubbed her lips together, then leaned forward, stealing another look around the preoccupied ballroom. When she spoke, she kept her voice just below the thrum of music. "I have the serum."

"Lovely." Lady Aria slipped a small satin pouch into Narissa's hand as she pretended to observe the ballroom.

Narissa quickly tucked the pouch of coins into the folds of her dress, wrapping her arms around herself to discreetly remove the slender vial from the banded waist of her gown. Her shoulder brushed against Lady Aria's, and she slid the truth serum into her open palm under the guise of coquettish laughter and genteel amusement.

"Thank you for this, Lady Narissa." Lady Aria nodded her head once and dipped into a slight curtsy. "I am most appreciative."

"Of course. Anytime."

Narissa watched as Lady Aria was absorbed into a cluster of enamored lords desperate for her hand, none of whom had any idea she would likely soon be betrothed to one of the younger Starstorm brothers. Her words rolled around in Narissa's head, and she found herself wondering which one Lady Aria would choose—Lord Tovian or Lord Nyxian—assuming she was given the option.

Well, she supposed she would find out soon enough.

Now, however, it was time for her to return to Windsong. She'd delivered the truth serum, and as much as she would like to stay and admire the couples dancing upon softly lit clouds, she couldn't risk Solarius going in search of her. It was only a matter of time before the flames in the hearth grew monotonous and he sought her out. At least she could hope. She sent one last look of longing toward the ballroom, then made her way to the grand hall to gather her personal effects.

Narissa ascended one of the winding staircases, counting her steps as she went. The intricately carved doors were shoved open, giving her a glimpse of the hall just beyond where the scent of winter wisteria hung heavy in the air.

With her gown gathered in both hands so she wouldn't step upon the delicate hem, she took the final step, when something snared her by the elbow, hauling her backward.

Narissa yelped and threw both arms wide to recover her balance as she lost her footing. She smacked into something solid, and the stench of ale and heavy pine slammed into her, causing her stomach to clench and her nose to crinkle in distaste.

The hand gripping her elbow yanked once more, spinning her, and she came face to face with Lord Calfair Skyhelm.

A thousand thoughts and terrors sprang to the forefront of her mind. The night he drugged her came hurtling back, planting crippling, traumatic images in her head. His sloppy mouth whispering crude obscenities into her ear. His cold hands groping and pinching her thighs and nipples. The lack of warmth emanating from him. And the sickening scent of dragon root mixed with mulled wine.

Lord Calfair's upper lip curled into a vicious sneer, and the whites of his eyes were red from exhaustion and overindulgence. The side of his face was a sickly green shade, likely where he was still healing from one of Solarius's well-aimed punches. He blinked hard as though trying to focus, and his lascivious gaze raked over her, lingering on her navel and the outline of her breasts.

The hand that gripped her elbow snaked its way to her wrist, dragging her closer, pinning her between the railing of the staircase and his body. His hold was punishing, his fingers dug into her skin, and she was sure to bruise.

"I believe you owe me a dance, Lady Narissa." Lord Calfair's words slurred, his hot, rank breath sticking to her cheek.

She edged back, grabbing the railing with one hand, piercing the wooden veneer with her nails. "You are mistaken, my lord. I don't owe you anything."

"Think of it as a way to make up for your rudeness." His mouth twisted into a heinous smile as his other arm snatched her waist, pressing her into the railing with so much force, she thought for certain he meant to push her over completely. He stared at her like she was a conquest, like she was unworthy of even being in the same room as him. "You come into *my* home, mingle in *my* ballroom dressed like *that*, and yet you do not even grant me the courtesy of your attention."

The curve of the rail prodded Narissa's back, sending a spike of fear into her heart, one that rattled her bones. She did not care to draw any unwanted attention, nor did she particularly like the idea of tumbling over the edge of the staircase. And she was not going to allow this slimy, depraved male to wield any kind of power over her ever again.

"Forgive me, my lord." She pressed one hand firmly against his chest and shoved. Lord Calfair swayed a bit but still he held his ground. She met his glare with one of her own. "But *you* did not invite me tonight. The invitation was extended to me by—"

"You think I give a fuck about my sister?" he hissed, spittle flying and clinging to the sparse black hairs protruding from his chin. "You are here, deliberately tempting me by wearing a dress like that, and if you think for one moment I will control my urges simply because you are now wedded, you are sorely mistaken."

He crushed her to him and her lungs caved, hollowing out as she struggled to catch her breath against the rank stench of him.

"Do not make a scene, Lady Narissa." The threat raked across her skin, and she stiffened against him, struggling to free herself from his hold. "You *will* dance with me. Unless you'd rather go somewhere more private."

Narissa shook her head, ready to object, to scream if she must, because surely someone would hear her. Surely someone would *see* her fight him off, someone was bound to come to her rescue. She wasn't invisible. Not now. But then a muscular arm shot out from beside her, and in a blur of color and movement, Solarius was there. His scent engulfed her, eased the erratic beating of her heart, as the bond steadied her, secured her. Solarius locked his hand around Lord Calfair's neck and squeezed, the veins of his hands straining with barely contained rage.

"Release my wife," he growled, venom dripping from his voice as the silver of his eyes darkened to an unfathomable shade. "*Now.*"

CHAPTER TWENTY-TWO

Solarius's hand around Calfair's throat was the best sort of vengeance.

He could feel him struggle to swallow against his grip, knew that if he squeezed a little bit tighter, then the air would cease to flow. Knew that if he used the full might of his strength, he could crush Calfair's neck, turn his bones to dust. Solarius enjoyed the way his former friend's eyes bulged slightly, and he delighted in the mottled shade of purple blooming over Calfair's skin while his mouth opened and closed like a dying fish. There would be no greater satisfaction than killing him right here, right now.

But a soft voice entered his mind, slinking past the fog of revenge clouding his mind.

"Let him go."

Narissa's delicate hand curled around his upper arm, and Solarius tightened his hold. Calfair struggled, gasping as the veins along the whites of his eyes popped.

"Solarius. Let him go." Narissa's tone was gentle yet firm. "I want to go home. Release him and take me home."

Home.

Not to Windsong.

Not to Azurvend.

But *home.*

To Celestine.

He released his grip on Calfair and the bastard started choking, swallowing greedy gulps of air as though that would somehow save his damned soul. Solarius was well aware of the fact that nearly everyone in the ball was staring at them. Nobles from every house in Aeramere stood in uncomfortable silence watching the altercation unfold. But he found he no longer cared what anyone thought—let them talk. They would know how easily he could end them if they so much as dared to lay a finger upon his wife.

Solarius draped his arm around Narissa's shoulders, curling her into his side as a means of protection.

Calfair was still coughing, rubbing one hand over his neck where the skin was swollen and bruised. His dark, watery gaze shot their way, and he sneered.

Solarius's jaw popped, and he pointed at him, his voice low and threatening as he said, "Consider this your final warning, Skyhelm."

He didn't wait for a response. He hauled Narissa out of that overbearing ballroom, grabbing her cloak and gloves from one of the servants on the way out.

"I'm going to kill him," he muttered, planting one hand on the small of her back as he guided her out of House Galefell and into the frosty winter night.

Narissa tucked her gloves into the pocket of her velvet cloak, and tossed it over her arms, refusing to look his direction. Instead, she inspected her manicure, adjusting and readjusting the golden rings on her fingers. "Another time, perhaps."

Her hushed dismissal only served to stoke his anger.

Solarius was no fool. He'd heard her scattered thoughts all day, he'd listened to her wage war against her own mind as she silently debated whether or not to talk to him, to figure out why he was broody and closed off. He was really going to have to work with her on barricading her mind, especially if she planned on keeping things from him. Like sneaking off to House Galefell to deliver some sort of tonic to Calfair's sister.

After all, he'd managed to keep her out of his mind all day. The letter he'd received from Ariesian last night had wedged itself between his shoulders like a blade of tension, and he'd concealed its infuriating contents from Narissa all day. Granted, it had not been Solarius's intent to be cold and standoffish toward her, but he was uncertain of how to handle Ariesian's message.

The letter was a warning.

After Drake had been denied an audience with Lord Aeolus Skyhelm, he'd slipped into the shadows and stolen into House Galefell anyway, as expected. He'd entered the house with the sole purpose of uncovering Trysta's reasons for being there and had discovered Solarius's mother in a secret talk with Calfair. That part of the letter had been shocking enough, but then it only got worse. Trysta seemed upset and was in desperate need of something only Calfair could access. The message was vague in terms of what exactly Trysta sought, but the price was apparently steep, as she promised Calfair more dragon root in exchange for the mystery item.

That slice of knowledge gutted Solarius.

His mother, his own fucking *mother*, had been the one to give Calfair the dragon root he used to take advantage of Narissa. And Trysta did not even bat an eye, not once did she bother to concern herself with why a lord of Aeramere might want such a harmful plant. Not only that, but Solarius didn't know if his mother had simply offered up dragon root for a trade, or if Calfair had requested it in return.

Either way, he'd held tight to his rage all day. He didn't want Narissa to know his fury, he didn't want her to think his family supported Calfair drugging her.

As it was, he hardly considered Trysta family anymore.

Solarius lost all trust for his mother many moons ago. Like when Trysta lied and claimed his sister, Novalise, was a simple star reader, then hid the fact that she actually possessed the legendary starstorm.

Or when she told all of Aeramere that Nyxian was star-touched when Novalise accidentally struck him with starfire. Then there were all the times Trysta knowingly fabricated star readings for other nobles to suit her own needs. But he supposed his first inkling of mistrust arose when she failed to shed a single tear upon learning about the death of his father, Zenos.

Trysta had lacked any emotion. She'd been somber, sure, but to not even cry? To not show the crush of devastation one must have felt when the supposed love of her life, the father of her eight children, was stolen from this living world far too soon?

Solarius had never let down his guard around her since.

Now, her clandestine meetings at House Galefell were only serving to further his suspicions of her wavering trust.

Beside him, Narissa shivered, drawing him back from his silent musings to the present.

He hailed the next carriage, bracing one arm in front of Narissa as the sleek Eponians with midnight coats and silver manes pranced to a stop before them. The driver leapt down from the seat in one fluid motion and opened the door for them, dipping his chin in greeting.

"To House Celestine," Solarius declared, his entire body attuning to the sweep of Narissa's eyes as they shifted over him.

"Celestine?"

"You said home." His tongue was sharp and his tone curt, his temper still boiling after she pulled such a ridiculous stunt. He grabbed her by the waist, lifted her into the carriage, and climbed in after her. The door closed behind him and he took the seat across from her, folding his arms over his chest. "So, we're going home."

The carriage lurched forward and Narissa gripped the edge of the leather seat, nearly toppling right into him. Her panicked gaze flicked out the windows toward the clear winter sky, and she pressed herself backward, chest heaving. Solarius may have been honorable and respectful, but the gown she wore tonight left so very little to the imagination that simply looking at her made his cock twitch and throb. If he had known *that* was the dress she was going to wear to

House Galefell, he never would have allowed her to leave Windsong without him.

Each time she shifted on the leather bench across from him, he got another glimpse of sun-kissed skin. She crossed one leg over the other, prim and clearly annoyed, but her shoulders bunched to nearly her ears as the carriage left the ground and launched into the night sky. If he wasn't so pissed off, he would find her mix of irritation and alarm slightly endearing.

But alas, he continued to grind his teeth, agitated by the fact that she'd chosen to sneak out of Windsong and attend a ball at Galefell, at Calfair's fucking *house*, without him.

"What of our clothing?" she sniped, her teeth grazing her plump bottom lip.

"I'll send for all of it from Windsong once we arrive."

Narissa huffed, unimpressed. "Fine, but what about the rest of my belongings? Everything I own is in Azurvend. My harp. My personal collection of potions. I have an entire room full of—"

"Of what?" Solarius bit out.

The coach bounced on a rolling gust of air and she inhaled sharply. "Of herbs and things."

He wanted to comfort her, to pull her into his arms and soothe her. There was no mistaking the bubble of fear surrounding her. "I'll send for all of it."

"But—"

"No more excuses, Narissa." He leaned forward, resting his elbows on his knees, linking his fingers together. "Do you think I don't hear what the servants in House Azurvend say about you? About me? About us? Do you honestly think I would just ignore their snide comments and outrageous claims?"

Some emotion banked deep in the heat of her angry ocean eyes, but Narissa said nothing. She rubbed her lips, then pressed them together so tightly, her entire body quivered.

Solarius responded for her.

"No. I refuse to allow you to dwell in a place where you are ignored and unwelcome. Your cousin, Lord Marintide, being the exception." He steepled his fingers, tapping them together lightly. "You will reside in House Celestine, with me, and if we must build a place of our own, then so be it."

She sniffled and straightened her spine, but it did nothing to disguise the glassy look in her eyes.

"Do not cry," he warned.

Her bottom lip trembled. "I'm trying not to."

Solarius leaned back against the seat and stretched his arms wide, his frustration mounting. "Have I done something to offend you? Is this not what you wanted?"

"No, it is, of course it is. It's just—"

"Then why are you upset?" Solarius boomed, expecting her to recoil from the rage in his voice, but she met him head on.

"I don't understand why you're shouting!" Narissa glared at him and her nails bit into the leather bench as a shudder of frustration wrecked her. "You're sitting here, telling me you're going to do all these wonderful things for me, for us, yet you're *angry* about it?"

Solarius shoved his hands through his hair and blew out a harsh breath. He pinched the bridge of his nose with his thumb and forefinger in an effort to calm his growing exasperation, but it was impossible to ignore her. To ignore how mindlessly furious he was with her.

He reached out then, plucking her off the seat as though she was featherlight, and plopped her onto his lap. Her legs draped over one of his thighs and her rosy pink skirts tumbled around them both.

"Why Rissa?" He gently grasped her chin, tilting her face up to him, while his other hand slid over the warm skin of her back, slipping beneath the soft fabric of her gown to her bare waist. "Why would you go to House Galefell without me? Why would you willingly put yourself in harm's way? I cannot protect you if I am not with you."

He meant every word yet could not help if they were charged with indignation.

Narissa lifted her chin, giving him a tempting view of her rather kissable neck. "Calfair's sister, Lady Aria, requested a tonic. I thought I could slip in and then quickly leave without being seen."

Solarius barked out a rough laugh, his fingers dipping lower to her hip. He released her chin and slowly let his other fingers graze the column of her throat, before he wrapped his hand around the back of her neck.

"Do you have an invisibility potion I'm not aware of? How in the world did you possibly think no one would notice you?"

"Because they never do!" she shouted, fisting her hands in her lap, and he fell silent as a swell of her emotions slammed into the bond, stealing his breath. "You do not know what it is like, Solarius. You have a wonderful, loving family. Your bloodline is without blemish. You are wildly handsome and most ladies swoon at the mere mention of your name."

He scoffed. "That's a little—"

She grabbed a fistful of his shirt. "I am *not* done speaking."

Solarius reared back. The coach jostled slightly, and he held her tighter, sensing the tremor of fear amidst the turmoil of her feelings. "Apologies, my lady."

Narissa's brow pinched together as she stared at where she clutched the fabric of his collared shirt in her hand. She swiped her thumb back and forth across a shiny black button. "I am a wallflower. I attend all the balls and seasonal parties, but I blend in with the papered walls. I am never asked to dance. No one ever brings me sweet wine or a refreshing glass of punch. I have no real friends and have spent the majority of my life alone. And tides be blessed, Reif tries, but there is only so much I can share with him."

Her words cut through him, torturously slow as she unraveled this layer of herself, as she laid herself bare before him.

He drew her face closer, fingers pressing into her delicate neck until they shared the same air. "How can you say that about yourself?"

"Because it's true, Sol." Narissa's eyes filled again, her lashes dampening, but the tears did not fall. Her nose crinkled and she blinked them away. "You were the first one who saw me. The first who made me think maybe, just maybe, I was deserving of something more. Of something greater."

Solarius followed the line of her plush bottom lip with the tip of his thumb. "Then Calfair happened."

"Yes." She swallowed, her tongue darting out, swiping along that luscious lip. "And then Rosalie happened."

Rosalie Davenport. The human princess Solarius obsessed over after he tried to purge Narissa from his mind. The first female who only used him for a good time. He supposed he had chased after her because she reminded him so much of Narissa. Similar golden hair, same spitfire attitude, but whereas Narissa threw carefully crafted insults his direction with heat in her eyes, Rosalie tossed them with ice. Cold and unforgiving, that one. He'd given Rosalie his heart and she ripped it out, then pierced it with the spiky heel of her shoe before she walked away from him for good. She only wanted the thrill of fucking a fae, and like a fool he gave in, thinking he might be enough to change her mind. To keep her around.

He wasn't.

She left him last Midsummer. He thought to propose, she acted as though he was wasting her time. Like she had somewhere better to be, anywhere else than in the same place as him.

Rosalie didn't love him, she loved the idea of him.

But Narissa…perhaps there was a story between them that had yet to be told. Maybe she could love him again.

"There was nothing between Rosalie and myself." The admission stung more than he cared to admit. But it was necessary. A truth he'd denied to himself for two full seasons. "She never wanted me."

"But *I* wanted you." Narissa grabbed his shoulders in earnest and her mouth spoke the words against his lips. Her frosty green eyes warmed with the reflection of desire. "I *still* want you. If you'll have me."

A single tear rolled down her cheek, and he caught the pearl in one hand without tearing his gaze away from her face. He tucked it into his pocket as the carriage dropped from the sky, landing smoothly as it rolled to a stop against the smooth drive of House Celestine.

Still, Solarius did not look away from her.

He held his breath and dove into the depths of her eyes, ready to drown.

"I want you, Rissa love. I promise. I have *always* wanted you." Then he captured her lips with his own, sealing that promise with a feverish kiss.

CHAPTER TWENTY-THREE

Narissa bit back a squeal as Solarius stepped from the carriage with her in his arms and carried her up to the front entrance of House Celestine.

The house itself was breathtaking, situated at the base of Moonfall Peaks, where it overlooked the starlit city of Celestine. Its deep purple walls were decorated with swirls of frost, it was surrounded by lush winter gardens on all sides, and incandescent light spilled from its numerous arched windows. Dizzying spires pierced the clear night sky, and sprawling balconies were illuminated with a silvery glow. The main door swung open, drenching them in warmth as he lifted her across the threshold and into the dazzling grand hall of the home.

Solarius's long strides crossed the floor, his boots clicking softly against the smooth stone as he headed for one of the twin spiral staircases of glittering blue sandstone. Gilded sconces sparked with faerie fire and the papered walls mimicked the night sky with shimmering moonstone constellations. He crossed over the inlaid crest of House Celestine—an eight-pointed star flanked by two outward facing crescent moons—and stalked past the formal sitting area just off the grand hall, ignoring the tittering of voices coming from within the room.

"Sol!"

Narissa recognized Sarelle's voice as she called out to her older brother. She peeked over his shoulder just in time to see Sarelle dart from the sitting room and follow them, with Caelian right behind her. "We weren't expecting you…both."

Curiosity sparkled in Sarelle's sapphire gaze.

"Nope." Solarius stilled, heaving a sigh of exasperation. He did not turn to face his sisters, but his grip on Narissa tightened.

"Are you staying?" Caelian asked, a flicker of hope in her voice.

Solarius ducked his head, dropping his chin to his chest, his windswept silver hair with its inky tips falling forward to hide his growing vexation.

"Yep," he called back, his tone curt and dismissive.

It wasn't at all like him to be so disparaging toward his sisters, or any of his siblings really, but Narissa imagined his brusque attitude had everything to do with the fact that the evidence of his arousal was straining against his pants.

Sarelle stepped forward, clasping her hands together, her round cheeks shiny with a smear of stardust. "Can we get you any—"

Solarius whipped around, clutching Narissa to him. "I know it may not seem like it, darling sisters, but I am incredibly busy at the moment."

Narissa dipped her head, smiling into his neck. Which proved to be a torturous mistake as the tempting scent of him addled her mind and intoxicated her senses. Tantalizing citrus. Warm, alluring spices. And that damning hint of bay rum. She inhaled deeply, lightly running her nose along the column of his throat, her lungs, her chest, the entirety of her soul filling with him.

A devastating rumble sounded deep in his chest, the reverberation of it echoing in her bones.

Solarius shook his head and started away from his sisters, taking the steps two at a time. He bounded up the winding staircase with exceptional speed as pulses of desire thrummed along the mating bond, a product of their racing heartbeats. Narissa thought for certain he would carry her straight to his bedchamber, but he surprised her by ducking into an alcove off the hall hidden away by a curtain of winterblooms. The pretty blue flowers and leaves of evergreen diminished the light, so slants of gold peeked in through the clusters of petals.

Like she was his most prized possession, Solarius carefully set Narissa down, but he left no space between them. Instead he backed her into the rough stone wall, planting one hand firmly above her head while the other remained in a tight fist by his side. His chest heaved. His jaw locked. And the silver of his eyes was molten, hot enough to send a spear of heat straight to her core.

Narissa splayed both her hands on the chilly wall behind her, clenching her legs together. "What are we—"

Solarius uncurled his fist and planted one finger against her lips, a scowl lining his brow. "This fucking dress."

Narissa's spine locked into place, and she glared up at him in challenge. "What's wrong with it?"

His low, answering chuckle caused her knees to soften and her nipples to pebble. "Nothing. Not a damn thing."

With his hand still propped on the wall near her head, Solarius leaned closer. He traced the line of her jaw with one finger, then it glided down her neck, between the valley of her breasts, all the way to her navel. He toyed with the diamond piercing there.

Rubbing his lips together, Solarius slid his hand beneath the deep cut of her gown, molding his palm to her hip. "I just need a moment to take you in, to admire you."

"Right here?" Narissa asked, struggling to form words around her hammering pulse. "In an alcove?"

Tingles radiated from his touch and goosebumps rippled across her flesh. Desire pooled low in her belly and her nails bit into the wall behind her in a desperate attempt to keep herself upright. His labored breathing became her own, his heart pounded in time with hers, and his mouth skated over hers in an almost kiss.

Solarius cocked a brow. "Are you nervous, Rissa love?"

"No." She stiffened, plastering her back against the wall, ignoring the rough scrape of stone against her skin. Melting when his hand coasted up her waist, to her ribs, to the curve of her breast.

He grinned while his thumb drew small circles over her skin. "Does it make you uncomfortable when I look at you?"

Yes.

"No." But the word escaped her on a pinched breath and her confidence faltered.

His hand, still snugly fit under the fabric of her dress, roved over her shoulder, catching on the thin diamond strap. "Do you know how easy it would be to snap this flimsy little strap in half?"

Narissa doubted it would take much effort. He could probably break them with a simple tug, shredding the ribbon, sending a waterfall of diamonds scattering around them.

"Please don't," she whispered, and he froze, his gaze snagging on hers.

"Don't?" he asked, watching her intently, and she saw the flash of concern in his eyes. The worry that hardened the silver to steel.

"It's one of my favorites," Narissa amended, arching away from the safety of the wall, offering herself to him.

"Then I will be very careful." He pressed a kiss to her neck, branding her. "Just like I will with you."

He hooked a finger beneath the diamond strap, slowly letting it slide down her shoulder, then he repeated the motion on the other side so she was completely exposed to him from the waist up.

Her nipples hardened to the point of pain and her breasts grew heavy, aching for his touch. For any kind of reprieve. He cupped her breasts, rolling her peaked nipples between his thumb and forefinger, and she loved the way she fit so perfectly in his hands. Solarius lowered his head, squeezing them both as his tongue darted out and laved her tender nipple. He showered her sensitive flesh with attention—sucking, licking, and teasing until the tension building inside of her sent currents of longing coursing through her. When his teeth scraped at her nipple and lightly bit, tugging it into his mouth, Narissa spasmed and squirmed.

She rolled her hips, peeling off the wall in a silent plea.

Solarius edged back, his hands gripping her hips, pinning her against him so she felt every swollen inch of him. His thumbs drew those agonizing circles again, and she grabbed his shoulders, her nails scraping along the stiff fabric of his collared shirt.

"Do you want more?" he asked, rubbing his lips together.

"You know I do." Narissa folded her arms beneath her chest, shoving her breasts directly into his line of sight. She lifted one shoulder in feigned disinterest, not wanting to appear needy or desperate.

"So pretty," he murmured, dropping to his knees before her. One hand vanished beneath the hem of her gown, and she inhaled sharply as his palm skated around her ankle.

Every inch of her was alive, vibrating with desire, and her knees nearly buckled when his hand slid up the back of her calf all the way to her thigh. Warmth spread through her, and the sensitive flesh between her legs grew damp as his fingers discovered the band of lace wrapped around her leg. Shivers of delight raced down her spine while his fingertips inched closer, brushing the inside of her thigh.

His brows rose in surprise. "What are these?"

"They're only stockings. To keep me warm."

"May I look?"

Narissa nodded, grateful he asked her permission, but knowing she would've let him look, anyway. If Solarius wanted to duck beneath her skirts and place those exceptionally kissable lips near the tender flesh of her inner thigh, who was she to stop him?

Solarius shoved the length of her gown up to her waist, carefully situating the shimmering fabric so it cradled her hips. Then he scooped the back of her knee and draped her leg over his shoulder. He rubbed and massaged, the pads of his fingers grazing the lace band of her stockings.

"I thought this dress would be my undoing." Solarius's words were rough and grating, and the knot of tension building in her core wound even tighter. "Yet I believe I was mistaken. These stockings are damning in the best way possible."

He was only distracted by the lace for a moment longer until his gaze snagged on *her*. On the way her satin undergarments were soaked for him.

"Fuck, Rissa. You're so damn beautiful." Solarius pressed a kiss to her heated skin, close enough to her slick center that Narissa's lungs caved and she almost toppled over the edge. She was strung and wired, so painfully responsive to his touch that one gesture, the simplest of kisses, almost wrecked her completely.

He glanced up at her from where he kneeled, his eyes dark with an unrecognizable emotion. "May I?"

Held captive by the way Solarius gazed up at her as though she was his only reason for air, Narissa could only nod.

"Let me hear you say it."

She hissed out a breath of frustration. "Fine. You can look."

Amusement danced across his handsome face, and he shook his head once, his low laughter causing her blood to hum. "I don't want to look, Narissa. I want to taste."

"Taste?" Suddenly, Narissa's complacency and bold declarations evaporated at the thought of Solarius tasting her…there. Her gaze cut to the waterfall of winterblooms, her breath hitching. It was one thing to be caught kissing in an alcove, it was something else altogether to be discovered with your husband's head between your legs. "What if someone sees us?"

She plastered herself against the wall, but Solarius drew her back to him. He tucked one hand behind her bottom, cupping her, while the other kept her leg firmly anchored over his broad shoulder.

"Then I suppose you will have to be quiet."

His warm breath fanned over her wetness, and she shuddered in his hold.

"I'm going to ask one more time." His fingers squeezed her leg, stretching her wide, baring her before him. "May I?"

"I…" Hesitation clawed at her, its sharp talons piercing through the cloud of her desire. She'd never had a male down there before, at least not with his face. "I suppose."

Narissa wasn't sure she would enjoy it.

Solarius chuckled, soft and sensual. He pulled the swath of satin to the side, exposing her fully. "Oh, you'll like it, Rissa love."

She intended to insult his blistering ego, but then his tongue slid along her seam, and Narissa unraveled.

He was sweet torture.

It was strange and exhilarating all at once, the way he seemed to enjoy feasting upon her, how each swipe of his tongue sent a jolt of energy pulsing down the bond. His teeth grazed her clit and it was as though all the air evaporated from her lungs, like every frayed nerve ending had been centered and entirely focused on that one particular area. And the moment Solarius showed it a shred of attention, Narissa's world came undone.

She grasped at his hair for purchase, threading her fingers through his silky strands before grabbing fistfuls and fusing his mouth to her center. She didn't care if she was wanton and shameless, Solarius was doing unspeakable things to her with only his tongue and she—her legs wobbled when he pushed a finger inside of her. And then another. He curled them in deep, powerful strokes and she rocked her hips, matching his pace.

"Come for me, Rissa love." Each word dripped with heady lust.

He applied the perfect amount of pressure once more and she bit her lip hard to keep from crying out.

The metallic tang of blood coated her tongue, and her magic roared to life, crashing into her like a tidal wave. Her release rose and crested in languid pulls, rushing in like the sea to the shore, then slowly withdrawing.

Solarius eased back and took his time adjusting her gown. He arranged her skirts and replaced the diamond straps, smoothed a hand down her unruly waves. His gaze locked in on the drop of scarlet beaded upon her lip and he crowded her, then flashed a wicked grin. In the next moment, his tongue darted out, swiping away the blood clinging to her mouth. A guttural sound rumbled in his chest. Solarius grabbed her hand, pulling her into him to ensure she remained upright and didn't melt into a puddle of messy feelings at his feet.

He led her out from behind the cascading blue flowers and into the dimly lit corridor.

"Where are we going?" Narissa was still in a post-lust haze, stumbling along blindly behind him, her legs trembling with each uneven step.

"My bedroom." Solarius pushed open a massive oak door with carved moon phases and flecks of glimmering moonstone.

Narissa lost her footing and pitched forward into the darkened bedchamber. Solarius caught her by the waist, kicking the door shut, and walked her backward until she was up against the nearest wall. She tried not to look around, to steal a few glimpses of her husband's bedroom, especially considering she'd never been inside before, but curiosity got the best of her. It was all moody, drenched in shades of gray and deepest navy, with a glass ceiling that showcased the whole of the night sky.

She knew it.

"Something bothering you, Narissa?" He kept one hand on the small of her back, the other planted on the wall over her head.

"No...I..." Again, her courage to speak her mind and never back down in front of him failed her. She lost her nerve to toss out churlish quips and sharp slights. Instead, honesty spilled from her like she'd been the one to take Lady Aria's truth serum. "It's just, well, you stopped in the alcove. So, I assumed you were done. That maybe you didn't necessarily want me anymore."

"Allow me to make myself perfectly clear." Solarius lowered his head so his mouth brushed over hers in a soft, nearly inconceivable touch. "I will always want you. The only reason I stopped was because I was about to erupt in my pants just by looking at you."

He spoke with such clarity, such calm composure, all Narissa could say was, "Oh."

"And I would much rather be buried deep inside that pretty little cunt of yours when that happens." His head tilted to one side, questioning. "If you don't mind."

"I don't mind," she rasped, and he smirked.

"Good." Solarius led her further into his bedchamber. "Because I'm going to take my time with you."

Narissa couldn't tell if it was a promise or a vow, and to be honest, she wasn't sure she cared. Because if there was one thing she wanted, it was to be absolutely ruined by Solarius Starstorm.

CHAPTER TWENTY-FOUR

Solarius had never wanted anything more in his life than he wanted Narissa. He craved everything about her—the way she rolled her lips whenever she hit him with one of those contemptuous remarks or caustic comments, the way her icy green eyes burned with uncontrollable fire whenever she was forced to share the same space as him. He'd gotten a taste of her in the alcove, he'd been gifted a brief display of what it would be like when she finally broke, when she finally shattered while he was inside of her, and he wanted to experience that again, more than he wanted air. Because Narissa patched up her broken heart and channeled that misplaced anger into an esteemed hatred for him, and now he planned on fucking the word hate right out of her vocabulary.

After all, they had to make up for years of lost time.

Time that had been stolen by away by Calfair.

Solarius shoved his former friend's name from his mind, refusing to let the bastard steal this moment from him as well.

No, he was going to be slow and deliberate with Narissa tonight.

He was going to cherish her.

He was going to take his time.

At least that was his plan until she dropped to her knees before him and reached for the button of his pants.

"Narissa," Solarius warned. "What are you doing?"

He snagged her wrist, tension coiling through him, his cock already straining against the tight fabric. It would be so easy to grab the back of her head and watch those pretty, glossy lips of hers take every inch of him.

She shrugged, lifting one shoulder with forced nonchalance. "Just returning the favor, my lord."

Solarius swallowed hard, capturing her chin with his hand. "You don't have to do this."

"Perhaps not." Narissa's frostbitten gaze flicked upward, and she watched him from beneath a fringe of dark lashes. The shimmery powder dusted across her cheeks glimmered in the faint light of his room. "But I want to."

His breathing grew heavy, each breath was suddenly pained, like his lungs were pinched tight. His pulse ricocheted, and her slender fingers—most of them adorned with delicate gold rings—deftly worked the buttons of his pants. Her hands explored him then, her perfectly manicured nails gently scraping the dip of his hips and lower abdomen, before sneaking into the waistband of his black shorts and tugging them down.

There was a quick inhale and then her warm breath coated his thick head as her eyes widened, round like tide pools, as she stared at his stiff cock.

Tentatively, Narissa reached out, running her fingers along his hard length, stroking him. Driving him absolutely mad with her dainty touches. He was already lined up with her lips and when her pink tongue peeked out, he fisted one hand on the wall above her head and groaned.

"Narissa, I swear to the stars, if you don't—"

Then she took him, every inch, into her sweet little mouth.

"Fuck," he bit out, his fingers tangling in her hair as he grabbed a fistful.

She drew him in hard, tongue swirling, cheeks hollowing as his hips jerked forward of their own accord. It would be different if she was *just* sucking his cock but fucking stars, her hands. They feathered across his thighs and over his firm stomach, her pretty nails scouring his muscles one moment, then dancing the next, sending a chill down his spine. Her hot mouth took him deeper with each thrust, and when he pushed in all the way to the hilt, she didn't choke or gag. Instead, Narissa gazed up at him with shining eyes and cupped his balls, squeezing lightly, urging him to keep going, to empty himself down her throat.

Maybe some other time.

Solarius pulled himself from her mouth before he exploded, ignoring the flash of shock on her face.

He grabbed her by her shoulders and hauled her to a standing position, shoving those flimsy diamond straps down so that her gown pooled around her feet in a puddle of dark pink silk and glittering beads. She stood before him, completely nude, save for those enticing stockings, a pair of moderately high heels, and an elegant—if not entirely useless—triangular scrap of satin. He took hold of the thin band and yanked, the ripping of fine fabric echoing in the space between him, as he tossed the satin barrier aside.

She yelped in surprise.

"Sol!" Narissa clamped one hand over her mouth, eyes sparkling, but the blush staining her cheeks faded the longer he stared at her. He fixated on the curve of her hips, the full and luscious slope of her breasts, the dip of her collarbone. All those sweet, tantalizing places he wanted to kiss.

It was fascinating, really, watching her reaction to the way he gazed upon her. He enjoyed the way her dusky nipples hardened to stiff little peaks beneath his intense assessment. And how she so cleverly tried to squeeze her thighs together, like she could somehow disguise her arousal from him. The most interesting tell was the way her body involuntarily arched toward him, as though she was silently begging for his touch.

Solarius scooped her up and carried her to his bed. He kicked off his pants and shorts, but she refused to lie down. Her eager hands clawed at his shirt, making quick work of the buttons, before she tugged it off him. Then her lips were on him. Kissing his chest, his stomach, then back up to his neck and shoulders. She traced the tattoo of his constellation, Azuralis, with the tip of her finger, memorizing each line. Each star.

She was up close now, on her knees, so his cock fit snugly between her thighs. Narissa wove her arms around his neck, pressing her breasts against him, rubbing every soft, lithe inch of her against the solid line of him. Her mouth slanted across his, their tongues meshed together in a kiss fueled by years-long hunger and misplaced anger. Their magic collided in a crush of glimmering tides and moonlight. He could taste the call of the sea as her power drowned him. Then her nails were digging into his shoulders, clawing up the back of his neck, and his hands found the globes of her ass. He gripped. Squeezed. His greedy fingers venturing dangerously close to where he knew she was already wet for him. She arched her back and his fingers slid lower, her whine of desperation sending every pump of blood straight to his cock. His heart hammered, frenzied and erratic, so all he wanted to do was splay Narissa wide open and plunge himself into her until she forgot her own name.

But this was Narissa.

His Narissa.

His wife.

And he wanted this moment to be full of gentle kisses and blissful lovemaking. Yes, he wanted to give her everything and more, he wanted to ruin her completely, but his threads of control were slipping. Unraveling. He pulled back and the bond spasmed. Narissa lurched back as though he'd slapped her.

"Enough," she spat, folding her arms across her chest, cutting him down with a vicious glare.

Solarius stilled, frozen with guilt. "What's wrong?"

"You." She waved one hand through the air between them. "Whatever is going on inside your head, stop it at once. I can feel you retreating. Pulling away from me."

Solarius raked both hands through his hair, tugging on the ends. "I promise, that is the furthest thing from my mind."

It wasn't quite the truth, and Narissa saw right through it.

"Liar." She grabbed his hands and forced them to her breasts, to palm them, to feel them. And she leaned into his touch. "I am *not* fragile, Solarius. Stop treating me like a porcelain doll that will break at any moment."

"I don't want to hurt—"

"You will not, and if you do, I will be sure to tell you. Yes, if you grab or pinch me too hard, it may leave bruises. And if you suck on my skin too harshly, it might leave a mark." She rubbed his palm over her peaked nipples, then guided the other hand between the valley of her breasts, and lower still, to where she urged two of his fingers into her slick heat.

Solarius wanted to die. She was fucking heavenly.

"But I *want* that, Sol." Narissa's voice took on that husky, siren-like quality, and he groaned, working his fingers inside her. "I want to be marked by you. To be claimed by you. So stop acting as though I might shatter and fuck me already."

"Sweet stars." Solarius dropped forward, pressing their foreheads together. "That mouth."

Narissa rocked against his knuckles and angled her head, sliding her tongue over the slick skin of his neck. "What about it?"

A violent noise, a cross between a groan and a growl, rumbled through his chest. As much as he wanted to keep pushing his fingers inside of her, as much as he wanted to watch her come undone again, Narissa had made it perfectly clear she wanted more from him than a safe and doting sexual encounter.

So, he would give her exactly what she wanted.

He yanked his fingers out of her deliciously wet center and snared her by the wrist. He dragged her toward the foot of the bed, where the large, ornate onyx mirror was propped against the wall, its lacquer reflective of the moon phases. With one quick movement, he spun her around so her back was pressed against his front, his throbbing cock nudging into her round bottom.

"Tell me how you want it," he demanded, wrapping a possessive arm around her waist while the other skated up her flesh and captured her throat.

"No," she answered coolly, nails toying with the dusting of hair along his forearms. "I don't think I will."

"Naughty midnight siren." Solarius's hand dipped lower and slid a finger along the seam of her lips, not surprised to find her soaking. "You're so wet for me, Rissa love."

"Really?" She arched a brow in the mirror's reflection, her gaze trained on his, her lids hooded with desire. "I hadn't noticed."

His cock jumped.

Stars above, this female would be the end of him.

"Grab the mirror with both hands. And spread your legs."

She willfully obeyed and Solarius took in the sight before him.

Her fingers curved over the detailed onyx frame, while the glass displayed her full breasts, her glazed eyes, and her swollen mouth. She shimmied a little, her heels scraping across the stone floor as she opened her legs for him, giving him a full view of her. Her slick folds glistened, primed and ready for him, and he roughed both hands up and over the backs of her thighs, tugging on the lace bands of her stockings before letting them smack soundly against her skin. The whimpering noise that escaped her almost made him come on the spot.

"I want your eyes on me the whole time, do you understand?" He gripped his shaft and pumped it twice, rubbing the head against her wetness as he lined himself up to enter her. "I want you looking right at me when you come on my cock, because from now on, it will only ever be me."

She nodded, sinking her teeth into that plump bottom lip in the way that drove him mad with desire.

Solarius didn't give her any warning.

He shoved into her, glancing down to watch her stretch to accommodate him. Narissa cried out, shoulders bunching to her ears as she arched, shoving herself backward like she needed more. Solarius grabbed her hips as he started to thrust, slow and methodical. After each push in deep, he drew himself back out in a lazy, languid stroke. He took his time filling her up, then edging her into oblivion as he pulled out to the point of pain, where barely the tip of his head was still nestled inside her.

Narissa clenched around him, broken sobs wrecking her. She shuddered. Thrashed. Her knuckles were white from where she gripped the mirror, and for a brief second, it looked as though she stomped her foot like a petulant child who failed to get her way. On more than one occasion, she attempted to grind her hips back, to take him harder, faster, deeper.

But he refused to give her that satisfaction.

Not yet.

"Solarius," she cried, squeezed her eyes shut. "Please."

"Eyes on me, Rissa love."

They flew open at his command, all sea green and full of fire.

"Say it again." He lifted his chin on another agonizingly slow thrust.

Her tongue darted out, gliding across her bottom lip, and she held his gaze. "Please."

That was all it took.

Solarius pumped himself into Narissa's tight heat and her answering whimpers only spurred him on to take her harder. Faster. Just like she wanted. Lunar magic channeled through him, spilling from his fingertips as the silver light washed over her golden skin. Those beautiful luminous wave tattoos appeared along the pointed tips of her ears and up her spine, and he reveled in the way she glowed just for him.

"Sol," she gasped. Her mouth fell open and her ocean eyes remained trained on him. "I think…I think I might…"

In one swift movement, Solarius yanked her upright, crushing her to him, his thumb rubbing her clit so her body quivered and seized. She clamped around his cock, throwing one arm over her head, grasping at the back of his neck. The bond thrummed as Narissa arched, taking him so fucking deep that she splintered around him. Her head fell against his shoulder, her pale green eyes fastened to his cold silver as he emptied himself inside of her. Her chest heaved and he jerked once. Twice.

"Rissa," he murmured, his mind emptying of all rational thought, and he pressed a kiss to the crook of her neck, where her skin was sweet and damp. "If that is what it will be like every time I bed you, I don't think I will ever be able to survive it."

"You must try, my lord." Her eyes fluttered closed and she sagged against him, all soft and pliable curves in his arms. "Because once will never be enough."

Solarius sighed, the truth of her words sinking into him.

He swept her up and carried her to his bed. She curled into him, warm and wonderful, draping one arm casually across his chest as she tucked herself under his arm. Solarius stared up at the glass ceiling, where the pitch of night stretched overhead, where the stars winked, keeping their secrets close. Narissa was absolutely right. Once would never be enough. Already his cock was thickening and she was simply lying there, her breathing deep and even.

The bond heated and a tempting whisper slid into his mind as Narissa hiked her leg up over him.

"Then do something about it, my lord."

Fuck.

CHAPTER TWENTY-FIVE

The next morning, Narissa awoke comfortably warm with Solarius's arm slung possessively around her waist and his hardened shaft wedged snugly between her legs. She blinked away the sleep from her eyes as gray morning light peeked in through the dusting of snow covering the glass ceiling. Soft sheets and a downy navy comforter were tossed over them, fire crackled and spit in the hearth, and Narissa let her mind drift. For a moment she allowed herself to imagine what it would be like to wake up every morning like this, sated and deliriously content, with the ache in her heart suddenly not so heavy.

Solarius's chest was pressed to her back, and with each steady rise and fall, she snuggled herself a little bit closer to him. His voice was heavy with sleep as he said, "If you keep nuzzling your perfect little ass against me, I'm going to flip you over and have you ride my cock."

Desire speared her and every inch of her skin tingled with awareness. Emboldened by his promise, she shimmied, squeezing his cock where it rested between her thighs. If she arched a little and slightly lifted one leg, then he would be able to slide right into her. But her squirming drew a seductive groan from Solarius, one that echoed down her spine, and caused her stomach to flip into tangled knots of anticipation.

His hand roved along the slope of her hip, then dove lower, his middle finger stroking her slit, discovering the proof of her arousal.

Solarius's lips feathered a kiss across her shoulders. "Are you not tender from last night, my lady?"

"On the contrary, my lord." She pivoted, turning to face him, trailing her nails down the broad expanse of his chest. His cock pulsed, pressing into her belly. "I am positively *aching* for you."

"Well, then. I cannot leave my wife unsatisfied."

He grabbed her by the waist and rolled onto his back, taking her with him so the length of her body was splayed over his own. He palmed her bottom with both hands, then reached for her thighs. Solarius hooked her legs so she straddled him, adjusting her position so her knees were planted on either side of his hips, and his head aligned with her center.

"Tell me, Rissa love." Solarius fisted his swollen length and rubbed along her wetness, coaxing a gasp from her. "How shall I ease this ache of yours?"

"Sol," she whimpered, grinding against him. It was like standing on the brink of despair. Her body was thrumming, alive with need, yet he refused to give her what she wanted. What she craved.

"Tell me, Narissa." His voice was a strained command. "I need to hear you say it."

She almost scoffed then, thought he was being a boastful jerk, but his eyes gave him away. They were filled with a kind of quiet desperation, a singular plea that touched her soul.

"Let me ride your cock, Solarius." Her whisper stretched between them, and she grabbed his shoulders, nails digging into his skin for balance as she anchored herself above him. "Please."

Gradually, she sank onto him, inch by blessed inch, until he filled her completely.

He guided her up and down, slow and methodical, but she could tell he was holding back. It was in the way his knuckles whitened with each carefully timed thrust. The way the line of concentration deepened across his forehead as though he was using every last shred of his own restraint. But mostly, it was the way he watched her too carefully, like she might fracture if he was too rough or too fast.

Narissa stilled, sucking in a sharp breath. "You're doing it again."

She knew why, of course. After what she'd suffered by Calfair's hands, after the shame she'd endured on her own, of course Solarius was mindful and protective. But she wasn't damaged. Her past did not dictate her future. And she refused to allow one male's unscrupulous behavior to impact her ability to own her sexuality.

She shook her head. "This isn't working."

A guttural groan of anguish escaped him when she climbed off his lap. He squeezed his eyes shut and scrubbed a hand over his face. "Rissa, wait."

"I will not partake in any more bedroom activities with you until you can stop treating me like I may fall apart at any moment. I told you last night that I wasn't going to break, and I meant it." Narissa raised her chin and climbed from the expansive bed, wrapping one of the thick linens around her. She knew what Solarius was capable of—she'd heard stories of his bedroom forays, his late-night revelries, of his prowess behind closed doors. All things she longed for, all things she craved. Yet still he insisted upon being a gentle lover with her, like she was somehow not worthy of his expertise. "If you wouldn't mind finding me something to wear while I wait for my belongings to arrive? Perhaps Sarelle or one of the twins have a day dress I can borrow."

Solarius sat up, raking both hands through his unkempt hair. The silvery strands with inky tips framed his face like midnight shadows. He leaned back against the headboard, his brow still pinched, like he didn't quite believe her. "Narissa, please. Let's talk about this, I know I—"

"If you wish to discuss this further, then we can do so. After breakfast." She huffed and tugged the sheets tighter around her. "I'm famished."

A partial truth. The reality of the matter was that the longer Solarius sat there, sprawled against a mountain of pillows with his shaft still ready for her, the more difficult it was becoming not to climb back on top of him.

He grinned, one brow arching in mock amusement. Raising both arms overhead, he stretched lazily, showcasing his muscled stomach… among other things. He fisted himself and pumped twice. "Are you hungry, Rissa love?"

Narissa bristled and Solarius reached for the hem of the sheet.

Damn their bond for being so telling. It made it impossible to keep anything secret.

She clutched the sheet, wrinkling the fabric in her grip. "Don't you dare."

"Or what?" he taunted and tugged hard, causing her to spin as he unraveled the linen from around her.

"Sol!" she shrieked, stumbling backward, arms flailing.

He vaulted off the bed, snared her by the waist with one arm before she toppled to the floor, then kissed her soundly on the mouth. Solarius grabbed her bottom and pulled her flush against him, and the skin-to-skin contact served as an aphrodisiac, heightening her senses. The mouthwatering layers of his scent. The abrasive quality of the pads of his fingers as they skated over her skin. The delicious press of his length into her stomach. But then he squeezed her bottom once and gave her a firm smack.

She jolted and he dropped his mouth to her ear, his words stirring something dark and delightful inside of her.

"It's a bold claim, Rissa, to refuse yourself pleasure in the bedroom when you're so clearly starved for my attention." Solarius reached between them and slid two fingers into her, pumping in idle strokes, until her knees turned soft and she could no longer stand upright without holding onto him. "I suppose I'll have to find ways to pleasure you outside of the bedroom instead. I do enjoy being creative."

Without warning, he pulled his fingers out of her, leaving her crestfallen on the edge of release. But when he popped those same fingers into his mouth and winked, Narissa almost sobbed.

He yanked on a pair of pants and grabbed his boots.

Narissa gaped at him, her temper flaring to life. "So, you're just going to leave me here, then? Like this?"

"Like what?" he mused. "Naked? Flushed and beautiful? Quivering with need?"

Her frustration stewed, boiled into anger.

"Yes." Solarius laced up his boots. "That's exactly how I'm going to leave you."

He stood then, grabbing her chin, and she scowled up at him.

"Right now, I'm going to find you a dress. And then we're going to get you some food, because you're a little snarky when you're hungry. And while you eat, I'm going to plan all the wicked things I want to do to you outside the bedroom." He lowered his head, letting his teeth trail and scrape up the column of her neck all the way to her ear. Her nipples pebbled. Her thighs clenched. And goosebumps raked across her exposed flesh. "Perhaps then you will realize that my caution with you stems from a place of reverence and years of pining, instead of just wanting to fuck you senseless."

Without another word, Solarius walked out of the bedroom, his last words hanging in the air between them, and Narissa was left shivering with anticipation.

CHAPTER TWENTY-SIX

reakfast in House Celestine was anything but boring.

The dining hall was ripe with uncomfortable tension, forced conversation, and awkward exchanges. Narissa knew the Starstorm siblings were a lively bunch, a loyal brood who stood by one another no matter the cost. They loved fiercely, teased one another mercilessly, and bickered amongst themselves as though it was a sport in which they all excelled beyond measure. Which was why it surprised Narissa to find the breakfast table stifled with strained silence and wavering unease.

Ariesian sat at the head of the table, stewing over a steaming cup of tea. The permanent scowl marring his brow was a testament to his current mood, but every so often, the steel of his gaze flicked toward his younger sister, Caelian. And for good reason.

Caelian looked…well…dreadful if Narissa was being honest. Smudges of exhaustion discolored the skin beneath her eyes, and she gnawed her bottom lip until it was red and raw. Sarelle was beside her, quietly encouraging her to eat, to hopefully gain back some of her color, but Caelian was forlorn. Positively lovesick over the hulking male seated at the opposite end of the table. Kjeld Holtstrom had been the object of Caelian's adoration since his arrival in Aeramere, and

Narissa couldn't say she blamed her. Kjeld was all hard, chiseled muscle with summer blue eyes and mussy golden hair he often kept braided or twisted away from his handsome face. He was an esteemed warrior. Breaking tides, he rode a *dragon*. And until recently, he'd been a human. But in a twist of events, Caelian's magic turned him fae, and in doing so, only enhanced his rugged beauty tenfold. Something he'd never forgiven her for doing.

And Caelian had paid the price. Dearly.

Solarius pulled out a chair for Narissa, seating her next to Tovian, while he took the chair on her opposite side. Nyxian was across from them and he flashed her a roguish smile.

"Morning, Lady Narissa." Nyxian grabbed a honeyed roll and slathered an absurd amount of butter on top. "I trust you slept well?"

His grin widened and Narissa flushed.

She dipped her head, unable to meet his knowing gaze. "Quite."

Oh, but Nyxian was relentless. "I imagine. It certainly sounded as though—"

"Nyx!" Sarelle scolded, her eyes widening like sapphire orbs at the same time Solarius kicked him from beneath the table.

"Mind yourself," Solarius warned. His hand found Narissa's thigh and he squeezed, possessive, as ripples of caution rolled off him in dense waves.

Nyxian bit off a hunk of bread and raised both his hands in surrender. "What? I was only going to say it sounded like—"

"Narissa, I must say," Sarelle interrupted her brother's antics smoothly and without hesitation, "that dress is positively lovely. Wherever did you find it?"

Narissa glanced down at the navy velvet gown that was a smidge too small and shoved her bosom up to her chin. It swept low with flowing ripples and was embellished with sparkly moons and stars made of diamonds. She met her friend's brilliant smile with one of her own and said, "Your closet."

"Nice save, Sarelle," Tovian murmured from beside her. He propped his elbows on the table, his swath of deep blue hair falling across half of his face, and turned in Narissa's direction. Whereas

Solarius's eyes were a molten silver, Tovian's held a glimmer of iridescence. "Tell me, Lady Narissa, do you have any inappropriate brothers or infuriating sisters?"

"Unfortunately, I only have one cousin who is annoyingly right most of the time." She thought of Reif and his panache for always knowing exactly what she needed to hear. With a small smile, she poked at the pile of fluffy cakes drizzled with honey on her plate. "Though I've always wanted a sibling or two."

Solarius scoffed and took a hasty swig of orange juice. "Be careful what you wish for."

As soon as he said it, Kjeld slammed his fist onto the table, rattling all the glassware and dishes. He muttered something about baby dragons and cursing stars as he stormed from the dining hall without a backward glance. Caelian, however, looked as though she might burst into tears at a moment's notice. She sniffed and blinked furiously, her bottom lip trembling as she slowly scooted her chair back. Her gaze never strayed from her shoes, never lifted to meet the heavy stares of those around her. She looked frail. Weak. And it broke Narissa's heart. She watched in silence as Caelian padded from the room—in the opposite direction of Kjeld—without making a sound.

"Blessed stars," Nyxian groaned the words out, shoving a hand through his unruly hair. "I hate it when the two of them are in a room together. It's fucking uncomfortable."

Ariesian's head snapped up and his gaze darted from Sarelle to Narissa. "Language, Nyx."

"Right," Nyxian muttered, tugging on the collar of his crisp violet shirt. "Apologies."

Narissa had the distinct feeling that he didn't mean it.

"Aries, are you certain you can't marry Caelian off next?" he asked, grabbing a fistful of sugared berries. He tossed one into the air and caught it in his mouth. "Her eternal pining over Drake's general is pitiful."

Narissa sat up straight, she was quite well-versed in the art of pining. "Lady Caelian and General Holtstrom would make a fine match."

Solarius leaned in close, as though he were about to spill a dark secret. "Except he wants nothing to do with her. Wish magic is dangerous, and Caelian made a foolish mistake."

Narissa was considering questioning Solarius further on the matter when Ariesian spoke once more.

"I'm afraid I'm busy securing another marriage for our family." The eldest Starstorm leaned back in his chair, his hands gripping the curving arms until his knuckles whitened, and for a brief moment, it looked as though he was preparing for battle.

"Is that right?" Nyxian's mischievous gaze landed on Sarelle. "Whose?"

Ariesian didn't even blink. His face was the epitome of calm neutrality when he said, "Yours."

Nyxian choked on a berry. He pounded his fist against his chest, then let out one barking cough that closely resembled an incredulous laugh. "You cannot be serious."

"Oh, but I am." Ariesian's fingers methodically tapped against the glossy wooden armchair. "Tov is returning to the seas in the spring, and you chose to remain here, in Aeramere. Sarelle is garnering the attention of Prince Aspen."

He paused then, because everyone at the table knew Sarelle's interest in Prince Aspen to be a ruse.

"And Caelian expended too much of her power. She's not allowed to court until she makes a full recovery." Ariesian notched a finger in Nyxian's direction. "That leaves only you, dear brother."

Narissa wasn't entirely sure what she expected, but it certainly wasn't watching Nyxian Starstorm explode on his eldest brother.

"I am *not* playing into your hand, Ariesian." Nyxian stood abruptly. His chair flipped back, and the echo of wood slamming against polished stone reverberated throughout the dining hall. Anger simmered beneath the surface of his usually carefree façade, and the scar marking the left side of his face only served to make him more menacing. "You don't run my life. You are not our father and you never will be, so drop the fucking act."

Sarelle clamped one hand over her mouth, and it was as though

Nyxian's word cracked his brother's icy exterior, because Ariesian faltered.

"Nyxian," Sarelle whispered, her voice a plea as her wild eyes darted between her brothers.

But he ignored her and bolted from the room, a volatile storm of emotions brewing in his wake.

Tovian cleared his throat and calmly set his napkin down on his plate. "I'll take care of it."

He stood and bowed slightly. "Brothers. Sister. Lady Narissa."

Then he, too, left, and the dining hall fell eerily silent.

Solarius clicked his tongue and popped one of the sugared berries that rolled across the table into his mouth. "See, Rissa love? Having siblings isn't so great after all."

But he squeezed her thigh, nonetheless.

Ariesian followed Tovian's suit, his expression solemn, his demeanor stiff and excessively formal. He offered them a curt bow. "If you'd excuse me."

The moment he abandoned the dining hall, Sarelle blew out a breath that sent her star-kissed midnight hair fluttering. "I am *so* sorry, Narissa. Their behavior this morning was inexcusable."

Narissa waved a hand flippantly through the air. "Think nothing of it."

In truth, she was almost grateful for the experience. It pleased her to see that the beloved Starstorms weren't perfect. That they were real and raw and sometimes even vulnerable. But perhaps what she loved most was that they'd chosen to not curb their behavior, her presence had not made difference. It was almost like they saw her as one of them. As part of their family.

"Are you staying with us long?" Sarelle asked, drawing Narissa's attention away from her sentimental thoughts.

"As long as you'd like," Solarius murmured, his voice a balm to her soul.

"For a while, I believe." Narissa finally took a bite of her honeyed cakes that had now grown cold.

Sarelle beamed, and the brilliance of her smile was near blinding. "Lovely! I've missed your company."

Again, Solarius squeezed Narissa's thigh, his touch now becoming a comfort.

"You have?" Narissa regretted the words as soon as they left her mouth. They sounded disbelieving and uncertain. They made her appear timid and doubtful.

"Of course!" Sarelle didn't seem to notice. Instead, her bubbly, if not slightly quirky, personality only seemed to shine even more. "We are going to have the best time now that you're here. It will be as though we're proper sisters."

Narissa ducked her head. "You already have sisters."

"But you do not. Besides, we're all quite keen to have another female around." Sarelle licked the last of her pudding off her spoon and stood from the table. "I hate to leave so soon, especially after the absolute catastrophe that was breakfast, but I do have some errands to run before the ball tonight."

Now it was Solarius's turn to choke. He coughed hard, and Narissa patted him roughly on the back.

"Ball?" he rasped.

"Sol…" Sarelle's shoulders dropped, and she rolled her eyes to the decadent chandelier above. "Don't tell me you've forgotten? It's Winter Solstice."

Solarius's head tipped back, and he rubbed at his temples. "It slipped my mind."

Whereas he seemed mildly perturbed about the matter, Narissa was attempting to disguise her growing dread. She had nothing to wear for House Celestine's yearly Yuletide Ball. All she had in her possession was the day dress she borrowed from Sarelle.

"All of my belongings are at House Azurvend." She worried her bottom lip. It was one thing to not be noticed at balls and dances, it was something else altogether to be entirely underdressed for the occasion.

"Come with me to Celestine! We can go shopping and find you a dress for tonight." Sarelle's deep blue eyes glittered with excitement. "I was going to purchase new gloves, anyway."

Solarius grabbed Narissa's hand and pressed a kiss to each of her knuckles. "Go shopping, Rissa love. I need to speak with Ariesian."

Narissa stood, but then Solarius caught her by the elbow and dragged his lips over her ear. "Purchase another pair of those stockings for me while you're out."

Her cheeks heated. "Yes, my lord."

Sarelle grabbed Narissa's hand and linked their arms together. "Don't worry, dear brother. I shall take good care of your lovely wife."

"See that you do."

"So," Sarelle whispered conspiratorially as they exited the dining hall. "What color stockings are you going to buy?"

An unexpected bubble of laughter escaped Narissa, and when she tossed a glance over her shoulder, she found Solarius watching her, a well of longing harbored in the depths of his silver eyes.

CHAPTER TWENTY-SEVEN

Solarius lounged on the sofa across from Ariesian's desk. He stretched his legs out before him, crossing one ankle over the other, with his arm strewn across the stack of plush pillows. Faerie fire glowed in the hearth, and though the air was warm, the atmosphere was cold. He'd remained seated across from his brother for a solid twenty minutes, and not a single word had been said.

Ariesian was in a foul mood.

He had the heels of his boots propped up on his desk, and the scowl he wore at breakfast had only deepened. In one hand, he cradled the Celestinian Wayfinder, the astrolabe given to him by their father. It spun and whirred, a sphere of glittery stars and the whole of the night sky.

Finally, Solarius spoke.

"He'll come around, Aries."

Then again, Nyxian was notorious for having a stubborn streak.

Ariesian spared him a glance but said nothing. He focused on the astrolabe, on the bursts of stardust sparking inside of it, on its ethereal structure. His brows drew together in a severe line, and he set the astrolabe on its stand where it floated and twirled before leaning back in his chair. It groaned beneath his weight, the wood creaking lightly, and Ariesian folded his arms across his chest.

Moments bled into minutes, until Ariesian loosed a heavy, burdensome sigh.

"I never wanted this, you know?" It was almost like he was talking to himself. His voice was low and hushed against the stillness and the crackling of flames. "I never wanted to be Lord Starstorm or High Councilor to Queen Elowyn, or any other ridiculously excessive title. But I was given no choice."

"You're the firstborn, you're heir to House Celestine." Solarius drummed his fingers along the back of the sofa. "It's been your duty since your birth."

Ariesian's cool glare cut to him. "Of that, I am well aware. But it would have been nice to have been given an option, to choose my own fate. My own destiny."

"Ah," Solarius mused, running his thumb along his jaw as he considered his elder brother. "Much like how you gave those same choices to Novalise, Sarelle, myself, and now Nyxian?"

Ariesian visibly stiffened. His muscles bunched with tension, the vein along his temple pulsed.

"Before Lord Firebane came to his senses, you signed a contract to marry Novalise off to the Shadowblade Assassin, without even telling her, I might add. You convinced Sarelle to entangle herself with Prince Aspen, whom you know is a notorious prick. And then you bound me to Narissa." Solarius drew his knees up and leaned forward, propping his elbows on his thighs as he steepled his fingers together. "Where were our options, Aries? Our choices?"

Ariesian bristled and his face became a mask of indifference. "I did what was necessary for the security and longevity of our house."

"Did you?" Solarius prodded, knowing he was getting dangerously close to pushing his brother over the edge of his calm exterior. "Or did you do it just to get it over with? Like our names are on your lengthy list of duties and we're only another check in the box?"

"The safety, happiness, and wellbeing of you and your brothers and sisters has always been a priority for me. You know that." Ariesian scrubbed a hand over his face, and for a moment, his mask fell. In a split second, all his emotions—fear, exhaustion, dread, worry—were laid bare. Then he blinked, and the stoic Lord Starstorm returned. "But it is also my responsibility to ensure House Celestine's bloodline."

Solarius stared at him. "Our."

Ariesian arched a brow. "Pardon?"

"You said *your* brothers and sisters. They're ours. Our siblings. Our family."

Solarius edged back, and it was as though a new light had been cast upon his brother. One that highlighted half of Ariesian as the strong, steadfast Lord of House Celestine. Confident. Fearless. Unwavering. And then there was the part of him lost to the shadows. The one burdened beneath an insurmountable weight of responsibility, the one who had forgotten what it was like to smile. To laugh. To live.

A bout of leaden silence stretched between them, and they stared at one another.

"It is not your fate to replace our father." Solarius kept his voice calm and even. "You must make your own way, Ariesian. We are not your charges."

"What would you have me do?" Ariesian raked his hands through his silver hair, exasperated. "Leave your future in the hands of our *mother?*"

The mention of Trysta struck a chord in Solarius's chest, one that radiated with quiet anger.

"Speaking of," Solarius began, forcing himself to unclench his jaw. "Did you or Drake ever figure out what it was she requested from Calfair in exchange for the dragon root?"

"Not yet." Ariesian's demeanor shifted from blatant displeasure to guarded tension. "Why?"

"Because I know why Calfair wanted the dragon root." Solarius launched into a detailed explanation, reiterating everything he and Narissa discovered. How she was drugged, taken advantage of, and ultimately used and misled.

By the time he finished telling the story, Ariesian looked ready to implode. His face turned crimson and his fists were clenched so tightly around the arms of his chair that Solarius worried he might rip them straight off the hinges.

"That fucking bastard," Ariesian barked. "Did you break his face?"

"Not badly enough."

"We need to figure out what Trysta wants, what she's so desperate to have that she would be willing to stoop to such low levels." Ariesian shoved back from his desk and the astrolabe tilted and spun at a dizzying speed. "Lord Calfair will pay for his crimes against Narissa."

Solarius leapt off the sofa after him. "Where are you going?"

"To speak with Queen Elowyn."

Shit. Why hadn't he thought of that?

The answer came quickly enough. Because he'd rather pummel Calfair until he was nothing more than a bloody, pulpy mess than allow him to spend the rest of his days in a dungeon.

As for Solarius's mother, whatever secret she was keeping must be detrimental. For years he'd been suspicious of her behavior, of the way she toyed with the lives of those around her, including her own children, as though they were the pieces of a game she wanted to win. She'd always been haughty, lacking compassion and affection, always caring more about herself. Her image. Her reputation. Her rank among Aeremere's five noble houses.

Sure, Narissa might be alone now, but her parents *loved* her.

Solarius, on the other hand, was never wanted. He wasn't the first-born, so he eclipsed his mother's attention. He wasn't a female, so she held no qualms about his personal life and refused to take an interest in any of his affairs. He was simply cast aside. Ignored. Forgotten.

Trysta never loved him.

She never loved any of them.

CHAPTER TWENTY-EIGHT

*E*ven in the winter, the city of Celestine was still magical. The frost-covered shops glittered like gemstones despite the fact that the sun was hidden behind a veil of thick, gray clouds. Fountains flowing with shimmery silver water that reminded Narissa of liquid starlight lined the main square. The rooftops were all made of glass, crystals like rainbow moonstone, selenite, and blue sunstone decorated many of the storefronts. She stayed along the main path with Sarelle, and they passed by an adorable bakery called Moonbeams—the front display showcased dozens of sweet treats—anything from tarts and pies to cakes and candies. Whereas strolling through Azurvend was like taking a trip to the bottom of the ocean, Celestine was like walking among the stars.

It was positively ethereal.

"Oh!" Sarelle tugged her toward an ornately carved door depicting the Faerie Star—a dazzling star with eight points. "This is it. Narissa, welcome to Divine Stars, my favorite shop in all of Celestine."

Narissa stumbled inside behind Sarelle as the bell above the door jingled softly, announcing their arrival.

Divine Stars was magnificent. There were racks upon racks of gowns and dresses in varying shades of the sky, anything from twilight to midnight. Dusky silver, sapphire blue, deepest amethyst, and pitch black. They were exquisite in detail, many of them embellished with pearls, diamonds, and other celestial-looking gemstones. Along the far wall were shelves fully stocked with bolts of delicate fabric, and there were display cases lined with velvet featuring a dizzying assortment of jewels—rings, bracelets, necklaces, hair clips—all of them looked to be crafted from the stars. Ribbons of lace and satin hung over the top of a glossy hardwood drawer brimming with gloves and…stockings.

Sarelle rummaged through the selection of gowns, pulling one from the rack. "I think you would look stunning in this one."

She hoisted it up and Narissa's jaw dropped. "It's…breathtaking."

"I know. *And* it's the only gold one of the lot." Sarelle shimmied a little, tempting her with the decadent gown. "I feel like it's a sign. Besides, gold will look fabulous against your sun-kissed skin."

"Fine, you've convinced me." Narissa gave her a playful roll of the eyes. "Though I must admit, I thought it would take much longer for me to find something to wear."

"Nonsense." Sarelle handed the gold gown to the shopkeeper and turned back toward the arrangement of dresses. "I have an excellent sense of style. And I know I said I needed new gloves, but in truth I wanted to find a new gown for myself as well. The Yuletide Ball is one of my favorite events of the year, and it's the first time I've been able to choose something for myself, instead of wearing whatever hideous garment my mother forces upon me."

The mention of Lady Trysta Starstorm sent a prickle of unease trekking down Narissa's spine. She was well aware of the Starstorm siblings' disdain toward their mother, and in truth, the Celestine matriarch had always seemed slightly off-putting and more than a little selfish to Narissa as well. There was something about her manner, the way cruel ambition seemed to glint in her eyes, like there was a film of deception coating her aura. Not to mention those annoying bracelets she always wore that jingled in the most obnoxious way.

"Will your mother be in attendance tonight?" Narissa asked, slowly making her way over to the drawer full of elegant, if not slightly scandalous, stockings.

"Most likely." Sarelle shrugged then and her midnight hair shimmered, a sheen of stardust coasting the luxurious strands. She fiddled with the long, gossamer sleeves of a gown. "She's not been home as of late. At least not since Creslyn and Drake's arrival from Brackroth. It seems the palace is a more important place to be at the moment."

Somehow, Narissa didn't find that at all surprising. Still, curiosity got the best of her. "And what of Prince Aspen? Will he be at the Yuletide Ball tonight?"

Sarelle paled and ducked her head. "I believe so, yes."

"Are things…that is, are you still…" Narissa found it difficult to finish asking. Sarelle was supposed to charm and court Aeramere's prince in order to learn why he wanted to overthrow his mother. But the supposed uprisings to the northwest had been silenced for some time now, and the last time there'd been any show of force was at Novalise and Asher's wedding, nearly three months prior. All of Aeramere had been oddly quiet since then, and Narissa secretly hoped all the dangers and talks of an impending war were finally over.

"I rarely see him. Ever since his impressive shape-shifting display at Novalise's wedding, he seldom leaves the palace. At least, that's what I assume based upon his lack of public outings. Save for his appearance at your wedding." Sarelle pulled a black silk gown from the rack, then added four more to the growing pile in her arms. "I've tried to make myself available at events where he is due to attend, but he always fails to show."

Narissa helped her carry the dresses to one of the fitting rooms at the back of the shop. "Do you like him?"

"I don't even know him." A pinched sigh escaped her, and she stole a glance around the small room to ensure there were no lingering patrons, no listening ears. Her voice dropped to a hollow whisper. "I just feel like this whole farce, or lack of one, will be a total disaster. And then I'll have let Ariesian, and all of my siblings, down. I do not wish to be a disappointment."

"Sarelle." Narissa hung the dresses on the hook in the fitting room before facing her friend. "You are *never* a disappointment. It is entirely out of your control if the prince is not around, you can only do so much. And you should not have to go out of your way to pursue him."

Sarelle opened her mouth to object, but Narissa held up one hand.

"I know." She drew the word out, then cupped Sarelle's cheek. "I understand the why. But you should not waste your time attempting to court a prince you want nothing to do with, especially not under false pretenses, when there are so many other lords who would fall at your feet if you accepted their arm."

"Do you really think so?" Sarelle asked, her sapphire eyes brimming with hope.

"Of course not." Narissa grinned. "I *know* so."

Sarelle laughed and sprinkles of stardust tumbled around them like faerie dust.

"Now, go try on these dresses for the Yuletide Ball." Narissa winked. "I have to go find a pair of stockings."

"Make sure they'd gold!" Sarelle cried as she closed the door to the fitting room.

Gold stockings.

Narissa shook her head but made her way toward the front of the shop to the massive drawer displaying dozens of gloves and stockings. The options were seemingly endless. She'd never seen so many different lengths, different colors, and different details. Lace with pearls. Silk with diamonds. Each set more fine than the last. Perusing through the extensive selection, Narissa's breath caught when she found a pair in gold.

The material was sheer, and would do absolutely nothing to keep her warm, but the back seams were dotted with aquamarines and the bands were intricate lace, woven with threads of pale turquoise.

Set on her purchase, Narissa scooped them up when the bell above the shop door jangled, and Lady Trysta Starstorm walked inside.

Narissa ducked behind the tall drawer of stockings and gloves. She wasn't exactly sure why she was hiding. Perhaps it had something to do with the fact that she and Sarelle were just discussing her mother.

Or maybe it was because the Starstorm matriarch was slightly terrifying.

She marched into the shop with a commanding air, decked in an excess of violet silk and silver beads. Her long white hair was carefully plaited and elaborate pins depicting stars pierced the coiffed braid. Heavy kohl lined her lids, though it did little to mask the deepening lines fanning out from her eyes. Her gaze was keen, her lips were pursed yet smug, and with each step, those atrocious bangles she wore clanked together noisily.

Narissa remained in her crouched position, carefully turning over the stockings in her hand, the perfect excuse would be to claim she dropped them if she were found out. But for now, the spot behind the oversized drawer was perfect for listening.

Eavesdropping, as a matter of fact.

"I just do not understand why it is so difficult," Lady Trysta muttered, her crackly voice grating like a shard of glass against rough stone. "All I want is a small vial of moonshade, how hard can that possibly be?"

Narissa frowned.

A vial of moonshade was an odd request. And to be fair, it was not easily harvested. The last time Narissa had seen it on any shelves was some years ago in Galefell, and even then, it was a rather elusive element. She couldn't even begin to imagine why Lady Trysta might need it, or what possible use for it she could have. On its own, moonshade was unremarkable. Yet mixed with the proper ingredients, and imbued onto tools or ornaments, it could become something of great power with the ability to turn the mundane into the extraordinary. Like the creation of glamour.

Lady Trysta's impudent tone drew Narissa from her thoughts, and she peeked around the drawer.

"Honestly, Livian," she scoffed loudly. "Hespira was far more adept at her position than you."

Hespira.

She was the one who came into the coffee shop with Lady Aria. As though she'd been drowned by a rogue wave, recollection slammed into Narissa. She remembered why Lady Aria's lady's maid looked so familiar—Hespira had come to Narissa a few years prior asking for honeysting. It wasn't in her interest to ask why a servant would have a need for honeysting, because the plant was often used to rid a home of pests. But honeysting also emitted a sweet-smelling lethal toxin, one that could be crafted into a poison, and if Hespira was employed by House Celestine all those years ago, then...

Narissa clamped one hand over her mouth, silencing her gasp. She twisted the stockings in her hand, wrinkling the fine fabric, as Lady Trysta swept from the shop with her cowering maid in tow.

Moonshade could create a glamour.

Honeysting could be used as a poison.

And the cause of death for Lord Zenos Starstorm, Solarius's father, remained unknown.

Oh no.

Oh no.

Narissa had no idea how she would prove it, but she was fairly certain Lord Zenos had been poisoned. By his wife.

CHAPTER TWENTY-NINE

Solarius took it upon himself to unpack and organize most of Narissa's belongings.

The whole of her wardrobe, along with quite literally everything else she owned, had been delivered while she was out shopping in Celestine with Sarelle. Solarius had to admit, he was impressed with the speed at which Lord Marintide accomplished getting it all packed up and delivered for her, but then again, being a fae had its perks. Unfortunately, Solarius now found himself overwhelmed with dozens of underthings. Who knew a female even owned that many nightgowns?

There were garters, panties, stockings, nighties—a damn plethora of lace, silk, satin, and other soft fabrics he was too intimidated to touch. He didn't even know where to put all of it, or if he'd set aside enough space. He might need to devote an entire dresser to Narissa's undergarments.

But Solarius had chosen his bedroom when he was younger for specific reasons. The first being, it was at the back of House Celestine and had a sweeping view of Moonfall Peaks, and in the distance he could see the Arcasian Sea. The second was for the adjoining sitting room. Granted, he had never actually used it for anything other than lounging or drinking the night away with his brothers, but now it would prove to be more beneficial than not.

The sitting room would double as Narissa's own personal space. An area where she could dry her herbs and flowers, brew her potions and tonics, and generally escape whenever she felt the need. Tovian and Kjeld helped him arrange most of her supplies. Together they sorted the numerous mortars and pestles, attempted to identify and group together her plants, and shelve her books and crystals. The only thing still needed was a place for her small, worn cauldron. He made a mental note to have a table especially crafted for her in mind, as well as to find her another, larger cauldron.

Lord Marintide had delivered the harp himself, warning Solarius that it was one of her most prized possessions and to take great care. Naturally, Solarius kept the harp in the bedroom. He had it placed near the balcony, overlooking the mountains and the sea, and already he could imagine the way the eastern morning light would illuminate her when she played. There was something oddly sensual about the way her fingers moved over the harp strings, the delicate strums and plucks, the way her eyes fluttered closed with each crescendo of enchanting music. It was a selfish decision, but he didn't care.

He wanted to be the only one to see her so vulnerable.

Maybe eventually they would get a new harp for another area of the house, depending upon if they stayed at House Celestine or built their own. But for now, he would keep her all to himself.

Unless she wanted to play for others, in which case he wouldn't stand in her way, but he would carve out the eyes of any male whose gaze lingered a little too long.

Solarius continued to sort through all the provocative underthings strewn across his bed when the door burst open, and Narissa swept into the room in a flurry of satin.

She drew up short and her eyes widened when she caught sight of her unmentionables covering the velvet comforter.

"Sol." Her gaze flicked from him to her things, then back to him, and she clutched the bag in her hands.

He grinned and lifted a pair of what he could only assume were panties, given their shape. The lack of material was interesting, but it was the string of pearls that had his cock thickening. The things he would do if he ever caught her in those…

"How come I've never seen you wear this?" he asked, arching one brow in mock amusement.

A rosy flush highlighted her cheeks, but she rolled her eyes to the glass ceiling, then reached over and snatched them from his grasp.

"Because *these*," she whispered, running two fingers along the glistening pearls, "are only for *very* special occasions."

He matched her, leaning closer and planting his hands firmly on the mattress. "Does the Yuletide Ball count?"

"I…" Her pretty full mouth fell open, and he seized the opportunity to distract her further.

Solarius reached for the bag filled with pale purple tissue paper. "Show me what you bought, Rissa love. More stockings? Perhaps another pair of pearl panties?"

She swatted his hand away from the goods. "I'll only show you after you tell me what's going on here. What is all this?"

Narissa gestured around the room, waving one hand wildly through the air.

"Allow me to show you." Solarius took her by the hand and linked their fingers together. He showed her the closet first, where all her gowns, capes, and shoes fit so tidily next to his own attire. "Don't mind the bed, that's still a work in progress, though I do hope you'll continue to share it with me."

He led her to the sitting room, showing off how most of her herbal necessities were somewhat organized. He gestured toward the window where bundles of dried flowers were laid on the sill, waiting to be hung. "You can change anything you like if it doesn't suit. I'm going to have a table made for you since we don't have anywhere to put your cauldron. And if you want a new one of those, I'll find you one. Just say the word."

Solarius nodded toward the main bedchamber. "And I put your harp by the balcony window."

"You did all this…" Her voice caught. "For me?"

"Well, the bed sharing thing is mostly for me." He gave her hand a squeeze and winked. "But, yes."

Her expression shifted then, and he watched as uncertainty clouded her pretty features, waiting to see if he had overstepped his bounds. The bag she carried dropped at her feet. She sniffled and her eyes took on a familiar sheen as a single tear rolled down her cheek.

The bond shivered with emotions.

Shit.

That was not the reaction he was expecting.

"Don't cry, Rissa love." He pulled her close, catching the small pearl with one hand before it could hit the ground. She burrowed her face in his chest, and he hated the way her body trembled in his arms. "Please, don't cry."

Wrapping one arm around her waist, he reached across the dresser and lifted the lid of a black jar and dropped the pearl inside. It tinkled softly in the round jar.

She peeked over from where she used his shirt to dry her eyes. "You...you collect the pearls."

It was more a statement of fact as opposed to a question, and Solarius suddenly found himself painfully uncomfortable. He kept his arm locked around her, rubbing one hand along the back of his neck, uncertain of how she would respond to the truth. He eased back only slightly, just enough to gauge her reaction, to see her face when he explained himself.

"All the ones that are because of me." Solarius nodded solemnly. "Yes."

"Why?"

"I thought to eventually make them into a necklace for you. Not to remind you of all the times I made you cry," he added quickly when a frown creased her brow, "but so that you know I will try my damnedest to never make you cry again."

Narissa was too quiet. She gnawed on her bottom lip, considering his words. The bond between them continued to thrum, gentle swells of the sea coupled with the radiance of the moon. Their magic blended and soared, but she remained silent.

Solarius hated to see her like this—timid and melancholy—instead of the passionate, if somewhat mouthy, siren he knew and loved.

Loved.

Fuck. Did he love her? Was that why he constantly sought to be near her, why he provoked her just to earn her attention, why he couldn't manage a single thought that didn't somehow involve her encompassing his every waking second? But she'd never said as much to him. Granted, she might have mentioned loving him once, but that was before. Before he fucked up. Before Calfair. There was a chance she hadn't forgiven him. Maybe her feelings were more forced acceptance of their current circumstance. Maybe she didn't love him at all.

He swallowed hard, blocking his mind from their bond immediately.

Narissa tilted her head, her wavy blonde hair spilling over one shoulder. "Sol? Are you alright?"

"Fine." The word croaked out of him, and he cleared his throat. He was being irrational, and told himself it didn't matter if she still loved him or not. Not all matches in Aeramere were tales of happily ever afters. While marriages were often required, love was never guaranteed. Again, he swallowed around the knot of tension. "Completely fine."

"Are you quite certain?" She placed the back of her hand against his forehead, then his cheek, checking his temperature. Her touch set his skin aflame, but his lungs hollowed out. Her scent consumed him. Owned him. She had to know he was positively burning, and it was all her fault. "You look rather unwell all of a sudden. As though you might be sick."

He needed to change the subject and fast, before he bolted from the room and abandoned Narissa completely. He would sort out his feelings for her later, preferably when she wasn't standing so close, when the nearness of her didn't devour him whole.

Solarius slid two fingers under her chin and gave her his most devastating smile. "Has anyone ever told you that you're exceptional in the art of flattery?"

A tiny scowl pinched the smooth skin of her brow.

"Forgive me for being concerned for your health." She suffered him a sigh and shoved out of his arms. "Trust I will be sure not to make such a mistake again."

Solarius smirked.

There she is.

He rather liked her that way. Quick-tempered. Passionate. A little bit volatile.

"Come." He grabbed her hand, tugging her toward the harp. "Play me a song, Rissa love."

"A song," she repeated, crossing her arms.

Solarius couldn't help it, his gaze instantly dipped to the full swell of her breasts. She still wore Sarelle's borrowed gown, and he immensely enjoyed the fact that it was a smidge too small. Narissa's ample bosom was on full display, and he swore if she took a deep breath, there was a chance the velvet would simply rip apart at the seams. In fact, he wouldn't mind lending the fabric a hand, if it meant he got to see his wife in all of her nude glory.

But first, he wanted her sitting at that harp, because his cock was aching and he'd fantasized about doing the most deliciously wicked things to her while she played.

"Fine," she muttered, completely oblivious to his blatant arousal. "Which one?"

She seated herself on the leather chair by the balcony and adjusted her skirts. Because they were more snug than usual, she shimmied a bit, hiking the hem to her knees, revealing the beautiful golden skin of her calves.

"Whichever is your favorite," he murmured.

Her eyes closed for the briefest of moments. When she opened them again, there was a distance in the swirls of frosty green. She angled the harp toward her, balancing it on her shoulder, and then she started to play.

Solarius watched, mesmerized as her fingers moved over the strings, as a familiar yet fragile melody filled the air between them. It was hypnotic really, how each strum, each chord, each breath she took elicited the most primal of urges inside him. Humming the tune, he rolled his neck as he casually strolled toward her. She tracked his movements, her lashes fluttering back as he knelt before her and wedged himself comfortably between the solid wood and her inner thigh.

She scowled at him and those ocean-like eyes caught on fire.

He summoned his magic then, the gentlest of lunarstorms, crafting and honing a shard of moonlight in his hands until it resembled a blade.

Narissa faltered, her fingers fumbling against the strings. "What are you doing?"

"Keep playing."

With slow, careful movements, he used the sharp edge of the blade to slice open the front of her gown. The velvet and lace ripped with ease so her breasts tumbled free, baring her to him. Her nipples peaked, practically begging for his touch, for the swipe of his tongue. The fabric slid down her arms, peeling open to reveal her toned stomach, and that sparkly little gem piercing her navel.

"I told you I was abstaining from bedroom activities," she hissed, but the erratic beating of her heart through the bond told him she wasn't nearly as pissed as she let on.

"And so you are." Solarius cupped both of her breasts, his thumbs swiping lazily back and forth across her sensitive flesh. He enjoyed the way she squirmed on the chair, how she arched toward him without thought. "You're playing the harp, and I'm doing this."

One hand trailed down to her hip, holding her in place, while the other snaked beneath the layers of her dress. His fingers inched along her thigh, slow. Cautious. Until they discovered her warm and wet, and lacking any kind of lacy barrier. His cock swelled, scraping against the seam of his pants. He wanted to show her, so she could see the effect she had on him. But her gaze was focused on his face, wild and aware, and for a moment, he worried he may have pushed her too far. But then he felt it. The faintest give of her leg as it fell open wider, granting him access.

Solarius slid one finger down her slick folds and Narissa gasped.

Her head fell back, and she struck a jarring chord. The dissonant sound grated against his ears, but he didn't care.

All he cared about was her. All he wanted was her.

He pushed one finger deep into her core, then added another. In and out, he kept his movements methodical, setting a leisurely pace. His other hand skated up her waist, brushing along the side of her breast. The most delightful whimper escaped her, carrying a whisper of his name on her lips.

"Do you like that, Rissa love?"

"Yes," she whispered, her chest heaving.

Narissa tried to keep plucking at the strings, but her impatience clawed down the bond. She rolled her hips, quietly urging him to increase his pace. Each time he curled his fingers, she stumbled over another chord.

"More," she begged.

"Play faster," he countered with a smirk, and the pale green of her gaze burned hot.

"Fine," she snapped.

Solarius should've known her temper would get the best of her, he should have taken more care in riling her up. Because he never saw her next move coming.

Narissa lifted her leg, so the velvet of her gown pooled at her waist, revealing his fingers deep inside of her. He bit back a groan, knowing he could absolutely sneak another finger in and she'd take it with no problem. But she surprised him further by propping her foot up, the thin heel of her shoe poking him squarely in the chest. Then she played, her fingers moving so swiftly over the strings of the harp that he could barely track them.

Stars above, she was wicked.

But a promise was a promise.

He pumped his fingers into her, following the hasty rhythm she set. She clenched around him, her body seizing as he drove her closer to the edge. The vicious point of her heel dug into him, but he didn't mind the pain, in fact, he reveled in it. It was fascinating, watching her writhe and grind against him, being witness to her undoing. Power hummed between them and when he worked her clit with his thumb, her leg spasmed, and she screamed his name. The blistering melody crescendoed, and Narissa vibrated in the wake of her orgasm, collapsing against the chair as the base of the harp dropped soundly against the floor.

Her skin flushed the pretty, rosy hue he loved so much, and he swore he'd never seen anything more desirable in his life. She was sprawled against the chair, legs spread, breasts out, and all of it was for him. Messy golden waves framed her face, and if he could ingrain this moment in his mind, he would. He let his eyes slowly drink in every inch of her, committing the finest detail of her beauty to his memory.

Solarius pressed a kiss to the inside of her thigh, then slowly stood.

"Don't worry, you don't have to participate in any bedroom activities." He pulled the hem of her gown so it covered her legs, then he adjusted his pulsing shaft. When her lust-filled gaze flicked down to where he strained for her against his pants, he rubbed his shaft a few times just to tease her. To remind her of what she would be missing. "But remember, Rissa love. The Yuletide Ball is *outside* of the bedroom."

Narissa's mouth fell open in shock and Solarius laughed, tugging off his shirt as he stalked toward the connected bathing suite. The sear of her gaze burned into his back.

CHAPTER THIRTY

Narissa stood on the balcony overlooking the ballroom of House Celestine, where a sea of nobles mingled and twirled, as conversations were drowned over the delightful thread of music floating through the air.

She gripped the railing with both hands, silently chastising herself for not entering the room on Solarius's arm. He said he would wait for her to finish dressing and preparing for the ball, but she'd sent him away, claiming it would take her far longer to get ready than him. In truth, she'd needed that precious extra time to recover after what he did to her while she played her harp. It had been more than his touch that left her reeling, the way he simply looked at her, like he wanted to *devour* her. She wanted him to lift her into his arms, carry her to the bed, and drive himself into her until he occupied every facet of her soul.

Instead, he'd stood up, then laughed and held her to her word.

No bedroom activities.

Narissa cursed herself for making such a foolish claim, clenching her thighs together as she considered all the ways he might make her pay for such a declaration. If he did indeed attempt to try something during the ball, then she thought it was only fair she take him by surprise as well. She opted to wear the pearl panties along with the new gold stockings she purchased for him. And she couldn't wait to see his face when he made that startling little discovery.

Still, she wished she didn't have to enter the ballroom by herself. Not that anyone would notice her, anyway. To make matters worse, Solarius had so thoroughly distracted her, that she'd forgotten to tell him about her theory regarding his mother. Granted, it was all speculation, but the timing of Hespira being in Lady Trysta's employ around the same time as Lord Zenos's death was entirely too coincidental.

Her gaze drifted past the brilliant blue winterblooms crawling up the pillars to where snowflakes danced along the ceiling in an enchanting display of magic. Rolling her shoulders back, she pushed away from the balcony and headed toward the spiral staircase.

"Are you ready?" Sarelle appeared beside her, looking stunning in a gown so deep of blue it matched her sapphire eyes perfectly. It was fitted at the waist, then ballooned out in heavy layers of shimmering satin. The bodice was encrusted with diamonds and sheer, gauze-like sleeves draped from her shoulders. There was the smallest smudge of stardust on her left cheek.

Narissa grinned and linked their arms together. "As I'll ever be."

They descended the staircase together, and for the first time in her life, Narissa became the center of attention. Every pair of eyes in the ballroom below snagged upon them, but when ones resembling molten silver met hers, she couldn't look away. She held Solarius's gaze, watching as he maneuvered his way through the ballroom without a care of who he shoved or interrupted, just to greet her at the bottom of the stairs.

"Chin up. Shoulders back." Sarelle gently patted her hand.

Narissa obeyed, whispering back, "Everyone is staring at us."

"Correction," she countered smoothly. "They see me all the time. Everyone is staring at *you.*"

It took every effort imaginable not to rub her lips together or appear nervous, but there was no escaping the discomfort needling its way along her spine. Narissa wasn't entirely sure she cared for the attention, after all. Passing by unnoticed was much easier and far less stressful. Right now, she had to make sure she didn't trip on the length of her gown or slip and tumble down the glittering steps.

"I was right, you know," Sarelle murmured as they neared the final set of stairs.

Narissa swallowed. It was difficult to find her voice with Solarius staring at her like she hung the very moon he controlled, and the word croaked out of her. "About?"

"That dress." Sarelle took her hand and passed her off to her waiting husband. "It's perfect for you."

Sarelle was more than right about the choice, the gold and turquoise stood out among the hues of navy, silver, purple, and black. Gold lace hugged her curves, dipping low in the center past her navel. Pale teal chiffon sleeves draped down her arms, and more of the gauzy fabric cinched her waist, flowing around her to the ground where the hem was dipped in a burnished gold. Yellow diamonds and beads of turquoise embellished the snug bodice, tumbling from her hips like dazzling, explosive starbursts. The gown was a statement. A choice. And Narissa owned it.

But her gratitude died on the tip of her tongue when Solarius grasped her hand and brought it to his mouth. He kissed one of her knuckles, his eyes trained entirely on her face. Narissa's heart flipped when he dragged her wrist across his mouth, his teeth scraping lightly against the tender flesh. She had no idea the inside of her wrist could be so sensitive, nor did she realize it would send a flood of heat rushing to her core.

"My lady." Solarius bowed deeply.

She dipped into an elegant curtsy. "My lord."

"Will my mesmerizing wife do me the honor of a dance?"

"If I must." But she winked and the whole of his face lit up in wonder as the bond between them flared bright.

Solarius led her around the dance floor in a series of slow, sensual movements. Lazy dips and sultry twirls. His hands skimmed all over her, sliding up her waist, grazing the side of her breast, capturing the small of her back, then venturing lower still. In each other's arms, they were fluid, an extension of one another. Together, they were a heady mixture of grace and confidence. They were effortless. A cadence of waves and moonlight. Narissa had never felt more alive than she did when Solarius danced with her.

The only thing that would make it perfect would be if the rest of the world fell away.

"Sol," she whispered below the undercurrent of entrancing music. "Everyone is staring."

"As they should." He dipped her low and gripped her thigh in a way that felt scandalously intimate. "You are a sight to behold, Narissa."

"I think I preferred it when I was able to move without notice."

His brow arched as he righted her. "Is that right?"

She nodded once, and he laced their fingers together.

"Then come with me."

She let Solarius take her by the hand as he hauled her out of the ballroom, the murmurs and whispers of partygoers and onlookers fading into a distant, droll hum. They darted through corridors of stained glass where Faerie Stars floated overhead, stopping only to catch their breath and steal impassioned kisses. With a fistful of fabric in one hand, Narissa hoisted the hem of her gown, keeping her other hand firmly locked in Solarius's hold as they raced across a frozen courtyard. This time, he dragged her beneath a tree with long, weepy limbs, pressing her back into its trunk. Its rough bark snagged and ripped at the fabric, but she no longer cared, because Solarius fused his mouth to hers. He captured the side of her face with both hands and their tongues tangled as he angled her, deepening the kiss. Teeth nipped and scraped, and she clutched at his jacket, clinging to him like she needed him more than the air he continued to steal from her lungs.

Narissa rocked her hips forward, desperate for some kind of friction, anything to ease the budding need building between her thighs. She swiveled her hips and the pearls shifted, rubbing her, making her slick and wet with need.

Solarius broke their kiss on a groan. "Not here."

The silver of his eyes was hot, scolding as they lingered on her lips.

Their breath misted before them, and the cold slowly began to seep into her bones.

Again, he grabbed her hand, guiding her through a maze of celestial halls until they rushed out one of the back entrances of House Celestine into a moonlit garden. It was a maze of smooth stone paths, shimmering fountains, arches of winter roses, and shapely evergreens. The gardens of House Celestine were lovely during the day and ethereal at night, for nearly every leaf and petal looked as though it had been kissed by stardust, and perhaps Narissa would have enjoyed it more were it not the fact that she could no longer feel her nose.

"It's freezing!" she shrieked, as they stumbled toward the expansive gardens.

Solarius pulled her against him, running his hands up and down her arms in an effort to warm her. An emotion banked deep in his gaze, one she didn't recognize, highlighted by a wash of moonlight and shadow. But then the corner of his mouth lifted into a careless smirk and her knees weakened as she softened in his arms.

Narissa's feet ached from running. The shoes she wore pinched her toes and with each ragged breath, a twinge pierced her lungs. She was quite sure her brand new gown was ripped in three places, as there was a distinct draft cooling the back of her thighs. But sweet shores, she was delirious, wild with obsession for this male who would willingly flee a ballroom with her and race through a house without a second thought.

His hand slid around the back of her neck and his mouth feathered kisses up her jaw to the lobe of her ear. His warm tongue flicked over the earring she wore, and a scrape of a whisper coasted across her cheek. There was a rumble in his chest and his rough voice sent heat pooling between her legs.

"Run."

Narissa faltered, pulling back to look up at him. A frown marred her brow. "What?"

"Run, Rissa." He dragged the pads of his fingers along the column of her neck, then further to the valley of her breasts. "If I catch you, you're mine."

She scoffed, folding her arms over her chest. "I'm already yours. We're married, remember?"

He leaned forward, pressing his forehead to hers, his nose lightly brushing against her own.

"You misunderstand me, Rissa love. I intend to make you mine in *every* way. Body. Mind. Soul. All of it. All of you." His lips met the corner of her mouth, the warmth of his breath fanning across her lips as he spoke. "That's what you want, is it not? To have me mark you? Brand you? Ruin you?"

Shivers wrecked her then, and it had nothing to do with the permeating cold. His questions thrummed down the bond, seeking the answers in her mind. In her heart. There was a nudge, a press of magic, of connection, and the rough desire in his voice made it impossible to deny him. To refuse him. Because of course that was what she wanted, it was what she had always wanted.

Him.

Solarius.

Always him.

But her defiance, her inexplicable urge to taunt him, reared its ugly head. "Are you serious?"

He flashed a wicked, ravenous grin. "On my mark."

"Solarius." She gave him her most stern voice, but her heart slammed against the tight wall of her chest, and her blood pumped with anticipation.

"Three." He started his countdown.

"Sol."

"Two."

Damn it.

Narissa hiked up her long skirts and took off running. She sprinted into the maze of flowers and manicured shrubs, panting as she raced past a gurgling fountain. Slivers of moonlight illuminated half of the path she chose, while the rest of it was doused in the shadows of nightfall. Behind her, she could hear the swift thuds of Solarius's boots against the solid ground, and she dared a chance look over one shoulder.

He was a few paces back, and the glint in his eyes made him look almost feral.

Her heels skidded across the icy stone, and she rounded a corner, grasping a hedgerow to keep from losing her balance.

"This isn't fair!" she shouted.

"How do you figure?"

Breaking tides, it sounded like he was *right* behind her.

"Because!" Her breaths came in aching pains as she dashed beneath an archway where winter roses and vines tumbled like a waterfall. "The bond will lead you right to me!"

"Then run faster." Solarius's voice skated past her ear.

A phantom hand grazed her waist, and she shrieked.

Narissa cut a corner, looked back once more to see if she lost him, then turned and slammed directly into his chest.

"Got you!" He snatched her by the waist and lifted her then, spinning her in a circle, and she threw her arms around his neck as laughter bubbled out of her.

Solarius went eerily still, lowering her to the ground in such a manner that she slid down his front with painstaking slowness. His inhales and exhales met hers, breath for breath. He kept his hands on her waist, the grip almost punishing and filled with tension. Steam rose from their heated skin and he leaned forward, resting his forehead against hers, closing his eyes.

"What is it?" Narissa asked, suddenly concerned by the change in his behavior. "What's wrong?"

His eyes flicked open, and in those deep pools of silver, Narissa swore she caught a glimmer of emotion. The sort that was filled with longing, desire, and something more permanent. A promise not yet kept.

"You laughed." The words were rough like gravel. Uneven. Unsteady. "Stars above, Rissa. I've missed that sound."

Narissa didn't have time to respond or process what Solarius said, because he captured the back of her neck and hauled her against him for a searing kiss.

CHAPTER THIRTY-ONE

The second the sound of Narissa's laugh rang out, Solarius knew he was lost to her. It was exactly as he remembered— a lush and sultry siren's call—and he hated that he almost forgot it. So long, he'd waited *so long* for her to laugh for him, and now that she finally had, he couldn't get enough of her. He wanted all of her. All of her laughs, all of her snarky comments, all of her time. Even when she was pissed off at him, even when she hated him, he wanted the entirety of her heart.

Her mouth was hot against his, a delicious inferno that tasted of sweetened mint and berries. Their tongues clashed, and he enjoyed the scrape of her nails against the back of his neck as she desperately tried to deepen the kiss. To fuse them together. But the gardens were frigid and despite the heat radiating off their bodies, it was only a matter of time before the winter temperatures would sink into their bones and freeze them from the inside out.

Solarius smoothed his hands down the back of her ruined dress and cupped her bottom. In one swift movement, he hoisted her up, anchoring her to him. Narissa wrapped her legs around his waist, her mouth roving over his, her hands tearing at his jacket and shirt. Each touch sent a bolt of energy through him. His blood stirred. His pulse hammered. His cock ached. He carried her through the garden and away from the house as snow started to tumble lightly from the sky, ready to show her the one place he knew she would love.

"Hold your breath," he murmured against her mouth.

She didn't question.

She didn't argue.

But the moment her lungs expanded, he locked his arm around her back, cradled the back of her head with one hand, and jumped.

The warm springs of the faerie pool engulfed them. Beneath the water, silence reigned. The world above was muted and there was only a gentle rushing sound, two synchronous heartbeats, and the soft hum of magic. Shock pulsed through the bond, followed by absolute delight, and their legs tangled as they kicked toward the surface.

Narissa gasped when they crashed through, and the second Solarius stole a gulp of air, her mouth was on his again. Lips sluiced over one another, and she dragged her teeth across his own, sucking and nipping. Her slender fingers raked through his wet hair, his hands molded against her curves, committing their shape to memory. The faerie pool was too deep to stand and each time they clashed in a burst of fervent kisses, they sank below the water's surface once more. Underwater, Narissa was a siren. The haze of moonlight splintered through the waves, casting her in an ethereal glow. Her hair rippled around her like ribbons of golden silk. The gown she wore floated around her, a harmony to the melody of her soul.

Fuck it.

If he drowned kissing her, then so be it.

But lucky for him, there was a submerged ledge of stone near the pool's edge. The perfect spot to ruin her like she so desperately wanted.

Solarius cut through the dark blue water where flecks of silver sparkled like starlight. His knee found the ledge first and he winced, but the pain was fleeting, because then Narissa was straddling his lap, and tearing at his shirt like she was starving for him.

He yanked off his formal jacket, tossing the sodden fabric onto the mossy shore behind him. Narissa's fingers made quick work of his button-down shirt, then she was clawing it off him, raking those finely manicured nails over his chest to his lower abdomen. His blood heated and she rolled her hips, rocking herself against his hard shaft, creating the most damning sort of friction. She linked her arms around his neck, her warm lips pressing kiss after kiss along his jaw until she reached his ear.

"I'm wearing the new stockings I bought for you." Her words sent a bolt of desire straight through him, and he grabbed handfuls of her wet gown, peeling it away from her body.

He wanted to *see* those stockings, but the shimmering water was so dark, it was impossible.

She nipped the lobe of his ear and whispered, "And perhaps a pair of pearls."

Damn the stars, she was too much. Narissa was too much.

"I want to see every inch of you." Solarius tugged the sodden fabric over her head, popping off beads and diamonds, then threw it into a heap behind them. "I want to see what's mine."

The wavelike tattoos on the tips of her ears glowed for him, and power thrummed beneath his fingertips as he traced the ones along her spine. She was radiant, a beauty of the night as tiny snowflakes danced through the sky above them. Beads of inky, starlit water slid from her shoulders to the tops of her breasts. Wet hair tumbled around her in wild waves, and he loved the way her damp lashes framed her ocean eyes. He loved the way she looked at him like he was all she ever wanted, and that ran deeper than his desire for anything else in this life.

More than anything, Solarius wanted Narissa to love him.

"Narissa, I—" he began, but she silenced him by placing a finger against his lips.

"Shh." The corner of her mouth curved, and she reached below the water. "Let me show you."

Her hands expertly undid his pants, and when his cock sprang free, she stroked his length in long, fluid movements.

"Rissa," he groaned, and then she was sinking below the water's surface, disappearing completely.

His brows pinched together, but then he felt it, the distinctive glide of her tongue over his length as she took him fully into her mouth. His head tilted back, and he rolled his eyes to the pitch of night. But there was a new sensation too—the motion of water. Each time Narissa pulled back, currents swirled around his shaft, surging and squeezing, while her tongue flicked over the tip. She taunted and teased, controlling the springs, clenching his cock in a channel of warm water until she sucked him back into her mouth.

When bubbles tickled the underside of his shaft, he nearly lost his mind.

He fisted one hand and bit his knuckle to keep himself from bucking his hips and fucking that pretty little mouth of hers.

In the distance, a twig snapped.

Alert and ready to protect his wife from prying eyes, Solarius reached for Narissa to pull her out of the water, but she only took him deeper.

"Narissa," he hissed through the bond. *"Someone's here."*

Sultry laughter was his only response while she intensified her magic, so the pressure built low, and his cock throbbed with the need for release.

"There you are." Ariesian's voice cut through the sound of blood rushing in his ears, and it was likely the only time in his life Solarius ever considered murdering his brother. "I was looking all over the ballroom for you."

"Well," Solarius ground the word out as Narissa scraped her nails down his thighs. He flinched. "You found me."

Fucking stars, she'd have to come up for air soon, and if she popped up while Ariesian was here, Solarius would have no choice but to follow through with his previous consideration of bodily harm.

"What are you doing out here?" Ariesian tugged on the sleeves of his coat, adjusting the cufflinks winking at his wrist. He scowled at the falling snow as though it had personally affronted him. "It's positively freezing."

Narissa sucked harder this time, tightening the channel of water she controlled to compress his cock. Solarius's hips jerked, and he spasmed against the divine assault. He dropped one hand in the water and tangled his fingers in Narissa's hair, attempting to pull her off his length, while he propped his other arm on the sloping shore in an effort to appear casual.

"Oh, you know," he drawled. "Just trying not to die."

Ariesian's dark brow quirked.

"Relaxing. Just relaxing." Stars above, Ariesian was a complete stick in the mud. Bet he would never be caught dead in a faerie pool with a female sucking him off underwater.

"Relaxing without your wife?" he countered, his face cut of stony, impassive boredom.

"She'll be coming soon enough," Solarius bit out, and another bubble of warm laughter echoed in his mind.

Fucking minx. She was driving him absolutely mad.

On purpose.

"Right. Well, I suppose our conversation can wait until tomorrow then." Ariesian shoved his hands into his pockets, strolling back toward the gardens when he paused and said, "Oh, and don't keep Narissa underwater much longer, we can't have your wife drowning. Wouldn't be a good look for the family reputation, you know."

The bastard didn't even fucking turn around.

He just kept walking.

And whistling.

Solarius plunged his hands into the faerie pool and hauled Narissa off him. Magic erupted around them, the tantalizing scent of sandalwood, soft flowers, and the tang of sea air. She laughed fully then, loud and rapturous, the sound of it like a song Solarius had known for the whole of his existence.

He raked a hand through his hair, shoving it back from his face. "I thought you were going to drown!"

"I control water, Sol." Again, her laughter sent another pulse of lust through him, but she shrugged as though it was the simplest concept in the world. "Moonlight bends to your will. The tides answer my call."

Her voice was soft, floating against his skin when she said, "Even when I want to suck your cock."

"Fucking stars," he growled, a dark thread of desire twisting through him.

He pulled her so she was straddling him again, and her squeal of surprise turned into a throaty moan as he hooked her panties with his thumb and tugged. Giving the strand of pearls a gentle tug, he rubbed them back and forth between her swollen lips, dragging her close to the edge.

"Sol," she murmured, burying her face in his neck as she bounced, desperate for him to fill her. She threw her arms around him, clinging to him.

"Are you sure?" he teased, barely sliding an inch into her. "It could be considered a bedroom activity."

She rolled her eyes. "Do be quiet. You're ruining the mood."

He chuckled, nudging the pearls aside, lining his head with her slit. "How's that? Better?"

"You're teasing me," she snapped, the tone of her voice slipping from frustrated annoyance to angsty desire.

"You started it," he countered, easing into her a little bit more. "My little underwater cocktease."

Another tight inch, another barely there give of her walls as she clamped around him.

"Yes. Yes, please." Narissa squirmed in an attempt to sink onto him fully, but he kept a firm hold on her hips. "Please."

"You're so lovely when you want something, and you ask so nicely." Solarius leaned forward slightly, letting his forehead rest against hers. Theirs gazes met, locked, and his hands cupped her bottom, spreading her wider. The tips of his fingers toyed with the pearls, stroking her with them.

"Solarius Starstorm Celestine, if you do not—"

"Let me fuck you in the faerie pool, Rissa love."

She inhaled, her nipples scraping against the wall of his chest, and on the next breath she whispered, "Yes."

One good thrust is all it took to be seated fully inside of her, and he was already so wound up that fitting into her so deeply nearly caused him to burst.

"Rissa," he groaned, moving her, guiding her in a painstakingly slow rhythm. Any faster and he'd come before her, and well...that simply wasn't allowed. After all, he was raised to be chivalrous, despite wanting to fuck her until she couldn't walk. So, he let her ride him, gradually building her up, enjoying the way the water churned between them, amplifying every sensation. Each pump inside of her was cruelly snug, like she was made for him, and each steady withdrawal sent him closer to the edge. He used the pearls she wore to tease her further, to apply the perfect amount of pressure to where she throbbed for him.

Narissa arched on a whimper, rolling and bouncing, taking him faster now. She tightened her hold on him, shoving his face into the swell of her breasts, clinging to him. Solarius allowed himself to be smothered, opening his mouth to lave, and suck, and bite. He jerked his hips forward, crushing the pearls between them, and she arched as her climax ripped through her.

His name fell from her lips on a hollow cry. She quivered then, her body convulsing as the swell of release crashed into her. His cock surged, hot and heavy, and he emptied himself inside her. Pump after heavy pump, she took all of him.

She collapsed against him, thoroughly spent, and he drew her in close, smoothing back some of the damp strands of her hair.

"Maybe we could do this again sometime." He twirled the golden ribbons around his finger, liking how they shimmered in the moonlight. Silver and gold. "You know, in the bedroom. As an activity."

Narissa snorted but he felt her smile against his neck.

"I hate you," she mumbled.

And Solarius just grinned, because he knew that was the furthest thing from the truth.

CHAPTER THIRTY-TWO

Solarius took his time strolling through the corridors of House Celestine on his way to Ariesian's office. After last night's interruption, he wasn't too keen on meeting with his eldest brother. Besides, his mind was still wrapped around the best blow job of his life, and it baffled him how Narissa hadn't any need for air. It also left him curious to see what else she was capable of doing with her tidal magic.

His mind drifted to her asleep in his bed, curled up under a moon-dust blanket, her golden waves sprawled across his pillow. He liked the way he caught peeks of sun-kissed skin whenever she rolled from one side to the other. A glimpse of her shoulder. A slip of her thigh. The tiny braided gold band on her toe. Just thinking about the unintentional teases of flesh was enough to make his cock twitch.

Unfortunately, walking into his brother's office blatantly aroused was probably not the best idea.

He needed to clear his mind, to think of anything else other than his wife's perfect body. Something boring or mundane. Something absurd. Like spelling each of his siblings' names backward from youngest to oldest.

N-Y-L-S-E-R-C.

N-A-I-L-E-A-C.

He was about to recite Nyxian's name next when someone called out to him.

"Solarius, darling." His mother's overly saccharine voice caused his blood to curdle. "I'm so glad I found you."

He stilled, shoved his hands into his pockets, and slowly faced her.

Trysta's dull white hair was twisted into a braid, complete with ornate star charms and threads of gold. The silver dress she wore looked more ill-fitting than normal—it was as though she'd taken a heavily beaded curtain and fashioned it into something suitable to wear. There were too many layers and the angles were sharp, jutting from her shoulders and hips like daggers. The skin beneath her observant eyes had taken on a grayish hue, and the lines creasing along her forehead and the corners of her mouth had deepened in recent weeks. Where once they were faint, they now resembled craters. Still, she stalked toward him like she was on a mission, her elaborate bangles jingling on her wrists.

"Mother." Solarius inclined his head in greeting.

She did not return the gesture.

"Walk with me." Trysta hooked her hand in the crook of his arm.

"I'm actually—" Solarius began, but she waved one hand through the air, cutting him off.

Like always.

"Your brother can wait," she sniped, plastering a counterfeit smile to her face, one Solarius had come to recognize over the years. "I wanted to speak with you about your lovely new bride."

At once, Solarius raised his guard. The hairs along the back of his neck stood on end and his jaw popped. Whatever business his mother had with Narissa, he planned on putting a stop to it. Nothing good could come of Trysta taking a vested interest in his wife, his marriage, or his life in general. She'd never made an effort before, and any concern she showed now was a warning.

"What about Narissa?" he asked, his voice cool and measured.

"To start, you two complement each other so well."

Her flattery was wasted on him, and he remained silent. Solarius did not want nor need her blessing. Or her opinion, for that matter.

"I had no idea Narissa was so adept with herbs and such." The heels of her shoes clicked noisily against the glittering tiled floor, and she peered over at him, eyes glinting with intrigue. "It's quite a novel skill to have, don't you think?"

Solarius ground his teeth, his hand in his pocket closing into a tight fist. He wasn't certain what exactly Trysta was getting at, or why she was even bothering to strike up a conversation with him. She never made small talk, and the only time she approached anyone of worth was when she wanted something in return.

"Indeed." He intended to keep his answers curt, to not give her anything.

Trysta prattled on, oblivious to his contempt.

"I fear my age is catching up with me," she continued, though she was hardly what any fae would consider old. "I've been in the market for a lightening cream for my skin, or perhaps something to assist with the tension lines around my eyes. Honestly, bearing and raising children has been no easy feat."

Her words set his teeth on edge. She hardly had a hand in the upbringing of himself and his siblings. She was scarcely around unless it was to patronize one of them or remind them of their disappointments and failures.

"What is it you're after, Mother?" he asked, cutting through her tedious bullshit.

"Do you suppose she could make something for me?"

Typical.

His patience snapped and his temper flared, funneling through him in a burst of white-hot rage. Of course, she would only see Narissa as something she could use for her own needs and then discard.

"Like what?" he spat, wrenching himself away from her. He glared at the woman he couldn't possibly believe shared even an ounce of his blood. "Some dragon root, perhaps?"

Trysta's gaze sharpened, the skin between her brows puckering.

"That's right, Mother. I know all about how you traded dragon root to Lord Calfair Skyhelm for some kind of concentrate. Or whatever it was you so desperately needed." His fury expanded, spurred by her ignorance. Her lack of care. Her complete and utter disdain for anyone save herself. Namely, his wife. "Do you have any idea what he did with that?"

Her dry lips opened and closed, but she remained silent.

"Calfair drugged Narissa while masquerading as me." Solarius took a menacing step toward her, encroaching on her space. Her eyes widened in shock, but she didn't step back from him. When he spoke again, he kept his voice low, a testament to his seething rage. "He pretended to be me while I was courting her, and then he deceived her and stole her honor."

There was a flicker of something in Trysta's eyes, but it was gone before he could decipher it. "Solarius. I had no idea."

"Stay away from my wife," he warned. "If you so much as look at her, I'll—"

"You'll *what?*" Trysta countered, baring her teeth, morphing into the monster she hid beneath a veneer of excess and opulence.

There was the female he didn't trust, the one who couldn't possibly be his mother.

Power boiled to the surface, and his magic simmered in his blood. "I will make you regret it for the rest of your days."

She scoffed, a vicious sneer tugging at the corners of her mouth. "I'd like to see you try."

It was the only caustic remark he needed, the one he'd been waiting for without even knowing. The opening he craved to release the dormant power of his bloodline.

Solarius unleashed the potent strength of the lunarstorm. Beams of violent moonlight exploded around him in a sphere of stellar energy. Shards of moon-dipped silver forged by the night ripped from the tips of his fingers as the air circulated in a violent frenzy. His blood churned, magic funneling from him like a maelstrom of archaic force. For generations, the magical starstorm coursing through his blood and that of his siblings had been thought to be extinct. But instead it was lying in wait, morphing, changing with each of them, revealing the truth of its greatness—a storm of celestial awakening.

"You are a poison to this family. You bleed us from the inside, you drain our soul with your lies. With your bullshit star readings and toxic nature." Solarius's chest expanded on a breath, his power building so the frosted windowpanes rattled and the ground beneath his feet quaked. "You lied about the starstorm and the truth of our bloodline. You lied about *everything*."

He stretched one arm back, ready to strike his mother down.

Something heavy and solid rocked him off his feet, slamming him into the nearest wall.

"Not like this." Ariesian's calm, controlled voice cut through the fog of fury clouding Solarius's mind. His brother's steel eyes bore into his own. "Not. Like. This."

"Her very existence is a plague," Solarius spat, glaring at Trysta from behind Ariesian's broad frame. There was something unnatural about the way she stared at him, like she was seeing past him, her eyes glazed with distance. She didn't look in fear of her life, she wasn't visibly shaken by his outburst, or angry beyond measure at the insults he hurled her direction. Instead, there was an eerie sort of tranquility about her expression, like she'd expected his reaction, like she'd been prepared for it. Prepared to fight back.

"Be that as it may." Ariesian spoke in clipped, measured words. He released the lapel of Solarius's coat and stepped back, flicking his wrists in annoyance. "The stars define our fate. Not ourselves."

"Yes," Solarius muttered, shoving his hands into the pockets of his pants to quell the urge to strangle his mother. "But even the stars keep secrets."

Ariesian said nothing. He turned slowly, quietly, and faced Trysta. Her sharp gaze slashed across them like a hot blade. Ariesian rolled his shoulders back, his chin lifting to an angle of distinction. When met head-on with the silent command of her eldest son, *the* Lord Starstorm Celestine, Trysta shriveled like a rotten berry, shrinking into herself before spinning on one heel, and stalking off in the opposite direction.

"Come with me." Ariesian led the way to his office, his pace quick, each click of his boots made with cold precision.

Solarius knew the way to his brother's office like the back of his hand, could find his way blindfolded in the dark. Yet the air thickening in the decadent halls of House Celestine was different now. It was charged with restless energy. With trepidation.

Ariesian shoved open the door, stepped aside to allow Solarius entry, then closed it behind them, twisting the lock into place.

The moment the lock clicked, Ariesian's wall of carefully built composure cracked and crumbled. He shoved both of his hands through his silver hair, mussing the perfectly coiffed style. He stormed over toward a cupboard along the far wall, grabbing two crystal glasses and a decanter of spiced whiskey.

"She must be hiding something." Ariesian poured three fingers' worth of the golden liquid and offered Solarius the drink.

"I need a clear head." Solarius waved him off, not wanting to indulge in anything that could prevent him from protecting Narissa. "What do you suppose she's hiding?"

"I wish I knew." Ariesian knocked back the alcohol in one gulp, then stared at the empty glass as though debating whether to refill it. He twirled it between his fingers, dropping into the chair behind his desk. "Distractions are popping up everywhere. Things meant to deter me from meddling with her doings. Intentional slips of information mean to divert my attention away from her dealings with Prince Aspen and Queen Elowyn."

Solarius rubbed the ache forming at his temples. Leave it to Trysta to misguide and mislead. She was literally quite good at nothing else in her miserable life save for fabricating truths and embellishing lies.

"What sorts of distractions?" Solarius asked, pressing his thumb between pinched brows.

Ariesian leaned back, the chair groaning beneath his weight, and gestured vaguely through the air. "The sudden demand to force Nyxian into a marriage with Lady Aria Skyhelm. The relative quiet we've experienced to give us some hope for peace. Oh, and then there was the sly mention of a witch queen."

Solarius's brows shot up, his headache suddenly forgotten. "I beg your pardon, did you say a witch queen?"

"Exactly that." Ariesian clicked his tongue in annoyance. "Apparently some witch proclaimed herself queen in Brackroth. As of now, she poses no threat to Aeramere, but I sent Creslyn and Drake to investigate, just in case."

"Creslyn," Solarius repeated, his tongue thick. "You sent our baby sister to go investigate some witch queen's rise to power?"

Ariesian rolled his eyes to the exposed beams of the ceiling. "In case you've forgotten, our sister is perfectly capable of handling herself against witches and bastard rulers alike. Not to mention the fact that she now has a dragon and is married to a *god*."

He hated to admit that Ariesian was right. But out of all of them, Creslyn was the only one who'd taken a life—multiple if memory served him—and was quite possibly the most fearsome of all the siblings. At least Solarius would think twice before crossing his youngest sister.

"Right." He huffed out a breath, his thoughts spiraling. "So, the real question becomes, how do we uncover whatever secrets Mother is keeping?"

Ariesian set the empty glass on his desk and when he looked up, the silver of his eyes had hardened, reminiscent of cold iron. When he spoke, his voice was a low rumble, like distant thunder. "We pry them from her through any means necessary."

Solarius nodded in solemn agreement. He would gladly go to any lengths to protect his siblings and, now, Narissa. He would walk through fire, take a blade through the heart, give his life for theirs over and over if it meant they were safe. For him, it would always be family above all else. Blood above all else.

And when that blood was poisoned, it was time to cut the vein.

CHAPTER THIRTY-THREE

arissa sat in the dining hall of House Celestine with one hand pressed firmly to her chest, trying to soothe the rush of anger funneling down the bond.

She knew Solarius was planning to meet with Ariesian this afternoon, so she could only assume the eldest Starstorm had said something to infuriate her husband. She'd seen Solarius lose his temper a handful of times, but this…this all-consuming rage, was entirely new. And to experience the effect it had on him through the bond was slightly terrifying. Never would she have thought Solarius capable of taking a life, but in that moment, it seemed as though he wanted nothing more.

Not only that, but it had been impossible to reach his mind. He'd completely shut her out. He'd shut *everything* out.

Helpless to do anything but search him out and perhaps make everything worse, she sat at the dining table with Sarelle and Caelian, pretending to enjoy the cute sandwiches and starberry punch, while acting as though nothing was amiss.

"Tell me, Caelian." Sarelle lifted her glass of punch and took a sip of the bubbly pink liquid. "Did you dance with anyone at the Yuletide

Ball? That is, after Solarius and our dear Narissa so effortlessly commanded everyone's attention?"

Sarelle winked and Narissa ducked her head, smiling at the memory of last night—everything from the dance, to traipsing through the garden, to the faerie pool.

"I'm afraid not." Caelian stared at her plate where the small pile of food remained untouched. Her silver hair, highlighted with threads of pale pink, icy blue, and lavender, tumbled around her shoulders, hiding most of her face from view. "I haven't danced since I…"

Her voice trailed off, but her sister wasn't letting her dismiss them so quickly.

"Since you saved the life of General Kjeld Holtstrom?" Sarelle suggested softly, her dark gaze flitting over her sister in quiet consideration.

A heavy sigh escaped Caelian then, filled with sharp agony and utter despair. She plucked at the starburst beads lining the opaque violet sleeves of her gown, then folded her hands in her lap.

"I should never have done it. He hates me for it." Rubbing her lips together, she pulled her shoulders back and straightened her spine, as though that would somehow erase the tears threatening to spill down her cheeks. "I should have let him die."

Sarelle instantly reached over and grabbed Caelian's hand. "No. No, no. Do not ever apologize for saving someone's life."

"I was hardly heroic, Sarelle." Hurt and torment were etched into the smooth planes of Caelian's face. "I used magic like a folly. I expelled too much, took too much, wished for too much. I was selfish, thinking only of myself. And now, the stars have taken—"

But Caelian's proclamation was silenced as a gust of wind stole through the dining hall. Ribbons of shimmery sky blue ruffled Narissa's hair like a breeze, stirring the curtains framing the windows, and caused the faerie fire glowing in the chandelier to flicker. It carried a crisp, cream envelope sealed with a wax emblem. The magical flurry of air swirled once, before delicately dropping the envelope into Narissa's lap.

"Oh!" She turned it over in her hands, running two fingers across the raised wax depicting the crest of House Galefell—pale blue clouds across the outline of a sun—and her stomach sank. Calfair wouldn't dare make any contact with her, not after the beating Solarius gave him, but her hands still trembled as she opened it.

"It's a letter. From Lady Aria Skyhelm." She pulled out a sheet of parchment with lovely, scrolling script, and quickly read the brief contents. It appeared Lady Aria required another elixir, one to help with exhaustion and fitful rest. A sleeping draught would do the trick.

"How curious." Sarelle cut into her lemon mousse with a spoon. "I wasn't aware you and Lady Aria were such good friends."

There was no jealousy in her tone, but more so an edge of curiosity. Caution, even.

"Oh, we're not. At least, not really." Narissa placed the letter on the table and reached for her punch. The bright, lively flavors danced across her tongue when she took a sip. She didn't miss the pointed look Sarelle sent her.

"I've always admired Lady Aria," Caelian mused, poking at the sandwich on her plate with a fork. She'd still yet to eat a single thing since lunch was served. "Her exceptional beauty. The awareness of her own self-worth. And her inexplicable ability to go after exactly what she wants."

Like one of your brothers, Narissa thought with a small smirk, recalling her conversation with Lady Aria the other day.

"Has she invited you for tea?" Sarelle asked, tilting her head so her raven hair reflected the deepest hue of blue in the afternoon light, illuminated by sprinkles of stardust.

"More or less." It wasn't quite a lie, but the words left an acidic flavor on her tongue. "She's asked me to this quaint cafe in Galefell. They have the most delicious desserts."

"How lovely, I do enjoy a good dessert." It was the first time Caelian had smiled in the entirety of their time spent together.

"As do I," a smooth male voice sounded from the doorway of the dining hall.

In unison, all three of them looked to see which of the Starstorm brothers had decided to join them, except it wasn't any of them.

There stood Prince Aspen, looking every inch the esteemed heir to all of Aeramere. He wore a rich forest green coat, the hem stitched in gold, and a stark white shirt underneath with the collar popped. The top two buttons were undone, revealing a swath of bronze skin, and a chain with what appeared to be miniature animal skulls dipped in gold hung from his neck. His pants were black, his boots were polished, and he bent at the waist, bowing deeply.

"Your Highness." Sarelle jumped out of her seat, nearly spilling her glass of starberry punch all over the oak table. She lowered herself into a prim, well-practiced curtsy. "I beg your pardon, we weren't expecting you."

Narissa and Caelian followed suit, each dipping into a curtsy, but neither taking their eyes off the prince, whose gaze had yet to trail away from Sarelle.

"Ladies." Prince Aspen tucked his hands behind his back, his broad shoulders encompassing the whole of the doorway. A lock of dark brown hair fell across one eye. "I've come to call upon Lady Sarelle."

Narissa glanced across the table at her friend, only to see Sarelle's color fade considerably. She smoothed away a few invisible wrinkles from her satin day dress, the bold hue of blue matching her eyes. She'd already confided in Narissa that she had not seen the prince in weeks and had very little success in attempting to woo him for Ariesian's cause. So, for Prince Aspen to make such an unannounced arrival was rather shocking.

And intriguing.

When she didn't answer right away, the prince continued speaking without interruption. "I thought we might take a stroll through the city of Celestine."

Sarelle's gaze darted to the nearest window, where the sun was shining brilliantly against a sky of the brightest blue. It was quite deceiving, for it looked positively lovely, but once outside, the winter season made itself known.

"Are you certain you wish to venture to Celestine?" Sarelle worried her bottom lip and there was the slightest hitch in her voice. "It's quite cold today."

Prince Aspen's face remained impassive, yet each word was spoken with calculated innuendo. "I am more than confident in my abilities to keep you warm, Lady Sarelle."

Narissa swallowed her gasp, and Caelian coughed loudly to cover her giggle of surprise.

Sarelle, however, turned a rather vivid shade of pink. The furious blush colored her cheeks and nose, chasing away her earlier pallor. "Of course, Your Highness."

She excused herself then and Narissa and Caelian watched in awed silence as she tucked her hand into the crook of the prince's offered arm without another word.

Once their footfalls could no longer be heard, Caelian expelled the breath she'd been holding.

"Narissa," she breathed, clutching both hands to her stomach, lashes flying back, framing her wide eyes. "Can you believe that? He just showed up out of the blue, no notice, no warning. Then to speak to her so *boldly*. And with *us* present?"

She laughed again, then snorted.

"Honestly." Narissa pulled her mouth to the side. "It was as though we weren't even here. He did not spare us a glance. Not once."

"Who didn't dare to spare my beautiful wife a glance?" Solarius's voice carried from the door as he strode into the dining hall.

Narissa sighed with relief. She'd been worried about him, hating how he shut her out of his mind, how she'd been blocked and unable to reach him. But seeing him in the flesh quelled some of her concern. The moment he wrapped an arm around her waist, she molded into his side.

"Prince Aspen," Caelian answered, tucking a few stray hairs back behind one ear.

"Prince Aspen?" Solarius looked down at Narissa, then over to his sister and back again. "Prince Aspen is here? In the house?"

Narissa nodded. "He called upon Sarelle just moments ago."

"He *what*?"

Caelian rolled her eyes at her brother's dramatics. "It's fine, Sol. He asked her to accompany him for a stroll through Celestine, nothing more. There will be plenty of onlookers milling about, ready to wag their tongues, and spread rumors as soon as they're both out of earshot."

But then Caelian's blue eyes locked onto Narissa, and they shared a look of secrecy—neither of them would hazard mentioning the prince's implications in regards to Sarelle's body temperature.

"Still, I wish either myself or Ariesian had been informed of his arrival." Solarius folded his arms across his chest, a line forming along his brow. "He should have asked one of us if he intends to court her."

Again, Caelian snorted, and Solarius's scowl deepened.

"Please, Sol. He's the Prince of Aeramere. He doesn't need your permission to do *anything*." She flipped her long hair over one shoulder and gathered her violet satin skirts to depart. "Besides, it's not like he asked for her hand. Merely her time."

She dipped her head then, leaving them alone in the dining hall, and Narissa found that she was pleased to see a glimpse of Caelian's former self make an appearance.

"What's this?" Solarius asked, plucking the envelope off the table.

His knuckles whitened the second he caught sight of House Galefell's crest.

"It's an invitation from Lady Aria to meet for tea." Narissa snatched it from his grasp, the corner of her mouth lifting when she saw the heat of desire flash in his eyes. "She's in need of a sleeping draught, and I plan on delivering one of mine to her."

His dark brow arched. "Do they not have sleeping draughts in Galefell?"

"I am sure they do. But I just so happen to make the best ones." She shrugged, allowing him a glimpse of skin where her aqua dress slipped off one shoulder. "Besides, there will also be tea."

"Fine, but I'm going with you." Solarius guided her out of the dining hall and into a large corridor where starlight danced along the ceiling and the windows reflected the purplish hue of the Moonfall Peaks. "The last thing I want is for you to travel to Galefell alone and possibly be anywhere within the vicinity of Calfair Skyhelm without me around to protect you."

"Okay, well—"

"And before you object," he continued, his fingers tracing idle circles along the small of her back. "I will keep myself busy so as to not intrude upon your time with Lady Aria. Now, when do we leave?"

Narissa smiled up at him, admiring his chiseled jawline, thinking about how she should plant kisses there. "Tomorrow."

"Tomorrow?" His hand slid lower, grabbing a handful of her bottom, and squeezing. "I'll be there."

"Do you promise?" she asked, throwing her arms around his neck.

"I promise."

"Oh, have our things yet arrived from Windsong?" she asked, pretending to ignore the fact that he was shuffling her backward into another alcove hidden away by winterblooms. "I'm missing my box of personal tonics."

"I believe so," he murmured, his lips leaving a heated trail down her neck. "I can confirm later."

"Thank you." Her head fell back against the curving stone wall as his hand hoisted the hem of her gown, dragging it up to her hip. Warmth blossomed between her legs, and she squirmed when his fingers caressed her upper thigh. "I need…"

"Tell me what you need, Rissa love."

"Sol," she whispered, intending to scold, but she was already reaching for the button on his pants where he strained for her. "It's the middle of the afternoon."

He flashed her a wicked grin. "My favorite fucking time of day."

And Narissa let him.

CHAPTER THIRTY-FOUR

Solarius spent the next morning searching through his and Narissa's belongings, trying to find her box of potions. Their belongings from Windsong had arrived in a separate shipment, and since it was only two trunks of mostly clothing and personal items, he hadn't bothered to sort through them yet. But Narissa was in need of her collection for her meeting with Lady Aria, and he'd promised to help her locate it before they left for Galefell.

He stood in their bedchamber, hands fisted on his hips, surrounded by piles of clothing and various accessories, but there wasn't a single box in sight. Narissa said it was carved cherrywood with a bronze latch, a little larger than a book, and might make a tinkling sound due to the vials cushioned in rows of velvet. But he'd sifted through everything, emptied both trunks completely, and still found nothing.

His brow furrowed.

Perhaps she'd misplaced it?

But she seemed adamant that she'd left it in Windsong with everything else when they made their hasty departure from House Galefell. He supposed he would have to check the cottage for himself when they traveled back later today.

A stiff knock on the door jarred him from his thoughts, and his head snapped up. "Enter."

The door to the bedroom creaked open and Nyxian appeared, the charming aura floating around him dimmer than usual. He shoved his unruly deep blue hair back from his face, and didn't seem to care when it fell in the exact same spot.

"Hey, Nyx." Solarius eyed his younger brother, noting the careless way he leaned against the doorframe, propping his shoulder against the solid wood. He wore wrinkled gray pants and his storm gray shirt was partially untucked, like he'd slept in his clothing of choice, and then simply rolled out of bed. Which, knowing Nyxian and his attitude toward expectations, was rather likely. "What can I do for you?"

"Mother is in her sitting room." He folded his arms across his chest, his blithe—if not slightly impetuous—personality all but diminished. "She sent me to fetch you."

Solarius had no desire to speak with the female who did nothing more than birth him.

"I am not a dog on a leash." He started folding the heap of clothing on the bed in order to prevent himself from punching a hole through the nearest wall. "And neither are you."

Nyxian merely shifted his weight, crossing one ankle over the other. It was clear he was still furious with Ariesian for planning his marriage to some twittering noble female, and from the looks of it, he'd taken to frequenting Celestine's notorious taverns. He stifled a yawn, but it did little to hide the red leaking into the whites of his eyes.

"What does she want?" Solarius asked, stacking his crisp shirts in neat piles.

"I don't know. She never talks to me." His tone dripped with resentment, and a line of irritation creased his forehead. "Did you know she never once asked me or Tovian about our sailing trip with the High Prince of Faeven? She didn't ask us about the realms we saw, the cities we visited, the people we met. Nothing."

Nyxian shoved his hands into the pockets of his pants, his gaze downcast. "I don't think she even cared that we were gone. If she noticed at all. She certainly didn't miss us."

His younger brother's admission bruised Solarius's heart.

He and Ariesian tried their damnedest to shield their siblings from their mother's cruel judgment, but somehow she always managed to snake past their defenses, to snare them with disparaging condescension and dismissive remarks. If there was one thing he could not bear, it was to see the light inside the souls of his brothers and sisters go dark.

"Tell me about one of your adventures," he said, taking an armful of Narissa's gowns to the dressing closet.

Nyxian sighed. "I already have."

"Tell me again."

"You're certain?"

Solarius nodded. "Of course I'm certain. Have I ever given you a reason to doubt me?"

A ghost of a smile passed over Nyxian's mouth. "Not as of late."

"Smart ass." Solarius smirked in return. "Go on then, tell me a seafaring story."

He listened intently as Nyxian launched into his favorite tale—one he'd regaled three times already—about a southern island where the waters are as green as precious jade and there's nothing but miles of endless sand for as far as the eye can see. Nyxian had fallen in love with the entire vibe, a balmy paradise where he could get drunk off rum-filled coconuts and lounge on a beach beneath the shade of a palm for hours.

To be fair, it sounded like a dream, the kind of place Solarius would love simply because Narissa would thrive.

Once Nyxian finished his story, Solarius stretched his arms overhead, popped his jaw, then headed for the door.

"Where are you going?" Nyxian asked, stepping out of the way to let him pass.

"I'm off to find out why our mother hates us."

☽✶☾

SOLARIUS strode into his mother's receiving room without knocking and without waiting for an invitation to enter. He knew it broke all sorts of social rules and norms, and he had no doubt Trysta would ream him for such inexcusable manners, but he no longer cared.

The sitting area was just off the main bedroom of the house—the one she used to share with his father—and though there was a small stone hearth where faerie fire sparked to life, a distinctive chill clung to the perfumed air. It smelled of fragrant tea leaves and withered roses. Navy brocade with silver-stitched constellations papered the walls, and a midnight rug stretched across most of the hardwood flooring. A bay window surrounded by inlaid selenite overlooked the gardens at the rear of the house and two stiff winged chairs were perched on either side of a small round oak table where a tea service was spread.

Trysta occupied one chair, her lips pursed as though she'd bitten into a rotten lemon, her hand flitting toward the vacant seat.

Just looking at her made Solarius's skin crawl with unease.

He was still furious with her after yesterday's events, and his mistrust toward her had evolved into a festering wound he wanted to purge from his heart. So he waited, counting each beat until her unforgiving gaze flicked to him with impatience. Until contempt dug its way into the wrinkles around her eyes and mouth.

Only then did he sit down.

She added two lumps of sugar to her cup of tea, then stirred, so the only sound was the clanking of the metal spoon against porcelain and the jingle of her excessive bracelets.

"I would offer you some tea." Trysta placed a slim glass bottle with a worn label on the table. "Though I know you prefer alcohol as of late."

The insult struck true, burrowing itself into Solarius's gut. But then again, if his mother had paid him any attention over the past few days, she would have noticed he'd intentionally forgone any sort of alcohol consumption, save for when he'd beaten Calfair in a local tavern.

"I'll have tea." He bit the words off.

Trysta's brows rose in surprise, and she reached for the teapot, pouring the steaming reddish-brown liquid into a cup for him. "Do you still require honey or sugar?"

"No." He hadn't added a sweetener to his tea in years.

"Very well." She placed the cup in a saucer before him and continued to stir her own, her movements slow and methodical. "I would like to apologize to you, Solarius. Not only for my behavior yesterday, but over the course of the past few years. I fear I have not been the mother you and your siblings deserve, as I've never quite been the same since your father died."

Solarius gripped the porcelain so tightly he thought for sure it would shatter. He downed the hot liquid in one long dredge, taking comfort in the way it scalded his throat, its bitterness coating his tongue. Of course, Trysta would find a way to blame her behavior on his dead father. She would never admit her actions were of her own accord, that she was selfish in nature. Her accountability was abysmal. No, she would rather fault her actions on the death of a male she hardly loved.

"Let me guess," Solarius drawled, leaning back in the rigid chair. "You lost part of yourself when he died."

His sarcasm was thick, but she cut through it, her own words like a serrated blade freshly pulled from a forge.

"On the contrary, my dear. I was made whole when that bastard died. It was like I was renewed. An awakening, if you will." Trysta placed her teacup on the table, canted her head to one side, and the world tipped on its axis.

Solarius blinked, struggling to focus on the harsh, mocking lines of her face. The colors of her sitting room blurred together, as though they were a wet painted canvas smeared in oil. Beads of sweat broke out along his forehead and a heated flush crept up his chest. He wiped the back of his hand across his brow, his gaze drifting to the hearth, where the fire had been snuffed out. His blood churned and the empty teacup slid from his hand, tumbling onto the thin rug. He watched it fall, his reflexes too slow, too sluggish to catch it before it shattered.

He knew this feeling, recognized this sensation.

For a while, he'd relished the rush of intoxication. But not anymore.

"What have you done?" he asked, his words slurring together in a string of incoherence.

Through bleary eyes he blinked, watching as Trysta dumped the bottle of rum into the teapot.

"Right now, you're likely feeling the effects of the amberwood and moon seeds. It's a lovely blend, you see. Capable of producing the effects of mild drunkenness in a matter of seconds." She left the empty bottle and cap on the table before him and when she stood, he slid toward the ground to go after her. "Though, I'll admit, I wasn't expecting you to drink the entire thing in one sitting."

His mother chuckled then, a wicked sort of cackle. "I doubt you'll be conscious much longer, though that only bodes well in my favor."

Solarius toppled out of the chair, grasping at the cloth fabric in an effort to haul himself to his feet. But his body wouldn't work. It was as though his mind was demanding a reaction, yet there was too much of a delay. His head lolled from one side to the other, he could barely feel his legs, and he was no longer sure if he was sitting up or lying down. He opened his mouth to speak but the words were merely nonsensical gibberish.

His tongue felt thick. His throat dry. His mouth was like paper.

"You know…" Trysta's voice sounded from somewhere above him, but looking for her was like trying to find the constellations on a cloudy night. Everything was dark and murky. Almost invisible. "I would claim that my morals kept me from killing my own offspring. I suppose in some way I was slightly against it, though not completely opposed. I never wanted so many fucking children, but your father insisted we have a large brood to carry on the *beloved* Starstorm name."

Even through the haze of forced inebriation, Solarius could hear the absolute disdain when she spoke.

"I imagine he suspected me after some time. Much like your wife, I've had quite the penchant for potions and tonics. It's only been a matter of finding the right ingredients. And Narissa, bless her, always had exactly what I was looking for." Trysta made a sort of *tsk*-ing noise and Solarius blinked, his vision caving in from both sides. "In a way, I suppose she's the one to blame for his death. After all, the deadly honeysting came from her garden."

Her footfalls sounded distant, more obscure than before, and he recognized the creaking of the door to her sitting room.

"But don't worry, my darling. Mother will be sure your sweet little siren pays for her crimes."

A cavernous, guttural growl erupted from Solarius as he crawled toward the door. He clawed at the carpet, his fingers biting into the stiff fibers, but it felt as though he was being crushed beneath the weight of a thousand boulders. He had to get to Narissa. To warn her. To save her. Again, his vision ebbed, and this time the world went with it. Solarius collapsed onto the ground as the snick of a lock clicked into place, and he tumbled headfirst into the pitch of despair.

CHAPTER THIRTY-FIVE

arissa was trying to contain her bubbling anger.

Twenty minutes.

It was twenty minutes past the hour and Solarius was nowhere to be found. The coach would be arriving any moment to carry them to House Galefell and if he didn't hurry, they would be late. Either that, or she would be forced to go without him. She knew she should have reminded him this morning or at least gone to check on him—she hadn't seen him since he disappeared after breakfast, claiming he had to go look for something. Then he'd never returned.

She bit back on the urge to expel a most unladylike sigh.

If she was in her own company, she might have cursed his name. But alas, Sarelle had opted to join her while she waited for him, and though she was furious, Narissa refused to belittle him in front of his family. No matter how deserving of it he might be.

She paced the grand hall of House Celestine, her heels clicking softly against the dazzling Faerie Star inlaid in the center of the floor. Every so often she would twist her fingers together in a show of nerves, then pretend to smooth the pleats of her gown instead. At the slightest noise, her gaze darted up to the length of hall stretching between the two curving staircases, but Solarius failed to appear.

Impatience gnawed at her and the gruff snorts and whinny of Eponians in the distance warned her she was running out of time.

Narissa knew Solarius was still somewhere within House Celestine. The bond continued its lazy hum, but each time she reached for him, she was answered with placid silence. Granted, she could have gone in search of him, but breaking tides, she was not his keeper. He was a lord of Aeramere, and he should've been more than capable of managing his time without her assistance. It wasn't her duty to remind of him of when he should be where or ensure he wasn't tardy. Besides, he was blatantly ignoring her at this point. If he truly cared about her traveling to House Galefell on her own, then he would've shown up for her as promised.

"I'm sure he'll be along soon enough." Sarelle's soft encouragement did little to ease Narissa's growing frustration. "Would you like me to travel with you in his stead?"

The massive doors to the grand hall groaned open just as two ashen gray winged Eponians touched down on the cobblestone drive. The sound of their hooves echoed across the smooth stone, and though the carriage they pulled was svelte black with gilded edging, it was the skies beyond that drew Narissa's eye.

Dense winter clouds blanketed the sky, shrouding the tops of the mountains in the distance. A howling wind whipped through the trees, the whisper of their branches a harsh cry against her ears.

Narissa's heart plummeted into her stomach.

She *hated* flying.

"Narissa?" Sarelle asked again, stepping into her line of vision, the blue of her eyes filled with concern. "Would you like me to go with you?"

"No, I wouldn't want to trouble you." Narissa adjusted the pin of her fur-lined cloak, fastening it at the base of her throat. "It's only Lady Aria. It will be a quick trip for tea, nothing more."

She'd had just enough dreamshade to concoct a sleeping draught last night since her personal box of potions had yet to be found. It would have been easier to give Lady Aria one from her own collection since her supply of dreamshade was dwindling. The dose she crafted last night was less than what she usually made, but given the circumstances, it would have to do.

"If you're certain." Sarelle dropped into a small curtsy, her indigo skirts fanning out around her. "I shall be waiting for your return. And I will be certain to reprimand my brother for his abhorrent behavior."

Narissa offered her a pleasant but tight smile. "You're a gem."

She left and did not look back, carrying herself out of House Celestine like a lady whose husband had not just trampled across her heart.

Straightening her spine and lifting her chin to disguise the swell of fear pressing down upon her chest, Narissa took the driver's proffered hand and stepped into the waiting carriage. She sank onto the cushioned bench, tucking the edges of her cloak around her for warmth. The minute the door closed behind her, Narissa's glossy composure failed.

She rolled her lips, clamping them together to keep the threat of tears at bay.

There was nowhere to keep the damning pearls that would inevitably fall, and Solarius wasn't there to catch them.

The past few days replayed in her mind, and she analyzed every second, every conversation, determined to figure out how she could have possibly gotten it so wrong. How could she have been so mistaken? As of late, Solarius's actions aligned with the idea of loving her, of protecting her. Surely he hadn't changed his mind. After all, he'd been intent on accompanying her. They both knew the chances were slim, but there was always the hazard of running into Calfair, especially considering Narissa would be in the city center of Galefell.

She chided herself for being so forgiving, for being too willing to accept him and his flaws.

Her life was far less complicated when she hated Solarius. When she assumed no good would ever come of their union. And perhaps she'd been right.

Too often he'd not held true to his word, and too often she believed each time would be different from the last. For not the first time, he'd chosen something else over her. Solarius continued to make decisions and live his life without fear of repercussions, while she was left with all the pain of his promises.

Narissa sniffled, squeezing her eyes shut, holding her own hands tight in her lap to keep from crying.

She would not waste any more tears—or pearls—on him.

He at least could have had the decency to tell her he wouldn't make it, instead of making her look so foolish for waiting for him.

To make matters worse, the flight to House Galefell was horrifying.

While Narissa told herself she had complete faith in her carriage driver, her body's reaction told her she was one more patch of bumpy air away from plummeting to her doom. Just like her parents.

The coach jostled through the heavy clouds, each rise and fall on the currents sent Narissa's pulse racing. Sometimes it felt as though her heart was stuck in the back of her throat, other times it seemed like it dropped into the pit of her stomach. She gripped the sleeve of her cloak in her hands, twisting the fabric between her damp palms. Every inhale was pained, a sweeping agony through her lungs that gave her pause, made her question if this was the perilous, helpless feeling her parents suffered before their carriage tumbled from the sky. It had been years since their tragic death, and though she could mostly recall their faces, the edges were blurred and the sound of their voices had long since faded from her memory.

Though she missed them fiercely, and often, she was not quite ready to join them among the stars.

Eventually, the thick embankment of clouds dispersed and the skies opened to reveal slivers of icy blue pierced by golden sunlight.

Narissa's breathing calmed. Her heart settled. And by the time the coach touched down on the wide landing streets outside of Galefell, she no longer felt as though she was waiting for death to claim her. Though apparently how she felt was nothing compared to how she looked, considering Lady Aria's amber gaze widened in shock the moment Narissa walked into the bustling cafe.

"Lady Narissa," she breathed, placing a hand to Narissa's clammy cheek when she sat down across from her, "are you quite well? You look as though you might be ill."

"It was a rough carriage ride from House Celestine." She tucked a few fraying waves of hair behind her ear and took another deep, centering breath. "The winds were rather vicious today."

"Here." Lady Aria handed her a pale pink confection that resembled a fluffy cloud topped with a glazed berry. "I find that sweets often settle my nerves better than any tonic."

"Thank you." Narissa bit into the dessert and immediately thought that perhaps she should start carrying a variety of sweets with her for just such an occasion. The delicate confection had a slightly crisp outer shell, but the insides were whipped magnificence, melting across her tongue and tasting lightly of sugary lemon. "This is wonderful."

"It's one of my favorites." Lady Aria's head bobbed in agreement as she sipped a frothy lavender drink. "I do apologize for the short notice of my invitation. I put the serum I previously purchased from you to good use, though now I'm regretting my decision."

She lifted two fingers, signaling for another purple drink, and when she faced Narissa again, there was a distinctive shadow in the depths of her rich eyes. "I fear I may have learned too much about my brother. About how truly merciless and monstrous he is, despite presenting himself as a proper lord of Aeramere."

The dessert Narissa ate was suddenly too sweet, and her stomach turned, roiling with nausea. If anyone else found out Calfair drugged Narissa, then bedded her, it would stain her marriage to Solarius. They would never escape the plague of his misdeed, it would follow them like a shadow the rest of their days. And Narissa didn't know if Lady Aria was one to keep secrets—or spread them.

"I...I should have warned you that a truth serum can be incredibly potent."

She danced around the subject, careful to not appear invested in Calfair's doings.

But Lady Aria waved off her concerns as another frothy lavender drink appeared before them, this one topped with whipped cream and a cherry. "Potency is neither here nor there. Did my brother admit he planned on marrying me off to one of the Starstorm brothers? Yes. Did he tell me which one or when? No. But before I could even ask, he started droning on and on about his pets."

She shuddered, twirling her straw around in her drink while Narissa's remained untouched, a dollop of cream dripping over the rim.

Narissa had heard rumors about Calfair's *pets,* as he called them. The humans he collected against their will. Men. Women. It made no difference. He kept them delirious on a concoction of herbs so they no longer knew their own minds, and locked them in rooms in the lowest levels of House Galefell for his own personal entertainment. Though sometimes other lords and ladies took part in the pleasure the mortals unknowingly provided. The entire affair was sordid, with Calfair more or less heading a secretive operation where Aeramere's nobles could partake in wild revelries, releasing their inhibitions for a night of debauchery. While Calfair claimed his pets were in Aeramere by choice, that they'd agreed to be *kept,* Narissa knew better. She'd seen the glazed look in their eyes when they wandered aimlessly throughout the ballroom of House Galefell, she'd witnessed the slightly slack-jawed, dazed expression they wore as though they'd lost control of their minds. He stripped them of their morality until they were shells, walking husks suitable for an evening of amusement and nothing more.

It was appalling.

Lady Aria dabbed at the corner of her mouth with a napkin, covertly muffling her words. "I should have known those poor humans weren't there voluntarily. He admitted as much after ingesting the truth serum. No wonder one or two mortals always mysteriously vanish right before Queen Elowyn closes the Veil at Midsummer."

The Veil was nothing more than a common glamour put in place by the queen to give the citizens of Aeramere a false sense of security.

But as far as Narissa knew, only the Starstorm family was aware of that well-kept secret.

At least Lady Aria did not seem to have an inkling about the torment her brother inflicted upon her, and for that, Narissa was only slightly grateful.

"I have the sleeping draught you requested." Narissa tucked it into a sewn-in pocket of her gown for safekeeping.

Immediately, Lady Aria's demeanor shifted. A newfound tension bunched along her shoulders, and her eyes flitted about the cafe teeming with Galefell nobles. She leaned forward across the plate of confectionary sweets, her voice low and sultry.

"Would you mind terribly if we stepped outside to make the exchange?" She smiled, her crimson lips turning up, but they were pinched. "There are a number of faces I recognize here, and I would hate for word to get back to my brother that I was pocketing potions or tonics. I can't afford to rouse his suspicions toward me."

A sensation Narissa understood all too well.

"Of course." She nodded readily, tossing a haphazard glance over one shoulder to ensure no one was loitering about or pretending to mind their own business. "Did you have another place in mind?"

"Actually, yes." Lady Aria stood from her seat, plucking the last cloud-like treat from the plate and popping it into her mouth. "We can slip out the back and no one will be none the wiser."

Narissa followed her lead, shaking off the twinge of remorse for leaving the untouched lavender drink behind. While it looked delicious, she knew a proper cup of tea would be required to soothe her nerves for the return carriage ride home.

She stayed a step or two behind Lady Aria as they wound their way through the darling cafe where the sun catchers dangling from the windows sent rainbows dancing around the space, and the plush, cushioned floor muffled the noise of footfalls. Lady Aria nodded toward a door at the rear of the cafe, its woodwork engraved with swirls and whorls, then brushed with shimmering blue paint. She grabbed the crystal handle shaped like matching wings and pushed it open, gesturing for Narissa to come along.

Narissa stepped out into the brilliant yet brisk afternoon when a burning pain pierced the side of her neck. She gasped, wincing against the sudden sting. Her balance faltered and she stumbled forward blindly, blinking against the harsh sunlight. Without warning, the radiance surrounding her ebbed, and the entirety of her world went black.

CHAPTER THIRTY-SIX

Solarius was dying.

Either that or he was suffering from quite possibly the worst hangover in existence, but that was practically the same thing as dying, was it not?

His head was aching. No, throbbing. Pain hammered at his temples, pulsing to the back of his neck, and behind his eyelids. His throat was raw, like he'd been forced to swallow gravel and sand. Though he couldn't be sure, he thought he was still breathing. Air continued to fill his lungs even though each breath was an agonizing feat of resilience. The beating of his heart was a slow thump, as though his blood was sludge moving through his veins. He felt lethargic, his bones too heavy, his muscles too limp to even move. To function.

Something cool and solid was pressed against his cheek.

There was a good chance it was the floor.

He groaned as someone peeled him from the ground, propping him up into what he assumed was a sitting position. His head lolled from side to side, and no matter how hard he tried, he couldn't quite open his eyes. It was like they'd been sealed shut with an adhesive.

"Come on, Sol." Ariesian's voice drifted over him, a familiar pull to his subconscious. "I need you to drink this for me."

The putrid stench of muddled herbs and sea kelp filled Solarius's nostrils. He recoiled, but someone's fingers clamped the sides of his face, forcing his mouth open. The foul-smelling liquid slid down his throat and he swallowed, almost choking, grateful for the faint mint aftertaste that lingered.

Consciousness bled into him. He could flex his hands and stretch his legs, and it no longer felt like his bones were so brittle they were about to snap. The pounding in his head rolled to a dull ache, a minor inconvenience given the gravity of the anguish he'd already suffered. Gradually he cracked one eye open, then the other, blinking the fog of confusion from his eyes. He was definitely seated on the ground while Ariesian held him up with one arm, an empty brown mug in his hand. Dim light slanted in through the window, illuminating five other figures yet obscuring most of their faces.

It made no difference.

Solarius would recognize Sarelle, Tovian, Nyxian, and Caelian anywhere. And given the strand of tension suffocating the space, the other hulking frame belonged to General Kjeld Holtstrom.

Easing out of his brother's hold, Solarius rubbed his temples and worked his jaw. "What happened?"

"From the looks of it, I'd say you drank yourself into a stupor." Tovian lifted an empty bottle of rum from the round table, then peered into the full teapot. He gave it a quick sniff, his lip curling in disgust. "But that's not the case, is it?"

"Not in the least." Ariesian stood, hauling Solarius to his feet, while his body protested the abrupt movement. "We all know Solarius prefers whiskey over rum."

What in the damned stars were they talking about?

He blinked again, taking in the heavily papered walls, the nearly snuffed out coals in the hearth of what he assumed was his mother's sitting room. It was a rarely used space, and he had no idea what he was doing there. Taking in his surroundings, he discovered the door was splintered, with chunks of wood missing, as though it had been busted open with an axe. Filtered evening light illuminated the mirrored looks of distress upon his sisters' faces—Sarelle gnawed at her bottom lip, eyes wide, while Caelian looked ready to punch a hole through the nearest wall. Her fists were curled at her sides and her small frame wavered with untempered rage.

Nyxian stepped forward, lines of dread tormenting his usually dashing face. "I'm sorry, Sol. I didn't know. I swear, I didn't know what she wanted."

Solarius sorted through the fog of his mind, grasping at bits of information as they slipped through his fingers. "What who wanted?"

"Mother." Nyxian swallowed, his throat working, and all the color drained from his face. "I had no idea she laced the tea with amberwood."

Amberwood.

Moon seeds.

Recollection of the past few hours slammed into him with brute force, each image tumbling into the next with startling clarity. Trysta's artificial apology. The tea. Her outrageous claim that Narissa was somehow responsible for his father's death.

Narissa.

The bond fired through him, hot and flaring, and he whipped around in a small circle, searching her out. "Narissa!"

Sarelle flinched. "She's not here, Sol. She left."

"She *left?*"

"Yes. For House Galefell. You...you were supposed to meet her." The depths of Sarelle's deep blue eyes glossed over with unshed tears. "When you didn't show, she went ahead on her own."

"And you let her?" he boomed, his voice thundering through the small space. "You let her go there by herself?"

"Of course not!" Sarelle cried, throwing her arms out in exasperation. "I offered to go with her, but she refused my company."

"Why didn't anyone try and come find me?" Solarius raked his hands through his hair, pacing, his stomach roiling with nausea that had nothing to do with amberwood and everything to do with the fact that Narissa's life was possibly in danger. "You have no idea what

Calfair is capable of, what he's already done to her. Our own fucking mother intends to ruin her, to trap Narissa in an outrageous scandal."

He shook his head, chest heaving. "I have to find her."

A strong hand clamped down on his shoulder, halting his frantic, jerky movements. "We're here now."

He tossed a careless glance over his shoulder to find Kjeld holding him in place. The former general from Brackroth rarely spoke these days and when he did, it was calm and with purpose.

"We will find your wife." Kjeld inclined his head, his dark blond braided hair falling forward. He met Solarius's gaze and held it in a silent vow.

"What's she planning?" Caelian demanded, a storm brewing in the depths of her deep blue eyes. For the first time in months, she didn't seem to care that she was sharing the same space of the male she loved, she didn't care if Kjeld was a few feet from her, staring at her in some strained mix of awe and loathing. "What is Mother attempting to hold over Narissa's head?"

"Father's death."

His words hung hollow, carving out years of pain that had been carefully buried beneath mountains of false bravado and feigned contentment. The sitting room was silent, save for the air stirred by uneven breaths, shaken exhales, and unsettled heartbeats. Each of his siblings looked as though they'd had their chests ripped open, their grief exposed for all to see, bare and unencumbered.

Kjeld's hand fell away from his shoulder, and a distinctive coldness crept into Solarius's bones.

"You cannot be serious." Ariesian's voice was hardened with disdain.

"I am incredibly serious." Solarius blew out a harsh breath, trying to recall Trysta's words, her threats. "She told me she never wanted eight children. You should have heard her, the way she spoke with such disgust. Such hate. Then she mentioned something about Narissa having honeysting and using it to concoct a poison. But Narissa would never, what reason would she possibly have to murder our father?"

"Narissa wouldn't have a reason." Tovian rolled his shoulders back, dark energy pouring from him. "But Mother would."

"Tov is right." Nyxian cracked his knuckles one at a time, his handsome features marred by a cloud of rage. "Father was powerful. Wealthy. It is no coincidence that he died suddenly and without a named cause the moment Mother secured herself a place in Queen Elowyn's High Council."

"If she had her way," Ariesian muttered, "she would have me banned from the council completely. As it is, she complains that my attendance is of no use, that *she* deserves to be the High Councilor from House Celestine even though I bear our father's title."

"You think she's behind it." Sarelle swiped at an errant tear that escaped down her cheek and lifted her chin. "You think Trysta is behind our father's death."

"Yes." Solarius spoke the singular word with coarse conviction. "I think she did it herself."

He supposed on some level he'd always known she was the reason for their father's untimely demise. Just as he thought perhaps a small part of him was never truly ready to admit it. All the warning signs were there—the lack of tears and regret, the disinterest in condolences and compassion, the ease with which she moved on afterward, like the gravity of his death wasn't enough to hold her down. At this point, he didn't even need her to admit it, he already knew. It was something he felt in his soul. Her culpability lingered in every word she spoke, it was in the sharpened glare of her eyes, the venom of her tongue.

"And now she intends to frame Narissa?" Tovian asked through a clenched jaw, his voice unusually low.

The very idea of their mother's callous scheme made Solarius physically ill. "Yes. I must go after her. I will not allow her to suffer at Trysta's hands."

"But Sol," Caelian interjected, her brow pinched in concern. "However will you find Narissa? House Galefell has so many levels, so many rooms. Even if we all go with you, it will take ages to search."

Solarius shrugged. "Then I suppose it's a good thing the bond will lead me right to her."

"What!" Sarelle shrieked, at the same time Caelian shouted, "You're mates!"

Nyxian tossed an arm over his shoulders, squeezing tightly. "Well done, brother."

"Yes, well, we can all rejoice in the fact that Narissa is bonded to me some other time. Right now, I have to get to House Galefell as quickly as possible." Solarius stole a glance out the window of the sitting room, where winter winds whipped against the glass, causing the panes to shudder.

Ariesian shook his head, his scowl deepening. "Eponians will take forever in this weather. There must be another way."

"There is." Caelian took a steadying breath, allowing her piercing eyes to travel over to the male who broke her so completely. And Kjeld met her gaze. Held it.

When their eyes locked, Solarius could've sworn the stars wept. Then Kjeld dipped his chin and turned away from Caelian, his voice rough with his Northernlands accent when he said, "I have a dragon."

CHAPTER THIRTY-SEVEN

*N*arissa gazed into the endless pitch. It was so dark she could scarcely tell if her eyes were even open. She blinked and long shadows stretched across her vision, slinking like serpents as she tried to peer into the painfully dismal light. Voices scraped against the walls, accompanied by the distinctive clink of metal. Excessive warmth suffocated her, each breath she took was like breathing in the heady heat of summer. Her back was pressed into a terribly stiff chair, but she was able to twist her wrists and roll her ankles, proof she wasn't shackled, yet somehow she was still being held captive. She shuffled her feet, the heels of her shoes scratching against hardwood, and a hoarse, bitter laugh filled the air.

"Oh, good," a feminine voice drawled, though she sounded far from pleased, "the siren has awoken."

That voice.

It tugged at the back of Narissa's mind, but each time she reached for it, the thread of familiarity slipped further from her grasp.

Without thinking, she reached up, rubbing at a tender spot on the side of her neck. She knew she followed Lady Aria out of the cafe, just as she knew she'd almost immediately been attacked, stabbed by something the moment she stepped outside, and it had apparently left her unconscious for hours. There were only so many types of tinctures that could render someone numb and immobile for a great length of time. Anything with sun thistle or writhing bane would certainly do the trick.

Whoever thought to inject her with one of those definitely knew their way around herbs, salves, and potions.

Faerie fire sparked to life in front of Narissa and she winced, drawing back from the sudden flicker of bright light. Beads of gray wax dripped down the tapered candle, and the flame spat, highlighting the lower half of Lady Trysta Starstorm's face. Her eyes glowed from within the shadows, shining pools of malice. She propped her elbows onto the wooden table across from Narissa, bracelets jangling against her thin wrists. The world shimmered slightly, the faintest warp of color and sound, as she steepled her fingers together. A cloying scent hung in the thick air—dried tea leaves and withered roses—coupled with an unsettling musty odor.

"We're so glad you could join us, Lady Narissa." Trysta wet her papery lips, gesturing vaguely to her left, where the air shifted and shadows swarmed. A moment later, Lord Calfair Skyhelm emerged, stepping into the dreary glow of light. "You see, Lord Calfair and I find ourselves in a rather precarious predicament. A scandal, to be sure."

"I have no idea what you're talking about." Narissa shrank into the rigid chair, unnerved by the way Lord Calfair's gaze slid over her, lingering on her curves for far longer than was respectful. He continued to stand, towering over her, his unnecessary nearness meant to intimidate and rattle her nerves.

"Oh, but you play the fool so well," Trysta said with a caustic laugh. "Do not tell me you don't have it all figured out by now. I know you are far more intelligent than you let on."

Narissa shook her head, her wavy hair sticking to the sides of her face, the heat melting into the room suddenly unbearable. "I really don't know—"

Lord Calfair's arm shot out and his fingers snared her jaw in a punishing grip. She bit back a gasp against his brute strength.

"Do not lie to us, Lady Narissa," he warned. "Why don't you use that pretty little head of yours? Feigning ignorance makes you look far less appealing."

"Easy, my lord." Trysta swatted his hand away. "Remember, damaged goods will be of little use to you."

Calfair scoffed, and his voice dropped to a deadly whisper. "I'd likely prefer her that way."

Icy fear streaked down Narissa's spine and dread curdled in her stomach. In the deepest part of her soul, she knew that whatever Calfair had planned for her was far worse than anything he'd done to her while she was drugged with dragon root.

"Now, Narissa darling." Trysta held out her hand and Calfair pulled a rolled scroll of parchment from the brocade pocket of his vest. She untied the ribbon and unraveled it, sliding it across the table to Narissa. "This is an admission of guilt, because surely your conscience is weighing on you by now. Your signature is needed at the bottom."

A feathered quill and pot of ink were placed before her.

Narissa clutched her hands in her lap, nails biting into her palms until she was certain to break skin. "And to what, exactly, am I admitting guilt?"

Trysta's sickly sweet smile stretched across her face, thinning her lips. "For the death of Lord Zenos Starstorm, of course."

"What?" She jolted forward, slamming both of her hands upon the rickety table. "That is absurd! I did no such thing!"

"But of course you did, darling. Don't you remember?" Trysta tapped the parchment with brittle nails. "You supplied the honeysting to Hespira, my former lady's maid. Because of your lapse in judgement, we were able to mix the toxin it excretes into a cup of herbal tea for Lord Zenos, which he unfortunately drank without a second thought. Therefore, his death is entirely your fault."

Narissa choked on a horrified laugh. This had to be some sick, twisted joke. A ruse meant to traumatize her and ruin her love for the one thing that brought her joy—potion making. Trysta was blatantly trying to contort the truth, to skew reality into having Narissa think the death of Lord Starstorm somehow fell on her shoulders. But she knew better.

"You poisoned him! You orchestrated the entire thing." The accusation must have struck because Trysta bristled against Narissa's sudden outburst. "I knew it from that day I saw you in the dress shop. I recognized your maid because she's the same one currently employed by Lady Aria. I know I sold her the honeysting, I only wish I'd known at the time she'd been working for you, then I could tell Solarius the truth."

Narissa's gaze flicked to Lord Calfair, who stood with his hands tucked into his pocket and a condescending smirk plastered across his stupid face.

She turned her attention back to Lady Trysta.

"See?" Trysta crooned. "You have it all figured out. Which is precisely why I need you to sign this parchment and agree to the fact that you took Lord Zenos Starstorm's life."

"I will do no such thing." Narissa lifted her chin in defiance.

Trysta loosed a sigh of annoyance and the candlelight wavered. "But you must. I cannot afford to have anyone know I use moonshade to create glamour. You see, I've woven a spectacular lie, I've crafted a life I wanted at the expense of those around me, and for that I hold no remorse."

She flipped her wrists, her bracelets clinking together in a grating jangle. They glistened in the wobbling light as though they'd been coated with oil.

The bracelets.

They were the source of her glamour. They had to be.

"Sign the paper, Lady Narissa," Calfair demanded coolly.

"Why?" She turned her glare on him, refusing to cower any longer. "How are you entangled in this web of deceit? What is Lady Trysta holding over your head?"

"You."

His response sent a chill deep into her bones.

"What?" Narissa hated the bobble in her voice, her confidence fading quickly.

"I'm not quite sure you understand your options, Lady Narissa, so allow me to be clearer on the matter." Trysta dipped the quill into the small well of black ink. "You are going to sign this, gladly I might add, and then you will suffer one of two fates. Either ingest a poison of your own making..."

She set a small, corked clear vial filled with a smoky blue liquid on the table. One Narissa recognized from her personal collection of missing elixirs.

"Or become one of Lord Calfair's pets."

Narissa's heart skittered and her lungs caved inward, making it almost impossible to breathe. She watched in horror as the wall behind Trysta and Calfair peeled back like curtains being drawn to reveal a glass enclosure where a dozen or so men and women idly lounged on sumptuous furniture. They were sprawled like decadent works of art, draped in finery to give the appearance of a satisfactory life. Their movements were slow and languid, their voices muffled beyond the glass, while mellow music filtered into the space, disguising their words. But nothing could hide the truth in their eyes —the glazed, distant expression of a shell of a soul. A lifeless creature.

"And how exactly did you find the moonshade?" Narissa asked, desperate to buy herself what little time she had left. "It's a rare plant and not so easily harvested."

"That was the least complicated part of this whole ordeal." Trysta's gaze narrowed, and the lines crinkling around her eyes sagged with the weight of extra skin. "Lord Calfair here is a most excellent supplier, even if he has been rather late on his deliveries recently."

"Your lack of patience never ceases to amaze me." Calfair folded his arms over his chest, an air of exasperation settling around his shoulders. He stared at Narissa, his facial expression devoid of any sort of emotion. "Your signature, Lady Narissa."

She reared back, defiant. "Absolutely not. I refuse to take the blame for a crime I did not commit."

Trysta's short laugh was punctuated by mocking ridicule. "I must say, I do admire your resistance. It's adorable that you think my plans will somehow be foiled. No one is coming to your rescue, Lady Narissa. I've made certain of it."

Solarius.

Narissa's chest caved at the thought of Trysta harming her own son. Icy fear mingled with burning rage, and her nails bit into the firm fabric of the chair. She wanted nothing more than to gouge Trysta's eyes out and rip that smug smile clean off her face.

"What have you done to him?" Narissa demanded, pitching forward. "What have you done to Solarius?"

"Nothing too outrageous. I didn't poison him if that's what you're worried about. Though it was incredibly easy to slip the amberwood into his tea. I'm surprised he didn't suspect a thing." Her wrinkled mouth twisted to one side, and she dusted the tip of the feather quill against her cheek. "Like father, like son in that sense, I suppose. Zenos never questioned me until it was too late, but by then I'd already married him and given him eight children."

She shrugged then, bracelets tinkling as she rolled her sleeves and dipped the quill into the well of ink to wet the tip once more. The stillness in the room wavered around Trysta. "Whether you willingly sign this admission is neither here nor there, Lady Narissa. Either way, your signature can be easily forged. It would be lovely if you could pick your demise and get on with it, as Lord Calfair and I are quite busy."

Narissa could feel Calfair's lascivious gaze seeping into her skin and the tiny hairs along the back of her neck stood on end. If she was forced to choose between a seemingly endless sleep or becoming one of Calfair's pets for the remainder of her days, then there was only one obvious choice. She could only hope her decision was not made in vain.

She snatched the vial off the table without hesitation and popped off the cork.

"Narissa!" Calfair lunged toward her, but he wasn't fast enough.

Tipping her head back, she swallowed the smoky blue liquid in one gulp, cringing as the intense flavors of bitter florals and moonlit honey coated the back of her throat.

Narissa squeezed her eyes shut, knowing it wouldn't take long for the effects to run their course. The racing beat of her heart echoed in her ears, accompanied by the devastatingly familiar thrum of the mating bond tying her to Solarius.

He would find her.

No matter what, she knew he would find her.

As her thoughts turned sluggish and her body grew heavy, as though her blood had turned to sand, Narissa reached through the bond to Solarius's mind, praying to the stars he could still hear her.

"The bracelets," she whispered.

The crush of nothingness slammed into her, pulling her under, and Narissa drowned.

CHAPTER THIRTY-EIGHT

"*The bracelets.*"

Narissa's voice stole through Solarius's mind, a swift and somber whisper, and though he reached for her in return, he received only unnatural silence as a response.

His wrath was soundless. It stole through his veins, freezing him from the inside out. He was numb to all other emotions, to all other sensations. He could no longer feel the burn of the brutally cold wind against his skin as Svartos, Drake's dragon, aimed for House Galefell. The reins were wrapped twice around his hands, and he knew the leather cut into his palms, but that painful feeling had ebbed away the second he heard Narissa's voice. Now, there was only cold calculation. He kept his gaze trained on the horizon, where the spires of House Galefell protruded through the inky clouds. There was nothing save for the rushing of his blood, the steady hum of a bond still intact, and the harrowing screech of a dragon.

The seat he shared with Sarelle gave him an extended vantage point, and he glanced over to where Odryss flew alongside them, with Kjeld and Ariesian atop his back. Svartos's onyx wings stretched wide as he leaned into the gusting wind, the graying light reflecting off his shiny black scales. Darkness chased them from the east, swallowing up the leaden winter clouds like spilled ink across a canvas of slate.

Odryss cut in front, and Kjeld guided them into a frozen courtyard surrounded by towering walls of pale blue stone. Solarius was grateful for the maneuver, because even though he found flying a dragon to be much like riding a horse, it was also slightly more intimidating. Horses didn't breathe fire, for example. Nor were they covered in massive scales with clawed wings and fearsome jaws capable of turning bone to dust. Basically, horses, and even Eponians, were far less terrifying to control.

The dragons touched down in the courtyard, kicking up bits of dead grass and frost in their wake. Solarius jumped down from Svartos's back without hesitation, then reached up, helping his sister from the seat atop the dragon as the beast lowered itself to the ground. He thought for certain they would be greeted by some malicious guards or an odious member of the household staff, but the last person he expected to see running out of the house, heading straight toward him, was Lady Aria Skyhelm.

Her usually bronze skin was pallid, as though it had lost some of its luster. Tendrils of loose midnight hair whipped around her, having fallen from the intricate hairstyle she wore. Wide eyes were framed with spidery lashes and her cheeks were flushed from the cold as she sprinted toward them.

"My lord." She dropped into a hasty curtsy, amber eyes flicking toward Sarelle. "My lady. You must come with me at once."

Ariesian stalked toward them and Solarius didn't miss the way a distinctive line of mistrust pinched across Lady Aria's brow at the sight of his eldest brother. Ariesian grabbed Solarius by the shoulder and halted him before he could take a step to follow.

"Not so fast, Lady Aria." Ariesian positioned himself before her, shielding his siblings. "Why don't you first explain why our mother's carriage is here at such an hour? Or at all, for that matter?"

"Mother is *here*?" Sarelle asked, clutching Solarius's sleeve and giving it an anxious tug. "Why would she be here?"

"She's conspiring with Calfair, there was talk of them framing

Lady Narissa for the death of your father." Lady Aria's back snapped straight, she did not shrink away from Ariesian so quickly. And her gaze latched onto Solarius. "If I was the wagering sort, I would imagine your beloved is in grave danger."

Kjeld stepped up on the other side, while Solarius shuffled Sarelle behind him. Anger bubbled to the surface, foaming and frothing. "Is that a threat?"

"No, my lord." Lady Aria didn't even blink when she said, "That's a fact."

"And how would you know?" Ariesian demanded, encroaching her space with his intimidating frame, looming over her. "What part do you play in their scheme?"

"I play no part, I was merely an innocent bystander in the wrong place at the wrong time." The brown of her eyes heated and if looks could kill, Ariesian would be dead where he stood. "Much like you, my lord, my brother controls all the pieces of my life. I am nothing more than a pawn. A bargaining chip. As you well know."

It would appear as though Ariesian had already negotiated a contract with Lord Calfair for Lady Aria to wed Nyxian, and she was none too pleased about the idea.

"Enough of this." Solarius interjected himself between them, turning his attention to the fuming female. "Lady Aria, where is my wife?"

"The lower levels." She cut Ariesian with another scathing look. "And I would suggest you hurry. Queen Elowyn is already en route to accept Lady Narissa's confession to the murder of your father."

Shit.

Solarius didn't waste another second of precious time.

He stole into House Galefell with the thunder of boots and voices behind him. The bond he shared with Narissa continued to pulse, but the beating of her heart was entirely too slow, its dull thump sounding as though it might give out at any moment. He followed its call like a siren's song, like he could hear the sultry lull of Narissa's voice through the maze-like corridors and spiraling staircases. His chest heaved with each painstaking breath while he sprinted toward her fading summons, the air growing thick and violently warm as he descended into the lower levels of the house.

Solarius was no fool.

He knew what Calfair kept hidden away beneath the excessive display of his family's wealth. The thought of Narissa being coerced or forced into becoming one of his pets, of her being dragged into that sickening world of sexual favors and servitude, made his stomach twist into unforgiving knots of dread. Bile scalded the back of his throat, hot and sticky, but he swallowed the uncomfortable sensation down.

Blinking away the disturbing images from his mind, Solarius bolted around a corner, then drew up short. He faced a crimson wall with no obvious windows and no latches for doors, but he could feel the tug of the bond coming from the opposite side. Narissa had to be in there somewhere, but he had no clue how to get to her.

"There must be a way in," he muttered, running his palms across the smooth red stone.

Sarelle stumbled into him, her heels sliding along the sleek ebony hardwood as she skidded to a stop, and Solarius grabbed her arm to keep her upright.

"Is Narissa in there?" she asked, throwing her arms out in front of her to examine the wall.

"Yes." Solarius pounded one fist against the fiery stone. "But I don't know how to reach her."

"Stand aside." It was Kjeld who spoke, his rough voice echoing through the dimly lit hall. He pulled an axe from the covered strap across his back, smacking the carved rustic handle against his calloused palm. Runes were engraved along the neck of the weapon, and a paralyzing metallic tang hung in the air.

Sarelle gasped, her hand coming round her own throat. "Is that iron?"

"It is," Kjeld grunted and hoisted the axe over one shoulder, priming to strike.

Every fae knew that cold iron was practically a death wish—the metal was their greatest weakness. It subdued them, dulling their magic until it was barely undetectable. The burns left behind if it touched their skin took ages to heal without proper treatment. And if left in close contact with the solid poison for too long, eventually, it would kill them.

But Kjeld had only recently become fae, and not by his wishes. He would've preferred to die a warrior's death. Yet he continued to fight with the very blade that could end his life.

Sarelle opened her mouth to perhaps mention that exact bit of information, but Ariesian silenced her with a look.

"Mind your eyes," was all Kjeld said before he swung the axe forward in a vicious blow. The blade made contact with the crimson wall, splintering it like a faceted diamond.

The sound rattled Solarius's ears, and he gritted his teeth against the noise.

Kjeld ripped the axe out and repeated the motion, sending bits of red glass flying.

Ariesian grabbed Sarelle, tucking her into his chest, and when Kjeld delivered the final blow against the wall of red, it shattered like a thousand broken rubies at their feet.

Solarius darted into the room, boots crunching over the shards of glass littering the floor. The space was lacking furnishings save for an old table with a candle that had nearly burned itself out—its flame spat from a puddle of wax. Trysta was seated in a wooden chair, her weathered face etched in severe lines of shock, while Lord Calfair stood nearby, rolling a scroll of parchment in his hands. He, however, didn't look the least bit surprised by their abrupt entry. Instead, it was remorse that clouded his features, and when his gaze slid to the high-back chair across from him, Solarius knew why.

Slumped and lifeless in the chair, with messy golden waves covering her face, was Narissa.

"Rissa!" Solarius shouted, and it was as though the heated blade of a dagger fresh from the forge tore open his chest and ripped out his heart. He rushed toward her, a swelling knot of panic clogging the back of his throat, making it impossible to breathe. His palms were damp as he gathered her limp body into his arms, hating the way her head lolled and her eyes stayed closed. Though he could feel the faintest glimmer of the bond, the thinnest thread of a connection, his magic churned with vengeful loathing as he turned to face his mother.

"You." He spoke the word like he was the cold hand of death sent to deliver her fate. "This is your fault. You did this to her."

"Well, this has been a lovely little reunion." Calfair let out a low whistle, tucking the parchment into the pocket of his vest. "But if you would excuse me, I suddenly have somewhere more important to be."

The heir of House Galefell had barely taken a step when swaths of shadows flecked with stardust circled around his throat, squeezing until Calfair's eyes bulged, and his mouth opened and closed like a fish out of water.

"The fuck you do," Ariesian growled, ribbons of glittering shadows pouring from the tips of his fingers. "You're going to stay right here, that way when Queen Elowyn arrives, she can see what a truly vile, insufferable prick you are and just how many Midsummer rules you've broken. I believe no kidnapping of mortals is at the top of the list, along with the assault of a lady."

Calfair jerked against his shadowy bindings. "You fucking—"

"Watch your tongue, air fae." Kjeld lifted his axe so the dull lighting reflected off the iron blade. "Or I'll cut it out."

Calfair paled, his skin turning a sallow hue as his eyes tracked the iron axe.

"You," Solarius repeated, gently setting an unconscious Narissa onto the chair. He stalked toward his mother. "Explain yourself."

She shoved out of the wooden chair, using it as a barrier between them. "I'm quite sure the circumstances already explain themselves."

"Do they?" he mused, tilting his head. "Because it looks to me like you're trying to pin my father's death upon my wife, when you know damn well it was your doing."

Trysta laughed then, short and bitter. But her eyes were rounder than usual, filled with a shadow of worry. "Don't be ridiculous. What benefit would I receive from poisoning Zenos? Besides, honeysting is almost impossible to find."

"How curious," Sarelle drawled, planting both of her hands on her hips, rounding on Trysta's other side, blocking her in. "I don't recall father's cause of death ever being determined. Yet you know he was poisoned, you even know the exact plant used to lace his tea."

Trysta's mouth fell open, then snapped shut. She took a hasty step backward, bumping into the table behind her. "Nonsense. I was only repeating what Narissa already told me."

She grabbed the edge of the table and her bracelets jangled noisily.

The bracelets.

Narissa's voice replayed in Solarius's head.

Fuck, the bracelets.

Of course.

The lunarstorm whipped through Solarius and razor-sharp bolts of moonlight formed at his fingertips. He was sick of his mother's games. Sick of her lying and her wretched behavior. More than anything, he couldn't stand what she'd done to their family. She murdered his father with little remorse, shamed Solarius and his siblings for showing any sign of grief. Hatred spewed from her mouth, proof she never wanted them. Never loved them. He threw his arms out, aiming each swirling shard at those damn bracelets she always wore. They scoured the air, spinning in dizzying circles. The fractals of moonlight hit the gold bangles with precision, cracking them, fracturing them into dozens of tiny pieces that fell to the floor like dust.

Trysta screamed, a haggard screech as the air shimmered, and the glamour she'd crafted for years fell away.

She stood before them as nothing more than a hollow husk of a decrepit female. Her snowy white hair turned ashen and thin, falling to her waist in stringy clumps. Her skin was blotched and discolored, sagging to the point where it hung off her sharp bones. The gown she wore displayed the wicked curve of her back as she hunched over, barely able to hold her head up. She was archaic. All the years of aging caught up to her in one fell swoop, stealing away the remnants of her life.

Sarelle gasped, horrified, clamping one hand over her mouth. Ariesian simply stood there, dumbfounded. Solarius wasn't sure he'd ever seen his brother rendered speechless before. Ariesian always knew what to say and how to say it.

"What are you looking at?" Trysta cried, her voice hoarse and scratchy. She pointed a bony finger at Narissa's unmoving form. "Your wife is dead!"

"She's not dead!" Lady Aria stood among the shattered red glass of the wall and raised one arm high, a singular vial in her grasp. "She took a sleeping draught of dreamshade. I swapped it with the honeysting poison when I learned my brother was an absolute disgrace to the Skyhelm family name."

She glared at Calfair, her boldly painted lips curled in disgust. To his credit, he didn't dare move, as Ariesian's shadows were still tightly wrapped around his throat.

A sleeping draught.

The tension coiling through Solarius's body instantly relaxed, eased to where he could finally breathe. That was why the bond still hummed. She was only in a deep sleep, saved by a potion of her very own making thanks to the wit and cleverness of one Lady Aria Skyhelm.

"I owe you the entirety of my gratitude, Lady Aria." Solarius bowed his head. "I am not sure I can ever repay you for saving her life."

"Think nothing of it." She lowered her arm, sighing quietly. "Lady Narissa is a wonderful fr—"

But Lady Aria's words were lost as Trysta lunged toward her, snatching the vial from her grasp.

It was like watching the world move at a pace that was so much slower than normal. Everyone's voices blurred together in a stream of incoherent words and shouts, a discordant melody. Their movements were drawn out and disorderly. Sedated. Solarius watched, catching only air as Trysta uncorked the vial of honeysting and swallowed it in one gulp.

The vial slipped from her hand, shattering against the hardwood floor.

Seconds bled by in an excruciating pace. It was as though time was nonexistent. There was only a collective breath of shock and the in the next moment, Trysta crumpled to the ground in a heap of bones and heavy silks. Her body twitched once. Then twice. A spasm jerked her leg and shoulders, causing her brittle form to flinch. Her final breath wheezed out of her in a wet, sucking sound, and then the matriarch of the Starstorm bloodline was no more.

A strange sense of calm passed over Solarius. There was no sadness, no devastation, no gaping loss. Only a quiet understanding of retribution. He scooped Narissa's sleeping form into his arms, cradling her against his chest. Words were lost to him, for all he cared about was taking her home and waiting for her to return to him.

He would wait for her forever.

Lady Aria gently placed her hand on his arm, a ghost of a smile edged around her lips. "She'll awaken, my lord. I promise you, she'll awaken."

CHAPTER THIRTY-NINE

$\mathcal{N}$arissa woke to the gentle hum of Solarius's voice floating over her and a spear of warmth spreading through her chest. Her eyelids felt heavy, as though she'd slept for a thousand years, but the familiar bloom of affection, of love, pulsed along the bond in time to the beating of her heart. His touch was gentle, his thumb tracing idle circles across the back of her hand as he patiently waited for her to wake from her slumber. A soft, languishing sigh escaped her, and she gradually blinked her eyes open, the corner of her lips curving as Solarius finally came into view.

He was seated by the edge of the bed—his bed—and Narissa swore she'd never seen anyone more forlorn in her life. Faint lines of sorrow lanced across his forehead, and there was a deep, ardent yearning in his eyes. He continued to hum her favorite song, the words replaced by the reverberations in his chest echoing through her soul. One by one, he laced her limp fingers through his own, and when she squeezed his hand, his gaze snapped to hers.

"Rissa love," he breathed, relief filling the lines of exhaustion on his face. He opened her palm and pressed a kiss to its center, trailing them down the length of her arm. With his other hand, he cupped her face, his eyes searching for something she no longer possessed.

"Sol." Narissa clutched their interlocked hands to her chest, drawing him close. She needed to apologize, to make amends for failing to warn him. For simply failing him. For not telling him the truth. "I'm sorry. I'm so sorry."

"You have *nothing* to apologize for, Narissa." He lurched from the chair and moved to the bed, seating himself beside her. "You're entirely without fault."

She shook her head, tucking a few golden waves back from her face so she could see him clearly. "You're wrong. I have much to regret. You see, I had my suspicions of your mother, and I should have given you some kind of notice, or at the very least made you aware, but—"

Solarius pressed one finger to her mouth, hushing her.

"You were right about the bracelets. About many things. I stopped trusting my mother long ago, and for good reason. But for what she did to my father, for what she did to you…the fact that she attempted to end your life." He brushed his lips across her knuckles once more. "For that, her name will be erased from the stars. Her memory forgotten. Her life nothing more than a void of time."

He stroked the line of her cheekbone, tracing it to her mouth. "Never apologize for that."

Narissa worried her bottom lip and his gaze tracked the movement. There was still so much she wanted to say, so much she had yet to admit. Her heart ached for him, longed for him, and she'd kept the truth of her feelings hidden because she feared that if she dared to admit it, then Solarius would walk away from her again. And she would be alone. Abandoned. But the way he was looking at her now, like he kept her soul and owned her heart, made all the words she struggled to find evaporate on the tip of her tongue.

His brow arched.

"Get out of my head." She scowled and amusement painted his handsome face. "I hate it when you do that, it makes it impossible to keep my feelings from you."

The corner of Solarius's mouth upturned into a cocky smirk. "Oh,

I am well aware. You're terrible at keeping your thoughts hidden from me."

Then his smile vanished.

"But what you don't know is that love pales in comparison to how I feel about you." He brushed a few strands of hair from her eyes, then slowly lowered his forehead to hers. "You are an ocean made of fire, and my soul burns for you. I would gladly drown in your tumultuous sea of emotions if it meant you were only ever mine. Moonrise to moonfall, so long as the tides continue to kiss the shore, I will forever in this life, and every life thereafter, love only you."

Something cavernous and empty inside of Narissa healed. Solarius's words, his vow to her, slowly stitched closed the wounds left behind on her heart. From the death of her parents. From her own loneliness. From him.

"I never truly hated you," she blurted out, and the burdensome weight she'd carried for so many years finally lifted. "Mating bond or not, I have wanted you, pined for you, since I first laid eyes on you. And I hated myself for it because I thought you didn't want me."

Solarius kissed the corner of her mouth, then whispered, "Say the words, Rissa love."

"I love you, Solarius Starstorm Celestine."

His smile returned, broader and full of devastating charm.

"And I love you, Narissa Seaborne Celestine." Solarius nuzzled his nose against the hollow of her throat. "I suddenly have the strong desire to make good on our marriage vows again."

A laugh bubbled out of Narissa, and she ran her fingers through his silky hair, enjoying the way his hand slipped beneath the velvet comforter to discover her bare thighs. "That sounds like a wonderful idea, but first, there's something else that requires my attention."

THE DUNGEON below Queen Elowyn's castle was cold and bleak. Serpentine corridors that looked more like caves snaked below the mountains of Terensel. Orbs of amber faerie fire glowed from sconces lining the damp walls, illuminating mysterious puddles along the uneven stone ground. In the distance, a steady *plop, plop, plop* clashed with the occasional groan, and Narissa hoped it was merely the sound of rainwater and not that of dripping blood. Though if the rank smell was any indication, it was the latter, and that thought alone caused her stomach to turn.

It was a rare thing for any fae of Aeramere to be imprisoned, but if rules were broken, the queen did not hesitate to dole out retribution.

And since Lord Calfair Skyhelm had committed more than one atrocious offense, Narissa wanted to ensure his penance was paid for the length of his stay in the dungeon.

She did not bother to look at him when his raspy voice called her name through the steel bars, and she didn't spare a glance toward the darkness engulfing him when she slipped a vial of terrifern into the hand of the guard who stood outside of his cell.

He offered her a stern, silent nod. Nothing more. Nothing less.

Though she winced slightly as the scrape of nails against rough stone grated her ears, she ignored Calfair's desperate, choking pleas for forgiveness. Her footfalls echoed over his broken sobs until the guard's callous voice silenced his weeping, and Calfair's shouts of regret morphed into a subdued sniveling.

Narissa carried her head high, chin lifted in satisfaction as she walked toward the silhouette of the male waiting for her.

He lounged against the dark stone, arms crossed over his chest, one foot propped against the slippery stone behind him.

"So," he drawled as she approached, shoving off the wall and offering her his arm. "Does the punishment suit the crime?"

She smiled up at her husband. "Every midnight hour, Calfair will be administered a dose of terrifern and be forced to endure his worst fear."

"Which is?"

"Drowning, of course. For how could a fae of House Galefell survive without air?"

Solarius chuckled, but it was dark and humorless. "Mm, such a naughty midnight siren."

Together, they left Queen Elowyn's palace in comfortable silence, for which Narissa was grateful. Though he said nothing, Solarius's presence calmed her mind, soothing the hardly recognizable ache inside of her. He was the peace she needed, and she supposed in some way, they saved one another. Rescued each other from a loveless fate of loneliness and broken promises.

It wasn't until they were seated in the carriage beside each other, with Solarius's arm wrapped snugly around her waist to quell her fear of flying, that he spoke.

"I have something for you." With his free hand, he reached into the pocket of his coat and pulled out a black velvet pouch.

"What's this?" Narissa asked when he handed it to her.

She peeked inside and gasped, lifting a beautiful handcrafted pearl necklace, the one he wanted to have made from her tears. Her heart twinged and her nose tingled.

Solarius cleared his throat. "It's a promise. To never make you cry again."

Her bottom lip wobbled. "But what if they're happy tears?"

He caught one as it slid down her cheek, turning into a delicate pink pearl.

"Then I suppose those will be the only ones allowed," he murmured, tucking it safely into the pocket of his pants. "And I'll have to make you a matching set."

Narissa laughed then and their mouths met in a tortuously slow kiss, a glide of lips, a slip of tongue, as though they were tasting each other for the first time. It was tender and delicate, an intimate meshing of souls. Turquoise waves crashed into incandescent moonlight as their magic claimed one another again, the tides dancing on the swell of a lunarstorm. Fate wove around their hearts in a decadent display of power, across burning oceans and moon dappled nights.

"I love you," Solarius murmured against her cheek, his mouth moving to the shell of her ear.

Narissa leaned into his touch, into a lifetime of love. "Do you promise?"

His words emblazoned themselves on her soul when he said, "I promise."

EPILOGUE

It wasn't that Kjeld Holtstrom hated Aeramere, or even the fae for that matter, it was just that he couldn't *stand* being one of them.

He was supposed to die. He'd lived by a very specific code of morals, he'd devoted the entirety of his life to defending Drake Kalstrand and training a legion of dragons. It had been his destiny to die in a war, whether on Brackroth's unforgiving shore, or some faraway land—but death would have claimed him either way. And it would've been his fucking honor.

When the sting of the Shadowblade pierced his chest after he threw himself in front of Lady Creslyn Starstorm, he'd tasted the bitter end. He'd known then, as the warmth of his blood mixed with cool, pouring rain, that Valorahan was calling his name. His heart stopped beating, his chest had ceased to rise, and it was only a matter of time before the glorious goddess of the battlefield would come claim his soul and finally carry him home. And again, it would have been his fucking honor.

Were it not for some faerie who deemed it her sole responsibility to save his life.

Lady Caelian Starstorm had stolen everything from him. His

morality. His honor. His soul. She'd wished to save him for her own selfish reasons, never once taking into consideration that he was destined for another fate. He was never supposed to become a fae, but she'd wished for that, too. Now, he had stupid fucking pointy ears, his eyes were almost too bright of blue, and the rune tattoos marking his shoulders and neck looked freshly painted. As a mortal man, he'd been strong enough. However, with fae blood coursing through his veins, his strength was amplified to a dangerous level. He had to be mindful, cautious, lest he shatter a pint glass in his hand or accidentally take out a doorframe.

It was exhausting to be in this constant state of awareness, to experience everything you've known on a more intense level. Music. Laughter. Food. Even the call of the dragons was magnified. He could hear them from within the walls of House Celestine, usually in the wee hours before sunrise, when the world was still and sleep evaded him.

To make matters worse, the longer he stayed in Aeramere, the more he wandered without purpose.

He tended to the dragons in the mornings, kept to himself in the afternoons, trying to find ways to whittle away the hours before he could return to the den in the evening to care for them again. Half the time he just sat on a stone rock, watching Astrylys—the only female of the three—tend to her eggs. He spoke to them, told them stories filled with ancient lore from the Northernlands, not that it mattered. They were alive long before he was born, and their kind had been privy to the world before, when gods and goddesses walked among men.

Unfortunately, even the dragons were bored with his company. He sensed their restlessness when he arrived, when he stayed too long watching them, waiting for a moment to arrive where he could feel alive again. So he'd bid them an early night, but again he found he could not sleep.

His hands curled into fists as he stalked through the midnight gardens of House Celestine. Even in the frostbitten winter, everything was too beautiful, too pristine. Lights sparkled through the glimmering windows, illuminating the cobblestone path and gushing fountains. Flowers that thrived in the coldest of seasons continued to bloom, mocking his foul mood. This was not the place for him. This world was too pleasing. Too whimsical. He was not made for balls and dancing, his blood was forged from earth and iron—and the latter was the kiss of death for a fae.

But Kjeld refused to give up his axe. He'd crafted it himself, carving the handle from ash wood, sharping the iron blade over a scorching flame. His axe—Kaldflam, as he called it—was his lifeblood. His identity. All that he had left of his former self.

It might do him good to go burn off some energy. Usually he stalked into the woods at the base of the mountains and cut down some trees, shaving the bark from the branches, and keeping the harvested logs for woodworking. Anything to feel alive, to feel the familiar sting of hard work seizing through his muscles, and the hardening of callouses on his palms.

But as he aimed for the baseline of evergreens, his plan was thwarted by the sound of soft crying.

Kjeld froze.

Another curse to being fae was his keen sense of smell. And he would know the scent of Lady Caelian Starstorm anywhere. Starflower, radiant amber, and creamy vanilla haunted his dreams, sometimes he swore he would catch the scent of her on his pillow when he woke in the dark morning hours with his cock throbbing. Because even though he was furious with her for taking his free will, for snatching away his right to a warrior's death, she would not escape his mind. He often imagined how she would feel beneath him, almost as much as he thought about punishing her for cursing him to a life he never wanted. Yet even those cruel notions turned wicked, and somehow almost always ended up with him envisioning her naked, and swollen, and aching for him.

It was a merciless world.

Kjeld shoved a hand through his tangled locks, the winter wind having knotted the loose strands with the braids he always wore. He debated in silence. Part of him knew he should keep walking, that he should just ignore her cries, and carry on without a care. Yet some sick, twisted part of him liked to watch her suffer, to see her endure the same agony inflicted upon him.

He kept his footfalls silent as he approached, careful to avoid stepping upon any fallen branches or frozen flowers, anything that might alert her to his presence. Tracking her scent and the sound of her hushed weeping, Kjeld discovered Lady Caelian seated upon the edge of a gurgling fountain, her back facing him, her tear-streaked face tilted toward the night sky.

"I'm sorry," she whispered, her silver hair tumbling down her back in wild waves, strands of pale pink, cold blue, and light purple woven throughout. "I take it back, I take all of it back."

She rocked forward, arms wrapped around her waist, as her keening gouged a hole in his heart.

"I beg of you, return it to me." Her shoulders trembled as another swell of broken sobs wrecked her body.

Kjeld roughed his knuckles across his trim bead, took one step toward her, then halted as a harrowing plea tore from her lips, and a falling star tumbled across the sky in a haze of lavender.

"I wish I had let him die."

A cold disquiet left him unsettled, its fine tip digging into his heart. He didn't move. He didn't breathe. He simply waited in the frozen silence of the night. But nothing happened. Her wish to the stars went unanswered and Kjeld didn't die.

He loosed a harsh breath.

The next time he died, it would be on his terms, with the honor he deserved. He would find a way to claim that fate for himself and it would have nothing to do with faerie wishes upon stars.

Kjeld walked away from her then, veering off the garden path, headed straight for the woods. But as he pulled Kaldflam from the leather strap upon his back, and took aim at the nearest tree, the tempting scent of starflower, amber, and vanilla surrounded him. Lady Caelian's devastating cries echoed in his ears. And he found himself searching the endless skies, desperately seeking a falling star, because he, too, longed to make a wish.

ACKNOWLEDGMENTS

I won't lie, this book was a beast for me to tackle. I had the hardest time connecting with Narissa in the beginning of the story, and I think a lot of it was because she was in many ways similar to me. But she finally started speaking to me, so I hope you enjoyed reading her as much as I enjoyed writing her.

To my fabulous team, Ashley and Amanda. Surprise! You're my team, in case you didn't know. I love sharing all the secrets with you, thank you for forcing me to keep them.

Thank you so much to my wonderful friend, Morgan Gauthier. For listening, talking, venting, reading, plotting, literally all of the things. To anyone reading this, get yourself a Morgan, because there is literally no one as lovely. Everyone should have a Morgan. (Dibs on this one, she's mine.)

To Kimberly, my deepest gratitude for creating the beautiful drawing of House Celestine when I was in a pinch. You're one in a million and I hope you know that you're stuck with me now. And to Lexie for giving me another gorgeous Starstorm cover, I can't wait to work with you on book four!

Because I took so long writing this book, it meant my beta readers had to devour it in record time. So, to Allison, Robin, Kristin, Cat, and Ashley, thank you always for reading. For giving me valuable feedback. For loving me even when I make you work under pressure. I appreciate you more than you will ever know.

To my editor, Emily. This book wouldn't be the beauty it is without you. Thank you so much for being on this journey with me. To QoC, for always supporting me, encouraging me, and having my back. To my hype team, thank you for helping me get the word out and making sure more people find Starstorm!

Thank you forever to my husband and daughters, I love all three of you infinitely.

And of course, I owe a world of gratitude to my readers. The ones who show up. Who wait patiently. Who share and scream about my books. Who stick with me. Who love my characters. I can't wait to see you in Aeramere again.

ABOUT THE AUTHOR

Hillary Raymer is a fantasy romance author. She's a wanderer, a storyteller, and believes in happily ever afters.

She has an unfinished Bachelor's Degree in English, because she ran off and married a Marine halfway through college. She loves the mountains and the beach, but would also like to live in a place where it was autumn year round. Currently, she lives in Virginia with her husband, two daughters, and two cats. When not writing, Hillary enjoys reading, doodling, and buying more plants she doesn't need.

Join her Court here https://discord.gg/EfHVy93Gvz

ALSO BY HILLARY RAYMER

The Faeven Saga

Crown of Roses

Throne of Dreams

Realm of Nightmares

Void of Endings

The Starstorm Series

All the Chaos of Constellations

All the Sacrifice of Shadows